HEWN

THE CEORFAN GARGOYLES SERIES

MIKI WARD
GARRETT WARD

Cover Design provided by Christopher Coyle at A Dark & Stormy Knight Graphic
Designs/Editing by Erica Collins/Formatted by Vicki M Duran

NOTE FROM THE AUTHORS

TO OUR READERS ...

Thank you for purchasing this book and reading it! Please don't be afraid to leave a review if you like it. This book is the last novel in the Ceorfan Gargoyles Series Trilogy. It contains violence, reverse harem relationships, graphic sex, and language.

Sincerely yours,
Miki & Garrett Ward

HEWN

By Miki & Garrett Ward

We dedicate this book to those who love saving the world, even if it's only a small corner. Also, to all the great examples of strong women like Taelor Reagan who gave us Michael, he will live in our hearts forever.

-Miki & Garrett

1

VISITORS

Kendra

Honoring Tana took a lot out of me. I snored, I'm sure of it because I woke myself up with a big snort. Oh, that's just great, especially when I have the most gorgeous set of arms around me, ones that just happen to be attached to a gargoyle I adore. Right when I think I've gotten away with my unladylike noise...

Mica beams and says, "Your snorts are even cute," as he turns toward me and opens his eyes.

"I didn't mean to sleep all day on my day off. I was hoping to get to that alone time we want." Right then, my stomach growls like a lion.

Mica smiles a panty melting grin at me and says, "We're alone right now. If you go with me to the lunchroom, I'll make you some breakfast, princess. I don't really want to get up. I like having you close to me here. But I do have a plan for tomorrow if you can wait."

"Well, if you put it that way. Waiting isn't going to be easy, but I'm kind of excited." I jump up and go to my bathroom to get dressed.

What!? I don't have the power to dress in front of him and not start something, holding back would be off the table.

He's waiting for me by the door when I finish dressing. I grab his hand as we take off toward the lunchroom. It really is just us, as almost all of Navan is torped and will be for several more hours. I understand Jared has some of his men here taking up the slack for the Elite Warrior Guard and working while the Guild is torpified. However, I never see the guards. When the gargoyle Ceorfan torp, it's their version of sleeping, but they've turned to stone. This is also when their wounds are healed in total. Even though Mica is a gargoyle, he can choose when he wants to torp. It's his gift.

I halfway skip-run on the way to the kitchen. Mica tries to walk slow for me, but one of his steps is three of mine. I don't mind at all, though.

We make coffee when we get into the kitchen area. Then my goyle asks me if I want to cut the veggies to make a pico-de-gallo for the omelets he's making that contain bacon and eggs. He's plating our food when I finish with the salsa. He adds the cheese, and I put the pico on top. We carry our plates to the table, and he goes back and fills us a cup of coffee and brings them over. My blond, amber-eyed goyle sits across from me, so we can talk. My face heats from the joy of his pampering me. It's the little things that are special to me. I never recognized that until I had to get my own when I was alone, and it hurt me to not have the consideration I'd been used to.

My breakfast date says with his head down and a little shy, "Princess, will you go back to Oahu with me for a couple of hours. I've arranged a little outing for us before we have to be in Scotland."

I take a deep cleansing breath and blow it out oooh... that's a prescription for happiness, one that I've been waiting on.

"What should I bring, Blondie?" I ask by way of answering, looking into his dreamy eyes. I could fall into those babies.

"You will?" His face is all screwed up and serious as he keeps talking. "I was afraid that I'd messed up too badly, and you were only keeping me around because of the bond. I was worried we wouldn't have anything more than what we have now." He hangs his head as his voice lowers to a whisper.

"What! Even after that... well, that... what happened in bed with everyone? I love you, Mica. I'm not letting you go. Stuff happens in a long relationship. I'm not saying I wasn't hurt at the time. I wanted to kill you. Then when I thought about it, I knew you loved me. Especially when you came home and apologized to us all. I'm not perfect; I'll probably mess up again, and will need you to forgive me. We're in this for the long run. I often wondered before I was etched if I'm being selfish and mistreating you all by having this poly-relationship. Now I feel different with all my grandmother's experience. It's very natural for me. This is what I want. I want you."

He scoops me up and presses me close to him. Tears are in my big goyle's eyes, and he's chuckling. His laugh makes me giggle. I can't wait to touch him and feel his touch.

Sitting me on the table, he kisses me lightly and says, "Then it's forever, babe. I have everything taken care of, let's not wait and go now. If you want to, that is? You need to bring a bathing suit. Maybe, a cover-up and something to wear to an outdoor restaurant... the alert alarm rings and interrupts him. The lights flash, but not red like they did when Kick infiltrated Navan. They're yellow, and the message is blaring that there are strangers at the cave entrance.

Mica and I jump up and head for the hidden opening where we're met by several of the human guards who are training to be Elites for the Ceorfan. Mega has been calling them cadets because they want to be part of the Elites. Mica takes charge and orders them to take point and our rear guard.

On the way, he explains that the warning or danger alert is more of a doorbell. When we get to the entrance, my partner pulses out a general query through the opening. He receives a pulse back. A pulse that I understand to mean the Hewn, the nomadic contingent of the Ceorfan Guild, needs to speak with the queen.

Immediately he says, "Babe, it's safe."

"Got it."

Then using his authoritative voice, he orders a big dark-haired man, "Cadet Sanders, please notify the Combat Information Center (CIC) operators that the way is safe. Then enter into the system that Navan has seven visitors, and they're torped at the entrance of the city. The contingent will be welcomed when the sun sets and taken to the allodium to speak with the High Guild (HG)."

The cadet responds, "Yes, sir," as he turns and reaches for his comm device and starts relaying his orders.

Kick and Jericho have reached us and are getting the information on what we've discovered. Sanders is still radioing in his orders.

I step through the crowd and push my way to the entrance to reach the Hewn. What I behold, are seven of the roughest looking gargoyles I can remember seeing. They're standing in a semi-circle, torpified in place. I'm shocked, putting my hand to my chin, and yes, I have memories of torped gargoyles pulsing. It's still a surprise because without bringing up the ancestor memory I wouldn't have known. It's sort of like I'd forgotten and just remembered. I realize they haven't been here long. They must have gotten here as the sun rose when the guards were changing out to the human sentries.

"I wonder what they want," I ask.

"I know exactly what they want," answers Kick with a dismal look having just arrived. He continues when I question him with a glance. "They need your help. Barat is carving up captured Hewn to add to his Crafted army. Because we have yet to thwart him, he's upping the ante and abducting more of them."

I pinched the bridge of my nose and rub my eyes. My hatred for Barat the Rat's Ass is making me fiery angry. My dragon wants to take over. I never thought about how the bastard is carving the Crafted. I get a grip on my anger long enough to ask, "Did you have no choice at all, Kick?"

His face is tortured with pain. The vein in his neck is pulsing, and his teeth are clenched as he grits out, "No, there's no choice with Barat."

I can't stand to see his agony, so I turn and pulse to the torped

Hewn in front of me. I tell them they're welcome in Navan, and I'll see them after sunset. "We will figure out a plan to help tonight!" I vow.

My breakfast date notices my anger escalating and starts talking me down. He thinks I might do something rash. But no, there's nothing I can do right now. I'm at a loss. I stare at him with a face full of 'Help me. I don't know how to fix this.'

He says, "Princess, let's assign these men some research and go to your chambers and see if we can find anything ourselves. Answers come to me better when I stop and think for a while. Are you alright with that?"

I nod yes, instead of voice the curses that I want to spit out. He retakes charge and orders the cadets to their posts with their tablets to search for information on missing or captured gargoyles that might be on the record. Facing the guards, Mica states, "We need their locations and pertinent details for the HG meeting tonight. The meetings are usually about thirty minutes after sunset, so be ready, and in the allodium at that time."

Shooting a questioning stare at the old mage, my partner asks, "Jericho, do you have anything to add?"

"Prince Consort Mica, not really, but I do remember some reference in a document I was reading in the Halls of History earlier this week. I will see if I can find it for the meeting too. Kick, do you think that you can look up some finder spells after you give the queen and her Ducere any details you know?"

The young mage answers, "I'm unfamiliar with the term Ducere."

"The Ducere are a small team of specially trained elite warriors whose primary mission is to protect the Queen. Queen Kendra's Ducere includes her Prince Consorts, among others," the ancient wizard says.

"Thank you for the explanation. Of course, I'll search the archives," the former prisoner says.

"I know that Barat is protected, and these spells won't work on him. I have tried every spell I know. I even tried one on you when you got here, and that won't work. But we might be able to use a spell on the taken Hewn," says Jericho.

The young mage tips his head to the side slightly and nods his assent.

Mica agrees. "That's perfect. I'll keep the queen busy pulsing our visitors and gathering information until the HG meeting unless you need me sooner."

Then I turn toward my handsome goyle and put a hand on his chest. He's so smart I can't help but be proud of how he handles himself.

He wraps me in his arms and lowering his head to mine, says softly, "Babe, can I have a raincheck for our date? I promise I'll make it worth your while."

I'm going to need to change my panties.

"Believe me, I'd rather have the date. You can have a dozen rainchecks," I say.

2

RELEASE

Kendra

First things first, I haven't forgotten that we have a mage in the cells who might be a friend. I'm getting him out. Mega and I've already discussed this, and my General agrees with me that we'll release the prisoner at sunset. However, forgiveness instead of permission is my prerogative. I need all the information I can get. It's a sure bet he has some.

I stop in my tracks and turn back to the retreating old mage that's several yards down the path with his protege and call out, "Jericho, we've forgotten the mage in the cells. Peter might have something in the way of information that could help. If not, I still want him out of prison, and we intended to release him tonight. Will you go with me now to release him?"

He waffles, "Your Ma... Kendra, are you sure you would not wish to wait for your Ducere to be with us for this undertaking?"

I answer, "I have my Ducere Mica with me. Mage Kick's here to help with his friend. I have a feeling this needs taken care of, and now is as good a time as any. The question is... will it hurt him the way it did Kick?"

"I have thought of that also, Edling. If Gortanik Lonato, or Kick as he is also known, were to assist with the spell, I believe I can adjust so that his friend is not injured and is still released from the compulsion spells placed on him," he answers.

The dark curly-haired mage, ducks his head. When he looks up, he says, "I'll assist you, Royal Mage Jericho. I know he isn't a danger and will speak to him so he can add his own magic to the spell. His talent is in shooting light streams. They look like what this generation uses for entertainment, but he can help boost the spell. With three of us, we should be able to release him without harm. He's in better shape than I was and has been eating wonderful food our gracious queen supplies even to prisoners."

When I turn, he watches me, his glance rakes me from head to toe. Sweat breaks out all over my body. I swallow hard before I ask, "What do you think, Mica? I think any information or even his support is worth the effort. If Mega has a problem, he'll tell me. Come on, let's get this done and not waste time."

We make our way to the jail, where I have a sense of deja vu. I straighten my shoulders and shake them just a bit before I still. What are my gut instincts saying? All good... I can assist if the mage is hurt and will be quicker than I was the last time. I'm sorry I waited, and it isn't something I'll do again. Waiting sucks.

My Royal Wizard walks to the transparent cell doorway with the young dark-haired man. Mica stands by my side.

Kick says, "Peter, I'm sure you've figured out that this is the Ceorfan Queen, Kendra."

Because of the compulsion spell placed on prisoners who've escaped Barat, he cannot speak. The captive nods to his friend and starts to kneel before me on the other side of the magical barrier. I shake my head and move my index finger in a no don't do that motion. That doesn't change a thing, he does it anyway. I take in his blond good looks and take a deep breath contemplating the meaning of his act. I don't believe he'll ever hurt me and am sure that Kick and Mica won't let anyone hurt me... that is if I need their help.

I step closer, hiding any pity, my face blank except for a lift to the corners of my mouth, and say, "Mage Jericho, please release my Ceorfan."

With a slight nod my direction the royal sorcerer answers and starts to mumble something that's almost a song. He motions to Peter and stands shoulder to shoulder with Kick. Mica stands beside me, his body tense, ready to take action. The three mages stand as close as possible then the magical cell wall goes down. I surge forward and add my own magic with theirs, placing my hand on the captive's head at the same time. I didn't mean to start singing, but with a low, quiet melody, I match Kick and Jericho's timber. Peter is starting his own tune. A sound similar to the crunch of wood breaking in a judo competition reverberates in waves through the air and fades. Jericho stops. We all do. Peter stands and hugs Kick. The newly freed mage sobs on his friend's shoulder. His brother-mage holds him until he calms, then lets him loose.

Kick takes his friend by the shoulder and turns him to face me then says, "My Queen may I have the pleasure of introducing my brother in the Warrior Mage Guard and my friend, Peter Ferris."

The blond wizard starts to kneel in front of me again. I grab his shoulders and stare him straight in the face and say, "No, no more bowing. I think you're mine, Peter. Is my heart correct? I need to hear it from you."

"Yes, Your Majesty, I'm your warrior mage until death or beyond," he says, his eyes glistening. He pulses the vow at the same time. It tingles on my skin. The way it feels when you see someone who cares for another with their actions. The way I felt when Kick held his weeping friend. I pulse back, telling him and the entire Guild that he is my warrior mage, and I've claimed him as one of us.

His eyes widen, and he says, "That's magnificent, Your Majesty. I noticed that you helped with the magic. Your song is why I didn't fall, there's healing in the way you spell. It would be my guess you have the healing and magic stones. Do you have all the others also?"

I answer, "I do have the green Earth healing stone it was given to me the first time I entered Navan. I also have the purple Magic stone. My grandmother Leta gave it to me when she called me to be etched. The magic I'm still getting used to using, but mostly I just go with my gut. I'm glad it helped you. So there are other stones? And please, call me Kendra, unless we need the formality in public."

His smile is like the sun as he brightens. His blue eyes flash when he answers, "Kendra, there are stones for Earth, Magic, Water, Fire, and Air. We need to get them all for you to have the power you need to conquer our enemies. Baratium and Walter are in the fae realm. Are the stones lost, or do you know where they are?"

"No, I don't have any idea of their location. I didn't even know there were other stones. I'll bring it up tonight at the High Guild meeting. You need to be there too. Now that I'm collecting mages, I need to address that with the HG. I know from a memory that the Warrior Mage Guard was a full division of the Elites. We need to bring back that section. What do you think, Mage Lonato?"

Mica smiles at me, confirming his agreement with my plan. I straighten my shoulders and grin back.

Kick is more than a little interested. His body becomes animated, moving his hands with excitement as he answers, "My Queen, it's something that needs to be done if you intend to exterminate Barat and the Horde. I can help. We have a great start, don't we, Jericho? Peter?"

Both of the mages agree with him, and they all chuckle and grip hands.

"In fact," the ancient sorcerer says, "We were just starting to do some research for our queen, Mage Ferris. We have a contingent of Hewn torpified at the entrance of Navan who would like an audience with our lady. She is granting them the audience so we can find out how to rid ourselves of Barat and his Hoard. We need to save the Hewn part of the Guild from being used and killed to supply more

Crafted to our enemy. Come and help with the search, and we will inform you of the new ways of the Guild. If you all will excuse us, we will meet you in the allodium, the Queen's conference chamber, after nightfall."

"Thank you. We should also get to our own searches," I respond, grabbing Mica by his hand.

On the way to my chamber, he says, "Princess, did I notice some sexual tension with one of your warrior mages, or did I imagine it?"

Knowing I'm caught, I tell the truth. It's easier than a lie. I recognize my own feelings, anyway. Looking down, I say, "I think I'm dealing with an attraction for Kick that can't come to anything. He's not ready for a relationship, and I'm not sure if it's right to add to our family yet."

"I understand. I think he'd be a good addition, though, when the time comes. I'll talk to the others about him as a possibility. You need to know babe, I don't think of it as sharing you, just in case you're thinking that. It's more like getting another brother. Our relationship is just between us. Sometimes, we can all have fun together, though."

I laugh and punch him in the arm and tease, "I love you, I'm glad we can talk openly. You're a big help... most of the time, you big lug."

I take off running. He accepts the challenge and chases after me. I let him catch me when we get to our chamber. His kisses are crazy good!

3

INFORMATION

Kendra

MICA AND I HAVE BEEN SCOURING OUR TABLETS FOR information. The day is getting late, we stop and stretch. We haven't found anything useful. Kick came to join us and let us know they haven't found much in their searches either.

We talk and go over the details again with the dark-haired mage, maybe it'll spark something. He tells us the details he knows. He had told the HG a while ago, but I didn't understand at that time what he was trying to say to us. I knew it was important, just not how it applies to my gargoyles.

Mage Kick asks, "What do you know about Resurgere, Your Majesty?"

"I know that Spar was made into a gargoyle by Resurgere when Mega was carved and gave the piece to him. The General also got part of Spar's bone in return. When it happened, the man I lost was raised as Spar, and now he's a gargoyle. I've seen Crafted in a skirmish and know they're made of wood and are controlled by their master's orders."

"That much is true. The Crafted are made of wood. They go through Resurgere only to the extent that they have a carved piece of a living gargoyle inserted into them to make them animated. Barat can't carve enough Ceorfan to make the number of Crafted he needs. In the old days, he abducted what was left of the warrior mages and had them create the evil beasts. He spelled and controlled us to do his bidding. He's down to one remaining prisoner from the Ceorfan Warrior Mages. He's my friend Steen, who we have plans to free. Our enemy also has two mages who are his, in every way. They are just as evil, and we can depend on them to do the most horrid things. Our wicked adversary has a few magic makers, but not enough gargoyle flesh. Apparently, the place he's decided to get it is the Hewn. They aren't as protected or missed as the Guild who live here in the city.

"I need to explain his process a little more. If that's okay with you?" Kick says.

I nod and say, "The more information, the better. I can take it."

He continues, "The gargoyles he carves aren't given anything for the pain, and many times they are carved to death for his pleasure. If he lets them live, they regenerate when torped to endure the pain again the next day. It's what happened to all the Cursed. My Queen, the Cursed are those Ceorfan who were captured during the Mage Wars. While I was a prisoner, I was able to use spells to numb their pain. Part of my magic is that I'm a finder-changer able to find things and ways to change instances in situations."

I interrupt and ask, "So you're saying, not only can you find stuff, you can change the outcome of this war?"

The handsome dark mage says, "Yes, I can find things and places, and ways to alter outcomes and spells. But not to shape the future, my gift isn't so specific in that area. To make it easier to understand, I'm able to manipulate circumstances, if I'm given time. Not being in Barat's castle with the ones he's torturing, I can't help the ones being carved," Kick admits with knit brows and a slight frown.

I ask, "Is that what happened to Kino and you when you were held by that ass?"

The sun is setting, and we feel the tingle of the waking of our gargoyle kind. We enjoyed the feeling for a few seconds as the gargoyles untorp and become flesh.

My two consorts jump off the torp stage and join us in the seating area. I stand and kiss Kino, my red rockstar, and Spar, my handsome blue goyle. I can tell by their looks they've been awake and listening to our conversation while torped. My rockstar's distant eyes and wrinkled brow are a dead give away.

My red prince consort takes a seat near me and answers my question, "Yes, it is, and we need to get the Hewn out as fast as possible. It is painful, and I wished for death in just a few days. Even with the benefit of friends to share my pain and make it more bearable until Kick altered the spell to numb the pain. It wasn't perfect, but we survived."

I wince, feeling his past pain in every cell of my body. "I'm sorry you had to go through that. From now on, I plan to do my best to make your life better. We need to shut that asshat down."

He takes my hand in his and lifts it for a kiss, then turns to Kick and says, "You told us that Barat is in the Faery world earlier. Is this where the prison is also? I never saw that prison. When I was held, we were still in the Earth realm."

My dark mage answers, "Not the one where you were held, brother. We were moved. I was told and believed you were dead. Then when I discovered where we were, I hoped there would be many Fae on this side of the border between the lands who could help me overtake Barat, so we could be free. Instead, I found border is now a barrier, and only the Fae people can cross and be admitted into their realm. Humans can get there if one of the magical ones is touching them and guards them on the other side. I can get an army there with a jump stone. This is one of the things we have to address to get an army over the boundary."

Kino says, "That is true. They closed the borders a long time ago.

There is so much I need to catch you and Peter up on. Maybe we can have time later, and I'll show you some things that will astound you."

The young dark-haired wizard says, "That would be good. I know a lot but still have missed much. Well, the travel between realms is the main thing. I need the High Guild to understand this to develop a solid plan. We need options, and I hope some of the others researching are getting some answers."

"So, are you the only one who can cross into Faery lands, Kick?" I ask.

"No, anyone of Fae blood or bound to a Fae person may enter without repercussion. The penalty is death for others. In fact, it's dangerous. The rulers there might just decide to kill any outsider for entertainment. The Faery people are very defensive and only think of their world. They haven't left in so long that people don't matter to them. I should be able to get us in to see the monarchy for a meeting. They're a selfish people, and it'll take a treasure to make them let in an army. Barat is part Fae and can come and go. He doesn't bother the Fae or even go around them except to give gifts. Magical gifts are always welcome to the king and queen there.

"Well, we have one we might gift, but I'm not sure we want it to be that close to Barat again. I wonder if they would make a deal with us in trade for it?" I ask and shudder.

Mica agrees, "That's a hell of an understatement. I mean, the part about the Caor Thintri being close to Barat. He would use it against us again. If that's the object, you're thinking of, Princess. I'm sure if the Fae king has it in his possession, it'd be foolish of the wicked mage to try to steal it back. I don't think he'd be that stupid."

"We could always hope," Spar interjects.

I can't help but giggle at my blue goyle, and Kino cocks his head in amusement.

Then Kick says, "The King of the Fae is a warrior with a large army, and they do not abide thieves."

I say, "Let's ask the HG. They might have more information for us to use. But you're right, the staff is probably the best thing to give the Fae king to get his favor. I've got to stop for a bit. My head is mush. Why don't we take a break? It's getting close to HG time, and the fun is just beginning."

I drop it but, I'm wondering how much time we're taking with TASS, The Alumbradai Sanctuary State's emergency meeting. The very one I called, so Kick can give the information he has. This will help us find the Horde of Barat so we can end them.

My princes and the dark mage, all agree. Spar gets up and makes us some fresh coffee, and I grab a brownie the chefs left out for us day-dwellers. Mica is right behind me. I can feel his breath on my neck, so I push my butt out a little to bump him in his man stuff. This earns me a slight growl. Damn, that's sexy. Maybe at work tomorrow we can make new plans to be alone for a few hours. I have more time than most people because I don't sleep that much, but I still have a lot to do in the time that I'm awake.

I ask, "Kick, do you want some coffee?"

He asks, "Do you have tea?"

"Yes, we do, let me show you how to make it. Feel free to get some any time you like."

I make sure he knows he's always welcome when he wants something as I plate him a brownie then hand it to him. I sit with my feet up on my chair and enjoy my coffee and dessert while we talk about everyday stuff so we can de-stress for a time.

Everyone's drinking coffee or tea and discussing whether to eat more or fly. They opt to wait for the food and fly first. We leave Kick and get to our exercise, telling him we'll meet him in the allodium in about an hour. I've had Clifton, the Count de Treon, move the meeting time to an hour after sunset so I can actually clean up for the members.

"Kick, do you mind gathering the Hewn and bringing them to the allodium for the meeting?" I ask.

He nods yes. I turn back to him as we are leaving my chambers and wave to him. I'm with my goyles, but I feel strange like I should have done something to bring him with us. Nope, not going there.

4

DISCOVERY

Kendra

Our flight was fantastic. But, now that we're back, I feel the weight of the serious decisions that need to be made. Well, after I shower anyway. Mica, Spar, and Kino have all gone to their rooms to shower, understanding that I need some time to myself. I want to meet the Hewn clean, at least.

I pull my hair into a clip and put some make-up on before entering my secret passage to the allodium. The stalactite by the entrance is where I pause, taking a deep breath and squaring my shoulders as I step into the conference hall. Dead silence... no, I hear Spar's deep voice telling Kino he needs a knife like one of the Hewn's.

When I sneak into the meeting, I notice everyone is seated. With my head held high and my back straight, I take my chair. I glance toward Duke Findare, or Fin as I think of him, and tip my head in question, asking if he wants to speak first. He nods at my silent query. I sigh quietly, glad for help who understands me.

"Duke Findare," I say, keeping it formal in front of our Hewn guests, who are also sitting at the table. "I'd like you to start this discussion. Please lead the meeting. We have garnered quite a bit of information and can add more as the meeting progresses." I motion with one hand, giving him the floor.

He surprises me by saying, "Krag, I introduce you to your queen, Kendra. Your Majesty, this is Krag, the leader of this group of Hewn and a past Elite Warrior Guard."

"I welcome you all to Navan."

The Duke stares at the warrior Hewn whom he has just introduced and adds in a gentle tone, "You may give your allegiance and introduce your men."

Krag bobs his head and kneels in front of me, giving me his sworn loyalty. Then motions for his men to follow suit. As they do, I check their auras. They all seem to be on the up and up. Tough as nails and some defensiveness but honest and willing to help.

Okay, I have no idea how to respond, so I check, my grandmother's memories and come up with, "I accept your fealty as my people and will return the debt with a covering in times of harm," I say. What the hell? I'm breathing fast, glad the words came to me.

It seems the visitors are happy with that because they're smiling those scary gargoyle smiles that I love so much. Their auras tell me they're glad about my response. All except one, even though he'd given his allegiance. I recognize flaring red anger in him. My thoughts travel to Eltira, and I shake them off, meaning to give him a non-judgmental chance.

Fin says, "Hewn of the Guild I give you the floor, put forth your petition."

Give me a break. The angry young man is who speaks. "Your Majesty," he says with a disdainful curl of his lip. "We're your people, whether you want us or not. Our number live away from cities, this one in particular. We like it that way. We normally can handle our own problems, but you've gotten us into a situation we can't get out of without help. So we're forced to come grovel before you, begging for help with a murderer you've set free."

The members burst into a noisy raucous. Mica is on the Hewn speaker like white on rice. He yanks him out of his chair and holds him to the wall by his neck.

The room erupts into motion. I take a defensive stance and watch as Spar holds back a couple of the Hewn warriors. His beautiful blue muscles ripple as he throws one to the ground. Then he steps on his foe, allowing him to grab the other one. This adversary is pulled to his feet and met with a never-fail back-kick to the nuts. When the nomad doubles over, my goyle shoves him onto his brother on the floor and holds them there.

At the same time, Kino takes another down and is singing under his breath. His melody is deadly. His red hair is flowing behind him as he swirls to find another to engage.

Kick is also in the fight. He's impressive as he backs off the last one with a vicious kick to the jaw, laying him out.

The newest mage, Peter, has one on the floor in a chokehold. One of the nomads rushes for me, but before he can touch me, I put him on his ass. Then I hold him down with a foot to the neck. A growl escapes that I didn't intend, and my head jerks around the room. The need to protect my people strong.

None of the guards in the room or General Mega needed to weigh in, until now. He picks the guy I'm standing on, up off the floor and tele-speaks, "They are all impressed with our strength... especially yours. They like that you were in the fight, Edling. They notice that some of the ones who overcame them in this fight are mages, considered to be weaker than themselves. Yet your senior personnel did not intervene. This let the ones they believe to be weaker contain them, speaking of their trust in your ability. They think that if they are weaker than these, the rest of the Elites must be mighty indeed. They had no idea our strength equals theirs."

I say, "Thank you for the information. I'm going to be on guard anyway, but I'll try to be nice."

My court is still holding the Hewn back as I walk to Mica and touch him on the shoulder and demand, "Let the asswipe down."

He drops him but doesn't let him go and says, "If you say one more fucking word or insult to My Queen, I'll nail your ass."

The douche nods his assent. Mica removes his hand from his foe's neck.

I smile inwardly and tele-comm Mega, "I'm so proud of the mages. It's an instinct for them to defend me already. They'll do."

"I had forgotten that you did not know the mages are warriors as well as magic makers. I will make sure that they also have training schedules to stay sharp and teach them about this century's warfare," he replies.

"Well, I really did know I just didn't have an idea how good at it they are," I smirk.

I nod to Fin, and he retakes control of the meeting and calms everyone. He orders, "Everyone, retake your seats, please. There will be no further violence unless you want to be detained forcefully."

All of the consorts and mages who defended me, stare daggers at the Hewn.

To further diffuse the situation, I make my way to the buffet and grab a jalapeño bagel and cream cheese and see that Spar has my coffee sitting in front of my seat. Now I can sit and not make them wait any longer. When I sit, I slowly look up and around, these men are hungry.

I say, "I want to eat, so if you will please take a minute and get yourselves something from the buffet, I would appreciate it. Hewn, please go first, as my guests." I raise an eyebrow and give them a 'I dare you' look.

One of them raises his own brow in return, stands, and walks to get his food. He murmurs under his breath, saying, "Now!" The others get up and, with their best manners, get some food. They're hungry but only take a little.

I tele-speak to Mega, "The Hewn are hungry and aren't taking enough food. Will you ask Clifton to get the chefs to bring in more, and lots of it."

He does as I ask. Clifton is clicking his fingers on his tablet then glances up at me with a tiny nod.

"Please continue," I ask with a motion to Findare with my bagel.

The Duke says glancing first at the table then up to the Hewn leader, "I understand that the nomads need our help. I want you to tell us what your petition is, old friend, but first... Your Majesty, I introduced you to Krag earlier, but there is more. Although he is widely looked to as the commander of the Hewn, he was Queen Leta's trusted commanding officer of her Elite Warrior Guard. He was also a survivor of the Mage Wars and one of the Cursed that our queen bought with her life. He is one of my friends and trusted allies within our own race. Krag, will you please explain to our queen what it is you seek and any information and facts you have that we need to know."

The immense gargoyle commander stands and bows in my direction, then ambles around the table. He says, "The Hewn are being abducted by Baratium and his evil troop. We haven't been able to recover any of our people because we can't find where they've been taken. I'll amend that statement because we have found one of our number, chopped to bits, and nothing but bones, laying out in the desert of the Sahara. The way we knew who it was is because her family ring was still on a finger bone. We have come here hoping you will help us, My Queen." With that, he bows again and returns to his seat.

Chuffing, I hold back a howl. These are mine! My dragon blood is ready to push my body into dragon mode and prepare for battle. I control myself and say, "Of course, we intend to help. We need as much information as possible to make our plans solid. Let me introduce you to, Gortanik Lonato, who has recently escaped from Barat, as we call him. I'll let the mage tell his story, then you can ask questions, Commander Krag."

He is nodding to me and starts to say something when Kick speaks. He stands and walks to stand in front of Krag. The handsome curly-haired mage kneels and bows his head. He says, "Commander, forgive me. I do know where they are and can help get us there. I'll do whatever I can to repay the debt I owe you for all the pain..." His voice hitches with emotion.

Krag stops him with a hand on his shoulder, "That's good news. We had all but given up trying to find the evil fucker. Let the past stay in the past, son. You had no choice. I forgave you and the others the minute we were carved. You had as much choice as we did. I'm glad to see you alive and free. I'm sorry I wasn't able to rescue you and the others. Forgive me also. Is anyone else still living?"

Kick answers, "Besides myself and Peter, he motions toward his blond friend, our friend Steen is still prisoner. I'm here to petition the HG so that we can send the Elites to save him. I'm afraid he might suffer the brunt of Barat's anger since I've gone missing. If he hasn't already."

I glance at Kino to see if he knows what they're talking about. I can tell he does. Pain, they have lots of pain, with these memories. It's thick and purple and hurts to see. I stay quiet and trust they'll tell me if I need to know. If not, I'll let it go, but I won't forget.

Krag interjects, "We have a mutual goal. Saving Steen, destroying the Horde of Barat, and protecting our people. This will help keep the Hewn safe."

I hear the name we've been calling our enemy, The Horde of Barat, and know that my Hewn have ties inside TASS.

Mega commands, "Dolo, please, take the notes for the strategy and plug them into the probability apps as we add information."

"Yes, sir. Already on it, General," Dolo clips.

We hash out plans without noticing how much time is passing when the chefs start bringing in a feast for the buffet. Clifton motions for a lunch break, and it carries. I let out a tense breath and relax. Then I make my way to the food so the others will follow. The Ceorfan get up and greet each other the way friends do before settling in to eat.

5

PLANS

Kendra

It's a new day. Spar and Kino are asleep on the torp stand in my room. Mica's getting ready for work in his own room while I clean up and change in mine. I don't have time to do everything I need to do. I start making a list in my head and laugh at myself. There's an excitement in me for this evening's London meeting. It will update TASS on the facts we've gleaned. It will be a challenge to concentrate on work today. But it's essential to give them the information concerning the Hewn of the Ceorfan. Adding Kick and Peter's report, too, will be crucial. I doubt TASS will be much help saving Steen, but I'll add that data. I don't want to underestimate them. They have a weird way of sometimes surprising me.

The secret society tries to meet in different places to keep the group incognito and the press in the dark. It costs to pay for the propaganda that refutes what they don't want the world to know. Although they'd rather spend their money differently, they'll definitely spend it to cover an episode of concern that might affect a member anytime. There are things other than gargoyles to have to hide from the population of the world. The Faery realm, for example.

At our meeting last night, the HG and I decided to steal the jump buoy while saving Steen. Following our routine, we give our information to TASS first. My General is planning the incursion with the Ducere.

My problem is... I will have to meet with the Fae royalty. I'll be in their land and have been counseled by the new young mages that it's a must to give a gift, or we might be in a fight. I hear the Fae don't fight fair and call their style clever.

I have no idea what I'll be able to give them. I'm leaning toward offering the staff Caor Thintri, but it hasn't been approved by the HG. Even though it's unlikely, we still need to ask if humans have anything to offer. Maybe we can ask for a search to find any other magical items which might be hidden within Earth. It's worth a try.

The HG is working on finding what we have that might be a magical treasure. Something that will be acceptable for now is the staff. It's our 'in,' and we hope they'll adore it so much they accept us as allies.

I hope they have an affinity for dragons. I have an idea they might.

I'm standing alone in my living room. It feels very different today. Here I am alone for once in a long time, and I'm not sure that I like it as much as I did before I met the Ceorfan Guild, my people, my family.

A familiar feeling wells up inside me. Where are my brothers anyway? I wonder if they'll be here to leave with me. As if on cue, I get a message from Jared. It reads;

Sis, I'll see you in London later, but I want to let you know Dana will be there to go with you from Navan. Don't forget a jacket. Love you, J.

My brother, always taking care of people. What a great guy.

It's time for Mica and me to leave for work. I hear a small squeak and look over to Elmer, who made the noise in his sleep on his upside-down perch. I pulse very lightly to him to calm him and get a faint pulse in return as Mica saunters out and calls from my door.

"Hey, Princess, are you ready? We need to get going. He rakes his eyes over my body and bobs his brows up and down before whistling his goofy wolf call.

My face reddens, and I duck my head and say, "I bet you say that to all the girls."

He huffs, faking offense, and says, "None that look as good as you. I only have eyes for one red dragon. Now, get that fanny in gear, so we aren't late."

WORK WAS THE SAME OL' same ol'. Nothing monumental happened, and my mind was on getting to London. I'm excited to get there to see my friends. As I'm heading to the reception hall in Navan, where we will open the portal for the trip, I sense someone coming closer and close my eyes. Within seconds I know it's Dana walking up. He should be rounding the corner right about... I open my eyes in time to catch him coming around the corner.

He circles me in his big arms and hugs me. Ah, brother hugs. This is how it is with my brothers, as soon as I think I need them, they're here or calling.

I sniff the air, and lightheartedly say, "You smell good."

He says, "Yeah, I got my weekly shower. 'Some like it fresh!'"

We laugh and sit on a short rock wall. My legs don't touch the ground, but his do.

Dana notices my feet swinging in the air. He uses his gift to create a rock platform for them to rest on. Then he bumps me with his shoulder and says, "Sis, you doing okay? I mean, with all the stuff that's happened, I need to be sure."

"I'm as happy as I can remember being in a long while. My life is full of good things. I'm strong. What do you think about this trip?"

He notices that I deflected and gives me a look that says very succinctly tell me the truth sis.

"Okay, honestly, I thought I'd never be able to live with what happened in the Jessup compound, but Dana, it feels like it happened a long time ago. Now that I have been etched, I have our grandmother's memories to help me deal, and they are very good at it. I have you and Jared and my consorts who love me. Our people help me cope with the hard stuff. I'm choosing to be happy and make the ones around me happy. You ever notice that if you're in a mood that the people around are affected too? I want everyone to be influenced positively—even if I sometimes have to practice to not be negative." Then I remember... "I had the funniest dream want to hear it?" We've always shared our dreams.

"Tell me."

I tell him about my dream about a city being destroyed and some treasure. I give him all the details, even that I believe it to be in the same area where we found grandmother Leta's head.

He says, "That could mean something. I'll look into it."

"Thank you, I love you, baby brother." I lean on his shoulder, and he pats me on the leg. In Dana-ese, that means I got ya.

That's how my consorts find us as they stroll up. I lift my head and take in the breathtaking view. Damn, they're quite the catch. Not only are they my vision of perfection, but they also have the best values. It makes them even more gorgeous. Those assholes, notice my stare, and exaggerate their struts. I laugh at them. I love that they're crazy!

Jericho's on his way right behind them with Kick and Peter, who in human terms are some of the best looking men I've ever seen. My face heats at the thought. Kino notices and turns to see who is behind them, then turns back to me by giving me a crooked knowing twinkle.

What am I even thinking? I just appreciate that my people are so good-looking, that's all.

Mega tele-speaks at this moment, *"Edling, we are on our way. I will be there with the Hewn in just a few minutes. I am assigning an escort for the nomads we are leaving here."*

I tele-speak back, saying, *"Almost everyone is here except, Clifton. Uh nope, he's walking up now. We'll be here when you arrive. See you in a bit."*

Clifton says, "Good morning, Majesty. Everything is ready, and the Ducere will be here with General Mega in a few minutes. Do you need anything?"

"Breakfast as soon as we get there. What do you think, Count? Do you think they'll be ready to feed this troupe?" I ask.

"Well, I'm sure that they are very prepared. Do you want me to go ahead and check?" the Count stammers.

"No, I was being flip. I'm sure TASS will take care of us. I just hope I'm bringing enough of the Ceorfan for this meeting, and it doesn't become a pissing party like the first one in Scotland."

Mega is here now with the Ducere team, who guard me, including Amber. I can't even tell that she's carrying a baby. I wonder if I'll ever be able to.

Flint is leading them in a rough military formation.

My prince consorts, Mica, Spar, Kino, along with Dana, walk near me.

Kick and Peter are in a group with Jericho and Krag, the Hewn leader. He has only included one of his men to come on this trip. He's an equally fierce-looking gargoyle with a pink granite hue.

The Count asks, "We are all accounted for, My Lady. Shall we leave?"

"Do you have the coordinates?"

"Yes, all that is ready, I gave them to Jericho earlier," he answers.

Mega nods to me. We are ready. Are you prepared to embark on this adventure, Pulse of our hearts?" Then he points toward Jericho, who inclines his head in Peter's direction.

The young blond mage opens a portal for us. I hear him tell Kick, under his breath, "Their way to travel is very quaint. We need to get them the jump-stone or find a way to make a new one soon."

6

LONDON

Kendra

As SOON AS WE GET THROUGH THE PORTAL, WE'RE STANDING IN puddles with fat drops of rain pouring on us. Clifton has an umbrella ready and pops it open with precision. The little gremlin checked the weather.

We're in an out of the way place to keep our travel undercover. I don't recognize the surroundings but say, "Thank you, Count."

Jericho points the way and says, "This way, My Lady Kendra," then sends Kick to the front of our group.

The dark-haired man moves, his elegant bearing begs us to follow him. Although he's never been here before, he stalks off into the dark night confidently, knowing exactly where we're going. He enters a building that appears to be a franchisee edifice and leads us through the lobby to the elevators. Then he walks past them and toward a column.

I watch in wonderment at how easy he leads us into the TASS inner sanctum without a guide. This gift of his impresses me. With a wave of his arm and a slight bow, he stops in front of an elevator door. It opens, and he says, "Please, this way."

We enter the cavernous lift. The doors close behind us. Then without pressing the floor button, we zoom downward. He then motions me to the front and says, "My lady, it's this way." He bows as the doors open, and I scoot by, followed by my entourage.

My brother and consorts are at my sides and flank me for protection. I spot Jared quickly and run to him for a hug.

He returns a brotherly embrace before pulling back to say, "I thought you might be ready for breakfast and ordered a buffet. Are you hungry?"

I answer, "Dragon style."

Glancing passed me he grins and adds, "Hey, baby brother, how are you?" He keeps me close, then steps over to Dana and gives him a squeeze.

Our baby brother says, cocking a brow, "I'll be better with some grub in me. Sissy needs something too before she blows away."

Jared chuckles, "Alright, earth-mover. Let me show you to the buffet."

"Sure thing storm-bringer," Dana retorts.

After we get our food, he takes us to our seats at a large business table outfitted with communications tech.

Now that we are eating, I say, "Jared, you look great! I kinda like the scruff, and is that a new suit?"

"Of course it is," the Duke of Stone answers for his older brother.

"Nice. Are you dressing up for a little redhead I've noticed you with here lately?" I ask.

He nods almost imperceptibly as an answer.

Dana has a slight lift of his mouth... that turkey knew! I wonder what else he knows that I don't. Boys and their secrets! Oh well, it never takes much to get them to spill.

José Brinker, the head of TASS, sits across the table from me. I beam and tell him hello as I finish my breakfast.

I search the room for Arden Kelly, my doctor friend, who faced death for me in the Jessup compound. I'll never forget that, ever. I feel a hand, soft on my back, and shiver. I check my senses, hoping it's Arden, and it's... Glen Hughes, that sexy man. He's not just Jared's friend anymore but mine too. I pivot in my chair, give him a brilliant smile, and reach for his hand to return the personal gesture.

I say, "Glen, I'm so happy to see you! How've you been?"

His blue eyes sparkle as he answers, "Your Majesty, I'm well, but not as well as you seem to be. How are you?"

Standing straighter from the compliment, I stare into his crystal eyes and, with all sincerity, say, "I've never been better, my friend. Thank you for asking."

I hope he can tell that I'm not just saying the words by rote but that I mean it. We leave the table and sit together in some comfortable chairs in the corner of the room. We discuss life until the waitstaff begins to clear the food and refill coffee.

I can always feel my consorts, but still, search the room for them. Then I tick off each and every one of their whereabouts in my head. My friend and I stand as I give excuses to leave and air kiss his cheek before saying, "We have to spend more time later. Please don't be a stranger."

He takes my hand before I walk away and responds, "You can depend on it, Kendra."

"*Mega,*" I telecommunicate to my general, *"I'm on my way over to you. Are all the Ceorfan in our member area?"*

"Our number is accounted for, Chuisle mo chroi," he says.

When I reach my people across the room, the vibe is wanting to get on with the mission of stealing back Steen. Waiting is hard.

We must work with our allies and give them this information to further our own causes. Ridding the world of the Horde of Barat and especially the man, then bringing my people into the world's presence safely. Thinking of it brings up questions.

I ask, "Is the plan for stealing the jump buoy part of the rescue for Steen, General?"

"Yes, Edling, it is. We will execute as soon as this meeting is concluded. Are you sure you wish to be part of this attempt? It would serve us better if you were in Navan."

I try to interrupt, but he stops me, "I think you would be an asset, but if we fail and Barat captures you, he will use you as a pawn against us. It will not be to our advantage."

"I'll think about it, but no promises," I return.

The gavel sounds with a sharp whack, and José Brinker begins, "I call to order this Transitional Legislative Assembly of the three thousand two hundred third Congress of The Alumbradai Sanctuary State. I would like to reserve reading of the minutes as well as approving our newly assigned representatives from our member States for the Executive Board. As we have a quorum, may I please have an appropriate motion?" The wrinkled old man looks up from his notes, awaiting a speaker.

A voice from the back, almost as if she's said this a thousand times, says, "So moved."

The chairman says, "We have a motion, do we have a second?'

Another monotone voice, "I second," bubbles out from the front of the assembly.

My eyes follow the speakers and return to the chairman.

"I believe a voice vote is appropriate. All in favor, please say, Aye," he appends.

An abundance of "Ayes," fills the hall.

"In the Chair's opinion, the Yeah's are enough to carry the vote."

I laugh, knowing my friend Mr. Brinker is shortcutting procedures. I'm sure he's in a hurry to get to the purpose of the meeting.

Unfortunately, there are always some procedures which must be attended to. One thing I've learned about my friend, when he gets to business, he wants to stay there and not be interrupted.

I patiently wait as he moves quickly through some tasks which must have been necessary to some primary member State. However, I'm having a hard time waiting for my turn, and my knees bounce in anticipation.

José's voice, droning and defiant continues, "It's of great importance to certain members as to who will be the up and coming power in the American movie industry. We have a special responsibility this year, as our newest member, the Ceorfan, must be brought into the open. It's known that Mr. Jason Briggs is coming to fame as a leading man. Mr. Briggs is known to accept persons with differences and fights a cause for individual freedom and is vehemently against slavery in any country. I demand a motion that Mr. Briggs and any other person similarly situated, be propelled to fame to aid us in that cause."

This time, the Chairman doesn't look around the room, awaiting a motion. He is looking directly at me. The members remain silent as a crypt. As I watch the smile spread across his face, it becomes evident that this is a way of TASS telling my people and me they're going to fight for our inclusion.

I speak, "Mr. Chairman, fellow members of TASS, I, on behalf of a grateful Ceorfan Guild, make the motion."

A tear of joy slides down from one eye as the entire room stands and in one voice shouts, "Aye!"

I feel several pulses of joy radiate against my skin, from my people.

Not another word is uttered as the whole of TASS remains standing, silently facing my people and me. I choke and bow a thank you to them before taking my seat.

My friend, the Chair, nods to me as the others take their seats. He says, "May I have a motion to suspend Robert's Rules of Order for the duration of this meeting. We have many issues to attend to, but only a few that are critical at the moment."

I adjust my posture and focus on regaining my composure as the rest of the meeting preliminaries play out.

José Brinker begins, "Now I would bring the notice of the members to our most important cause. We have a guest today who can give facts concerning our enemy. He's a magic user and part Fae as well as a trusted confidant of the Ceorfan queen and court. His word is to be trusted. Without further ado, I introduce you to

Gortanik Lonato." He moves back from the podium for Kick to move up to it.

Kick fidgets a little then takes command with a perfect ambassadorial demeanor. Clearly, he lays out all the information concerning the whereabouts of Barat and the Horde.

He adds, "I've been held prisoner to this mad man and his cohorts for generations. Ladies and gentlemen, there's nothing our enemy considers off-limits. He has no problem with any type of killing or torture if it suits his purpose. His cause and motivation are to eliminate all human-kind. He's found long ago that gargoyles make the best slaves for building his empire. He's concentrating on creating an army of Crafted with the mages he has left.

"Now that you know the whereabouts of this evil mastermind, I suggest you make a plan to find a way to placate the Fae king and queen. Without their admittance into the Faery kingdom, all of our plans will be for nothing. They do not abide by just anyone entering the realm. Understanding that the Fae were abused by humans, which resulted in war, that lack of trust is understandable. They trade in highly valuable magical items that they lost in the wars. That is one of the things we have of value they will accept as trade. I can get us there, but you will have to do the barter. I caution you to be clever, they will not fail to be themselves. Master Chairman, I return the floor." With that, Kick strides across the room at a quick clip, but with the same grace I see in Jericho. He sits with the Ceorfan delegation close to Krag.

The committee chairman asks, "Queen Kendra, would you like to take the floor and add to the discussion your Ceorfan contingent has shared."

I stand and start, "This is definitely why we're here, Chairman Brinker. I do have more information to share with this forum."

He returns, "Then, by all means, Your Majesty, please." He reaches for my hand and guides me up the steps to the podium before leaving me to have my say.

I begin, "Fellow TASS members and honored guests, we have

plans to rid the world of Barat. You know he's holding one of my Ceorfan mages prisoner, and I intend to retrieve my man tonight. What you don't know is that in the process, I also hope to grab the item Barat uses to transport his army. In the past, it was rumored that the staff, the Caor Thintri, was the power behind the travel. We were mistaken in that theory. The staff is a weapon akin to a laser vaporizer. He travels with a large stone called a jump buoy. You can understand why it was thought the staff moved the army because he uses it as soon as they arrive. There was a time when these buoys were used and made by the Ceorfan frequently. The formula for them has been lost, we intend to add it to our list of things to rediscover. Until then, we will abscond with the one that he has in the Fae realm."

The silence is prominent, you can hear a pin drop.

7

CHAOS

Kendra

THE DEAFENING SILENCE LASTS FOR SECONDS, THEN THE ROOM
bursts into chaos as several members shout for the floor.

I'm not ready to give over and hold up a hand and say, "Please, let
me continue. I understand that you feel more planning is needed.
That there are considerations to add for failure, and you probably
would like a piece of this pie. However, we don't intend to leave our
Ceorfan in the madman's hands any longer than we are forced.

"This is a small covert mission planned for by the best I have.
We'll slip in and retrieve our man and our magic stone. We don't
intend to go to war tonight. Even though this mission may force the
battle to a head, and begin the end of our enemy. This is one reason I
felt that the plan needed to be shared in this forum because you need
to prepare.

"We have inside information and can sneak in and out without
anyone being the wiser. I intend to go to the Faery king and queen
and offer a gift of a magical staff we call Caor Thintri unless you have
a better option. If you don't have a better option, the staff will do. I

hope it will garner favor and give us permission to be in their realm. After meeting with the Fae royalty, I, along with my Elite Warriors, will rescue my mage and gather intel in our pursuit to annihilate Barat.

"In the meantime, we need to search for more of the treasures that the Fae nobility will envy. Doing so will allow us to enter the realm at our pleasure, as my mage warrior explained. It would be a benefit if it also helps gain their trust so they can learn to trust humans again and ease up on the barriers to their realm, at least where this forum is concerned. Questions?"

Arden Kelly, bless his soul, stands and without asking, begins, "Queen Kendra, I want to be part of this contingent. As a member of TASS and a doctor, I can be of value. This will also satisfy our membership that we have other people to advise and garner support from the Fae nobles. Please, be advised that I will definitely accompany you tonight."

Stumped by the galant shithead, I have no recourse but to accept his offer. He has given me the best solution as well as affording the members relief for having a TASS presence. Nothing sort of genius. He's adorable. I also don't want him hurt. It's maddening.

"Well, Arden, it looks like we have a human and TASS contingent for the trip. Thank you for your offer," I grind out through gritted teeth, fake smile plastered on my face. He better not get himself hurt. That will really piss me off.

"Mr. Chairman, I yield the floor." I watch José as he stands and takes my hand to help me down the stairs of the stage. He is communicating his care. I see a little hot pink tinge in his aura that I sense is fatherly love.

My general and consorts stand while I take my seat beside them. The air is full of approval from the Ceorfan, especially the Hewn leader.

Member 209 has taken the podium and begins her speech. She spits out, "How, and if the Ceorfan enter this supposed realm, how much influence can TASS have? And how can we acquire more?"

Now the argument ensues. The member's statement isn't really about greed but wanting to direct the realms into a peace agreement to further commerce between the realms.

I don't think the Fae royalty will agree to anything close to this as it would require humans to travel between the realms, and they don't trust them at this time. Maybe with people like Arden, they will learn a little trust. Yes, perhaps him going is a good idea.

Spar reaches out and takes my hand in his and softly rubs it, calming me even further, making it possible to think more precisely of the plan tonight. "General, I did consider your idea of staying behind, but that's not going to happen."

"I do understand, Edling. You need to go to meet with the Fae and plead our case. I agree. You will need all the consorts and the mages in your company. Might I suggest you dress the part of queen? They are people who love all that glitters and the showiness of riches."

"Well, son of a biscuit eater. I guess I need to see if Amber brought me something that'll impress."

"Pulse of my heart, I can assure you she has. We knew that it would not be within your power to stay and let us do the dirty job."

"Dirty work, General. The phrase is 'dirty work,' and you're correct, but I did really consider it for a few minutes."

The weight off of my shoulders, I can finally relax. I glance over at Spar, who is sitting to my right. His blue eyes sparkle as I smirk and blow him a kiss while everyone is paying attention to the speaker. His hand tightens on mine.

I just managed to hear Member 209 ask another of her pointed questions.

"I also would like to ask the Ceorfan Queen what intentions she has concerning the stone they're retrieving tonight, and if this membership will house the weapon," Member 209 states as if she has a right to our country's belongings.

I stand at the same time as Mega and begin, "I decide what happens with all Ceorfan treasures and if they'll be shared."

"That may be your right, but you will invite contention and possibly criminal behavior if we aren't able to share in such a device."

Now Krag and my consorts are standing. Spar pulls me close to his side. I pat the air and motion for my people to return to their seats. Kino is singing under his breath. I nod to him to continue and whisper my thanks to him.

"Member 209, I'll consider using our tools to further the case for this forum when it's put forward and not as a pressure technique. The tools and weapons of the Ceorfan are no more yours to demand than your country's arsenals are for me to demand to use in any combat situation. I will consider all offers and safe uses of our supplies within this forum as needed and only in a civil manner. I've said before the Ceorfan are here to help." I'm not sure if it's my words or Kino's spell, probably both, but the tension is relieved.

The Chairman moves, "The committee will break and be recalled in two hours."

We all head to the buffet and continue the discussions within our own groups. Our semi-private conversation doesn't last as many of the members vie to speak with me on friendly terms. Even the stand-offish members are waiting for my attention. Good thing I've been practicing my blank face.

I'm relieved to see Glen nearby. He takes my hand and says, "Kendra, thank you for saying you'll go with me for a walk. I do wish for a moment alone. I need to catch up. He bends and kisses me soundly putting his arms around me and pushing slightly toward the door."

I'm wondering what he's up to since we've just spoken.

Under his breath, he says, "Please, play along."

I nod, and we move toward the door.

"General, please send my Ducere and inform my stiff consorts this is a ruse to talk privately. I need José to know that I won't be returning. Stay and recon the room, then follow us when the meeting resumes," I order Mega.

"Yes, Your Majesty, it is being done. I am sending Peter to follow. Also, you might need magic, and others will be noticed faster."

The door is open, Glen and I leave, and he hurries me into another room then hands me a long coat and hat. I recognize the need for putting on a diversion and the disguise. He dawns one himself before we rush out of the building.

He says, "Kendra, I overheard Member 209 making a plan to follow you and the Ceorfan to steal the jump stone. This particular member will stop at nothing to get what she wants. I'm saying it's dangerous, and I'm taking you to my hotel and leaving with another operative to throw them off."

"Are you sure? Listen, Glen, I can handle myself in a fight."

"I believe you, but we don't need an international incident that we can avoid. I'll leave it up to you."

"I agree, let's go."

I check my senses for my guard. They're behind me. In fact, they're all around me, even in the air. We enter through a beautiful old hotel. Then hurry to his room where we meet his female accomplice, who he introduces, "Pam, this is my cousin Kenni. She works with me and isn't feeling well, so I brought her to nap. Let's go get a drink and leave her to rest, shall we?"

That fast, they're out the door and gone.

Pam? Okay, I understand subterfuge, but why not call me Victoria or Kassie?

I'm going to the roof. This is no place for me. As I swing the door wide to leave, there's Peter standing with a wide grin.

He says, "Well My Queen are you ready for some adventure?"

"You better believe it, mage, let's go."

He chants a short phase and says, "I put a spell on us so that no one will give us a thought or pay attention to us and then will forget we passed."

When we reach the roof, my entire team, along with Arden Kelly, is waiting for us. Adrenaline is high. Excitement is in the air.

I grin and say, "Amber, did you bring me a dress I can at least fight in?"

She rolls her eyes and says, "I'm always prepared, wench." No one is surprised at her comment and moves on.

Peter hands my hand that he has been dragging me with over to Kick. He says, "My Lady Queen, I'm taking us to the fortress that belongs to my family in Fae. It'll be a ruin. It's unused but will afford us time to get you ready for the Faery court. Are you prepared?"

I answer, "Yes, let's go get our man."

8

FAERY

Kendra

Not only is it dark and dank, but it stinks in here. We entered the portal and came out in a pigpen. The look on Kick's face is full of shame, and he says, "I'm so sorry to bring you to such...

I hold up a hand to stop him, "I've been in much worse places, Kick. This is perfect."

Amber butts right in, "Now get out of the way, all of you. I need to get Kendra dressed, turn your backs." Kino raises an eye. "Yes, you too, Prince Consort."

Kino turns slowly and mutters, "You know this is not what I thought would happen, but listening to my sexy dragon queen dress, it is very erotic."

Spar hits him in the gut with a teasing blow, "Shut the fuck up. You're making it worse." Grinning at his friend, he leans into him and continues, "You know we could do this for fun." He bobs his head with a smirk.

Kino is nodding with the same evil smirk.

Mica laughs, "You're sharing private stuff. Stop it before I have to fuck you up for telling secrets about our lady."

In reality, several of the incursion group feel an uptick in sexual tension as they nervously listen to the rustle of clothes coming off, then back on. Arden never moves. They all generally behave until Kino sneaks a glance and touches Spar and Mica to turn slightly and see what he is watching. Amber is standing on a chair, closing a tab low on my back. Crazy goyles think I'm blind, so I wiggle my butt just a little. The dress is very revealing compared to most of my formal clothes.

I ask, "Amber, are you sure Jamie made this dress for me?"

She smiles, "Unless the humans are sporting tails now, My Queen."

"No way, chica. I'm staying in my human form for this. Though, I'm glad the clothes he makes me can be worn when I only morph halfway," I say.

There's no answer. We both hope the day will come when it'll be okay to sport our own forms in public.

This dress is perfect for the Faery court. Champagne pink sparkles cover my body. My consorts appreciate the view until Mica sees that Kick is grimacing in their direction. He motions to him to come over and leans into him and whispers, "You're welcome to ask her out mage. As Kendra's consorts, we've spoken and decided we trust you. We feel that you would be a good fit for our family. I just want you to know that it's a possibility."

One split second of gladness covers Kick's features then it's quickly replaced with shame before he schools the look and goes blank. "I'm not interested."

No way to un-hear that. I'm hurt and take a too loud breath that they all hear. I pivot and stare at the mage and give him a cold nod. I should've known the attraction I have for the warrior is all for nothing. I should be happy with the men I have. What was I thinking? This one is definitely not for me.

Mica touches the mage's forearm getting his attention and, in a low voice, warns, "Never hurt her again. I forgot about dragon hearing. Now that she knows you aren't interested, she won't look your way again, but I warn you... keep the choice you have decided on and don't mess with her or you mess with us."

The pain Kick feels shows on his face for a flash. Mica recognizes it before the mage nods his agreement and says, "My Queen, I apologize, you're the epitome of every man's dreams. I'll never be more than your most ardent guard. I intend to be the best of your mage warriors, and you won't have to wonder if you have protection from this day forward."

Still feeling the burn of his rejection, but happy for the compliment and promise I answer with prim authority, "Thank you, I have plenty of protection and can take care of myself just fine. I won't expect more from you than what's expected from any Ceorfan warrior. Now, are we ready to meet the Fae nobles?"

Kino's beside me in a flash and says, "Beloved, you are gorgeous and will be sure to impress the king and queen of this realm. Please, let me escort you." He holds his arm out for me, and I place mine on it.

Mega, who has been to the Faery court before, opens a portal with a stone. We put on our best courtly manners and walk into a magnificent foyer. It's everything you'd imagine a fairy castle to look like, opulent, bright, and sparkling. I feel a tingling on my skin and brush it away. I know it's a spell to dampen our magic. Yeah, it won't dampen my magic. In fact, I make a motion and brush it off of all my Ceorfan.

They don't even flinch, but I can tell they notice when Mega blinks his agreement and says, "I did not know that they have spell protections here that are placed automatically, Edling. Good job getting rid of it. I understand the value. I wonder if they know it failed."

"I guess we're about to find out," I answer as a tall, regal Fae man stands before me and asks for our credentials. I snort and giggle then roll my eyes. Well, so much for courtly manners.

The Faery steward reaches a hand toward me to shake my hand, but Kino blocks him, "This is the queen of the Ceorfan Guild, Kendra Macbard. You may call her, Your Majesty. She will invite all touches, until then she is not to be touched by common hands. We have come to offer a gift to the Fae king and queen and seek an alliance."

The man purses his lips and says, "Please, follow me."

We're taken to a lounge, and the doors are left open.

The steward says, "I'll leave you here. Please, make yourself at home, Your Majesty. I'll make your presence known then return for you."

He leaves us in the opulent living area. I hate sitting in my dress, but I need to get off my feet; these heels are killing me. I need to tell Amber and Jamie next time I can't be wearing these, my feet won't take it.

I smile when I notice Spar, Mica, and Kino are all standing in front of me like guards. Jericho's with them, Peter and Kick are closer to the doors with the rest of my Ducere.

We're here only minutes when my retinue parts like the Red Sea to show the entrance of a couple who are the most beautiful people I've ever seen. I was expecting beauty but not like the two before me. I stand, my eyes going back and forth between them. The strength of them isn't just physical but also part of their bearing. It flows off of them in waves.

They smile. I take a deep breath and relax. The soft, kind expressions make me feel welcome. I move toward them, reaching out to take the woman's hands as if we're old friends. She literally glows with happiness.

The Fae King says, "Your Majesty, you're welcome in the realm of the Fae. I'm King Dag, and this is Queen Dayna. We're pleased to welcome you to our home. Please Dwion, get our guests some refreshment." He asked his serving man so nicely it doesn't come off as a command.

I reply, "Thank you for the welcome. Let me introduce my

company. These are the prince regents, Spar Megason, Kokkino Petra, and Mica Jacobs. This is Jericho, Royal Mage, and his Mage Warriors." I leave out their names holding back some secrets, then continue, "Megahir is my general, Arden Kelly is our TASS representative, and the others in attendance are my Ducere."

King Dag responds, "You're welcome here and free to move between the realms without consequence. We're familiar with the TASS fellowship. I'm surprised to see you have a member with you, though. How can we be of assistance, Dragon Queen? And please, sit, let's get comfortable to talk."

A shimmer of light goes through the air at his words as if making my welcome law. He holds his queen's hand as she sits before sitting beside her himself. The steward returns with a large tray with a coffee carafe and teapot. There's an array of finger foods on the shelf under them complete with plates and napkins.

Curious I move to a chair close to them and ask, "That's wonderful, how did you know I'm a dragon? Do I look or smell like a dragon? If you don't mind my asking, this is all very new to me."

Spar offers me a cup of coffee the server had given him. Now that I'm relaxing, so are the rest of the Ceorfan, and we all begin to talk freely.

The queen answers, "It's known that the queens of the Ceorfan are dragons, and that must be the case. However, yes, you do look like a dragon. In fact, you look like a red dragon. We've been without dragons for so long. It's a dream come true for you to be here."

Oh, that speaks volumes. They must have needs that only I can address.

The Fae Queen's cheeks flush red, and she's jittery with excitement when she says, "I can't wait to see you shift and fly in the Faery skies! Please, call me Dayna."

Her eagerness makes me beam. I know how it made the Ceorfan feel that I'm part of them and I get the gist of this couple much quicker than I did with my own people. I'm taking the chance at honesty with them. I want to be known for it anyway.

"I hope my presence can help you here, and I'll do what I can to make that happen. I brought a gift for you and your kingdom."

I motion to Jericho, and he brings forth the Caor Thinrti and hands it to the king.

The noble couple breath faster and have tears in their eyes.

King Dag says, "Kendra, this is the most unique gift you could have given to us. One of my own people made it and used it for a terrible and bloody cause. Long have we coveted the return of this tool. It's been used as a weapon long enough. It has much more valuable uses," he adds cryptically.

"We also have a gift for you, and call me Dag if you will." He reaches into the air and pulls out a small gold box like a Magician. Jericho takes the box and hands it to me.

"It is safe, Edling. Jericho says to let you know it is one of the five jewels of the dragon queens," Mega tele-coms.

I take the treasure and open it, there inside is a brilliant red gem on velvet. My memories say this is the fire jewel. It whispers to me the way the others spoke, but the voice is silkier. Each gemstone has its own personality.

Peering at the stone, I ask, "Please wait for me. I can't answer here, but will soon."

Then I look towards my new friends and say, "I had no idea this was here. I'm more than glad to accept this gift. This is precious to me too. Dag, Dayna, I think I can be honest with you. Let's be friends as well as allies. I need to tell you why I'm here."

9

UNITY

Kendra

Now the room is silent, and everyone is waiting for what I say next. "Leaving politics by the wayside, I want to lay out why we need to be here. It's not just a pleasure trip.

We have an enemy in the Earth realm that's causing problems, and we know he's located here in Faery. He's holding one of my people prisoner. I'm here to get him back. I won't stop there either. It's my intent to kill this madman who's murdered thousands of humans. I'll do so with as little damage as possible to the Fae realm."

You could hear a pin drop. I'm afraid I may have just erased all my welcome in the place.

The couple both have horrified looks pasted to their faces. I'm going to have to ask... they're not saying a word. Maybe they don't want to disappoint me or something.

"I'm asking for help or at least approval Dag... Dayna, what is it? You don't have to be there in the fighting if you can't, just let me know what you're thinking. I'd really like to count you in."

"Kendra, what you're asking is a hard thing for us. We don't sanction violence in any way here in Faery. You're such a boon to us that I'll have this discussion, but know this, it won't be shared with the Fae people."

I return, "Dag, it's essential, I understand. Talk to me, so I can better understand your culture and know where you're coming from?"

Dayna holds my hand, so I don't feel rejected, and Dag starts, "I'll explain. Long ago, most honored dragon, there was no barrier between the realms of Earth and Faery. The Fae people were free to wander the Earth, but soon there were abuses. I'll admit they were on both sides those injuries created wars. To protect my people, Dayna and I separated the realms and have a strict no entry law where only the Fae can enter or leave and requires all Fae, under penalty of death, to adhere to our rules of non-violence whatsoever.

"I understand that one of my people has failed to comply with this law. His land, his home, even his life is forfeit. To my shame, we have ignored him and his behavior, what little we have known of that, that is. As soon as we capture him, we'll deal with him and report his death to you. It's also our wish to have an alliance with you. It's to our advantage.

"Kendra, you must know that your presence gives life. It has been hard on my queen to be barren and your presence gives us hope. The dragons of old were able to make the daily lives of all people they came in contact with, not only healthier but happier. We didn't expect violence from you when you entered the realm because it isn't what we've experienced in the past dragon queens.

"Not only do we want this alliance to prosper our people, but we also want to be friends with you for our own reasons. Please, Kendra, My Queen, and I have waited for much of our lives to have children, and your presence will give us that gift. There's no reason for us not to have heirs, but it isn't easy for anyone in this realm to procreate. Is it acceptable to you that we deal with the man?"

"Not really. I have a lot against the scum. It really isn't my style to manipulate. I like to let others be who they are and accept them the way they are, but in this case, I want to sway you to my cause. "If you will let me... covertly, rescue my mage, then I'll consider letting you deal with the criminal. But please, let me know of his capture and death with facts that I can share with the TASS members."

With a flick of his graceful hand, the king closes the doors to the parlor. He says, "Give me no details, and we will ignore any circumstance or gossip that you are committing a crime against Fae law. I promise we're good at this." He grins at me with a pleading demeanor.

"General Mega, sneak Kick and Spar into Barat's fortress and rescue Steen now. Tell them to return here as if they'd never left."

In seconds Spar cries out as he stumbles into a table.

I get up and move toward him and whisper, "I love you." Then I transform a hand and cut him with a claw.

I exclaim, "Oh no, please help us, Mage Gortanik, take care of your prince? Your Majesties, do you have somewhere my mage can clean up my gargoyle prince?" I hope I'm not overdoing the formal, but I'm keeping the mage at arm's length.

Kick comes over and holds the blue gargoyle's wrist at the artery and watches for the king or queen to show him where to attend to his friend. The queen leads them from the room. Arden follows without a word.

Kino says, "Here, I'll help my brother. We will be right back, beloved."

I hadn't included Kino on purpose to spare him, but my tough rockstar isn't going for that, so I nod my acceptance as they leave the room. Mega stays having given the orders. I trust he knows best here.

Dayna comes back in just seconds and informs me that she's taken them to a particular room where Spar can be helped privately, and then they can return at their leisure. Then she covertly winks at me. Oh goodness, I love this lady. I duck my head, so I don't laugh out loud but let her know with a touch to the arm we're in cahoots.

King Dag raises an eyebrow fractionally then ignores any thought that something could be going on behind his back.

The steward refills my coffee cup and asks, "Would you like anything else, Queen Kendra?"

"Actually, I think I'll fill a plate, thank you. Do you mind telling me your name, I heard but not well?"

He nearly gags as he gulps and manages, "My name is Dwion, My Lady."

My plate full, I take a bite and say, "What I want to know Dwion is if this is a recipe I can make or if all this delicious food is just Faery dust?"

The king coughs and spits his own drink into the air and laughs. His steward stiffens and blinks then says, "No, it's not Faery dust, my lady. This was cooked in the king's kitchen. All I did was use magic to set it before you." He is fidgeting with a button and then wringing his hands, "I can see if our cook will share some of the recipes with you?"

I answer, "I'd like that. Yes, I think especially these spicy, cheesy things."

He's off to check immediately.

"Well, Dag, Dayna, do you trust Dwion, or have I just let Barat know we're on his trail?" I ask.

"That remains to be seen, My Lady. However, he's accepted the house spell and won't repeat what he hears in the palace. I think it's safe that he won't be the leak if there is one. I've seen the spell broken, but it's excruciating, and only a master can thwart the magic... or a dragon queen."

"Is that so?" I say understanding that he knows I rejected the spell upon our arrival.

Queen Dayna, giggles and admits, "It's been long years that we have felt the magic dismissed. Now, tell me, Kendra, where did you get your dress?"

We spend the next while talking a sharing like friends do when a knock on the door halts our reverie. In walks Kino and Spar with a bandaged hand. Kick is behind them with another mage that I haven't met and a Fae guard. I school my features and accept the stranger as one of mine.

I say, "King Dag and Queen Dayna, I think we have made a deal. I think our visit is up for this trip, though. Is there anything I can do for you before we leave?"

The king answers, "You can grace us with your company any time young queen and soon. Please. I'll contact you as soon as our business is completed. Thank you, Kendra, for your alliance and friendship. To contact us, just say our names in a clear pool or basin of water."

Dayna adds, "Please, say you'll come soon, Kendra. If I can do anything for you, just let me know." The queen hugs me, and I feel my donum tingle with genuine care from the monarch.

When I stand and step to the door, the king says, "Just a second. I'll open a way home for you and reset your time so that you don't return years later than when you left. Just imagine where you wish to be my friend."

I respond by putting a hand on his then drawing him in for a hug. He's surprised as if he isn't used to hugs but pulls me in for a generous and warm embrace that I sense is genuine.

10

NAVAN FIRST

Kendra

WE STEP THROUGH A GLIMMERING WALL OF LIGHT INTO MY allodium in Navan. I snap into action. I don't wait and pulse to Clifton that I need him in my meeting room. As part of my Ducere, Dolo is with me. I ask him to send a message to the High Guild that they're needed here. I have to give them the information from today, before my gargoyles torp. "Wait! What time is it, Dolo?" The time feels wrong, maybe I'm tired.

"My Lady, we have returned to the minute we left the roof of the hotel. Morning is still hours away."

"That's wonderful. Making friends with the Fae nobility is going to be to our advantage," I say as the HG members begin to file into the room.

Clifton responds, "That is wonderful, Kendra. They are not always easy to get along with. You have a way of making even the hardest to get along with comfortable. I think your gift of persuasion may be part of it, but you are rather likable too."

Arden is still with us and seated. I'll ask him as soon as we hear all the information if he'd like to be our guest or return to London.

I glance at my assistant and say, "Maybe they want to have all the advantages that being friends with a dragon queen entails, Count."

I stand beside the beautiful chair crafted especially for me, and add, "If you'll all be seated. We have lots of information to get through. I haven't even heard some of it. Mega, will you please order the meeting?"

He bows just slightly and answers, "Yes, Pulse of our hearts. For the HG members benefit, I will start when we get to our destination in London."

"Did you just say HG?" I tele-speak.

He doesn't answer me but raises a brow, lifts the corner of his mouth just a fraction, then keeps speaking. "The TASS meeting started as usual with the business that was voted in as a world government. Dolo, please add the information to the guild member's tablets."

Without waiting, he continues, "The queen is making a name for herself and us by proxy, for defending her people and putting us first. She let them know her plans to save her Warrior Mage, Steen, and take the jump buoy that Barat had stolen during the Mage Wars."

Several murmurs of thanks scurry around the room. They know that I'll do damage when it comes to defending my own. The members and the Hewn express their appreciation.

Mega continues, "With the help of the Duke of Storms friend, Glen Hughes, our queen made it out of the den of cutthroats wanting to use the stone for their own greed. She met the Elite Warriors on the roof of his hotel, and we traveled to the Fae realm from there.

"Please note the palace in Faery has an automatic magic dampening spell that attaches to those who enter. However, our Edling brushed it away like mist. The monarchs did notice the Dragon Queen disposed of their spell without trouble. She then struck a secret deal with the Fae in which Spar, Kino, Kick, and Arden Kelly left to free Steen and take the jump buoy. Spar, will you take over from here and give your account of the rescue?"

Spar stands and walks toward Steen, who hasn't been introduced and says, "I first want to introduce you to Steen." Then taking a page from Findare's book, he asks, "Steen, do you pledge yourself to the Ceorfan Queen, Kendra Macbard?"

Steen bows before me and answers, "Your Majesty, I'm your warrior mage until death or beyond."

"I accept your pledge," I return and pulse the news in the manner that I had with Peter. Steen isn't surprised by the way Peter was. He's intrigued, and respect shines from his features. I motion for him to return to his seat and nod to Spar to continue.

Spar continues, "Just so the members understand I'll start from when Kendra cut my hand."

Jewel, one of the oldest HG members, barks defensively at Spar. "What would make our queen cut you, young goyle? Did you offer offense?"

"No ma'am, we needed a reason to leave the room and be alone so that we could travel to Barat's fortress to rescue Steen."

The member is satisfied and sees that there's no need to defend me or worry about my safety. She waves a hand for Spar to continue his speech.

"When Arden, Kick, Kino, and I were shuttled into a triage room by the Fae queen Dayna. She sent all the guards away except one. Queen Dayna told him to go with us, help with whatever we need, and ask no questions. Then she told him to bring us to the parlor when we were done.

"I first made sure that Kick felt it was a good idea to take the Fae with us. Or, if not, then Kino would sing him to sleep, or I'd just knock him out. But the dark mage let us know to take him, and it was good that we did.

"Kick opened a portal. When we got to our destination, the protection spells on the place had diverted us to the front doors. Kino and Kick sang a spell that made us unnoticed by this crazy mage who'd opened the doors.

"The queen's guard immediately said he was sent to investigate a problem and needed to question the inhabitants of the fortress. The mage was bending over backward to do what the guard wanted. He introduced himself as Walter and his apprentice as Bladriell. There were some ladies there too. The guard said he needed them all, including the master of the castle. They all left without ever looking in our direction. I thought we might be caught when the one called Walter looked around, closing the door, but he just sniffed and left.

"I grabbed Kick and Kino's hands and sunk into the stone and through the walls. When we were through, Kick lead us to a locked room where we found Steen chained to a bed. It was easy work to get him loose and leave. He was thrilled and said he was afraid that he was about to die, so we hurried with our mission.

"In fact, none of the operation was hard, but something did happen when we went to steal the jump buoy. I was informed that it's a big magical rock that makes it possible to move several people, and their stuff, simultaneously to another place. Interestingly, a buoy can also anchor a soul, so the user doesn't get lost and can be recalled."

"Wait, this seems different than a portal stone that I've used before," a clearly excited Jared says.

"Jare, it is very different. This stone can magically transport lots of people and their equipment simultaneously to any other place. I guess we could if the user is powerful enough, transport the entire city of Navan to a new location. A portal stone, though, can only transport items or personnel in single file, like they're going through a tunnel," Spar adds.

"You are entirely correct, young Spar. Three of these were developed by warrior mages for our Ceorfan Queen Iphigenia. One was stolen by Barat during the Mage Wars. They function as a link between the physical, metaphysical, and magical realms. That is how large masses can be instantaneously moved and a person's soul can be retrieved, all by the same object," interjected the wrinkled mage Jericho.

"So there are three of them? Where are the other two?" questions Jared.

"That remains to be seen. We know that Queen Iphigenia had them. I believe she hid them within hidden treasure vaults," the old mage added wistfully.

Not wanting the conversation to spin out of control, Spar holds up his hands to call for quiet. "The jump buoy we stole back, you can see it over there."

Spar points, and everyone looks at the massive crystalline rock. Its enormous size is its most prominent feature. If it had a shape, it would almost be similar to a Mayan temple. It has a sizable square-ish base, tapering toward a pyramid. Except the top doesn't reach a point. It's more of a jagged edge, like the top of a rugged mountain.

"We brought it here, and the funny thing is that no one was here, and the room looked a little dusty. I know that's not important, but it feels like it is. Kick told us he'd made a mistake because time in Fae is different, so we went back to Barat's lair, and then he did something, and we came here again, leaving the stone before we returned to the castle and waited for Queen Dayna's guard. With all the shielding around Navan, Kino said it wouldn't be tracked, but I need to be sure if that's correct. Kendra, do you think there are enough defenses?"

I look over at the stone, and nothing is attached to it, so I know that much is right. My memories come forward, and I know that I can test the stone with magic. I throw out a hand much the way I closed off my chamber door before and say, "Show me your magic."

I'm shown just like an etched story, from its beginning to now, the history of the stone. Ha! Now I can tell the Mage Guild how to make another if we need one.

"The stone is free of any spells to track it. However, checking it just now, I learned something. I now know its history and have information to make another when we're ready."

I'm happy to know this and might have a new way to appease TASS.

"Please continue, Spar."

His sexy grin and those flashing baby blues kill me. Maybe we can sneak away later. Holy crap, his eyes sparkle, and I'm a lizard if he doesn't know what I'm thinking.

"Yes, My Lady. While we waited for the guard outside the fortress, we saw some little broken... what I'm going to call brownies, trailing out of the place as fast as they could go. We talked to them and scared the tar out of them at first, but Kino calmed them, and Kick healed what he could. Then he gave them some food from his pack, and they left laughing and dancing. It made me glad that we could do that for them, but Kendra, the sense of urgency to get rid of Barat and his minions, went up ten notches seeing those little abused fairies. My heart hurts for everyone that devil is abusing afresh."

I nod to my love, then he finishes.

"When the guard came out, we met him, and he opened a portal and took his time entering so we could go first. As we walked into the parlor where you were waiting, the guard said he has much to report, and his king will not be happy to know that his Fae are torturing other Fae. That's when we went in, and you said your goodbyes to our new allies." He sits with his legs apart; his sexiness turns me on. I'm going to melt into goo if I keep watching him.

Changing my tactics to control myself and finish this meeting, I move on. "Kick, do you have anything to add?"

"No, My Queen, your consort, has given a good account of the excursion." I watch as my redheaded rockstar agrees. Holy crap, he's a doll. I have to get out of here.

"Clifton, will you contact the TASS chairman and give him the information that the Ceorfan will return to the meeting tomorrow with more intelligence concerning our enemy. Also, see to our guests that they have enough space and food."

"Yes, Your Majesty." He takes his cue and asks the members if they have anything to add to the meeting or questions. After a few minor issues, he dismisses the HG.

I need to make sure the Hewn are taken care of and know they are part of my people and say, "Krag, please consider this your home while you and your group are here. If there's anything you need, let me know. We'll talk before we leave for London tomorrow night." He nods, and I see that his eyes, if nothing else, are smiling.

11

FRIENDSHIP

Kendra

I'm tired, but I have a friend to see before resting. Kino and Kick split off with Jericho while Spar goes with Mega. Bummer! Mica is with me, though, as I walk over to Arden and ask him if he'd like a tour of Navan and some food.

"I'd love a tour Kendra, but no food. I think I've eaten enough between TASS and the Fae nobles. Do you mind?"

"Of course I don't mind, we're friends, and I want to show you my home. I have hours until I have to be at work."

Mica excuses himself by touching me in the middle of my back. Then giving me a small bow, he says, "It was nice to meet you again, Arden, but if you'll excuse me, I have work to do. Kendra, I'll leave you in his capable hands and will see you before dawn, babe." He bends with a sweet kiss and is gone.

"Well, it's just you and me, Arden. Let's start this way, and I'll show you the lunchroom first so you'll always be stuffed. The food is wonderful too. At first, I'd forget that gargoyles are people; they only look different. That they could make such amazing food would surprise me. Now, nothing my people do surprises me. In any case, if you get hungry, go there; they always have food."

Arden offers an arm to me, and I take it. He says, "Kendra this place is amazing, do you ever get used to it?"

I'm surprised when I say, "Yes, but I still see how beautiful it is."

That's when Elmer flies right up and attaches to the front of my shirt. "Awh, I missed you too, little boy. You feel fat from eating tonight." I say, scratching his tiny head. "Meet Elmer, my pet bat, Arden."

"Kendra, you know that bats can carry rabies, right?"

"Yes, but not Elmer, I've made sure. Thank you for thinking of my health, though."

"That's my job," he laughs, and we take a short tour showing him some of the most beautiful formations and making up names for them until we're laughing so much our faces hurt. When we finally get to the lunchroom, we stop and get drinks. Of course, some guards start to shoo out the goyles, but with a stern look from me, they quit. Sitting and talking, I tap a quick message on my tablet to Clifton to ask where Arden's room is. My old college friend drops a bomb on me before I get to tell him I'll take him to his chamber.

"Kendra, I need to ask you something serious," Arden says.

My heart stops. Oh my, I hope he isn't going to say he's interested in me... I'll have to friend zone him hard, and I don't want to hurt him.

"Arden, you are one of my all-time best friends. Of course, we can talk about something serious." That at least was soft... and he doesn't appear hurt.

He begins, nervously looking at his fingers as he wiggles them anxiously, "Okay. I don't want to get anyone in trouble, especially my girl. But Kendra, I need to let you know that I'm dating one of your Ceorfan. I'm hoping that she and I could take our relationship to the next level. I very much enjoy spending time with her, and I want to spend time with her away from Navan or in secret. Is that something that will get us in trouble?"

Thank God!

"Holy crap! How... Who... no, really, you don't have to tell me, but really?" I sputter my questions and statement out in a mishmash of words.

"I am certain it's a lot to ask of you. But I want to show her my world too and not hide all the time."

"Oh, sorry, I didn't mean to sound that way. I have no problem with you dating one of my Ceorfan. You've got to spill, though, because I might need to help if you get some haters in the human public. In fact, I love this idea. Maybe... Do you mind waiting just a day or two? I need to get with TASS and tell them we're going wide. Haha, and the world governments need to get ready to publicize our secret. Oh, I'm so excited!"

He takes a deep breath and smiles. "I'm so relieved we were afraid that you wouldn't be happy and say no. My girl's name is Peri, and we met when you got... you know... taken. While you were gone, she was the specialist who was assigned to help us to get weapons to use in the Jessup encampment. Even though I had to come clean because they searched me to death. She was there, secretly providing gear to the team. We've been FaceTiming ever since and even met once incognito in the night. I can't thank you enough. I need to call her!"

My old friend reaches for me and gives me a great big friendly hug. I'm caught up in his excitement when my tablet chimes a notification.

I check the message and say, "Clifton told me where your room is, so let me take you there, and you can have some privacy to call her and clean up, then maybe she can take you and show you more of Navan while Mica and I are at work. What do you think?"

"Just show me the way."

I wonder how many times Jared called me Kens to his friends? Whatever. It's a name I accept. I almost skip taking him to his chamber.

12

SOME INTEGRATION

Kendra

I'm still on cloud nine when I enter my own chamber and see Ferre leaning over with her obviously enhanced boobs in Kick's face. I recognize the magic as it cups her breasts, keeping them perfectly shaped, no matter her... position.

Instant dragon anger pours through me. I'm gonna kill her. I pause and run a scenario for her death in my head, slowing time like I do when I'm in a battle. I don't smirk as my thoughts create the perfect end for her. Then one side of my lips inches up.

I hear Kick politely explaining, "I have eyes for only one woman. I'm not worthy of such a woman. But while she lives, I'll never be interested in any other."

Damn, he is Lancelot.

She says, "I understand big boy, but if you ever need a friend I'm here for you. I need to go help my sister, Barhaine."

When she sees me, she startles a little. I glimpse a flash of surprise, as her eyes widen and jaw slackens. The oranges in her aura let me know she only wanted to have some fun with Kick. It becomes obvious she wasn't trying to do something behind my back. If anything, she's excited to be in the room with me.

Ferre does a quick, little off-kilter curtsey. I can't help but love her as I forget my earlier anger. Old cougar!

Thank the Lord, everyone's here. My visit to Faery has given me a sort of jet-lag. The time is still off for me. Usually, I feel the setting and rising of the sun. I see the sunset as a new day because that's when the majority of the Ceorfan un-torp. Oddly, I guess because of the jet-lag, I wonder how close it is to dawn.

I take out my tablet to verify the time. It's half an hour before sunrise.

"Hey, guys. I have some news. And how are the Hewn? I think we should have a party to recognize they're part of us. How about it?"

"Great idea, now tell us your news, hun," Spar asks.

"Well, it seems Arden is enamored with Peri and wants to date her in public." I'm excited and keep rambling about how happy I am and how I think this will be the beginning of the reintegration of the Ceorfan back into society, and, and... It takes me a bit to notice their silence. When it finally penetrates my excitement, I stop talking. "What is it, what's wrong?"

Spar rubs the back of his neck and isn't looking up. In fact, none of them are looking at me.

Finally, Kino glances my way with a pained expression. My stomach sinks. What have I done wrong?

Kino says, "I know what you are thinking, beloved. You have not done anything wrong. We are wondering how the world is going to take this change and how they are going to accept gargoyles. Change is hard on some people."

"When you guys torp, I'll send a message to José Brinker and see if we can do a massive media kit on how the Ceorfan are good and protect. I'm tired but will take a nap after work. I'll get some opinions and answers before sundown."

Mica takes my hand in his and says, "I'm sorry, Princess, we aren't trying to rain on your parade. I know most people are gonna be very kind and accepting, but there'll be those who'll cause trouble. I don't want to see any of our people hurt. I feel a little like the Fae king wanting to make a barrier to protect them from humans. I know it's not right... you did the right thing. I'm happy, and we'll deal with problems as they arise."

"We can talk more when we wake, hun. I've gotta go pee. I learned a while ago that I might be stone when the sun comes up, but if I torp needing to pee, it only gets worse until I change back," Spar chuckles.

"Get going, yeah, we can talk tonight. Mica, are you ready for work. We need to leave. Kick is here, and I'll let him know I don't mind if he stays."

My big partner turns to the mage and makes sure he knows he's welcome. "You have enough to do, but don't be afraid to rest while we're gone. We'll see you in eight hours," Mica says.

"Yes, I'll be here. I have nothing else to do today but research and make a guard training schedule for the mages. That's going to take some time."

My Rockstar heads over to the torp stage as my blue heartthrob comes running out of the bathroom with his pants still not buttoned and hanging low. The mage and Mica walk with me to watch them torp.

The dark-haired man says, "Do you mind if I soak in the magic of the torp with you? It's always refreshing, and I could use the energy?"

"Oh, that's interesting. Yes..." putting my finger on my chin thinking... "I do remember. There was a time when humans, dragons, and mages commonly enjoyed the torp magic. And there's another good thing we get from it besides the long life and the healing of my loves. Of course, join us."

My goyles are listening as we feel the sun rising; they strike a pose together. The stinkers have hardened into another pose.

Kick is soaking up the magic as it prickles our skin. I watch him out of the corner of my eye. I think he's a good fit for the Guild. Also, I'm sure he'll help my people. He helps me.

When I take in the final pose of my goyles, I note Kino looking straight at me with puckered lips, his hand near his mouth, blowing me a kiss. Or, I guess it could be for whoever stands in the way of his lips. I giggle then move to watch Spar.

He, on the other hand, is just being Spar. His pants have dropped enough that half his ass is now visible. That round butt is toward me, my blue goyle having turned his back to me. With his knees bent somewhat, he's twisted his upper body back to me. His eyes are wide in feigned shock at his backside being exposed, and his hand is near his mouth, which is open into the shape of a big 'O.' He looks like that little girl on the suntan lotion from a long time ago.

The feeling of their torp didn't energize me. It makes me feel happy, though. My ranger partner and I sit at the table with the mage. I send a few messages from my tablet. The first one to José to let him know we'll be at the meeting tonight. I have a question to put before them. I describe my request to him. My thoughts are, if he has any concerns, he'll be prepared ahead of time.

I wonder if I should use the jump buoy as a carrot for getting what I want at the meeting. "Kick, do you mind talking to me for a minute? I need an opinion."

Mica looks up, squinting in my direction, while still paying attention. Our eyes lock. What a hottie. I've got to get some time alone with him. I squeeze my legs together and shift, forgetting my question until I hear the mage's voice.

"I don't mind helping you, My Queen, ever," Kick answers.

"Call me, Kendra, please. You heard that I want to have the Ceorfan gargoyles be seen in the human public. In fact, I put it before TASS when I was first introduced to them. It was one of my primary goals for my people. What will it hurt if I get what I want by offering the jump buoy as an incentive?"

"Kendra, it can be used as a weapon so you'd have to be in control of the magic and not share the use to them. That aside, it's a good chance that it'll get you what you want fast. Especially considering the greed on some of their faces when you told them you intended to retrieve it."

"You're right. I want you and the Warrior Mage Guard to be in control of it. Also, the Guard should be the only ones able to approve its use and to operate it. I think I need to talk to Jericho some more about this. But it's time for Mica and me to leave for work. We'll see you later."

Together, my golden goyle and I move toward the door. I turn before stepping through and wave. I notice that Kick flinches when he sees that I saw him watching me. Not sure what that means, but Mica and I continue on our way.

13

A MOTION

Kendra

WHEN MICA AND I RETURN TO NAVAN AFTER WORK, HE GOES TO his room, telling me he'll be with me soon so we can rest before the others wake. He needs to report to Mega even when we have uneventful shifts, and I know he wants to shower. What I wouldn't give to be in there with him.

I enter my chambers and find Kick there at the table where we'd left him this morning.

"Have you been here all day?"

He grins and says, "No, My Lady, I did rest and have a meal in the lunchroom. How was your day?"

"Oh, just making sure. It was another boring day at work. The most interesting thing is always Mica. If he hadn't been with me, I would've gone nuts." My shoulders sag, and my eyelids droop.

Kick says, "I think you're asleep on your feet. Please, consider a nap. I promise to be here if you need anything. I can contact the Royal Mage for you and set up a meeting to discuss the jump buoy and how you want to handle its uses when you wake."

"You're right, I do need to rest. Mica will be here soon. You can stay if you want. No one will care." I want to reach out and hug him. But, no, that's not our relationship, and it would probably strain things. I pivot in a circle, trudge to my bed, and lay down fully clothed. Elmer swoops down from his perch and is on my chest in seconds. Rubbing his soft little head gently, I drift off to sleep.

Funny that I actually sleep. Mica is snoring softly beside me, and I know I slept longer than I wanted, but feel much better. I peek around my room, instead of looking toward my consorts who I can sense through our connections. I discover Kick is walking around my seating area with a big book in his hands. Those hands! So sexy!

He must sense me watching him and glances over to me. My heart lightens when he smiles. Amazing. I'd gotten used to his brooding appearance, but his playful look is brilliant. Shut-up! I scoot to the end of the bed and get up.

"I'm going to take a bath, then I'll be back, will you..." wash my back... is what I want to say, but I behave. "I mean 'with' you. I see you have something to share. Do you mind waiting?"

Shit, yeah, he probably does have something to share, but not with me.

"Yes, it can wait, and I don't mind waiting. But I do need to give you this information before the meeting with TASS."

"Okay, we can talk after I wash up." I go without waiting for an answer.

I should hurry, but I don't. Instead, I lean back in the heat of my bathing pool and rest. It's sunset; I can feel it. My goyles are awake. I have my eyes closed, but hear every sound, and know when Amber enters. Her little feet smack the ground in soft clicks.

She asks, "Kendra, would you like me to wash your hair?"

"You know, I do. It won't bother your back being pregnant or anything, will it?"

"No, that will take a few more weeks. How are you doing?"

There was a time when I couldn't talk to another female and thought I'd only have men for friends. I think men are way easier than women anyway. Having Amber and some of the others for friends has opened up my world. I love having female friends. I didn't know what I was missing until now.

"Amber, I'm doing better than ever and hoping the bottom isn't going to drop out of my wonderful life."

"Lean forward a bit. I can't even begin to imagine how that is for you. I don't think any of the princes would let that happen, and you know what? I don't think a certain tall dark and handsome mage would either."

I gulp and share, "You know when I was changing into that pink dress in Faery? I was hoping he would want me and was let down when he made sure I knew that he doesn't."

"Kendra, my friend, I don't think it's as easy as that, but yeah, I was too."

"It won't keep me from checking him out, though!" I laugh and plunge under the water when she pushes on my shoulder, encouraging me to rinse.

"You and me both girl," she laughs.

"Now, tell me how it is to be pregnant, and how Mason is doing with the baby coming?"

"He's completely over the moon and trying to baby me. I'm not letting him all the time, but not having to do my own claws, and cleaning is wonderful. There are times I admit that I'm getting tired easier. I'm always warm now, but nothing bad. I think being with child agrees with me. Gargoyle babies grow fast. Now get out, and I'll fix your hair."

"Getting out."

We sit, talk, and experiment with my makeup until she says, "I have to go. Mason will be getting nervous that I'm... she jumps and puts a hand to her little baby bump then says, "That's the first time I have felt the baby move. Feel it," she all but demands.

I reach out a hand, and she presses it firmly against her stomach. I wait and feel movement across my hand, take a sharp breath, and squeal, "I felt it!"

She's jittery with glee and says, "I've got to go show Mason. Love you, see you later."

She's out the door before I have a second to think or say goodbye. I dress in my flying gear and leave the bathroom. My handsome princes aren't here; they must have already gone to get breakfast.

Elmer is and flies over.

Kick is still here sitting on my sofa reading. He has dark circles under his eyes, which prompts me to say, "You need rest. If you want to sleep in my bed with Mica, you can or lay on the couch, but you will get some sleep. You're dead on your feet."

"Your Majesty, I agree and am going to crawl up with Mica and rest for a while. I know that you and the others will go flying before the HG meets, and I'll need to be fresh for the meeting later too."

"Scoot then," I say, pointing toward the bed and ogle his fine ass as he crawls up and drops to sleep almost instantly.

Fuck me! I grab a muffin the chefs had provided in my little kitchen area with Elmer firmly attached to my shirt, turn, and leave.

14

HIKERS

Kendra

THE LUNCHROOM IS STUFFED WITH GOYLES EATING. I'M HERE TO find my princes. A hush falls over the cool room when I enter. But, thankfully, the guards don't try to hurry everyone out at my presence.

Spar looks up with his wicked grin and whistles. I smirk at him. I can almost feel his desire, and it heats me to the melting point. I must have walked over to the table but don't really remember. I shake my head to clear it.

"Are you three ready, or am I flying on my own tonight? I need the exercise. My wings are getting stronger, and I don't want to lose that muscle."

Kino asks, "Beloved, are you hungry? You might need to eat something first. We burn a lot of energy flying."

Mica, his golden eyes gleaming adds, "Yeah, babe, I'll get it just tell me what you want."

I couldn't love them more if I tried. My center throbs as the memory of their hands on my body fills my thoughts. I'm a goner.

I straighten my back, huff softly, and say, "I ate a muffin on the way here and will get more when we get back to London. I'll take some coffee on the way to the cave entrance, though."

No sooner is that out of my mouth than Spar's returning with a thermal cup and handing it to me. My goyles and I move as one, and we're out of the cave in no time.

I put my hand to my chest to protect Elmer, and he shifts to my neck and settles under my hair as I take off. The air cools my skin. I sense the guys want to hurry, so I set a faster pace. We've gone far enough, and I glide on the wind getting my bearings there's something amiss. I glance around and notice that the others feel it too. All of us concentrate on the ground under us.

I say, "I want to land and figure out what's making my donum kick up. How about that ridge?"

There's tree cover and large boulders to hide behind if necessary. My wings blow up the dry and powdery dirt. Spar points to the north, and I spot a couple lying on the ground.

"Mica, me and you," I whisper, then stare into Spar's eyes, touching Kino's arm. They both nod and slink into the tree line and disappear. I'm covered by rocks and shift into my human shape with Mica doing the same. His change is graceful and elegant but so powerful. I can only hope to look as sexy when my body is morphing. He grabs my hand, and we run to the couple. I sniff the air, and so does my guy-goyle. No danger is apparent.

I say in my best Ranger voice, "Federal Ranger Macbard, can we be of assistance. Not even a finger moves on either person. I move closer and morph one hand back to red and black claws since I don't have a weapon in my exercise clothes. I don't need them like I did not long ago, anyway, Mica's here too.

Both of the people are breathing, male, dark-skinned, and wearing hiking gear. One has a canteen in his outstretched hand, so I reach for it, and sure enough, it's empty.

The man groans and turns over. I hop back and ask, "What happened here, are you okay?" His eyelids flutter, but he doesn't answer or wake.

Mica checks the other man and says, "They're incredibly dehydrated and out of it. They won't live unless we get them to safety. He taps his tablet and calls the others.

They arrive in seconds, Kino says, "I checked, and the Cueva Hallow News is reporting missing hikers in this area. Be on the watch for rescue workers and change I'll carry one if you get the other, Spar. We can take them to the Ranger Station to get them help."

Elmer starts moving, and now that it's dark, it's feeding time I pulse to him to go, and he flies off into the night sky.

It only takes minutes to get to the federal facility. We land as quietly as possible in the back buildings away from all cameras and morph again. Mica picks up the smaller of the two men and gets him over my shoulders. I could have gotten him in a fireman's carry position, but it would take me longer. As soon as the dehydrated man is on me, Spar places the bigger hiker on Mica. He nods his thanks and takes off with me right behind him. He buzzes us in as the night watch runs towards us. My guess is they saw us walk up on the monitors.

Jerry Gonzalez is one of the city police officers who responds to the calls for enforcement. He and his partner, a new guy named Tyler Elles, are carrying a stretcher toward me. They set it down, and I lean forward to let the hiker down into their waiting hands. I make a puffing noise and struggle a bit. I adjust my back, in an attempt to make it look like it was a harder job to carry the guy than it really was.

There's only one medic on the night shift, and he's giving the necessary triage to his new patients as Officer Elles calls for an ambulance. The hospital is over an hour away on the northeast side of Cueva Hollow, so the medical officer is going to be the one who saves these men. He's already started one IV on the big guy and is just starting on the smaller of the two.

"Jerry, do you want my information? I'm in a hurry to get home and get some rest for my shift tomorrow, so if you don't mind, I'll let you write the police report," I say to him so that Mica and I can leave.

"What the heck were you doing out here anyway? You both need to go home and get some sleep. I'll do the reports, just give me the specifics."

"Mica says, "It's my fault we're still here. We were rock climbing, and then I planned on taking her to dinner. We were on Wal-eye ridge, and being so high, we spotted those men unmoving on the ground below us. We went to offer assistance and found them unconscious and carried them to my truck and got here in minutes."

"It looks like they had water, but it was gone when we got to them. Why wasn't it reported that the two were missing sooner?" I wonder.

Jerry answers, "They are here with a huge group visiting the caverns, and they have been gone for two days. Their friends didn't worry until they missed a meeting today at three when you both were off the clock. The friends say they thought they were in Tarone, the next town closest to Cueva Hallow, checking out the cowboy museum."

"So they've been wandering around in the ninety-plus degree New Mexico heat with no water for two days, no wonder they are dehydrated," I say.

"You said it. Did you see their ride anywhere by any chance?" Jerry asks.

"No, did you, Mica?" I ask.

"No, I didn't, they must have gotten too far away before they got lost. Well, Jerry, we'll leave them in your capable hands and see you next time." Mica pats the smaller officer's shoulder before we leave.

We hightail it to the trees without being seen and find the others sitting there waiting leaning against the big tree trunks. Kino has his long red locks in a hairband and has let a little scruff start to grow on his chin. Damn, mother, may I have another? Oh yeah, the blue stunner with the messy blonde mohawk next to him is just as fine, and he's all mine. Not to mention the gorgeous hunk-a-goyle beside me. The two sitting stand and start toward us. Their muscles ripple under their tight flying gear. Now that's something I dream about.

"All taken care of. The EMT's have the hikers, and it looks like they'll be fine. Thank you all for being the best support and caring about others." Shit! That is such a turn on. "Ready to go home?" I gush.

I morph when they affirm they are. I better go now. Surrounded by these three is making me sweat. All shifted, we fly high to minimize our chances of being spotted. Even though it's dark, we aren't taking chances.

When we sit down in front of the cave entrance, Jericho meets us with Krag and some of the Hewn. There's a little path in the dirt where he's been pacing. He says, "I hope everything is alright. You aren't usually gone for so long, and it's time to go to London. Should I cancel for us, My Lady? I don't mind calling the Duke of Storms for you."

"We found some lost hikers in the hills, and they needed medical attention that my dragon didn't need to take care of. No, call Jared. But just tell him we're going to be late. This is an important meeting, we need to show up."

My eyes widen, I blink, tilt my head in thought, and placing a finger on my chin, I say, "Yes, let's be late. That will be good if they miss us for an hour or two. Because of the attack, the committee may want to take action against the perpetrators. They may also be more open to us. Especially if they think they may lose our help."

Krag laughs a croaky gargoyle chuff and says, "I like how you think, My Queen. You'll have their attention when we arrive. Are you hungry? Your chefs made a delicious meal in your war council room," he asks, extending an arm.

I take his arm, cock a grin, and say, "You betcha, big boy. I like how you think too! I call it my allodium because that's what my brother called it. But I might just add the war council to it for fun."

Now we all chuckle and find our way to the food. When I've showered and dressed, we can leave to inform TASS of our new information.

15

MEETING TWO

Kendra

KRAG WAS RIGHT, THE CHEFS DID MAKE A WONDERFUL MEAL, and I'm stuffed, and I'm miserable and rub my abdomen in an attempt to feel better. Note to self... don't keep eating when I'm full.

I exit the bathroom dressed in queenly fashion, Sunny, my stylist is with me beaming over my appearance. I'm wearing a short dress, backless to make room for my wings and tail. It's a gorgeous cream-colored taffeta with pleats in the front. Matching silk shoes with gold embellishments finish the look.

Kino comes forward, offers his arm with a nod of his head, ducked a smidgeon, and says under his breath, "My beloved, you look good enough to eat."

I bite my lips, then raise them, letting the glee shine from my eyes and say, "You're killing me, and I'm on the edge with no relief. Let's call in sick."

With a satisfied pucker, he kisses my hand and says, "Soon, I'll take care of your needs. I promise."

Then we truck off with Spar and Mica to meet the mages and our other Ceorfan for a trip through the portal to see the TASS members.

When we get to the waiting area, we're the last to show. We've done this before and know the drill. Kick opens a portal, and we're through quickly. He guides us to the meeting of the heads of the world. We were right. It's quiet as a mouse in here. No one moves until José walks over to the podium and replaces a sour-looking chubby member. He throws a hand in the direction of the American member's seating, and the man heads toward them with a huff.

The Chairman says, "Your Majesty, Queen Kendra, would you like the floor, or would you like to wait to give us the information you wish to share with this forum?"

"Yes, Mr. Chairman, I believe I would like the floor. There's quite a lot to share, and it's time I get started," I say, walking up the steps.

José helps me up the few steps. I put on my most queenly visage and square my shoulders.

I say, "First, let me apologize for my tardiness. My prince consorts, and I had found some lost hikers in a desert area that needed urgent assistance."

A rumble of nervous murmurs makes their way across the room in waves. It only takes a few seconds for the interruption to abate. When I look back across the membership again, the faces are far more welcoming than before I said anything.

Next, I tell the members about the attack, leaving out the subterfuge of Glen Hughes. If they knew how well he fooled them, they would be able to adjust in the future. I don't want them to know he was in on saving me to the degree he did.

I speak firmly and say, "Second, I'm not happy that members of this group had me followed and attacked my Guild and me. This calls for strong deliberation on my part with my people. We believe it's in our best interest to remove ourselves from this forum."

The intake of air from the members almost sucks me forward.

I tele-com my General, *"Good, let them squirm. They need us more than we need them as always. We have a better chance of defeating our common enemy than they do. This will push back inte-grating into the population and making ourselves known, but I can find another way."*

I step away from the podium and add another thought to Mega, *"Commander, will you block anyone from coming forward to help me off this stage? We're leaving."*

He tele-messages me back as he moves forward, *"I am organizing the Ducere now, My Queen."*

Mega is speaking very formally. That isn't unusual, but he's been trying hard to update his language, and he didn't this time.

I ask, *"I take it there's some kind of danger, or are you playing the ever alert Ceorfan General?"*

"No one here is feeling the need to hurt you. However, this group needs a show of power. I'm making a point," Mega says as I'm encircled by my Elite Warrior Guard and Hewn.

It is an effort on my part to not cackle as the humans in the room stay perfectly still for our show.

Jared is lined up with us and ready to leave too. My army is impressive, and I know before my dragon self became part of me, I'd have peed my pants viewing the monsters around me. I follow their lead, and we file out of the hall.

Once out the door, Peter activates the jump stone, and we're out of here. I step into my allodium and watch as my contingent head straight for the buffet. Good, at least they feel that they can finally eat in my presence. Besides, for the most part, they're big and need lots of food.

My little green assistant, Count de Treon, says, "Your Majesty, I hope you don't mind that I took the liberty of ordering food."

The phone rings before I have time to answer him. He looks up at me and says, "It is the TASS chairman. Shall I answer or make them wait until we've eaten?"

I answer, "Let them wait and hand me a damn bagel... I mean, please."

There are grunts and growls around the room of approval. We eat, but I just pick at my food. I'm not hungry yet.

Kick says, "We have the upper hand, but it won't last. We need to get everything we could possibly want before their attitude changes, and the party is over if you know what I mean."

Mica answers, "Yes, I agree, we need a list. This is one time that we know for sure we're getting our way, so let's not go easy on them."

Spar agrees, "I like that idea. Not only do we press the fact we won't share our jump buoy willy-nilly, but we should also stress only those who play nicely will have the advantage of using it. Only at our discretion, though, as we discussed. What if we force the issue and make them start the propaganda machines now so that we can walk Earth again sooner? No waiting."

I say, "You're right. I was going to bring it up, but now I'll make it with a deadline. What about the end of the week?"

Smiles and satisfaction fill the room, and pulses tag me. I wonder if the mages feel this. And the phone is ringing again, so I nod to the Count.

He answers, and of course, it's José Brinker.

He says, "Kendra, that was well played. Some of the members are beside themselves, others are cleaning up their pants from your military display. I have to say it took me back even, a very nice maneuver."

My eyes brighten with glee, "Thank you, José, I bet that was a sight. All those suits rushing to the bathroom. We are eating and making a list of demands while we are the golden children."

He answers, "Good thinking. Add that you want exclusive access to all TASS installations and news media for your people at all times. Some of the members have been withholding from the Ceorfan, and it needs to stop."

Okay, thank you again, Chairman, and we'll be back after we finish our meal. You can tell them you twisted my arm," I say with a giggle.

Krag asks, "Your Majesty, could I suggest that you also ask them to release any and all Ceorfan they may or may not have in custody. It is my belief that some of our people are being experimented on in countries with the capabilities. My brother hasn't been seen in a long time, he dropped off the radar without letting us know, and that isn't like him. I've always thought a government found a way to capture him for research."

"Yes, that's a wonderful addition to our demands," I say, sipping the coffee Spar handed me earlier. We made quite the exit and have enormous demands. Now what kind of entrance do we make when we return in a few minutes. I need some rest before I go to work and would like to get this over with."

"My Queen," Mega says, "I would like to use the jump buoy. We will be well-served if our entire group materializes in the meeting. This will show what we use daily, as well as emphasize what humans don't understand. I am speaking about magic. They need to see our strength but also to know that we live differently and with magical gifts. Of course, we don't want them to know all of our secrets, but they need to know we have more than they know."

"I agree. Is there anything else? I'd like to add that we have options and don't have to stay on Earth. We can go to Faery now. If humanity wants our help, they need to speak up. They don't know that we help others daily. I want to stress this is our mandate and charter. They'll have to figure out if they want us or not," Kino says.

"Yes, it'll be a change, but we're getting used to change, right? If you're ready, warrior mages would you do the honors?" I say, rising from my seat and moving closer to the jump buoy.

My elites surround me as before, and Kick moves to the crystalline stone. When we're all assembled in an impressive military formation. A slight uptick in the corner of the mage's eye is the only question I see from him. I nod, and the next second we've all returned to the TASS meeting area. Groans and surprised squeaks emerge around the room. I walk straight to the podium, taking the proffered hand of the old Chairman as I climb the steps.

The results of this meeting will be much different.

16

GETTING OUR WAY

Kendra

I'VE BEEN PRACTICING MY BLANK FACE FOR SO LONG IT FALLS into place without effort as I glance around the room. I verify that I'm everyone's focus, and my brothers are grinning at me. They're the only ones in the room, smiling. I almost smile back and look down to stay sober. Those two could paste on a smirk while watching an IRS auditor dig through piles of receipts. Everything is entertainment for them. Their happy faces give me strength. A toughness that I'll need to get what my people deserve, especially from this room full of self-serving vipers.

I start, "TASS members. I won't withdraw my earlier words."

Again, the room is filled with a mild form of interruption as members speak to one another. Only a few of them were loud enough to catch my attention.

Continuing on, I say, "What I will say is that we will consider remaining on Earth to assist this world where we can."

Letting them know we have options is sure to surprise them, especially some of the more vocal antagonists. Knowing we can leave

Earth ultimately should serve as a sharp undercut to any negotiation point they opt for.

I continue, "Members, we have a list of requirements in exchange for our service with you."

This interruption is much more boisterous than the others. Our allies in the room, demand of our opponents, a more significant number, time for me to present our needs. I hear, "Just hear her out!" shouted more than once.

José brings his gavel down with a sharp crack that brings immediate order to the room. Chairman Brinker glowers at the members before saying to me, "Your Majesty, we wish for you to stay and be a part of us and our world. If you continue, we shall consider your list. We will offer you as much as it is in our power. If approval from our members' governments is required, I would beg for the time needed for those approvals to wend their way through the bureaucracy. I return the floor to you, Queen Kendra."

I add, "Thank you, Mr. Chairman. Our list isn't long, but it is required. One thing isn't any more important than another. What we will give you in return is Barat on a platter. We'll begin an outreach campaign to help further peace in the world. Our mages and gargoyle negotiators have generation upon generation of knowledge. My people were present before either side in the Middle East. We saw the Great Wall of China being constructed. There isn't a single conflict area in the world where we don't have a greater depth of knowledge than the entire human race combined.

"We'll assign teams to assist your archeologists. The Ceorfan will provide first-hand accounts from the fall of Troy, the rise and fall of Rome. The Lost Legion... It was never lost. Many of them are members of our society and stand ready to help you understand your own past. I have memories dating back thousands of years. Memories that will rewrite your flawed version of history.

"We'll help you with any legitimate task, big or small. The Ceorfan gargoyles and mages are helpers. We want to help."

I pause here to let what I've offered sink in. I want the members to truly grasp the scope of knowledge alone that my people can and eagerly will provide. The transition isn't long. I wait just long enough for the members to begin to shuffle in their seats and for a slight muttering to begin.

As it does, I continue. This time deliberately lowering my voice, forcing my audience to listen carefully. "What I didn't tell you earlier is that we have found the Horde and their leader Baratium Mezacain. We are closing in on him. As a further incentive for this body to treat with us with respect, we'll destroy the Horde and kill its leaders. Soon, the Horde will no longer terrorize your towns and villages.

"For all that we have offered, we can provide more... much more. In return, we ask for comparatively little;

1. We want your country's propaganda apparatus to bring knowledge of the Ceorfan people to the world. This must demonstrate our desire to help. It must also begin by the end of this week.
2. We require access to exclusive TASS installations and news media for your people at all times.
3. You must agree, our weapons are our own. We don't mind sharing if the cause is righteous. The jump buoy that you undoubtedly saw us use to re-enter this meeting undeterred is one of the items we intend to share. But it will only be shared by approved plans that have been researched by us. Its use will be at our sole discretion. Once I make a decision, it is final and shall not be questioned. Only my Warrior Mages Guard will operate the stones, and only at my expressed command. In any case, most humans can't make it work; even though some humans do possess magic.
4. Within the next twenty-four hours, I want all Ceorfan people in your countries released. Regardless of the reason they've been detained, they will be delivered into

the care of the Dukes of Storms and Stone. Any country that does not fully and immediately comply, or who harms a Ceorfan in their country, will be in a de facto state of war with the Ceorfan. That country will also be excluded from any technology, knowledge, or magical assistance until I'm confident this requirement has been met. There is no appeal. I retain the sole power of decision in this regard. I hope I've made myself clear."

I STOP and stare out across the hushed crowd. My eyes trace from left to right, then back again. I want them to see me looking directly into them, wondering if I'm using some sort of magic to read their thoughts. They must understand me, they have no chance to defeat us. Either they agree, or we pick up our toys and leave.

"*Mega,*" I tele-speak, "*How does the room read?*"

"*They are considering. Some are surprised you know about those detained, and some aren't fazed at all. Members are excited, to say the least that we can end the Baratium problem. Some are working out how to start their own propaganda programs today while others are trying to figure out how to use us for gain.*"

I finally end my pause. "It has been a long day and night. I'll retire for the evening. If you have any questions, please ask them of our representative, the Duke of Storms. I'll return when the situation warrants. Until then, goodnight."

Jared directs his gaze at me and nods. José stands and offers me his hand. I take it, and he guides me down the steps. My Ducere and Warrior Guard form-up on Kick and he returns us to Navan.

The entire Guild sat in stoic silence throughout my presentment. Doing so provided me a perfect backdrop of cooperation and support. This evening, there was little doubt as to the strength of the Ceorfan, both socially and militarily. The stoicism ends as soon as the glow of the jump buoy fades. The Ceorfan break into pulses and hoots as we settle into the allodium. The scene is raucous as the vibrations massage my skin, and the cheers and huzzahs ring through my ears. Quickly, I feel the rest of the city energize as the news spreads, "The Ceorfan will be known once again. We will be free to be seen in public. Our eternal isolation is at an end."

I tele-com, *"Mega, will you dismiss this group and give them my best congrats, and thanks for the spectacular show tonight."*

"Yes, Your Majesty, I will, and I will see you in the evening."

Dana is beside me, he hugs me and says, "Great job, Sis. I think this is gonna work out, but I have something I'm working on. I need to talk to you later."

I answer, "Not now?"

"I need to get some information, but I'll know tomorrow and will get back. It concerns that crown and the treasure from the dream. I might've found something."

"How interesting, I can't wait. Are you sleeping at all, little brother?"

"No more than you do, I'd bet," he answers with a wry smile.

I chuckle at my crazy brother, putting it back on me and say, "Touché, little brother, touché. I'll see you tonight then. I love you."

"Love you too, Sis."

Dana walks away and, choosing to not use my own shortcut, I walk the long way around to my chambers. I'm not sure why because so many who are welcome in my allodium know about the not so secret passageway. When I get to the door, I overhear Mica telling someone he's taking me on a date while they are torped today or just after they wake.

Kick pipes up and says, "If you would like to take her to Faery, I'd be your guide and make sure and give you some privacy... just a thought."

I walk in and don't pretend I didn't overhear and say, "Oh Mica, that would be so nice. Unless you have other plans that is."

"Nope, my plans are fluid and can always change. Let's get some rest now. Then after work, we'll start out unless you'd rather nap after work, then go."

"I love the idea. Is that alright with you, Kick?"

"Of course it is my lady, I did offer. I'll plan while you two are at work and meet you here before sunset."

I sit in Spar's lap and kiss him and say, "I wish I could stay awake and watch you and Kino torp, but I need some rest before work. Do you mind?"

It's become a personal time to share, but they understand there hasn't been much time for me to sleep the last few days.

"No, honey, go to bed now, or I'll have to spank you," Spar quips.

"Promises, promises. What do you think Kino, would you let him spank me?"

"No, but I might do it for him and let him watch." He smiles with a wicked grin.

"Uh hmmm," Kick clears his throat and adds, "I think I have some planning to do somewhere else. His face is red, and he is fidgety when he turns and walks out the door.

My goyles laugh, but I fail to see the humor. I motion with my head to Mica toward the bed, and all my goyles get up and walk with us. I lay down, and Spar and Kino lie on either side of me. Mica is on Kino's side. It only takes me minutes between my loves, and I'm asleep. There isn't a safer or better place to be. It's been a long night, and I need some rest.

17

THE NEWS IS OUT

Kendra

I͏ᴛ ɪꜱ ᴀɴ ᴏꜰꜰɪᴄɪᴀʟ Aᴘʀɪʟ ᴅᴀʏ ɪɴ Nᴇᴡ Mᴇxɪᴄᴏ. I͏ᴛ'ꜱ ᴏꜰꜰɪᴄɪᴀʟ because there's a dry wind blowing in from the west at a steady twenty-two mile an hour. The gusts, which have been topping out at fifty-two miles an hour, make dealing with this frustratingly consistent wind more difficult for me. When in my human form, I don't weigh very much. Every time I get out of my Forest Ranger SUV, I have to fight to stay on my feet. The dust is so thick we are gritty from it. It's worked its way into every nook and cranny of my body.

Mica calls in that we're finished with our last call. "Hey Princess, the comms are dead. We need to get back to the station. It's too dangerous to be out here without anyone knowing where we are and with no backup."

"Yep, standard operating procedure," I say as I make a 'U-ey' and head back to the station.

When we get back, one of the large pecan trees near the building has fallen onto the roof of the main building, causing a lot of damage. The roof has collapsed in places, and I can see the steel beams in one wall. There's a group of office workers and emergency personnel standing outside, on the leeward side of the building, talking. Captain Murphy meets us as we park.

He says, "Well, I'm glad to see you're adhering to procedure. I called the home office, and we all have emergency leave until the building is safe, and the electricity is back."

"Damn wind, I'll make a report manually and send you an email. I guess you'll be calling us?" Mica asks.

"Yes, but this'll take a few days. Don't expect to hear from me until sometime next week. Signs and trees blew down in town too. All the electricians are tied up. I'll message you both when I hear any news. Just take your gear home and note that you've got it in your report."

"Yes, sir," we both say, getting out of our SUV to leave it in the parking lot. I grab a bag out of the back and Mica, and I walk off into the woods everyone knows we park at the old ranger's cottage by now.

At least that's what they think. When we're hidden, we change our clothes, morph and then fly to the La Caverna to see Jimmy and maybe Vanessa. It's also where Jasper, my truck, is really parked today.

We fly high because there are so many people who might see us, and the wind is terrible at ground level. As we fly higher, I'm perturbed to see it isn't any better flying high. The change from winter to spring and the longer days, has the ground heating more, causing further turbulence in the lower atmosphere. Unless we get above ten-thousand feet, we're stuck fighting our way through the tumultuous winds.

When we arrive, we pulse to check the area. When we're sure it's safe, we touch down on the roof of the apartment building and go in to see our teens.

After them telling me so many times to not knock, I don't hesitate before I barge in. If they are getting to 'know' each other, they'll get over it. I'm astonished to find those crazy kids sitting on the couch doing homework eating pizza and wings. Although, after reflecting for a second, these two are serious about finishing school with good grades. It shouldn't surprise me that they're acting so maturely.

"Oh, wings, can I have one?" I ask.

"I hope you know you don't have to ask. The question is, do you want something to drink, and are those spicy?" Jimmy corrects.

"I just want some water. I think I swallowed a sand dune on the way over. We can't stay. I just want to tell you something."

Vanessa, who lets us call her by her nickname Ness or Nessa, gets up and grabs both Mica and me a bottle of water from the fridge and says, "Well shoot, we could use a break. Forty-seven days and we're out of school. So right now, that means we're covered up with studying for finals in five classes."

"This week, the gargoyles are going to get to see the world again," I say, my words coming fast and high with excitement.

"What? How? And what can we do to help?" Jimmy asks.

"I'm not sure how the world will react to our introduction. I know there will be some who are scared and will call us demons and stuff. But I think most people are like us, pretty inclusive.

Maybe if we can be seen in public together with you and a few of your friends, we can ease the stress on our allies. It may also put pressure on others who don't feel comfortable with anything different. TASS should be announcing our presence to all the governments soon. It will hit the news soon after that. If you and Nessa can tip your part of social media in our favor, it can only help. I'm open to any ideas you have. I'm nervous and want to limit the backlash."

"It'll be alright, Kendra. Like you said, most people are going to be okay and inclusive. Yeah, there are always a few troublemakers. We understand we go to school and battle bullies. In school, we set up a partner program where certain people would walk with a football player or a group of cheerleaders. Maybe you could do something like that. Find a group of humans who will always escort any gargoyle. We probably wouldn't be helpful in a fight. If it reaches that point, it's probably best to get out of that place anyway. Maybe, we could get a group started at school... at least until the novelty dies down?" Jimmy suggests.

"That's a great idea. I'll announce it to the Ceorfan if you can get a group started. We want this to happen and hope it is a smooth transition. Is there anything I can help you two with while I'm here, groceries, or something?" I ask.

Ness answers, "Not unless you can do the mind-speak thing for us to ace our test," Ness laughs.

Jimmy adds, "We've got plenty to eat. So we're good."

Mica says, "You both will do fine, just keep studying. Let's go home and nap Princess. Then we can call a conference of all Ceorfan before our date."

"Ooo, a date. You two behave, and I want you home before sunup," Jimmy jokes.

I can't help but cackle, "You sound just like my brothers. We'll only be gone for a few hours and will see you tomorrow. The wind took out the Ranger's station, so we're on leave for a few days. Let's be seen together in the park tomorrow. What do you think?"

Jimmy nods and says, "We've got a plan then. See you tomorrow; we can barbecue some more wings."

Mica and I give hugs and go to the roof, where we portal home.

My chambers are empty except for stone Spar and Kino on their torping platform. I'm just finished dressing in shorts and a tank when José calls.

"Kendra, I wanted to show you the news that the governments are sharing with the world. I'm sending you video links. It's going well, and most countries are responding favorably. We do have a few groups who are different. One is claiming that they have known about the Ceorfan and been helping keep you hidden in an underground railroad. We've used some of the old shots from our security cameras, but need you to be seen with the heads of the governments being accepted tomorrow morning. If that's alright with you?"

"It is, but please ask if it can be tomorrow night so all my consorts can be by my side. The world might need to know how different we really are from the beginning."

"I understand and agree. My personal assistant, Cecile, and Tito, who helps you when you're with me in Fiatril Hall, are working hard. They have a mass of people who can swarm any negative story overwhelming it with our story. They'll make this project work. We're calling it, project Hard Head, for amusement. Pun intended, after the spectacular stunt you pulled last night. I hope you understand it's all in fun. There is no insult intended."

"Why you old devil. I love that!"

"You won't be thanking me soon. You're scheduled for a whirlwind tour around the world."

"Uh, now that you mentioned wind, I need to break it to my boss," I say, I better get on that. See you soon, Beelzebub."

He laughs and says his goodbyes.

I call Captain Murphy. He's already seen my mug on television and is fiery hot himself. I spend the next half hour explaining that I still want my job and why I had to keep the Ceorfan Guild secret. He calms down a fraction. I promise I'll see him on the weekend to talk more about how to handle my job and my position as a dragon queen. He all but hangs up on me. I stare at my phone in disbelief before saying, "So much for being a queen. I get no respect."

18

DATE NIGHT

Kendra

I'M FINALLY ON MY DATE WITH MICA. WE'RE IN FAERY, BUT instead of noticing all of the fantastical creatures and greenery, I'm drawn to the massive redwood trees surrounding us. This forest would surely be familiar to anyone who's visited the grove of giant redwoods in California. There's even one that includes a hollowed-out trunk. A particularly colossal specimen, the path passing through it and all.

We're floating in a gondola, similar to ones used in Venice; only this gondola is much more ornate. The river is flowing only a little faster than I could walk, giving me plenty of time to take in the gorgeous scenery.

"It belongs to the Queen of Faery," our gondolier says knowing what my questions are. A flash of kaleidoscopic colors interrupts the gondolier. Kick is our gondolier? That's interesting. When did he get here?

The Fae queen must have let Mica use her boat. That's another fascinating point. I didn't know Mica knew who to speak to pull this off. Maybe Kick spoke to one of the queen's servants or something. It doesn't matter. I'm in heaven right now.

Mica is keeping me seated with my back facing the direction we're going. He said it's to focus and not look too far ahead. He's right, except I'm focused on the men in this boat mostly.

However, I do notice my surroundings too. The meadow-green grass is shot through with swirls of bright crimson and umber. The perfectly trimmed turf is broken by flawlessly lined pebble-stone walking paths that are decorated with small pink and white flowers. I spot some little gnome's playing in the flower beds along one portion of the trail.

One path leads to a beautiful arbor bench that has blue and yellow roses covering the large rectangular trestle. "Kick, will you please take me to that bench later," I ask, before suddenly realizing I'm with Mica right now.

Mica, utterly unfazed by my question, turns to Kick and says, "You can take her if you like, my friend."

Kick blushes demurely, before nodding an acceptance to me.

This day is hot, but with the shade of the trees, we're perfectly fine on the water. Ever so gently, our gondola begins a turn. It only takes seconds. But when the one-hundred eighty-degree reversal is complete, I see the most beautiful castle.

Another prismatic twinkle as I catch a glint of the sun. Suddenly, we're out of the gondola, and Mica's carrying me up a beautiful set of stairs and through a broad set of wooden doors into a lavishly decorated bedroom. "Princess, this room is fit for you," he growls. He lays me gently on a massive oval canopy-bed.

He takes me in his arms and kisses me moving to my neck his hot breath heats more than my skin. His foreplay is gentle... at first. Then, his claws rake my naked back as his teeth tease a nipple, biting it before releasing it, then letting his tongue massage it. He deftly removes my underwear and takes me.

The ecstasy is overwhelming as I begin to rock back and forth. My eyes close as he brings me close to climaxing.

I sense someone else in the room and open my eyes. Kick's standing in the door. His nakedness causes him no shame as he glides over to me.

"I told you he was part of us," Mica says.

Kick touches my shoulder...

The smell of coffee pulls me out of the best dream ever!

Elmer is my first thought as I let go of my fantasy. It's funny because a few seconds ago my men were my only thought. I reach my hand up to feel my pet's soft body. I scoot out of bed, holding him to me and head straight to the coffee maker.

As my pulse calms, I check the time. I slept for two hours on the dot. I pour the fresh brew and wonder how someone could have entered my chamber and made the coffee without waking me, not just me but Mica too.

I tip-toe over to the table and sit down to flip through the links José had Cecile send earlier. They're lovely and should garner positive publicity from the press as well as from the humans of this world.

Kick comes in, humming a tune and bringing his gaze up to mine and says, "I see you've already gotten a drink. Do you mind if I join you?"

"I never mind if you're here. You could drag your bed in here and be here all the time, and I wouldn't mind." What the hell am I saying? I roll my eyes and blink, hoping he doesn't kill me for that statement.

The tall, dark, handsome mage looks away quickly and turns red. I should probably introduce him to Jadeite. He isn't into me, that's a fact.

He changes the subject and says, "I have a perfect spot for your date in Faery. There's a place that's so magical you'll want to stay for hours. It's a type of carnival but Faery style. What do you think?"

"I love the idea, and the Fae king and queen did say we're always welcome. I'd like to see them before we leave or maybe we can message them, and they could meet us there? Is that possible?"

"Of course it is, My Lady. I can do it with a spell when we arrive," Kick says happily.

Mica stirs, scoots out of bed, and heads over to me, scratching his head. He kisses the top of mine, then pours himself some coffee and says, "Babe, I need to change then talk to Mega. I'll be back in about an hour to go on our date. Is that okay?"

"Yes. I need to get ready too. What does one wear to a Fae carnival anyway?" I ask turning toward the mage who is staring at me.

My consort kisses my head again and leaves, saying, "That's my cue to leave. I'll be back as soon as possible."

Kick says, "What do you usually wear on dates?"

"Well, here lately, mostly ball gowns," I laugh. "I haven't been on that many dates I did go with David before he became Spar to a human carnival. I wore a summer dress with flip flops then."

"That's actually a great idea minus the flip flops. Make them flats. You still need to look royal. The Fae will know who you are and will expect some pomp and ceremony, even if you don't. Now I'll leave you to that and be back in about an hour." He bows and kisses my hand. I almost groan with pleasure but manage to hold it back and let him leave.

I call Amber, and she helps me pick out an outfit and pull my hair up. I look regal enough, but not over the top. No jewels except earrings and a ring. Amber is just leaving when Mica comes back and whistles at me.

Amber socks him in the knee and says, "Have a good time and be back early, we have a world tour to plan."

"Yes ma'am, that's what I just heard from Mega, gravel bits. How are you doing?"

"I'm fine, now get going and have fun."

Kick comes in, and we're on our way to Faery. When we step into the carnival area, it's like a dream. The air sparkles, and the music is so incredible it makes me want to dance a jig. I bounce from foot to foot and rub my hands together. Mica and Kick glance at each other and burst out laughing.

"Stop snickering," I say playfully before adding, "I want to swing.

Look at that. Take me there first." I point to a massive round swing. It holds at least fifty Fae around its circumference. It must move by magic and in different directions.

We spend a couple of hours on rides, eating, and laughing. The Faery royalty can't be with us but say to enjoy and stay as long as we like when our friend the mage and guide petitioned them.

Soon, Kick buys a basket from a stall and informs us we're going on a boat ride. We are shown to a little river and a small boat that brings to mind the boats I've seen in pictures of Venice. Wait, didn't I just dream this?

This boat has a covering on the ends. The curly haired mage gets in and reaches for me. I step forward, and the boat rocks just a bit, and I slam into him. He wraps his arms around me to steady me. His lean body feels good. When we notice we've stayed embraced a little too long, we hop away from one another.

Mica gets in, and we sit under one of the overhangs in a plush lounging area, then lean back in soft pillows. Kick mumbles a spell, and we start off down the river. I sit in my partner's arms and rub a muscled leg. He flips the little covering over us and kisses me.

The remaining tension from the past few days leaves my body. Suddenly Mica's kiss is all my boneless body knows. I could stay this way forever, but feel weird because Kick is out there guiding the skiff. We hear him make a grunting noise, and Mica flips open the covering with a wide grin.

Our guide for our date says, "I wanted to stop here and let you both watch the sunset. It'll set in a little while. I'll be on the shore if you need me. Use your dragon magic, My Lady, and call my name." Then he's gone, the way Jericho leaves with the breeze. It makes me think that he may have a mini jump stone or something.

Mica growls, "Alone at last. I want you, Kendra. You can say no, and I'll stop...

I slam my lips on his to shut him up, then back away and say, "I'm not saying no to you, not now, not ever. Now kiss me like you mean it."

He ducks his head and kisses me deeply then moves down to my neck. I growl, and my legs shake with anticipation. My hands move over his chest, unbuttoning his buttons.

I say, "Take your shirt off. In fact, take everything off I want to see you."

He stands and takes off his clothes, then raises a brow in my direction.

I stand and do the same for him as he reclines. His eyes are hungry, and I can't wait, so no posing.

I want to crawl onto him and sit on his hard cock, but what I do is lean forward and kiss him. He holds my head with a large hand and takes out my hair clip. I shake it loose for him then touch my mouth tenderly to his. He sighs into my mouth, sinking his hands into my hair. His groan goes straight to my core.

I shoot into action. Straddling his hips, I cover him with kisses and travel down his neck.

I bite his shoulder and say, "I'm so ready."

He grinds his hardness into me for an answer. I reach for his hard dick and rub it on my wet slit. He moans for me, encouraging me, so I aim his throbbing thickness at my entrance and slide down.

Holy crap, I'm going to come fast. The stretch is a bit painful, but just enough to feel amazing. I start to rock on him with a slow rhythm. His hands hold my ass and he thrusts in rhythm with me. In only minutes I feel an orgasm building and moan, "Mica, I love you. I'm about to come. Come with me, baby!"

He answers by shoving into me hard. That's enough to get me over the top, and my vagina starts pulsing with a hard throb. He keeps me throbbing as he keeps thrusting up. Oh, that tickle is almost too much.

I hold my hands on his hard chest and concentrate, sweat on my brow. I open my eyes and watch him come.

He squishes up his features with a grunt. Fuck, he's gorgeous. I ride him a couple more beats until he stops me with his hands. His face screwed up from the intensity. I'm all out of energy and fall forward on him and kiss his chest.

After a bit, I roll over and snuggle close. My golden goyle holds me tight, and we both rest. My leg is slung over his, and I stare at him as we talk about everything for a while.

He says, "It's sunset; let's watch it, beautiful." He opens the cover, and we watch the sun go down in each other's arms.

When it's fully dark, and there's only the light of the moon and the carnival far away, we stand and dress.

I call up a touch of magic and call Kick.

19

BRIDGE

Kendra

My warrior mage comes back to the boat in the blink of an eye with a breeze on my sensitive skin and says, "When I was on the shore, I saw a bridge up ahead. Would you like to go see it or go home now?" He's looking at his feet and not us. I wonder if he could have seen more than I thought.

"Bridge," we chorus then laugh.

Kick grins and starts the boat forward. In a little while, we see the river widens, and before us is the massive stone edifice of the bridge itself. This bridge has one pier in the center, which allows for two perfectly formed barrels that support the main deck itself. The construction makes it look like a giant 'm.' The boat will go under it easily, so we continue forward. It's well lit by what looks like stone sconces every few feet. This bridge is a work of art with both of its arches covered in carved fantasy icons. Well, not fantasy but well-known beautiful things and people that humans don't believe are real.

I'm so engrossed in the art that I don't notice one of the fantastical forms as it begins to move. As we get closer, I start to squint into the darkness, trying to make out the figures. I stand up to get a better look at the lavish artistry. The light from the sconces playfully dances on the various creatures. My eyes wide, I stare transfixed at a particularly wonderful image of a unicorn flying with a dragon.

My gaze wanders. A monster with no hair, evil-looking, and misshapen glares back at us. Its demented yellow eyes have locked on to me. It is clinging to the underside of the bridge and holds my stare. I watch in surprise as it takes out a large chunk of the bottom of the deck, a piece that includes the keystone. Its aura is totally red and black! Holy shit, this thing literally reeks with hatred.

I see the piece of the bridge as it flies toward us. It hits the water, mere feet from where I'm standing. The action of the water slams our boat against the center pillar. We're beached on the base of the structure that makes up the cutwater. With the keystone missing, the structure of the bridge is compromised.

"Kick, get us out of here. This bridge is going to collapse!" I yell to our mage tour guide.

I couldn't finish my command before the bridge begins to crumble and fall on us. Kick slams into me and covers me with his body even though Mica is closer.

Time slows, every detail is evident. The feel of the wind, and the soft material of his shirt. I cover Kick's head with my hands as tiny dust particles obscure my vision, and larger rocks fall in slow motion. Mica moves into my view and is covering our friend and me. My massive goyle changes, his wings extend, and he covers us, torping before the rest of the bridge covers us.

That was beautiful! His wings are like black velvet. If it wasn't dark before it is now. We're covered by my lovers' wings, and he is covered by debris. Kick's head is close to mine. I can feel him as I struggle to move in the confined space, but I can't. It's useless. Time speeds back up and the dust is choking me as I speak checking on my sexy mage, "Are you okay?"

His head is on my breast, and I feel liquid. I hope it isn't blood. It is, though, I can smell it. He opens his mouth, and I feel his jaw move on my breast. What I wouldn't give for the circumstances to be different.

He says, "Yes, Kendra, are you?"

"I am, but I can't move much. How about you?"

He shifts a little and digs into my stomach. When I grunt in pain, he puts a hand on my waist and says, "I'm so sorry. Did I hurt you much?"

"No, I was just surprised. Kick, thank you for sacrificing yourself to cover me from getting hurt. My skin is so tough now I don't think I'm bleeding, but I can smell blood? Are you sure you're okay?" I put my hands on his face for comfort and can't help but play with his curls.

"I think I have a gash on my head from a flying splinter of rock, but it's not bad. I hope I'm not getting blood all over you."

I can fix that. I feel around Kick's head and feel the wound. Morphing a claw, I poke a hole in my hand and drip some blood on him. Things go woozy for a second as I feel a wave from his magic and mine. It is passing quickly, but I enjoy the feeling almost as much as I enjoy his body on mine.

He says honestly, "Kendra, thank you. You're all a man would ever want and more."

"What? I don't understand. I thought you never noticed me that way. In fact, I was sure I repel you," I blurted out holding nothing back.

"You never repelled me. You are perfection. Oh, I noticed, and if I was in any way deserving of you, I'd have made it known long ago, but I'm not worth your time."

His fingers smooth my sides and press into me. The drunk feeling that my blood mixed with Faery magic has loosened both our tongues. Not that I hold back much, ever.

"Kick, let me be honest with you. I've never forgotten you since I was in Leta's body, and it's only gotten worse. The you that I know is a wonderful man. We all make mistakes, and it's how we live in the now that matters. I can overlook yours if you overlook mine. I'd love for you to be in my life as more than just a loyal subject. If that isn't what you want, then I'll take what you're willing to share. But know this, I do want you."

He sucks in his breath quickly and says, "There isn't a man alive that would say no to that, my lady. If you consider me worthy, I'll make myself a better man for you, if you're sure?"

I pull his hand up to my lips and kiss it, saying, "I'm sure. And as much as I like having you plastered to me, I have a plan. If you don't mind? I wish I would have thought of it when the bridge was falling."

It takes ages for me to reach into his pocket and find his small jump stone. "I'm going to make your stone take three of us." A search through my grandmother's memories gives me the perfect magic and the words to use to get us all out of here.

As I tighten my arms around Kick, I say, "Mica, I'm getting us out of here. Hang on."

With one arm hanging onto Kick, I reach my other hand to Mica's face and breathe slowly, concentrating on building my magic. Purple light flares. We drop so fast my stomach is in my throat. Then the stone floor of the lunchroom stops my fall, and I hit my head too hard. The last thing I see is Krag, the Hewn leader's surprise, then the lights go out.

20

JUST A BUMP

Kendra

THE NOISE AROUND ME IS BOTHERING ME AS I OPEN MY EYES TO complain. When I do pry them open, I notice Jericho's wrinkled old visage hovering above Krag and me standing beside him. Mica is at my side, and it appears that I landed us in the lunchroom in Navan. In fact, I landed on one of the stone tables next to one of the buffets! Well, that's one way to make an entrance. I feel for Kick, and he isn't on top of me, so I move to get up.

The old wizard pushes me back and says, "One moment, Your Majesty, the medical team should be here for you in minutes."

"Fuck that mage. I'll be alright, just give me a few. Dragon, remember?" I say, pointing at my face, then pushing him back and swinging my legs off the table. I realize I pushed him right into the enormous Hewn leader, which would be funny at any other time.

Spar catches me when I wobble unsteadily. I lean into him and hold on for life. Then I turn around and roll my eyes as I see the packed cafeteria and my Guild watching me with concern. I sigh and whisper, "Just get me to our rooms, and I need something to drink. Water will be fine, but let's go now."

Without asking, Spar picks me up and leaves the room. I can hear Mica saying, "She just needs a few minutes mage. I'll let you know, but my guess is, she's just fine."

In seconds he's next to Spar walking at a fast clip to our chambers. When we get there, I'm already starting to feel better but snuggle into my blue goyles hard muscles anyway. Why not enjoy the ride when I can?

He sits with me on our couch, and Mica hands me a cup of water. I sit up, taking it from him and give him and Spar a crooked grin, then say, "Okay, so I muffed the landing a bit, sue me." When they don't grin back, I add, "I promise I'm better, my head is already clearing. And where is Kino? Is Kick all right?"

Spar answers, "Kino took the mage to the medical facility. He'll be here in a bit, after Dr. Ogman gives him a prognosis. He had blood on him and hit the table harder than you. When you landed, he bounced off."

As if on cue, both Kino and Kick walk into the room and sit with us. Kick bunches a pillow in his lap and asks, "My lady are you all right? I was so worried..."

"What the hell mage? You should be in medical and resting," I say, pointing to the sling he's sporting on his right arm.

Mica pipes up, "Isn't that the pot calling the kettle black, Kendra?"

I can't help but giggle, and once I start, I can't stop until I have tears, and my jaw is aching. In fact, we're all laughing. Everyone except Kino. He has his arms crossed over his chest, waiting for an explanation. When I see him standing that way, I just burst out cackling again and point because I can't speak.

That at least that gets a smile, then he says, "I love to hear you laugh, but I fail to see the humor. Will one of you please tell us what happened? Were you attacked?"

We sober up, and Mica begins to tell what happened, leaving out the part about the thing that collapsed the bridge. Kick then takes over and provides that bit. I add that the attacker was indeed evil.

"It was a wild troll," Kick says. "They're different than civilized trolls and often their mind is warped and demented. I didn't notice the monster until we got right under the bridge. I saw its treasure first. That's why I made it to you so fast, Kendra. As soon as I turned to you, I caught sight of the beast. I knew it was protecting its treasure. I am sorry to both of you. I should've been looking for problems, instead of staring at Kendra." The smile is big and bright. It is obvious he doesn't mind sharing it with everyone in the room.

Then I add that our mage friend protected me with his body while Mica covered us both and torped, saving us until I got us home in the most dramatic fashion.

"Thank you both for that, by the way," I say.

Kino asks, "I'm missing how you managed to magic home, beloved. Did your magic do it automatically, or did you make it work for you?"

I'm embarrassed to say and bow my head some looking up, wrinkling my forehead and say, "I had noticed Kick moves the way Jericho does, so I dug in his pocket and found a little jump stone. I found a memory from my grandmother Leta and adapted my magic to the stone to bring us home. I'll do better next time. I certainly won't think about dessert in the lunchroom first, though! Did someone find the stone? It was in my hand when we dropped, but I don't have it now?"

"I was in the lunchroom when you fell onto the table beside me. My heart almost stopped. I saw the stone drop from your hand, and I picked it up. I thought it might be a clue as to where you were and where I should start a search for information. Here you go," says Kino placing the stone in Kick's hand.

The dark-haired mage says, "Thank you, it isn't supposed to be able to transport more than one person, My Lady. You're strong to have gotten the three of us home together. Thank you for that. I should've thought about it myself. I knew there are wild trolls in

Faery. I wasn't used to being free there and wasn't thinking. Please, forgive me."

"There isn't anything to forgive. You saved my life along with Mica's. Don't beat yourself up. We're a team here, in fact, should I tell them now?" I ask.

He ducks his head, bobbing it a few times, then gets up nervously and says, "Let me. Gentlemen, I would like to date Kendra, with your blessings, of course."

My goyles slap him on the back and welcome him to the family the way I knew they would.

Kino says, "We welcome you, mage, but there are standards, and I ask you to treat our queen like the treasure she is, or we will all have to kick your ass." He smirks proud of himself, and the others agree.

"I intend to treat her as the best treasure on Earth. Now, if you don't mind, I'll leave you all to each other's company. I need some rest." He winks at me and turns to exit.

I watched him leave, wishing he would stay. Looking at my goyles faces, I ask, "Well, flying is out for me tonight. I want a nap too," I say, getting out of Spar's lap and laying down.

Spar and Kino lie on either side of me, and I snuggle into them and doze off. When I wake, Mica has me wrapped up in his arms. I move away waking him as I do, and walk over to my other goyles who are sitting reading tablets and making notes.

Spar says, "Kendra, you haven't been asleep long, how do you feel?"

I answer, "I feel refreshed and ready for business. What are y'all doing?"

Kino says, "I received a message from the Count that José has contacted him. He says that all the PR machines are primed and ready. Knowledge of the Ceorfan has already begun to leak out to the news stations the PR team has the best relationships with.

He also says you're expected to meet with several Heads of State tonight. I'll put him off, but if you really feel better, maybe we should go to a few and watch the beginnings of our future play out, live."

"I think you're right. Do you mind messaging the Count while I get ready?" I ask.

"I will do it now. What do you think fellows, shall we dress formally for the occasion also?"

There are groans all around from the men who would rather not wear much or only flying clothes. But they do agree, for the good of the Ceorfan Guild, we need to put on a show. Maybe showing just how different we are will be appealing to the world. I message Sunny, and he says he'll be here in minutes. So I head off to the bath.

21

TREASURE MAP

Kendra

WE SPENT THE REST OF THE NIGHT WINING, DINING, AND visiting with the dignitaries of the world while being photographed and taped. It was a whirlwind. Although we are welcomed at every turn and made to feel at home, it's strange to be seen in public, sporting our tails and claws.

We're in the White House ballroom, mingling with the rich and famous. My brothers and consorts are here too.

Dana says, "Sis, I've found something, and you need to know about it. Can we meet in your allodium after this shindig is over?" He's talking about an event at the White House while the Ceorfan are being introduced to the President. I don't think anything phases, my little brother.

"Yes, in fact, I'm tired of this and want to go home anyway. Jared, come with us, please. Let's say our goodbyes," I answer.

I, along with my brothers, their dates, and my large contingent attending me, make our way over to the President and his First Lady. We let them know that we'll be happy to meet with them again soon.

We also thank them for the wonderful night and for their help in making the Ceorfan welcome in America.

The President says, "It's our pleasure to help. I hope to make this a mutually beneficial friendship. I'll need to set up a meeting for negotiations and terms of our relationship with you later."

"I understand, Mr. President, have your man call my man, and we'll get it taken care of," I answer with a laugh.

His wife, the First Lady, smiles and offers her goodbyes and well wishes. So we can open a portal in private, one of the President's bodyguards escorts us to a secluded area underneath the White House.

Mega tele-speaks, *"It is all clear, Edling, we can open a portal."*

I nod to Peter, who is standing alongside several of the Hewn. They've been acting as a contingent of bodyguards for all my trips since coming to Navan. I still keep my Ducere with me. The Hewn need to feel they're part of our nation. Protecting the queen is one of the most coveted positions. So it's natural that they would want to be included in that task.

The mage opens a portal, and we step into my waiting chamber.

"I really need coffee," I say.

"I'll make some," says Spar, who takes off toward the drink bar and begins to make a fresh pot.

Jared and Dana walk over to me with another goyle. "Well, hello, Steen, how are you? How do you like Scotland?" I ask, knowing he's been there with my brother.

He bows his head in my direction and answers, "I love it, but it's taking me a little to get used to the new ways and modern facilities.

Jared chuckles and says, "He means malls. I took him to get clothes and almost lost him to an escalator, then he demanded ale at a fast-food restaurant in the food court. I've had the best time."

I pat Steen on the shoulder and say, "Don't let him push you around. If he gets too out of line, call me, and I'll whoop him for you." I'm turning to face Dana as Steen's eyes go wide at my comment, and he blinks, gapping like a beached carp. "Dana, what is it you wanted us to know?" I ask, still amused.

He takes a scribbled-on map out of his pocket. After pointing to a spot, he pushes it toward me and says, "I've been thinking for a while now about whatever happened to the dragon treasure of the Ceorfan. It's been brought up several times, and we need money to improve the lives of the Ceorfan people. Really, Jared and I can't finance the whole Guild. Especially now that we're going to be able to live in the open.

"Homes and safe places to torp are needed. So I started searching and found a map of the area where the gargoyles lived in Ilioilion. I also found this record in the Halls of History. It explains that when the city burned, and the Ceorfan left, a treasure was left behind. I know there's more than just the kilt pin we found. I want to take some of the gargoyles who remember the way it was when Leta was the queen and find that treasure. What do you think?"

"I think that would solve a lot of problems. I'm not even sure I still have a job, so I have no problem with you looking for it. Does anyone here want to volunteer to help? You know, Dana, I had a dream not too long ago about a city burning and a treasure that was taken," I answer.

Krag says, "I want to help. I know the area well and can sail us there. We escaped with as many as we could when the enemy came and burned the city after Queen Leta gave her life to end the war.

"Our enemy had no honor when he burned the city, killing many of us before we fled. That's when Navan was founded, and most of our nation hid here for ages. I had just been released from my prison in Faery and refused to hide underground, so I became one of the Hewn. Can I see the kilt pin you mentioned?"

Kino says, "I have it; I'll be right back."

As he walks off to get the pin, Jared says, "If the Guild can support itself, it'll go a long way to our acceptance in the daily life of the world. We need our own industry so that people don't feel that we're taking what is rightfully theirs or even worse, begin to think we're poaching their jobs if you know what I mean."

Kino returns with a little box containing the pin and hands it to Krag. He removes the pin and studies it, before saying, "It's definitely Ceorfan made and a style that we commonly used, but there's something familiar about it."

Kick moves over to the Hewn man holding the pin and gingerly takes it from him, then says, "This was my father's. You would have seen him wearing it in Queen Leta's court."

No one speaks and lets him continue, "It has magic and makes the bearer able to fly."

Krag starts to hand him the box it was in then stops, glancing at me. I nod in assent to him, and he says, "Here, it is rightfully yours then."

"I agree. I didn't know it had magic, but now that I look at the light around it, I see that it's purple. Is that how to tell with an object? It would be nice to be able to tell."

"Yes, it is, and sometimes you can see the purple and the element color of the magic it controls. This controls air, and that is clear magic, so there is no color difference."

"That's interesting." Then I turn back to my youngest brother. "Dana, I'd like to find the lost treasure too. Not just to help us, but if there are some lost Fae magical items that I could return to them, it will help cement our relationship with the Faery King and Queen. When do you want to leave, brother?"

"Well, as soon as possible. What do you think, Krag? How long will it take to outfit a ship, or shall we fly there first?"

"Let me message my people, and we can fly or portal there and meet them," answers the big Hewn leader.

Dana answers, "Okay, then I'll put my business in order while you're torped today. We'll meet here tonight at sundown. Anyone who would like to come with us and help, please be here and ready to go at sunset. Jared, can you go, or do you have business to attend to?"

"My business manager can handle almost anything for a few

days. I want to go. But I have other duties, and I'm sure you can take care of it, little brother," Jared says.

Looking at Jared, then Dana, I answer, "It seems we have a plan then, and it's close to daybreak, so let's go get ready for the day. I have something I need to do. My boss, Captain Murphy, will be up in awhile. I need to call him and apologize to him. He should not have found out on the news that I'm a dragon Queen, and Mica is a gargoyle. Have a good torp all, and I'll see you tonight." I hug my brothers and watch them leave by way of separate portals.

How did our lives get to this point? I shake my head and take a sip of my coffee.

22

BREAKING THE NEWS

Kendra

Spar, Kino, Mica, and Kick follow me to my room, and we sit in my lounge without saying a word. We're happy to be together and enjoying the moment relaxing.

I break the silence, "Do any of you want to go on the treasure hunt with my brothers?" Each of them says yes and no.

"We want to, but need to think about it," says Spar leaning forward with his elbows on his knees and speaking concernedly.

Each of them has a reason to remain with me. Unfortunately, the amount of work we need to accomplish seems like it will not allow that. Getting the Ceorfan accepted into the world is number one on my list. The treasure is essential too. We need it so humans won't be able to accuse us of stealing either money or jobs... or both. Human economics dictate that both are critical and cannot be inhibited in any way. In other words, our economy must be an asset to humans, but it can never be a drain.

In the middle of this back and forth, Kino blurts out, "Gortanik, I want to say something I have thought about since we found out you are alive. I am so sorry you were held as a prisoner. We would have come to get you if any of us had any idea that you were alive. You were my best friend and me..."

"Stop! You don't owe me an apology. You didn't do anything to me. I know you love me. I am certain you would have come for me, had you known I was alive," Kick says, staring at Kino then taking his hand. They nod to each other and walk together to the torp stage.

Mica and Spar go with them. They pose, and the tingle of the magic starts. I fill up on the warmth of the magic and am left with a glad heart.

I reach for Kick's hand, and we walk back to the couch and talk like dating teenagers until I say, "I better call Captain Murphy. I owe him. He has always been a great supervisor. For him to find out about the Ceorfan and me on the news, was a discredit to the relationship he and I had established. Kick, I hope this doesn't change my position at work, but I need to be sure."

"I understand. While you are doing that, I have something I'd like to do. Do you mind if I leave and come back? I have something for you," Kick asks.

"You're always welcome here," I respond.

He gives me a sly grin and leaves as I pick up my phone. I take a deep breath and slowly blow it out, giving me time to collect my courage. Then I press my bosses number from my favorites list.

I hear a brusk hello and say, "Captain Murphy?"

"Yes, Ms. Macbard, or should I say, Ceorfan Queen Kendra?"

I wince. "Sorry, Murph. You have to believe me, I was hoping to call and let you know before you saw the news. I don't blame you for being so mad at me the other night. I guess this changes things a little, doesn't it?" I ask, hoping he won't start yelling again.

"Now that I've gotten over the shock of seeing you on television, it doesn't change much for me. I trust you, Kendra. Some things even make so much more sense now. Still, there is a problem, I'll have to work on. With you working for the Federal government, though. Your security clearance has been revoked. The Feds argue that you lied on your background check, so they canceled the whole thing. Also, I've got no idea how the higher-ups will look at you. Are you another government or something? I'm sorry, you can't come back to work until I've got this figured out. Hell, they may just ask if you'll be an ambassador between our two nations. That's way above my paygrade, though. I'm sorry, Kendra, but unless something changes... Listen, do you really want to keep working here, or is it better if you resign?"

"Murph, I love working with the Rangers Service. But, I have to say, it is getting pretty hard to keep my schedule. I agree with you, the ambassadorship is above this conversation. Maybe I'll bring it up with the President when I see him next. Heck, Murph, I'm sorry that it's worked out like this. I wish it would have been possible to bring you in on my secret. Everything has just happened so fast... shit, it's all going to sound like excuses. At least it's in the open now. Maybe you can bring the crew a few at a time and come visit us in Navan. You would always be welcome. I hope that I would still be welcome to visit you and my friends at the Ranger station, too," I say hopefully.

Murphy answers, "Of course, Kendra. You are always welcome. I will take you up on your offer of visiting Navan too. Since you live here... you do live here, right?" he asks pensively.

"Yes, I do live in this area," I waffle.

"Good, then I hope I can count on you if things get where we need your help," Murphy says.

"Captain, whatever happens, you can count on my people and me to serve and protect, as always."

"That's good for us then. Thank you, I'll call you when the bureaucrats in Washington give me an idea on how we're supposed to interact with you and your people. Have a good night. Oh, wait a sec," the good captain hurries to get the words in before I hang up.

"Is there something else?"

"I was wondering... I think I know I just need to be sure, though. Mica is a Ceorfan gargoyle and isn't working for me anymore either, right?"

"Yes, he's one of my people, and won't be coming back. I promise

Murph that we'll be watching and help protect and serve as much as we can. Please don't be afraid to call me if you need us. It can always be off the record," I plead.

"It's a deal, little lady. It couldn't happen to a better girl. I'm happy for you. I'll be calling." He hangs up before I can say anything else.

The breath comes out of me in a loud, humming blow. I can't help but feel the loss of that job as I change out of my formal clothes and put on some comfy pajamas. I sip my coffee, thinking of how my life is changing while tapping messages into my tablet. I need to keep track of what I have going on, or I'll forget. When I open my calendar, I smile. The good Count has already filled in the things I need. I shoot him a message to thank him and see that he had left me one. It reads:

Your Majesty, I've been in touch with the American president's man, Angelis Castle. He'll be the acting liaison to our people. You'll need to appoint a contact for our government, and perhaps for all the countries, you have relationships with. I'll put forth the motion in tonight's meeting of the High Guild so that you remember. Have a beautiful day.

Your personal assistant,

Count de Treon, Clifton Danby.

I hadn't thought of that. I do need liaisons and ambassadors. I can't do it all myself. I tap a thank you to Clifton when Kick pulses at my door. I pulse back automatically, making sure he feels the happiness I feel at his presence.

The serious look on his face has me searching his aura. It's violet and silver. That shows me so much, mostly how connected he is with his magic. The silver, in his case, is a gift, his gift, I think. Personally, I think he's a gift for me, those dark, brooding looks are all mine, and I can't get enough.

He takes a cleansing breath and approaches me, then goes on one knee when he reaches my chair. I reach out to stop him but stall waiting to see what he's doing first.

He says with a deep trembling voice, full of emotion, "This isn't how it's done traditionally where the queen makes the first move toward a consort. This is more of a human tradition, my heart. I offer you my love and life and ask for your hand. I love you, Kendra. You have been in my dreams since I met you. Even when I thought to wed a woman I loved beyond understanding, you were always in my thoughts. I was able to love her because you were not a possibility for me. Now that you are, I don't want to take a chance I might lose you. Will you be mine?"

He stretches out his hand, and in it is a stone. I don't recognize it, but I do see the love in my mage. I gently take the rock in my hands, it's power hits me. This is one of the five stones of the Ceorfan. This one is called Air. It calls to me and wants me to press it to my forehead the way I had the other stones. I answer quickly, so that Kick knows I love him in case I pass out as I did the first time, "I love that you asked this way. Today, and all days forward, I name you my consort. With all of my heart, body, and soul, I'll love and cherish you and bind us for eternity." Then I press the stone to my head.

The room tilts, or is it me, fighting off the magic of air as I start to leave my body to dream walk. I bite my lip and taste the salty tang of blood, then lean into Kick and bite his lip as we touch. Magic slams into us as SPIRIT, we are dragon bound by spirit. I let the power cover me as my mage's arms surround me. He lays my body down on the floor softly and lays beside me, holding me in his strong arms. I'm out of my physical form, looking around as the energy of the atmosphere swirls around me. I see my dark-haired consort coming toward me floating in the dream world. I glance toward our resting forms and know that they're safe.

With his face full of joy, he says, "My Queen, we're united

forever. Look around you. This is an area you reign. Don't let it scare you, you can control this realm the way you do the other, no difference."

"I'm not used to this, but with you here, I feel like I can do anything." I reach for his hand, and he squeezes my fingers, letting me know I can feel here.

"What do you say, will you take a short trip with me?"

"Where, where will we go?"

"Anywhere you want. The possibilities are endless in this realm. But I warn you we have to get back to our bodies before too long, or we'll be stiff and sore from the floor. You'll feel rested, though, because, in essence, we're sleeping."

23

EVIL UP CLOSE

Kendra

Kick and I are in the spirit or dream realm. I am amazed at the eddies of energy rippling around us. The energy even has different patterns. The spirit energy is lighter and billows, forming cloud-like patterns, before dissipating and reforming in another area.

"Kick, if it doesn't hurt you, I'd like to go to Faery and see the place where Barat had you imprisoned. I want to see if he's still there or if we can find him." I'm wondering if I can use this new dream walking to search for our common enemy.

"We can do that. Let me show you the way."

He puts his arm around me and urges me forward. Like a sideways elevator, we're moved forward and into the evil mage's home in an instant. What I see is a castle-like old European stone monstrosity. We move through the walls as if they are a mere suggestion of reality. Kick shows me where he was held and where he had to carve Kino and Krag and the other Ceorfan. My heart goes out to him as the passion pours from his tone, and his words hitch and stop. I kiss him on the cheek, and he comes back to himself.

An old hunchback with rusty red-gray hair comes into the room. His arthritic fingers working the latch to the door as he closes it behind him. My man is suddenly transported back to a day, hundreds of years before... before Drusey was murdered. Kick stares at the withered old man, the pain fully transparent on his face.

"What is it? What's wrong?" I ask.

"That's one of my tormentors. He's a mage named Walter Deveros," he answers while pointing directly toward the mage at the door. "He's the one who first carved Kino, the one who forced me to carve..." His hand rakes his hair away from his face.

I turn, hate building bile in my guts as I watch the old mage. The queen consort inside me, warring with the peacemaker. My blood boils wanting to destroy him, but the queen regent inside me stays my hand... for now.

Despite his age, Walter's green-gold eyes are full of energy. They're cold and cunning, yet not crazy. His tan is so dark it must reflect his soul. The years in the sun have taken their toll on his leathery, wrinkled skin. In the broadest and possibly strangest sense, you could consider him handsome. If you like bespectacled wrinkled arthritic old mass murderers, that is.

The door opens, and another younger man, dark hair, and a look that would provide the poster for 'creepy' enters the room.

"That's Walter's assistant. He's called Bladriell," Kick blandly states, grimacing as he rubs his temples. He quietly adds, "I haven't called them by name in a very long time."

"What did you call them, or did you just avoid names?" I ask quietly, still fighting to suppress my rage and desire to seek my revenge for the pain these two have caused.

"I called Walter "fuckwad" or anything that starts with fuck and Bladriell "shithead" or anything that started with shit," he says matter of factly without a single emotion showing. I used the same terms with Barat too.

Despite my fury, I giggle and say, "We're more alike than I thought."

"Oh, what did you think I was like, darling?" he questions, without the slightest hint of agitation.

"Very proper for one, super-hot for another. Now how can we use this dream walk to find Barat? We found the fuck-shit minions. The more I'm here in front of them, the more I want to kill them."

"Well, you have the magic stone in you, and we're linked by blood and love. I might be able to call on my finder gift, but it'd be an experiment. I don't know what will happen with all of the magical protections on this place."

"Let's try, anyway."

Kick reaches holding me close, sings a few lines of a melody, and we move forward into a room in the castle, and there is Barat asleep.

"He's in a druid sleep. We need to tell the others and the Fae King if you want him to conquer this evil." Kick notes, the calmness of his voice almost impossible to believe.

I'm still in his arms, my breath coming in gulps. Here is the piece of shit who I can't wait to kill. A million thoughts go through my mind, but mostly, how can I kill him now, without causing a rift between the Fae and me. My eyes search to room for a weapon that I can send into his heart using magic.

Kick turns my face to him, "My Heart, now is not the time. You can't kill him in spirit form. We can come back, now that we know where he is. He'll be here in the long-sleep for a while.

The others need to know what we've found. We need a plan, one that maximizes your safety. Also, we can't make the Fae our enemy. It would be a mistake on our part as they have much to share. We can come back here after our ally knows. If they don't end him, we can. This blight on the world isn't going anywhere right now. I have full confidence in your ability to take care of yourself, but he's mighty and sets traps everywhere. Now that we're finally together, please don't get hurt."

My breath hitches, I blink, and nod, "You're right. Let's go home and get some rest. Then when the others wake, we'll give them the fucker on a platter."

As Kick and I turn to each other, preparing to exit the dream walk and return to our bodies, we see something that stops us cold. Walter and Bladriell are now standing in the room with Barat.

Kick reacts first. "Kendra, wait. Let's see what they do."

"Bladriell, you must wake our Lord Baratium. You must tell him about Sass. That satyratrix could ruin everything if she gives away our plans. I don't care if she is my sister's best friend," pleads Walter.

"No, Master, don't make me wake him. His anger is fierce. He'll hurt me and not let me die. The satyratrix's have a lot of power that makes men crazy for them. They are better than the sirens," cries Bladriell.

"You must wake him!" Walter screams. "We can't take a chance on her giving away our location to the enemy. If the Ceorfan finds out where we are, it'll be a war, and we aren't ready. Tell the master it's good news. Say that we know how to find the whore. Tell him that Trix, my sister, will go find her friend for us. Yes, tell him that. He'll be happy that we can find the wretched Sass," answers a self-satisfied Walter, the smug grin spreading across his twisted face.

The ancient mage can see that he's won the fight as he watches the shoulders of his assistant drop and his head bow forward. The deep breath taken in by him solidifies his surrender.

Bladriell moves to Barat's side and mumbles a chant, softly, rhythmically. The sound slowly builds until he's speaking clearly and with purpose, "As the ancient ones commanded the spirits, I now command yours. My Lord Baratium, return to the Fae lands. Return to your body."

As Bladriell speaks the final words, Baratium opens his eyes and commands, "You scum, why have you woken me? I commanded none to wake me until the final battle was readied."

"Yes, my lord, but..."

Without waiting for another word, Barat strikes. He rises from his bed and, with a single word, 'vasanízo,' hits Bladriell with a devastating slash spell, tearing a broad strip of flesh from Bladriell's back and right arm. A second slash rends even more skin and muscle.

Blood streams from his gashes and pools on the floor beside the younger man.

"Please, Lord, I was ordered to wake you by Walter. I begged to not bother you. Please, don't hurt me," the bloodied shithead begs. Walter's eyes go wide, and he moves to the door.

"I'm awake now, you cur. Tell me why before you pay with your life!"

"My Lord, it's Sass. She left. But we have found her in the human world. She's living with the Hewn. We don't know where. But, Trix wants to leave you to join her too. We can trace Trix and find Sass," whimpers the flayed apprentice.

Barat's arms relax and move to his sides, his eyes widen with the knowledge of what his servant said.

"Walter, is this true? Does your sister wish to join our enemy, the gargoyles?" whispers wicked Baratium, a sneer on his face showing the depth of his disgust.

The old-ass mage, sensing the problem inexpertly looks for a way out, "My Lord, Bladriell has slightly misspoken. What he should have said is, Trix wants to find Kick. She doesn't want to leave you, she wants to see that wretched mage Gortanik.

"He was hers. She wants him back. That's all my Lord," mewls the skinny mage. "Please, my lord."

"Where's Trix now?" asks their Master in a tone so cold and without mercy, it leaves his wrinkled old servant temporarily dumbstruck.

Walter stands and stares, amazed, at his master, mouth opening and closing like a fish on the bank of a lake. "My Lord, she's not here. She isn't set to return until the evening tomorrow."

Barat looks directly into his servant's eyes, his own black pits of hate. In a cold, calculating voice says, "You will bring her directly to me upon her return. Do you understand me, Walter?"

The meaning of his master's words is clear. He intends to use Trix as an example of what disloyalty brings.

For the second time in almost as many seconds, the wilted old coger is struck dumb again. His mind racing, he searches for an answer for his Lord. He has to fix this. This isn't what he wanted to happen. His sister is innocent in this...

Brutally, Walter is slammed against the wall. His feet are several inches off the floor. The force of the magical wave is enough to knock the wind from the overmatched mage. Without having to hear the question from his master again, he blurts out, "Yes, Master. I'll bring her to you immediately when I find her?"

"Thank you," purrs the vile Barat, condescendence dripping from each syllable. "Just bring her unharmed. I'll see to her personally. I'm going back to sleep. Don't wake me until you've found her."

24

THE NET

Kendra

K<small>ICK, AND</small> I <small>RETURN TO OUR BODIES WITH ONLY SECONDS</small> remaining until sunset. Almost immediately, I feel the thrum of the gargoyles untorping. There's a crackle in the air. It's electric. With the air stone now part of me, I can see their magic as it spills into the air. It's glittery but not thick like I thought it would look. It's more of a white light and feather-soft. Then my goyles are awake, and the exhilarating rush of their magic, as well as their return, fills me with indescribable joy. Much of the murderous feelings brought on by seeing Barat are washed away by the arrival of my goyles.

Kick stands with me, receiving a refreshing dose of the magic that radiates from my consorts as they un-torpify, a look of shock on his face.

As soon as the sun sets fully, my goyles rush us with hugs and pats on the back. I know they can hear and see when they're torped. Still, I'm never sure if they're asleep or attentive to what's going on around them. This time they must have been awake when Kick proposed to me.

Kino says, "Yes, we heard you pop the question to our beauty and couldn't be happier. We knew you would come around."

Mica seamlessly adds to his brother of the heart's statement, "Well, I wasn't sure you would, but I knew if you quit resisting how you truly felt you would. Welcome to the family."

Spar warns, "We have set a precedent for those who hurt our woman, so expect a beat down if you ever hurt her. This is a forever family you're now part of, so get used to handling problems, we won't let you go."

I say with a joking tone, "I don't think that'll ever be necessary, but if it comes up, I can handle my own fight."

They chuckle and agree I can handle myself. Then Kino adds, "Yes, beloved, you are a wonderful fighter, but you will not keep us from helping or defending you. We are a family."

Mica says, "Yes sir, we're a package deal. All for one and all that shit!"

Spar adds his two cents, "We should have a party. But shouldn't we pulse the Guild, so they all know how happy we are? What do y'all think?"

"You're right, hun. But right now, Kick and I have news that won't wait. We have to tell you before we go to the HG meeting tonight." I say.

I tell my goyles what the Air stone does. Then I add all about the dream walk Kick, and I took and how he saw fuckhead and shithead for the first time in a while. I keep an eye on my mage as I relate this part and notice as his face goes blank. There's something here that I need to help Kick with.

"We also found Barat, and we know how to find him again."

As I finish this sentence, Mica begins to stand, a flood of color flushing his face, the anger clearly gaining the upper hand.

I reach out to him and place a hand on his chest to calm him and ask, "How about we fly and get the excitement to a manageable level and Mica I really want to talk this out. Please, don't charge in without us and our allies. They need to learn to trust us and have our backs.

This gives us the perfect opportunity to forge a tighter alliance with the world."

He groans, "Okay, but it can't happen soon enough for me. I'd just as soon go kill the bastard now and just report to everyone he's dead. Are you sure?"

I answer, "Yes, I'm sure. Now let's get going so I have time for a shower before the meeting."

We quickly change into our flying clothes and head to the cave's entrance. Now that Kick has the kilt pin, he can fly with the rest of us, and he probably needs the exercise and practice.

WHEN WE EXIT NAVAN, we're high on a hill with a smooth-faced cliff. This place also allows no room for error. I pause and watch Kick, excitement in my eyes, expecting to see the same from my new consort.

I ask, "Kick, are you sure you can fly with that pin?"

Kick's sober answer is a simple, "Yes."

I take notice of the sadness in my consort's eyes, but I also recognize that this isn't the time to discuss it.

"Alright, if something happens, you guys be ready to save him," I tell my other consorts. Then I jump. My red-tipped black wings take the wind. I don't have to flap them much and land in an updraft.

Kick is right behind me. His movement is very different from the rest of us. He is basically floating and moving at a fast pace.

Kino points at the dark-haired man and says, "I remember now. I had seen this before when we were at the academy for warrior mage training. I saw your father fly with Queen Leta. I didn't know it was the pin that enabled him to join her, I thought at the time she did it with her magic."

I ask, "How is it? Does the wind bother you, or is it hard at all?"

Kick answers, "No, it isn't hard, but it is taking a lot of my will to keep up with you. I think it'll get easier with practice."

Spar holds his elbow and takes some of the pressure off of the mage. "Does this help at all?"

"Yes, actually it does. If I begin to run out of stamina or magic, I'll call you, okay?"

"You bet buddy, I'll be here for you," Spar says.

Glancing around at them all, Mica says, "Ready now, let's exercise these wings for real!" He races off and flies hard.

The others follow easily, even Kick can keep up. On the way back to Navan, when we've exerted ourselves, he begins to tire. Kino notices and pushes his wingtip under his friend's arm, and Spar holds up the other.

Kick nods with a grimace and says, "I definitely need to build up to this. It's been a long time since I even thought about training for anything, but this could come in handy."

We pulse the guards at the entrance and circle waiting for their return pulse, allowing us to enter, when a flight of bats goes by us. Elmer is with them and pulses to me as he passes. He lets me know he's hungry and will be home before daylight. That little bat is so cute. He makes me happy, and a grin breaks out on my face as I pulse him back just as the guards to Navan pulse the 'all safe' message.

UNDERSTANDING

Kendra

SINCE BLOWING DIRT AND DUST ARE A REGULAR PART OF LIFE around our city, we disregard the powdery chestnut brown irritant erupting from our downdrafts. It fills the air around us as we land. I pulse a quick message to Clifton, asking him to ready the High Guild for a strategy meeting in one hour.

Instead of pulsing me back, he messages me on my tablet; "My Queen, I scheduled the meeting as soon as you pulsed your arrival to the guards."

What will I do if I ever lose that goyle's service? So the entire Guild will know how I feel, I pulse a compliment to him for his diligence and dedication. One aspect of pulsing that I've gotten better at 'reading' is the emotional undertones carried within all pulse messages.

In his reply, it's clear that Count de Treon is over the moon with excitement at being singled out so publicly.

Before I let the beginning of the evening's business overtake me, I pause and simply enjoy standing at the entrance of our great city.

Standing at the ingress of Navan has always been a surreal experience for me. The hidden opening is difficult to see from the air or ground. Jericho has magically made it impossible to find, unless you know where to look. But standing here reminds me of my role in the Ceorfan Guild and their unrepentant joy at my happiness. I also know how important it is to share that happiness with them.

Now is the time for an announcement, so I take Kick's hand in one and Mica's in the other with Spar and Kino taking their other hands, respectively. The feeling of oneness in our family is palpable. When we pulse the excellent news about my newest consort and our latest family member, the whump from the vibration is more significant than I recall from any of the others. I chalk it up to the fact the Air stone gives me more sensitivity to what is in the atmosphere now. It also makes me remember the look on Kick's face before we flew because he gave me the stone.

I watch him closely. The surface melancholy is still evident on his face. I signal my other guys to give us a moment with a look and nod. Wordlessly they acknowledge, and one by one makes their excuses until it is only Kick and I left.

"Kick, you know you can speak with me about anything. Right?" I ask softly and lovingly, my voice carrying just to his ears. Still, I obviously startle him, which he covers exceptionally well. Anyone who doesn't share the blood gift that links me with the hurting mage wouldn't have noticed his slight start at the sound of my voice.

"I have to admit, seeing Bladriell, Walter, and Barat have unnerved me more than I thought it ever could," he returns without looking at me. His voice is just as soft as mine but with something like disappointment weaving throughout. "It takes a lot for me not to return and attack them now, even if it means my life. I'm holding back because of you and our people," he finishes, his ruefulness replaced by a potent bitterness.

Now that I know what to look for, I see the conflict, buried within spirits of his elegiac past. Kick is torn by losing Drusey, the torture he's endured, as well as inflicted upon his friends, versus the joy he feels by loving again.

"They made you do horrific things. They tried to take who you are as a person," I respond trying to understand more deeply while hoping he'll share more.

"It's more than that, My Heart. They stripped me down to nothing. They took my fiancé. They took my friends. They took my humanity, my joy, everything that made me, me. Slowly, I fought... we all fought, Peter, Steen, me... we all fought to find something human, some connection." Kick stops and stares at me, the pain etched deep in his face. It's clear he has more to say, but he's unsure of what it is... or maybe whether he should say it at all.

"My love, Kick--I'm here. I'll hear you. I won't judge you. Please, tell me what you need to," I say as comfortingly as I'm able.

"Kendra, since I met you, I have loved you. Even so, it was a love I never hoped to have returned. When I was trapped in that Fae prison, it was Trix who saved me. Well, not really saved me. She used me more than anything. But I think it saved us both for a while. Now, because of Walter's stupidity, Barat fully intends to murder her."

"I've been thinking about that, my love. I think I have an answer to it. But we have to get to the HG meeting so I can get it in place," I answer him softly.

Kick turns to me, his eyes a little wider and alive than they were a few seconds ago.

"Kick, I'm sure our people sense the danger growing as our tactical situation has Navan on a stricter defensive posture. And while I know we have to get ready for the coming battle against Barat, my experience has taught me, stress can bring out unwanted aggression," I say.

Just then, thinking of that, I remember it was Peter who tried to kill Spar in his integration tests. The Ceorfan must fight unified. Many of us haven't had time to meld into that brotherhood of trust. The kind of faith where you know everyone has your back. I need to know that Spar and Peter have put this behind them. I need to know that every Ceorfan will defend the goyle beside them.

"Kick, we have a few minutes before the others will meet us here to go to the meeting. I'd like to dream walk and check on them," I tell him.

When I glance up into his eyes, I see they're full of understanding. His expression is comforting as he takes my hand and leads me to the sofa where we sit.

In his typical Kick unagitated way, he entreats, "Come, My Lady, lean on me, and let's check on the people of your heart."

Since he and I are dragon bound by spirit, slipping into the dream walk is as easy as taking a deep breath. No sooner had he finished his words than we entered the spirit dream world where we float to the people I'm most concerned about.

Peter is standing outside of Mega and Spar's chambers, nervously pulsing for entry. Spar calls out to him instead of pulsing back, "Mage, come in." The blonde mage enters, wringing his hands his head down.

Peter nods a tentative hello to Mega, who excuses himself, saying, "I'll see you both in the High Guild meeting presently." The big blue goyle swaggers to the doorway and, after a brief glance back at his son, leaves the two alone.

They stand in silence until it grows awkward. As it does, they both start speaking at the same time. Peter backs up a half step and offers Spar a full bow complete with a little wave of his hand, extending the courtesy of speaking first to the gargoyle in front of him.

Spar is so much like his father, big, blue, and intimidating softens his tone and says, "I know you're here to apologize for trying to kill me, mage. I'd like to hear what you have to say because I want to understand. We have to fight together, and I need to know if I can trust you. Tell me, was your life with that fucker anything like what Kick went through?" Spar asks, his tone never growing harsher than if he were speaking to a child.

Peter knows Spar's asking about his imprisonment and grimaces at the memories that quickly invade his thoughts. Peter pauses, before taking a deep breath and banishing the incursive memories, "It was the most horrible position I can imagine. I don't know how I survived... I don't see how any of us, including those we carved, survived.

"Spar Megason, I can't beg your forgiveness because I'm not fit to be forgiven. I do hope one day you may find it within you to not hold ill-will toward me," Peter says, speaking in circles. He waves his arms about, gesticulating without purpose, as his words seem to flow without direction.

"Here sit, we have a little while before we have to go. Tell me what you need to," Spar asks as he motions to a chair in the eating area of the room. After they sit, Peter relaxes and tells Spar in a short, succinct way that he was forced to do Barat's work, or his loved ones would suffer. On the night he attacked Spar, his mind was clouded with magic, drugs, and even sex. Peter truly believed that Spar was just another enemy.

Spar sits processing the information, grief, and concern fighting for purchase on his large handsome face. Again when he speaks, the care of his tone is evident, "I can't fathom what you've been through. From what I know about it, it would've broken a lesser man. Also, that you came here to talk with me knowing it might not be an easy conversation speaks well of you. So, can I trust you to have my back mage?" he asks without the danger Peter expected.

"Yes. Unequivocally, yes. I promise to do the best I can for you and the Ceorfan people. I'd be honored to count you as my brother, if you'll have me," Peter answers, relief flooding through every word.

Then let's put this behind us and get on with our lives. Still, if you ever do it again, you can bet your fucking-firetruck, I won't be as forgiving," Spar grins his scary gargoyle grin at his new brother in arms.

"Peter takes a breath and says, "Thank you, you won't regret it."

I share a look with Kick before we speed back to our bodies. We return happy and secure in the knowledge that we don't have to worry about two of the people we both love most.

"Well, we better clean up," I say, thinking of the nightly meeting.

Kick asks, "I don't suppose you want to give a guy a clue to your plans for the High Guild, do you?" "Not a chance! Waiting is half the fun!" I say cheerily.

He laughs.

26

SHARING INFO

Kendra

NOW THAT MY CONSORTS AND I ARE CLEAN AND DRESSED, THE five of us enter my allodium together. We stop in the doorway to verify everyone is here or if some are coming in still. I take advantage of this pause to admire the work that Dana and his team had done in constructing this magnificent conference room.

Looking around, it becomes evident that not everyone is here yet. The Hewn are missing, along with my brothers. Well, maybe I'll find out they started the treasure hunt early. I hurry to my seat and open my tablet, concentrating while the others settle.

Spar knocks knuckles with Peter as he pours coffee at the drink table. Before he sits, he sets the cup in front of me, and I take it, offering him a wanton smile as payment. I brush his fingers as he passes to the other side of my chair to sit beside me. The members were notified by Clifton that this is a strategy meeting, so they're already sitting, waiting. I nod to Duke Findare to start the session.

Kick, still tired from his first flight, looks around for a place to sit, unease building on his brow. My other goyles intend to stand and form a protective arc around both Kick and me. Since Jared isn't here, I motion Kick to sit in his spot so he can stay close. Oh well, Jare, you snooze you lose! My mage takes the hint and sits. He slumps into the large seat, and leans back, all his muscles letting go of the tension he'd built up.

Duke Findare begins by asking, "Clifton, will you please bring the meeting to regular order and proceed with approving the prior meeting minutes? We will spend as little time on procedures and formalities as possible."

I add, "I agree, we have a large amount of work to do and very little time to accomplish it all." All eyes are on me as I speak, and I notice as several members sit straighter in their seats.

The Count de Treon quickly and efficiently makes it through all of the parliamentary procedures before turning to me, "My Queen, the floor is yours."

"Thank you, Count," the seriousness of my tone conveying a meaning the words don't announce. "Members, I'll give you the good news first. As I pulsed earlier, "I have taken Gortanik Lonato as my consort. As my engagement gift, he's given me the Air stone. Kick had kept it hidden from Baratium and his ilk during the entirety of his centuries-long imprisonment. I now have all the stones, save one... the Water stone. As with the other stones, I feel my magic has been increased again. Also, like with the other stones, I'll learn how to use it through daily practice."

The spattering of applause was a little disappointing until my other three goyles heartily joined in. The other HG members must have decided that if those three were okay with Kick, then they had no reason not to be. Immediately the room is filled with happy pulses that grow to a roar with a feel of something like hip-hip-hooray or something similar. Still, with more awe and respect thrown into the mix.

Kick slowly stands and offers a gracious bow to the assembled Ceorfan High Guild. His genuine smile chiseled on his face, and it reaches his eyes for the first time since we returned from the Fae realm. "Thank you, my friends, of old as well as my new friends. I hope to be worthy of your respect and happy wishes. Please take your seats. We have more good news and lots of decisions to make," he finishes the redness burning more brightly on his cheeks than he would have liked.

More murmurs and nods of appreciation are offered to the mage. With the member's earlier questions regarding his suitability wholly gone, the HG members retake their seats. The smiles in the room fade to pursed lips and squinted eyes of anticipation, as they settle to do the business of the Ceorfan.

"Now that I have the Air stone, as I mentioned previously, I only need the Water stone. Does anyone have information on it?" I ask earnestly.

Member Jewel pipes up and asks, "My Queen, would you like us to search for the stone? If it could make the difference in finding our enemy, I'm sure that we will have many volunteers to help."

I answer, "That's what I want to talk about, Jewel. Now, it's common knowledge that when I receive a stone, it asks to become part of me. It becomes a part of my consciousness by joining with my head. When I do this and believe me, it's hard to wait even minutes, I dreamwalk. This time, being bound to Kick, he traveled with me to the spirit realm. While there, we went to see if we could find Barat and Horde." I pause.

"As the stone melded with me, Kick and I dream walked to the Fae lands. He showed me where he'd been imprisoned. He also showed me his torturers, as well as our enemy, Baratium.

Grunts of disapproval and gasps fill the air as I pause. I can see the emotion floating like waves in the atmosphere. They're the colors I've always noticed in the auras surrounding people. That's interesting.

The Count's eyes blink, and his shoulders perk up as he asks, "My Lady, did you find him?"

"Yes, we did."

Just as the room erupts with people clamoring to be heard, I continue, "We know how to find him again! We won't have a problem finding him when we want." I all but shout the final words to be heard above the growing din.

I make out phrases shouted around the room, "Kill him now," and "Why wait?" Others bark for calm. Knowing that sometimes the most important thing a leader can do is be the stone in the middle of the storm, the fixed point for all to attach to, I sit calmly. I carry no smile, no hint of hate, or desire for immediate revenge. I begin to gaze around the room, confidently, rationally. As I catch a member's eye, recognition piles on them as they realize they need to allow the meeting to continue. One by one, I meet their eyes. One by one, they quiet.

Once the room has silenced, I speak, "We have many tasks to accomplish to reach our goal of destroying this worthless piece of shit. Our allies are new and wholly untested. They don't have a reason to trust us. We must give them reasons. We can't rush headlong into this battle without considering all of its implications. The last thing we need is to make more enemies now."

Mica's holding my hand and gives it a squeeze while Spar puts his on my leg under the table. It provides me with strength.

"Our enemy is in a druid's sleep in his castle in Faery. He has a few servants remaining with him. They spend the majority of their time working in a laboratory. All the Crafted we could see were still as statues and remained inanimate. They should be an easy target.

"My consorts and I believe that it's in our best interest to enlist the help of our new allies, both human and Fae. As a people, we need to find a way to become closer to them.

"The Fae King and Queen have said they'll capture or kill Barat since he's one of their people. Since we want to stay on friendly terms with them, I suggest we don't attack from outside Fae. What I desperately need are tactics that will build bonds of trust with both the Fae and human realms. Also, just as importantly, we need permission from the Fae King to take out the Horde and Barat. We need his permission even though he's already told us to leave Barat to him. General Mega, will you start first?" I ask more hopefully than I feel.

My massive general stands and postures as he begins, "Over the years we have found that it is important to include our allies on the information. I would first appoint your ambassadors to the more powerful countries of this world. From there, we can both send and receive information. In Faery, I think you should handle the King and Queen yourself. You are the dragon queen of the Ceorfan, and diplomacy is necessary where they are concerned. Offer them magic treasure from the vaults that we are searching for at this time. Offering the treasure is a must. But don't take no for an answer. They need to understand that we are going to take the evil mage's life and will do it with humans at our side."

After several of the members play devil's advocate, we agree to Mega's proposal.

I say, "Slateri, Jewel, and Gem will be the first ambassadors along with Tobert and Igneous. When we find my brothers and Krag, I want to add Krag to the list, but he might be used elsewhere. If we need more Mega, we will have to draw from the Elite Warrior's Guard.

"Clifton, I can't do without you, I hope you don't feel slighted, but I need you coordinating all of our ambassadors." I don't give him time to answer and say, "I need you to reach out to the human governments and tell them our ambassadors must meet with them about the murderer Barat.

27

WHAT TREASURE

Kendra

THE IMPLICATIONS OF MY DECISIONS ARE STILL HANGING IN THE air when I feel the pull of something familiar. I smile, and I glance toward the doorway expectantly. I don't have to feel their ingress-pulse to know my brothers are about to enter the allodium. Still, their pulses, along with several other ingress-pulses, tickles my skin and reverberate gently through the room. My guards relax after they return a pulse to my brothers as well as Krag and his Hewn.

Jared is the first to speak, but only after he greets me with a brief hug and a kiss, followed by Dana repeating our brother's greeting, "Hello everyone, I'm sorry we're late. But, we've found something astonishing that we need to report," he says cheerily, his enthusiasm in total contradiction to the mood of the room.

Jared, a man who can read a room as well as anyone I've ever met, stops. He quickly surveys the room. When he continues, after the slightest pause, his tone has changed to one more in line with our current discussion, "It appears as if we've missed something important. Maybe I could ask if you would please bring us up to date,

Queen Kendra? After that, we'll give you a piece of news that should make everyone's day better."

"Sure can, little brother," I grin, using my nickname for him instead of Duke of Storms to pay him back for calling me Queen Kendra when we aren't in a formal setting. I get to it and provide a recap of what we've been through so far, including why I believe we should wait on our allies and not go straight into Faery to kill Barat and his henchmen.

Dana gives me a knowing look along with a goofy lopsided grin. Raising one eyebrow, he says, "Well, if you need treasure for the King and Queen of Faery, then I guess it's a good thing that we're hot on the trail of the Ceorfan Queen's treasure," he says. His smirk turns into a full-blown shit-eating grin.

"Seriously?" I ask.

Of course, he's serious. Dana isn't one to exaggerate things of such importance. "So the rumor that the Hewn have it isn't true? Yeah, never mind. I'm not sure why I even asked that."

"Only one small problem... getting to it. Tell 'em, Jared," he adds more seriously, all traces of a smile disappearing.

Jared clears his throat and brings up one corner of his lips and starts, "Krag and the Hewn knew where the treasure was last seen, and that's where we began our search.

"The map that Dana found in the Halls was critical. Because although, with the help of the Hewn, we had gotten to the correct area of the world. We couldn't find another clue as to where the treasure is hidden. We assumed it'd be in a nearby cave or buried near the location we found. In reality, we've found that this was just the first of several clues we have to follow to find it. It also appears that there isn't a single hiding place for the treasure. There are but many.

"We're going to have to follow these clues to find it. That is unless we can find someone who helped hide the treasure." Jared pauses and looks around the room hopefully.

Continuing, "On the map that Dana found in the Halls of History, was a clue which reads, 'To get the prize, one of stone and one of wing must work together to open the well.' We couldn't find a well. Krag said he remembered there was one. Dana used his gift to quickly move tons of dirt and rock, where Krag indicated the well should be.

"Right where he said, we found an old cistern head that Krag recognized as having Queen Leta's crest, which in itself is a lock. Being privy to the secrets of the time, it only took seconds before it was open. On the inside of the well just under the lip, we found another clue or set of instructions, depending on your mood. We're going to need more help to get to it, Kendra. The next piece of evidence makes it obvious. It states that 'The Dragon Queen of the long-lived must fly over the Great Wall and find the hermit, Achor.'"

"You're kidding me. We're going to be searching forever if this keeps up. Do you have a map or something we can see?" I take a quick breath and shake my head. Now that we're close to our dreams, my head is spinning.

"Yes, I'll send it to you, and all the High Guild," the Duke of Storms answers and quickly sends the maps as well as a summary of action items he had made to the members' tablets. I quickly review the information and find his list of to-dos is almost identical to the list we've been discussing in council before Jared even arrived.

Interjecting, I say, "Jare, I'm not sure how you do it, but your task list is what we've been discussing. I believe several of these items are important and can't wait. I'm convinced my most important task is ensuring a quick and painful death for that low-life worthless fuckwit Baratium. Next, it's continuing the integration of our people into the community of nations within both Fae and human worlds. I don't mind flying over somewhere, but it's going to have to be a fast trip," I say as I glance at Dana. His nod of agreement helps lower my anxiety level a little. Maybe from a ten to a nine...

Murmurs of agreement spread around the room.

"Also, since neither Mica or I have a paying job, we need a way of paying for our necessities," I say, embarrassment creeping into my voice and coloring my cheeks a bright red in the process. I've always had to work hard for every penny I've gotten. Not that Jare and Dana didn't work for theirs. They did and continue to do so.

Jared made millions writing a piece of software while he was in college. Dana has been so good with his hands, he's always had money following him around.

I, on the other hand, have never had the specific talents of my brothers. I'm smart and work hard, but the pay of a Park Ranger isn't something that'll let you retire early. Both of my brothers have tried to 'help' me financially. But call it pride if you want, I want to make my own way. I've always wanted it that way.

A few outbursts of laughter, which quickly quieted, threaten to push my embarrassment into full-blown tears... a few giggles...

"Ummm, am I missing something?" I ask hesitantly, the tears of anger hanging on just behind my facade of coolness.

"Your Majesty," Amber starts, "you know you have your Queen's Treasure... right?" She finishes, hopefully.

"Queen's Treasure? What treasure?" I ask in a shocked response. I remember her saying something about treasure one of the first times she helped me dress. I thought it meant like the crowned jewels, not something I can use to live on.

Amber smiles a knowing and comforting smile. "Kendra, you're the richest person in the world. Your treasure is vast. It's been held in trust for you for hundreds of years. It's here, in Navan. Much was lost but not all the treasure of our people. We aren't poor by any means, no Ceorfan is," she adds.

My breath is gone, and I hold perfectly still as her words sink in.

"My Queen," Clifton starts, "you have always wanted to feel you were not a burden. We did not believe you would feel you were worthy of this inheritance if we were to disclose it to you at an inappropriate time. This birthright has been used for your welfare as needed since you have come to us. This treasure has always belonged to our Queens. It's a legacy of your grandmother and mother, not a burden to your people."

"But what about the Ceorfan, my people? Where is their vast wealth?" I ask, struggling to gather my mind around the events.

"Your people are well cared for. We have a wealth that far exceeds most small countries."

"Oh, okay," is all I can manage.

It's the Duke of Stone that comes to my rescue. "Sis, Jare and I are glad you're all taken care of, but I've been itchin' to tell you 'bout the treasure for a while. I've been working with Jericho, but I need some help finding the rest of it and bringin' it home." He finishes with a raised eyebrow, something Dana likes to do when he knows he has made an important point, and I'm not paying enough attention.

"Right! Got it. You need help finding it... the lost treasure?" dread at being spread thin seeping into my voice.

"Well, Sis, if you gotta put it that way. Yes!" He laughs.

Finally, the surprise begins to wash away, and my thinking clears. "Alright, little brother, I'll get you some help. Jericho, I'm guessing you'd like to keep helping the Duke of Stone?"

A nod of his head is all the affirmation I need.

"Is there anyone else in the room who can provide assistance?" I ask as I peer around the room.

A hand raises. "My Queen. I was one of the architects of the hiding places," Peter says. "I'd be grateful for the opportunity to help."

"Very well, Peter, thank you. If anyone else would like to help, please see the Duke. I think we can move on and let Dana handle the details of this little hunt. Duke of Storms, Jared, I have a special task for you and Dr. Ogman."

"Sure, My Queen, Sis. Whatever you need," Jared responds, grinning ear to ear.

"You may not want to accept so quickly. This is going to put you on the front lines without your bodyguards. I need you to find a Faery named Sass and another named Trix before Baratium murders them."

"You got it, Sis," my brother pipes up almost before I can finish.

I know I can always count on these two to never ask the uncomfortable question in public and help me get done what needs doing.

"I'm assuming someone here knows who these two Faery women are and can help me...," Jared asks without making it a question.

"I can help you," came a voice standing with Peter. It's Steen.

Jared stares intently at the mage before nodding approval.

Steen responds with a nod of his own.

"Well," I begin, "these are three crucial things..."

"Sorry, Princess, it's four," says a smiling Mica. "Integrate the Ceorfan into the human world, find the treasure, rescue Trix and Sass, and kill that fucker Baratium." Mica holds four fingers up and wiggles them to everyone, satisfied he caught a potential loose end, a bit too much pride in his posture.

"I stand corr–"

Kino sighs loud enough to interrupt me. When I look over at him, he's shaking his head while he's looking at Mica, humor and annoyance warring on his handsome mug. His suppressed grin tells me fun had already won the day. "Once again Mica, I must teach you to count,"

Kino happily interjects, "It's five things, not four. We also need to get the Water stone." He pauses ever so slightly, satisfaction on his face for the briefest of moments before turning serious as he glances at me.

Damn, I forgot about the Water stone.

"It could be anywhere," he continues, "I suspect the Hewn have information on where to find that most important final stone for you, my darling," says Kino his ramrod-straight posture doesn't change as he takes a small peg out of Mica.

Mica's grin to his friend could mean anything, but in this case, I think it says, 'It's on Kino!'

Krag's gaze locks on Kino's as he gives my red hunk-a gargoyle a curt nod, indicating his potential willingness to speak with Kino later.

Maybe they can find the stone together.

"Ok, so it's five things. That's enough for tonight. My brain can't take anymore," I laugh in exasperation, then add, "Anyone hungry?" I glance up quickly and, hopefully, somewhat expecting to hear more pleas for action items to be added to my already overburdened load.

I have one of the best chefs in the world in Chef Morgan. He happens to be the chef for all HG meetings, as well as my personal chef. On important occasions, Chef Ron from TASS has portaled in. Tonight is essential for me. I want a surprise dinner for the entire Guild after the HG meeting in recognition of mine and Kick's announcement and, more importantly, the happiness at having the Hewn in Navan again.

The Guild has a right to meet the Hewn gargoyles as well as the reverse. Maybe that will help cement their decision to work with us. We didn't have time to go all out on the buffet, but between both our chefs, we have time to have a pleasant surprise for everyone.

The smell of cooking food begins to fill the allodium. Mixing scents of smoky BBQ beef, honey baked ham, yams, roasted nuts, and so many variations of pies fills the room. The sight, alone, of the pies being prepared, filled me with delight at the prospect of trying several of them. My mouth is watering. So I guess I shouldn't have been surprised as the entire room shifts out of their seats, the Hewn included, and make their way to the extensive buffet being delivered.

The tension in the room has lifted. Now, since my brothers will be attending to their own tasks, I contemplate ways of accomplishing parts of the list without them or my harem of gargoyles. It's going to be different, but I think I can get it done. I'll also tighten the bonds with our allies at the same time.

My problem, as usual, doesn't lie with my brothers succeeding in their assignments. It's with me. Can I let them do their job without worrying so much about their protection that I slack on my own duties? I guess we'll see.

28

REST BEFORE THE STORM

Kendra

THE INDIVIDUAL PLANS FOR EACH OF OUR TASKS HAVE US deliberating well into the morning hours. It only breaks up when we grab food and drink, mostly from the leftovers from the buffet. Eating aside, I think the real reason we all agreed to take a break is that it's getting close to the time for all good gargoyles to be home to reach their stands and stages to torp.

My guys and I are exhausted, so we leave to get some rest. Even Mica chooses to torp today. His thinking is it'll add to his strength for the coming days.

Kick and I lie down, and he looks at me with a questioning look of 'can I touch you again.'

I smile at him and snuggle into him. His arms wrap around me, embracing me tightly. In seconds I'm asleep. We sleep for hours before we find each other in the dreamscape. It is so easy to find him again that it doesn't even surprise me when I see him.

After we join hands, I think of a place at the foot of the green mountains and rolling hills in Ireland. As quickly as I think of it, we're standing there. The fresh smell of the green grass is heady, and I reach for my handsome mage's hand and turn him around like children playing a game. The beauty surrounding us is totally entrancing. I release his hand, encircle his waist with my arms, and reach up for a kiss. The light in his eyes all for me. I can easily see that he cares and wants more, so together, we decide to wake.

Now I feel his erection pressing against my back, his hands already on my breasts and pulling me into him. I moan in pleasure as he pulls me harder and kisses my shoulder.

"Kick, you know the others can see and hear us. Does that bother you? If it does, we can go somewhere else."

"No, that isn't a problem. Is it for you?"

I raise a brow and grin. "Not for me, kiss me like you mean it."

His hand goes to my chin, and he holds my face for the softest press of our lips then I giggle and slam him against the sheets and kiss him deeply. He flips me over, and I feel his erection grind into me and groan, "You feel so good."

He moans, and I'm so turned on. I flip him back over and watch his face to make sure it's okay as I hold his hard flesh close to my throbbing entrance. He nods, and I press him inside my hot opening and begin to glide back and forth slowly to a rhythm in my head. Knowing the others might be awake turns me on even more, thinking they might one day all be here at once, and I growl, "Oh, I'm almost there, Kick!" I sit up taller and arch my back in pleasure.

His hands on my ass never leave, but now he's moving harder with me.

It's everything I can do to keep going and not stop moving. My orgasm feels fantastic, but I want to see his face when he comes, so I keep up the rhythm. In minutes I'm rewarded with what I want as he reaches his own climax and spurts hot cum inside me. His face is beautiful in his pleasure but tight with his mouth pursed. I lean into him and enjoy his warmth, loving the feel of him before I roll off beside him.

We lay breathless staring at the ceiling of my room, our fingers interlaced. He turns on his side and looks directly at me, "You're even more beautiful now," he says playfully.

"You bet your sweet ass I am. I hate to be so quick with work, angel, but I want to get up and start on our plans. Want to shower with me?" I retort giving him a soft kiss.

"Wait, what did you just call me," he asks, incredulity dripping from each word. A look of surprise on his face, as his right eyebrow arches above his other.

"Ummm... what? Angel?" I ask, caught somewhat off guard.

"Yes, if I get to be part of your life then I should be able to help you pick my pet name. Do I get a say?" he asks quietly, almost as if he wants to tease me and isn't good at it yet.

"Well, I hadn't thought about discussing it. I just sorta picked them out for my goyles. It just came out," I say hesitantly, hoping I don't hurt his feelings. I wonder why calling him "Angel" would bother him?

"I'm not like the gargoyles," he says with a slight grin still appearing totally serious.

I squint my eyes a bit, wondering if he's playing with me. He's so serious I can't tell.

The dark mage points a thumb over his shoulder at the guys posing together in a silly position, and says, "I mean they're great guys and all, but coming up with a name for them must have been easy." He's clearly playing to amuse me and our torpified audience. Who'd have ever guessed he has a funny side?

Now that I get it I spur him on saying, "Oh and what name would you come up with mage of mine?

"You could call me Stud Muffin. It perfectly describes me. I'm amazing in bed, and you like to eat me," he finishes with a decidedly non-Kick goofy grin.

"Well, sir, I'm glad to see you speaking so easily for a change. What brought out your inner joker," I ask.

"You're amazing, Kendra. You've saved me in more ways than

one. Now you are going to help, Sass and Trix. Two people you don't know and you're so relaxed about the whole thing. Helping people is just who you are. I'm in awe of you."

"Thank you, you're sweet," I say as I rub my hand gently on his face, pulling him in for a kiss. Just before our lips touch, I push him away. "Back to the pet name, Lancelot," I exclaim mockingly.

"No! You can't use that one. I knew Lancelot, and I'm no Lancelot," Kick deadpans.

"Ok... knockout! You're good looking, and you dream walk with me, and I gotta be sleeping..." I finish.

"Let's go back to angel, except make it dark angel. How about that," he asks.

I giggle and shove him away. "Hey, Dark Angel, I think you forgot that my goyles are listening to this little exchange. If you didn't, you might want to consider the consequences of talking about this in front of them," I add teasingly as I shake my naked ass at him and walk to my shower.

I glance over my shoulder and see him sitting there, slack jawed, one hand over his mouth. I swear I could almost hear him as he mouths the words, "Oh shit!"

Kick regains his thoughts and follows me into the shower. We finish and dress just in time to return to my chamber and bathe in the magic of the guys de-torpifying.

As soon as they're free, they line up to kiss me. Kino is first. After his passionate kiss, he says, "Good day, beloved." Then, without missing a beat he looks straight at Kick, "Hello, Mr. Cheeky," he says with a shit-eating grin on his face.

Next is Mica. His passionate kiss makes my toes curl and feel like they're going to explode, "Hey, babe." Then again to Kick, "Hello there, Faery Princess," as he turns to join Kino.

Finally, Spar takes me and spins me and dips me backwards before giving me the deepest kiss of the three, "Morning, Honey. Hey there, Romeo," he adds with a sly grin.

Kick's holding his head in his hands, and covering his face as best he can, his head shaking with laughter--I hope.

After a few moments, he removes his hands and starts, "You three are..." Then he sees them posing. Spar and Mica stand ramrod straight, their arms bent at the elbows, holding Kino, who is lying down on his side across their arms, his head resting on his elbow, blowing a kiss to Kick. Spar and Mica each have one wing up, meeting the others wing and forming a heart around the three of them.

All I can say for sure is, it's a good thing that my mage wasn't drinking his coffee because it would have been spit across the room; he's laughing so hard. I think he's even more handsome with a smile on his face.

After the boys were done giving each other the business, we meet in the lounge to discuss the previous day's HG meeting.

"Guys, I'm not comfortable with where we left some of the tasks last night," I start.

"Ok, hun, what's the problem," Spar asks.

"Well, we're technically in a state of war," I say hesitantly.

Nods and a few "Uh huh's" drift around, so I continue. "Dana and Jared are heading out on some pretty important missions without warrior protection."

The look of understanding on each of their faces.

"I know they're dragons and can protect themselves, but it's not what they're trained to do. Is it? I was hoping I could get a couple of you to go with them to watch over them," I plead, searching each face for help.

"Babe, you know you can count on us. But don't you think we should be here with you. No offense to your brothers, I love them and all... but you're the one we're sworn to protect," Mica says, hesitating just enough that I know he was uncomfortable with what he said.

Kino rescues me, "Beloved, I believe I understand. I agree with you. Jared will be in Faery, and Dana is chasing the treasures. Barat will have plenty of opportunities to strike either of them. You will have your guard, and two of us can stay by your side. I feel secure with that level of protection for you. As I have the most experience with the treasure, I will help the Duke of Stone in his search," he finishes.

I see the others slip into a resigned agreement with my red goyle.

"I'll help out, Jar... I mean, the Duke of Storms," Spar says a little too excitedly. I gaze at him questioningly, to which he responds, "Hey, I've never been to Faery for a visit. This should be fun," he exclaims.

I roll my eyes at him.

"I do need you all to know," Spar begins, his head down, his arms outstretched, hands pressed hard onto his knees.

It's a position I know well from our time together. Spar is clearly working up to saying something he's very uncomfortable with.

"I have to talk with Peter. The last time I was alone with him, he tried to kill me. I know he was under a spell. But I," he emphasizes the 'I' and pauses to catch not my eyes, but Kick's, "need to make sure that our new mage is good to go."

My dark angel looks at my blue goyle long and hard before answering. His reply is simple and filled with trust as I could hope for, "I trust you. Do what you need. I have seen and am sure he is legit. Let me know if you'd like me to go with you."

The answer sends relief washing over Spar and is as evident as the tide cleaning away a child's sandcastle on a sunny afternoon. He responds simply, "Thank you, brother."

"I just want to spend the last few moments with y'all before we all go our separate ways. I'll stay in touch with magic. Promise me you'll call or find me if there's a problem. No, not only then. Message me every day. I'll miss you all terribly," I add.

The fear rising out of the blackness representing our approaching separation begins burning deep in my gut. Maybe it's not so much fear as it is the idea that's been festering inside me that I won't be able to protect everyone. The idea that tells me, I'm left sending others to do some of the most dangerous tasks, outside my ring of protection.

No matter how fast I can portal to them with an army of the best fighters in the world at my back, it may not be enough. I have to face the realization that, at some point, I may never see some of the most influential people in my life. I let my hair slip in front of my face. I feel a pulse and turn to it as Mega enters the room. This draws the other's eyes also. They don't notice the tear that slides down my face.

29

GETTING TO WORK

Kendra

IT'S TRANQUIL IN THE WAITING AREA JUST OUTSIDE THE reception hall. We've been making a habit of gathering here before we depart on any vital mission. This time is different. Since the last HG meeting, the tension's been building. My muscles are bound tightly. Already, I'm almost in a fighting stance.

We'll be leaving in three separate portals. I feel the strangeness of today working its way into my consciousness. A cold shiver runs down my spine... This is it. For better or worse, we're about to realize all of our plans.

"Edling," Megahir tele-shouts in my mind. The insistence of his baritone voice reverberating in such a way that it's obvious this isn't the first time he's called to me.

"Yes, General?" I start, "I'm sorry Mega, I must have let my mind wander a bit."

Based on how close the blue-gray behemoth is standing without my noticing, I'd apparently let my thoughts wander further afield than I'd intended.

"What can I do for you?" I ask after regaining my composure.

His black eyes flick up and down me in pride. He adjusts his posture and stands tall, with his chest out then answers with the authenticity that's common from the massive mohawked gargoyle.

"My Queen, please, you never have anything to apologize to me about–ever. I consider it my greatest honor to be the leader of your people's defense. You are both our most revered treasure as well as our greatest weapon," Mega says in his typically serious way. As he reaches his hands to hold mine, he tele-speaks, *I am proud of you, Edling.*

Some day, I hope he's able to find enough peace and security he'll be able to take off the burden of protecting everyone and everything. For now, I need him as he is.

"Thank you, Mega. Let's hope our plans are as successful as we think they will be. Excuse me, I need to speak with my brothers before they leave," I beg-off, hoping my voice is as loud as my General needs it to be.

As Mega bows, I look around and watch the room fill with gargoyles and mages. I notice Duke Findare Magnus, Jadite, Flint, even pregnant Amber, and her guy goyle Mason have made their appearance. I spot Jimmy and Vanessa, the teenagers, from town and wonder what they're doing here. Jimmy sees me watching and comes over with a big hug. Vanessa hugs me too.

Before I say a word, Jimmy says, "Thank you so much, Kendra, for giving us jobs as pages in the Ceorfan Guild. We won't let you down."

I smile mentally thanking Findare for remembering to give Jimmy a job. That he also gave one to Vanessa is a bonus.

I say, "I know you won't. We can talk later. I have to get this show on the road now, though." I pat him on the shoulder as he ducks his head and moves away with his girlfriend.

The energy in the room is a surreal mixture of excitement, trepidation, and fear. The three combine to cause an overreaction of a dominant psychological trait for each person to come forward.

Jared is his larger self, smiling and sidling throughout his team while reviewing tasks and objectives. He's preparing them as if he were about to take the field for one of his football games. His team, Spar, Flint, Steen, Peri, and Dr. Ogman, carry confident smiles and greet the well-wishers gathered nearby.

Dana has drawn inward, concentrating on his tasks, in doing so, he's taken his team with him. The core of his team, Kino, Apex, Jericho, and Peter, all stand quietly with him. There are more who stand ready that'll be helping with his mission. When his team speaks, it's with a specific purpose and without any bull-shit.

I find myself thinking of ways to protect them all, all the while knowing, intrinsically, that this is the moment I'm sending my people into danger. Risks will arise from situations we can't plan for. It'll put them in positions where I can't possibly protect them all.

I find the desire for one last touch, one final goodbye overwhelming my knowledge that I mustn't allow any of them to see my distress. I wade into the crowd to find my baby brother.

When I look up into Dana's blue-green eyes, I see he's feeling many of the same emotions as I am... except for fear. I have rarely seen Dana express any type of fear. I can't help but want to hug him. A euphoric surge of sadness hits my heart as the realization of possible pending loss fills my head, and a tear slides down my cheek. I can't do this for him or fully protect him while he completes his part of our plans. I'm going to trust him to do it. I'm sure he'll do it well. I reach for him and give him a big sister hug letting him know I love him then say, "Baby brother, I'll be there if you need me. Use your donum, and I'll know... I'll come. I know you'll find the treasure. Just stay safe, okay?"

"I'll do that, Sis. I love you too. Now go hug Jared before he leaves without it," he tells me without a hint of agitation and his dimple on full display. I hold him for just a second longer before I turn him loose. As I look into his eyes again, I'm pretty sure I see the glassy twinkle. He quickly turns and begins talking to his team, who are gathering around him.

I find Jared by his voice, a commanding modulation within the sea of worry and doubt. That's my little brother, he rarely doubts anything he does. I don't hesitate when I find him. I quickly turn him to me and pull him close, ensuring he knows his big sister loves him.

Before I have a chance to speak, he says, "Sis, you use your donum if you need me."

I smile at his astute perception. "I was going to tell you that," I say and playfully punch him in the arm for taking my line. "Stay safe, Jared. You're beginning the most dangerous part of our plans. I won't have you hurt. I mean it, stay safe. If you have any doubts as to your or your team's safety, call for reinforcement," I order, a little more sternly than I'd intended.

If he is hurt by my directness, he shows no sign of it and responds with cheeky disregard, "Yes, My Queenliness! You command, I obey!" His mock stand to attention and salute providing all the evidence of his confidence in his team and himself.

"Sis, I know you're worried. This is the first time we've split up like this, and you can't help everyone at the same time. Dana and I are pretty good dragons. You're the one who needs to remember to ask for help when things get too tough!" He chides me gently. "I love you. I'll do my best to bring them all home too," he adds as he pulls me in for a final hug.

"Jare, don't worry about Navan or me. I've got Mega and most of my Ducere and the Elite Warriors. You've also stationed more security around every place any of us may go. Good luck, Duke of Storms." I return his mock salute with one of genuine sincerity.

With that, he turns his back and yells, "Circle up, Blue Team!" while he's twirling his hand above his head in a circle.

Across the room, I hear Dana, "Green team, bring it in."

I begin, "Red Team...," when I feel a touch on my arm, gentle but insistent, it's Krag. His eyes are wide with concern. As I turn to him, my head tilts upward to him, a disquieting sense of confusion, causing my donum to tingle. This gargoyle has something in mind that scares him. He suddenly takes my hand with far more force and strength than he should have with his queen, pulling me the rest of the way around to face him.

Out of the corner of my eye, I notice Jared react, pushing his way through the small crowd which has gotten between us.

In all of my fights, I've been able to slow the battle to the point I'm ready to react much faster than I could, had I not been gifted as I am. Again it proves useful, as I watch Krag and verify his aura is not red or displaying any color of violence but respect and care. He drops to one knee, his head bowed.

I send an urgent "Stop" command with a pulse. Jared and Dana react before I send it. The room has fallen silent with all eyes on us.

Krag kisses my hand and speaks, "My Queen, I was sent by the Hewn to determine your fitness to lead. Many Hewn have questioned your experience, others your determination to do what is needed. Still, others have questioned your loyalty to the Ceorfan."

My heart is racing as I listen to the large gargoyle, and my hand goes to my chest. All of the concerns of the Hewn are the same demons I battle daily. If they are worried about the same worries, I have...

Krag continues, "I've watched as you helped build these plans, even agreeing to them knowing they place your brothers at great risk. While here, I've listened to your people, and they universally adore you. Without success, I've searched for ways your selfishness would risk the Ceorfan. My Queen, I've searched for failings which a Ceorfan Queen shouldn't have, to no avail. I believe it's time for the Hewn to come in from the desert and join with our Ceorfan sisters and brothers. No more holding back, will you have us," he finishes, looking earnestly into my eyes.

My racing heart feels like it's going to burst through my chest and explode in a giant pyrotechnic starburst. My grandmother's words come to me without me even searching for them, "I eagerly and joyously accept the Hewn into the bosom of our Grandmother Leta's city-home. Your reintegration has been earnestly sought for more than a millennium. Krag, rise and be welcomed by your brothers and sisters," I finish with a feeling of great relief, like a great sin finally being atoned.

Krag stands but continues to face me. "My Queen, I have one other thing to tell you. I know where the Water stone is. Terin, Jericho's daughter, has it. She's the leader of all the Hewn. When I call, she'll bring it to you," a grin broadening across his face.

The shock of what's just happened hasn't even finished sinking in. Jericho has a daughter? She's the leader of the Hewn? I'll have to find out more about that later.

I give him a brief answer, "Thank you for your trust and the stone. It's going to be needed in the upcoming days. Call Terin and give her my best. For now though we have to go." I dismiss him gently.

It's time to get the teams moving. With the teams ready and grouped together. I tele-speak to Mega, *"General, anytime you're ready."*

"Yes, Edling, you're the head concho."

I bow my head and wipe the grin off my face knowing he meant head honcho.

His voice booms as he orders, "Mages of each team, head your group and open your portals. You know your orders and responsibilities. I'll be monitoring your progress with your team's assigned communications officer and in the Queen's daily briefs. Good hunting warriors."

The senior mage of each team had been decided on in the group planning meetings. Three mages step forward and weave their magic into place. No jump stone is used for this part of the mission. Shimmers of light glow on the faces of the prepared Ceorfan, and they begin to transfer through the portals to their respective target location.

Amber and Mason, along with Koke, who is second in command of the Elite Warrior's Guard after Mega, are to stay behind and defend Navan if the need arises. The worry, as they gaze at us as we leave, stamped on each of their faces.

Before stepping through the portal, I feel the pulse of Koke's first order, "All Ceorfan, this is Commander Koke. Effective immediately, all entrances, as well as exits to Navan, are closed. No one will be admitted or allowed to leave the city until... until this situation has been resolved or further clarified. Defense and Reaction Team (DaRT), report to me in the Combat Information Center (CIC). Communications, sound the Defensive Incursion Alert. Set condition, Modified Zulu, and Weapons Status Yellow One."

Within a heartbeat, I hear the clanging of a tocsin... and my portal closes behind me.

30

GREEN TEAM GO

Dana

JERICHO OPENS OUR PORTAL, AND WE STEP THROUGH. ALTHOUGH we've opened it onto an area we know to be safe, we don't take any chances.

First we send through one of the Elite scouts who accompany each team. This particular scout has a gift similar to Mica and can avoid torpifying for several hours. After she returns with an all clear, we step through.

When we arrive at our new location, the sun is shining brightly, causing me to squint for a few seconds 'til I get my sunglasses to cover my eyes. We'd known that the time would be in the daylight hours, and the gargoyles with us have only seconds to pose and harden to stone.

Jericho and I had prepared for this. I say, "Go ahead, Royal Mage, make them invisible."

He nods and proceeds to do that with a wave of his hand.

"Jericho, please remain here with our team while Peter and I take a tour of the area. Maybe you could read them a book or something," Dana says with a devilish grin.

"I shall protect our torpified friends while you are gone. I had not considered reading to them. But, if you command it, I will obey," Jericho states as if he were telling me water is wet.

I laugh and hand Peter a tiny earbud. He's our head mage even with the ancient royal mage with us. The young blond has more strength. "Peter, here, this is our earbud communications system. Dolo secured them for us a while back. I'm told it's got a long name. I've been calling it ORCS. It stands for something, but I can't remember what. Besides, I like ORCS. Sorta gives it a hobbit feel. Anyway, after you seat it in your ear, push it three times. That'll put it on channel three. This'll allow all of us to talk to each other. But it only works if you're within a hundred feet of another ORCS earbuds," I say, happy I remembered to tell him this final important detail.

After we verify we're both on the correct channel, we have to pause for a few minutes for Peter to practice using the ORCS device surreptitiously. He keeps putting his hand to his ear, which will give away the fact he's wearing a hidden communications device. After a bit, he gets the hang of it, and he and I make our way to a nearby path. He waves the direction, and we start walking. As we walk the two miles or so to the road, I tell the young mage about our last visit to this castle. I finish, proud of our accomplishments that day, despite the brutal murder of Alexandritana.

"When I was last here, my best friend was vaporized as I watched unable to help. Impotently, I watched as many Ceorfan die that day, my family... my friends. That day was the end of my happiness," Peter finishes with his hands going to cover his face.

The emotion pouring off of the mage is palpable as if it transformed into a corporeal yoke and placed itself upon his shoulders to be carried with him throughout time.

He jerks his hands away after angrily wiping away the tears he's trying to stifle. He stands straighter and adjusts his clothes, then looks at me for guidance.

My jaw aches from grinding my teeth, anger at my lack of tact. Unable to recover, I placed a callused hand on his shoulder, "Peter, if it helps, we're going to kill that motherfucker," I firmly state.

He looks up to me and nods weakly. One new task on my To-Do list, help Peter find his purpose again.

We finish our hike to the road without another word being uttered. Jared's given me a specific landmark. In this case, it's a unique set of wooden structures used to mark the entrance to one particular field. We're to wait near them for our ride. A truck, driven by one of my brother's Turkish guards.

He arrives, sliding on the dirt near the shoulder of the road, a plume of dust following in his wake. The driver leans out and yells, "You must hurry. You cannot be seen walking in this area. There are police constantly patrolling this road," his English broken by the Turkish accent of his home country. I'll never know how Jared can find these people in such faraway places.

We squeeze into his freaking tiny and filthy truck, and he starts the short drive to the ruins of the once-great Castle Ilioiliom. The same place where we were attacked by hundreds of Crafted and that bastard rat, Barat.

After a short drive, maybe less than ten minutes, we slow as we near our stopping point close by the once-great gargoyle city.

As our vehicle slows, our driver says, "I will wait only fifteen minutes. After that, I must leave. Good luck."

Those are his final words as he pulls over and stops. I pat him on the shoulder and give him a one-hundred-dollar bill from my wallet for his trouble. I know 'his richness,' my brother, is paying him. I just feel like I need to add my thanks too.

"Thank you for the ride and your silence, friend."

He takes my money and bows his head, patting my hand on his shoulder. After that he pushes my hand away and adjusts the scarf around his face then looks forward, waiting for us to depart.

Supposing I've been excused, I unfold my long legs from his vehicle and get out. Peter slides out after me. When he closes the door, the driver takes off, spewing more dirt into the air and onto both of us.

"Fucker, come back ya varmint, I want my money back," I growl, knowing he can't hear me. It still makes me feel better to say it, though, and so does the one-finger salute he can see if he looks in his rearview.

Laughing, I look to see how my partner is taking the 'dust-up.' The inimical grimace haunting his eyes tells me all I need to know... I've got lots of work to do to help the mage return to his humanity.

He turns to me the emotion fading from his face, he points to a path and tells me, "Let's go."

We follow many paths, not straying off of them due to the many guards. I smile as we pass the healthy apple tree that I caused to grow.

The mage looks at me oddly. There's a sign near the tree that speaks of the tree's miraculous appearance. Most of the tourists laugh it off as another 'fake miracle.' Well, I suppose they're right, in a way... it wasn't a miracle, 'twas Dana magic!

We continue along the imposing outside wall of the castle, but inside the great city and pass the place where Alexandritana gave her life to capture the staff from fuckwad. I look away, not wanting to remember the pain of that day. I want to think of her beauty and courage instead.

We finally weave our way to the end of the wall, and Peter is turning to go into the castle itself when I stop him with a touch on his arm. Then I point to the wall above us, telling him where we'd found the great dragon head of Queen Leta.

"I'm grateful to all who risked their lives to help Queen Kendra through her etching and to recover our Queen Leta," the young man says.

The emotions from earlier are mixed with what he's feeling now, evident in his word. However, he must be in a state of shock at standing here again and keeps his features blank.

Again he motions me forward. This time, I let him lead me up a grand stone stairway that ends in a large ruin. The ruin is obviously a tattered remnant of a once beautiful building.

Peter says, "This is where Priam held court. Just over there," he points at a large area that was obviously once a beautiful fountain. "This is called the king's pond. At least that's the spell name we put on it to identify it."

"Ok," I answer, convinced he knows what he's talking about. "But where's the 'Great Wall' and this hermit 'Achor'?" I ask, hopefully.

Peter turns and points directly north of where we're standing.

"You see that wall in front of us?"

I nod as he continues, "Below that wall is a large cliff. When you're on the plain to the north of the wall, it looks enormous. We called it the 'Great Wall' because of that," Peter concludes, a small shrug of his shoulders being the only indication he's finished speaking.

"Fine, the map and other clues have told us that 'the Dragon Queen of the long-lived must fly over the Great Wall and find the hermit Achor,' what's that all about?" I ask, before realizing that I've asked about Achor before. "Tell me about the hermit first," I ask a little more stridently knowing our time is limited.

Again the mage turns and only points. This time he's pointing at the statue in the middle of the 'king's pond.' "She's there!"

"Wait, what? It can't be that easy. Why didn't you just tell us in Navan?" I question, worry creeping into my voice.

"The Hewn were present, and they hadn't made their intentions known. I couldn't take the chance that a Hewn would find the mask and keep it from our queen. Besides, it was too late to say anything after Krag pledged his loyalty," he says with all the sincerity he could muster.

"Huh," I breathe out and shrug my shoulders. No use gripping now, but I need to know more. "Is there anything else you need to show me," I ask, then remembering how difficult it must be for Peter to be here and soften my tone, "or is there any other part of this city you'd like to visit?"

"No," is his only response.

"Let's get back to the others before un-torp time. I need to store up energy." Finding our driver was easy. I knock on his hood as I pass to get into the truck. He acknowledges with a wave. He must have noticed it was a large American bill I gave him as his attitude has vastly improved.

I bark, "Home, James," adding a broad smile, letting him know I'm not holdin' onto a grudge.

The man doesn't even remark, he just takes off down the bumpy roadway.

Peter and I don't speak on the ride back to our beginning point. It's almost dark by the time we arrive, so it's easy to get out of the truck unobserved in the gray twilight. I let my mage friend's silence continue, thinking that Peter will break it if he needs it. He's quiet until we're within a few hundred yards of where Jericho and the gargoyles are waiting.

As we make our way over to the Green Team, he says, "Dana, I appreciate you trusting me and taking me back to my city. You know it's difficult for me to be there. When I told you 'no' about seeing other parts. What I really mean is, not now. I need to wait for my brothers, Steen and Kick. We three have a pact to return to this city together after Baratium is dead," his voice insistent and beckoning no response.

I let him have his privacy on the matter and walk toward the torped gargoyles and the Royal Mage just as the magic of the untorping starts. It hits me. Then like my Sis had told us to do, I soak it up, rub my arms, and arch my back. When all the goyles are moving, Kino walks up to me and waits for instruction. We have basically the same authority, but since I'm head of the team, he's deferring to my leadership.

I stretch a hand and hold his arm, walking with him a few steps explaining, "Kino, I need you to reach out to Kendra. We'll be ready to go into the city in an hour. I need her to portal in, north of the castle, and fly directly south over the large fountain next to the king's chamber. She and I have gone over this map so many times, she'll know what I want. Then we get with the digging."

"I can do that, anything else?" he says.

"No, like I say, we'll have a little time before we go, so if you need to do anything, that'll be a good time to do it," I say.

"Well, I must work with Jericho some. He needs to know how my bard spells are evolving and work with me on the strategies of how to use them if needed."

"Oh, what are you telling me? I'm not getting it."

He answers, "Being with Kendra is affecting me to the point that my speaking voice is even having magical effects on those around me. I can control it myself and have, but the ancient mage has a way of using spells in surprising ways."

"I get it, believe me. Until Jared called and told me how to transform into my dragon, I thought I was dyin'. Communication is key."

The red goyle nods and says, "I'll let you know what she says in a little while."

He turns and heads off to sit on a nearby rock. While I get with the rest of the team and discuss what we saw today and what we're gonna do now.

A round of cheers erupts, breaking the silence of the moonless night as they find out our queen will be here.

Then her consort walks over to us without a hint of cheer and says, "She understands, Duke." He's obviously worried about his love coming to this isolated location again.

"Kino, she's gonna be fine. She's tough, ask me, she can make a shampoo bottle into a horrid weapon. She can do this little number in her sleep. The night's black. All she's gotta do is portal in, fly over and portal out," I encourage him.

He shakes his head at me, but I can see the determination in his posture to not let her be hurt. "I bet my right ball, he's gonna fly with her," Dana mutters.

31

BLUE TEAM IN FAE

Jared

THE MUSCULAR BALD STEEN WAVES, SING-SONGS A SPELL, AND opens the portal as instructed by Mega. The blue team steps through. The big mage has gotten healthy in the few days he's been with me. I'm used to him already and hope he sticks around for a long while.

It's early evening in Fae, and just after the sun has set. It's odd. The time difference I mean, but we know we can't account for the time differences between Fae and Navan.

The Faery land is shining with the glow of twinkling lights in the dark.

Dr. Ogman stops after entering the wonderful new world place and takes a deep breath then smiles... and I thought gargoyle smiles were ominous. He has two rows of pointed sharp teeth, giving him the look of a giant piranha. This doctor has hidden depths I don't want to know about.

Spar is hyper-vigilant and scoping the area. He's my muscle, but I'm sure his gift of sinking into solid objects will be needed. I think of him as my brother in law because of his time in the human world. All my sister's consorts technically are, but this blue goyle is special to me. He's a skilled member of the Elite Guard. He spent twenty-eight years as a human, seven of them in the Army special forces. He walks with a confidence that only a human can carry. He's whispering to Flint. If anything gets past my dragon senses, those two will notice any problems before it can hurt my team. I'm sure of it.

The pretty lady Peri is our weapons officer and acting communications officer. The seriousness of our mission has her intense pale eyes flicking around the area. She sinks down on her heels. Her strong long legs hold her without a tremor. She taps a note into her tablet and puts a finger to her chin when she's finished. I think she might have been testing to see if it still works because she has a satisfactory visage before she puts away the tech.

"Alright, team, here's your ORCS. Remember, they only work within one hundred feet of another ORCS device," she says sternly.

I hadn't noticed before, but she's quite beautiful. The blue of her eyes perfectly complements her blue hair and dark skin. I find myself staring at her when I hear Spar.

"ORCS, that's some sort of acronym, isn't it? What's it mean, Oreos R Cookies Stupid, or some shit like that?" he asks with a mocking laugh, not meant for Peri. They have been friends since he was first carved, having met in the training pit in the gargoyle cave.

She'll tell you, she told him he trained like a gargoyle who had his grrr metaphorically removed before offering to train with him. They've been huge friends since. Which, if you think about it, is very funny because he's so big... well, never mind.

She quips back, "Yes, it's an acronym. No dumbass--but Oreos are delicious! It stands for Operating Radial Communications System. We only use it for operations, and each device talks to each other, kind of like a hub and wheel, radially, and obviously, it's a communications system. Now quit giving me shit, or I'll have a talk with Kendra," she tells him, only looking at him at the end, and then with a broad toothy grin.

My team's small, but I believe, powerful. I wave them on into a covering of lush vegetation and whisper. "We all know the plan, let's get going. Remember, Kendra said, there's a nice pub near the castle on the right side of the path. She said it's obvious. If we reach it, we've gone too far. The one we want is on the other side of the path. It's more of a working goyles bar, let's call it chthonic. Ironically, it's called The Friendly Badger. That's where I want you two to find a dark corner and chill. Listen in on what is going on. When you finish, return here and set up a base for us to return to as needed," I finish.

"Jared, I've known you forever, and I still feel like I sometimes need a dictionary when you're talkin,'" Spar interjects. "I've never had Fae beer, though... They do have beer here, don't they," he says with real concern carrying through his words for the first time since we gathered to leave for Faery.

I know, long-term, Kendra wants to count the Fae as allies. That means we can't do anything which might upset that. Our plan is simply to gather as much information on where Trix may be hiding and maintain a low profile. Peri and I will raise our profiles some, but only enough that we can twist some information out of some lower-level bureaucrat. In fact, remaining low-key is a primary imperative to our overall plan.

"Well, if they don't have beer, I know they have a great Fae whiskey. You'll love it!" Peri comments nonchalantly to him, knowing his penchant for Scotch Whiskey.

Jared continues, "Dr. Ogman is going to the Faery Memorial Infirmary and Sanitorium for Supernatural and Other Disorders where he'll find out if she's been treated, or is actually there.

Peri and I are heading over to the castle. I doubt the King or Queen will take time to meet with me as they did Kendra. But, that's not a problem since I'm only hoping to speak with a few minor officials. Maybe we can talk one of them into helping. Doc, we'll meet Spar and Flint at the Friendly Badger at ten o'clock pm local time. Let's synchronize watches, six thirty-seven pm local... mark," I order, realizing this may be the third time I've had everyone sync-up. Nods around the group and at least one set of eye rolls, from Spar, confirm both aspects of my request.

Since the hospital is near the castle and The Friendly Badger, a known Hewn establishment and tavern. We head in the same direction and shed people along the way, first Spar and Flint, at the inn, then the doctor. The communications officer and I go only fifteen minutes further to reach the castle where we're barred entry.

"Excuse me, humans, we don't allow human scum or gargoyles within the castle grounds," the guard sneers at me while simultaneously giving Peri a disdainful glance.

"Excuse me, footman," my partner interjects without missing a beat and using the same disdainful voice the guard used while saying 'human,' "This is Duke Jared Macbard, dragon Duke, and brother to Queen Kendra Macbard of the Ceorfan. Please, be so kind as to fetch your Captain," she adds, a sly grin sidling across her lips and eyes. "I'm Peri Blackstone. My father is Fae, so I have as much right to visit this castle as you have to protect it," she finishes, her ample chest puffing out proudly.

I maintain my composure as the two trade insults, letting them pass as if beneath me. We'd anticipated this type of reception since we deliberately hadn't announced our arrival ahead of time. In fact, we were hoping it would turn out this way...

"Mr... I mean Duke Macbard--my apologies sir. I meant no disrespect, sir. You are a most honored visitor to the castle. Ms. Blackstone, as you have requested, I'll happily bring my Captain to your service, if you would, please accompany me inside to the parlor. I'll have my commander here as soon as possible," the guard concludes, the worry palpably hanging off each word.

Another guard opens the door for us while ours shows us to the parlor, where he ensures the staff knows our identities and importance. A well-dressed valet bows as he enters, and the guard exits. Another valet, I assume, is accompanying the first and standing at a discrete distance.

The first man introduces himself, saying, "Your Grace, my name is Gwion. I'm the castle steward. This is Lazuli Pollenfleck. He will be your personal valet while you're in Faery." Gwion turns, and with a simple hand, gesture points to Lazuli.

Damn, did he say Lazy-Luli? When in doubt, use sir or ma'am!

I reach for the steward's hand and shake it, saying, "Thank you, sir, the service is appreciated."

"May I offer you a refreshment or collation? Their Majesties will take their evening meal at eight o'clock pm. I've notified the chef of your visitation and assure you, he and his wonderful staff are making the proper arrangements. I've also alerted him that you'll have a guest as well," as he pauses to look respectfully at Peri and offering her an honorific bow. "Both the King and Queen are quite excited to meet you, Duke Macbard," he adds with a well-practiced smile.

I pride myself on being able to react to unforeseen circumstances. This isn't one we even remotely expected. I stall for more words. Our research primarily leads us to believe I'd be little noticed by the elite of Faery. In fact, our plans call for us to make a bit of a fuss at the door, then using that 'disrespect' to gain access to several lower-level officials for afternoon tea. Now it seems we're invited to a State Dinner.

I respond, glancing in my partner's direction, "Thank you, we graciously accept your invitation. Yes, Peri and I would appreciate a beverage."

Knowing that I'm considered royalty, I understand the etiquette of waiting on Peri to order first would go over like leaving a turd in the toilet, so I order first, "Since this is my first visit here I don't know what to try. I'd love to try a wine or liqueur of your choosing. Wait," holding a finger up to him, "Kendra, said the brandy is amazing. That's what I'll have," I say as I glance at Peri for her request.

"I prefer chilled water if you please," she adds quickly almost to the valet's back as he quickly turns and hurries away to retrieve our drinks.

"I'm sorry, Duke, since I'm your weapons officer as well as your communications, I can't imbibe," she concludes an energetic smile on her perfectly structured face.

She knows that I have standing orders to not use that moniker during the duration of this mission. If maintaining a low profile is essential, having 'Duke' floating around our lexicon seems counter-productive, yet with what just happened, all bets are now off.

In minutes the door to the parlor swings open, and the guard as well as a person I suppose to be his captain enter. Both offer me a crisp salute.

Standing, I straighten my clothes and step over to greet them both, respectfully returning their salute, "Hello, my name is Jared Macbard. I'm sorry if I've caused any problems or confusion. That wasn't my intention. Your guard was doing his job... a good job. I want to compliment you and him on his work. I also need to find out who to speak with relating to a personal matter. I assume you are well placed and can help in that regard," I say, hoping it sounds believable since I have no desire to see the guard punished for what, now, would be a mistake.

The look of relief on both their faces is priceless. Their shoulders shift relaxing stiff posture. The picture of the before and after faces would have made a great gif... if I only had a way of saving the moment. It's only later that I find out that, indeed, my communications officer has the entire display recorded.

The new soldier introduces herself as Captain Treefly. "Duke Macbard, what is the personal matter you seek assistance for?" she asks, relief still washing off of her in waves and a gracious business-like expression glued on her face.

"I'm looking for a Fae. Her name is Trix," I query directly.

Both guards noticeably stiffen, unmoving except for their shallow breathing, their demeanor becoming perceptibly frosty as they stand to attention, the tension back, both jawlines hard and unmoving.

"I'm sorry, did I say something wrong?" I ask tilting my head and bringing my brows up as confusion drifts across my face.

A guarded Captain Treefly answers her lips curl in a slight sneer, and her eyes hood, "No sir, her types live on the edges of polite society." Polite isn't evident in her tone as she tilts her head back, affecting an even more judgmental pose.

I remain still holding my hands together in front of me and say, "I don't understand."

"We don't speak of them. Especially within the confines of the king and queen's home. I'm sure you understand. However, if you're considering female companionship... the King has already made certain arrangements," she finishes with a rigid bow.

"Wait... what? No! Thank you for your help," I conclude, trying to get out of the now very uncomfortable conversation. I bend forward with a slight bow of my own. The guards politely exit the parlor. I hope my mouth isn't catching flies as they left. I glance at my tall gargoyle comm officer. I must look as ridiculous as I feel. How in the hell has this gone so wrong? I scrape a hand down my face. This is a big mess. Not only am I not keeping a low profile, but the freaking king is providing me some of his court for sex!

"Peri, do you have any idea how to get out of this mess? Surely you have some knowledge of their traditions... anything?" I ask, frustration filling each word with a desperation I rarely feel.

Her return expression, a mixture of shock and chagrin must somewhat mirror my own, eyes and mouth both wide and free of anything useful. Her retort is as unhelpful as the guard's, "Well, if you just want sex, all you had to do was ask," with a cheeky but fucking sexy grin.

Well, that makes it worse but funny. I point at her, my fingers held like a gun as I play shoot at her with a chuckle.

"I'll have to figure out what to do now. Peri, please go find Spar and Flint and let them know we won't be there for dinner. You can also ask if they have any ideas on how to get me out of the mess I'm in. I'm sure they have more experience with this than I do," I say, grinning.

"Yes, sir," she says, jumping a bit as she salutes with a grin of her own, and walks to the door.

After she leaves, a stream of beautiful Countesses, Princesses, and even the Queen herself make their way to meet me. I spent the next hour speaking with every female member of the King's court. It was delightful, but a certain redhead remains in the back of my thoughts.

The group of women leaves to prepare themselves for dinner as Peri returns. She's just in time for us to be escorted to the main dining room. Unfortunately, we don't have time to discuss what she's learned from Spar and Flint. My partner is seated toward the middle of the table, several seats away from me. Lucky for me... not, I'm seated next to the Queen, who happens to be drinking a great deal.

The room is a dream world of twinkling light and wonder. It is truly magical, and my eyes travel to admire the scene; however, dinner is a bloody affair.

The chefs start the menu with fresh kills. I don't move a muscle as the blood runs down the table. I stare as the redcaps vie for it, making their malevolent appearance even more so. Their faces are covered with gore as the chefs butcher a giant deer and boar for the main course of the dinner. A coppery tang hangs in the air of the beautiful room after the slaughter is complete, and the carnage disappears along with the redcaps. The butchery is graphic in its gore and offensiveness to humans. Unfortunately, another, less easily navigable surprise awaits me.

"Duke Macbard, how do you like our kingdom so far?" the Queen asks while taking another generous sip of her wine and rubbing her foot down the length of my leg.

Unwilling to show a reaction to the physical advances of the Queen, I answer her as I genuinely feel, "Your Majesty, yours is a beautiful and special kingdom. My fiancé would find this fascinating," I say hoping the Fae Queen will take a hint.

"Pshhh. She is a mere mortal. What could she hold for a dragon to find so compelling?" she coos, not put off by my remark in the slightest.

Luckily the King steps in to help me out, "Dearest, you must remember that the Duke grew up in the human world and only recently realized his dragon form," he manages to condescend and complement in the same sentence.

I raise my glass in a toast and stand. "If I may," I glance at the King, then the Queen. Both offer me a nod of their heads, which I take as approval to continue, "May you continue to find favor within the realm of Fae, may the number of your children cause you to build an addition to your beautiful home. And most importantly, may you continue to rule with the same compassion and justice as your enemies hate and your people love." I raise my glass to the King, tip it to the Queen, then lift it to the rest of the gathered assembly before slamming it in one gulp.

After I sit, the Queen leans over to me to thank me for the kind toast. As she does, she places her hand on my leg before letting it slide to my crotch. One rule I learned ahead of time was I can't, under any circumstances, touch either the king or queen. Instead, I make a show of standing and offering her a polite comment. This time when I sit, her hand isn't on me.

The rest of the dinner and dessert are uneventful until we're preparing to leave the table. "Duke Macbard, I have had quarters arranged for you and your guest," Lazuli Pollenfleck, my personal valet says.

I keep my features blank and answer, "Thank you, we can leave now. My partner has other duties and won't be staying."

"I'll show you to them now," he says in such a way it feels more like a command.

I get the notion from his strange half-grin that he's pleased Peri isn't staying the night. He motions for me to follow him. After I make my goodnights to the royal couple, and with Peri following behind me before she departs. We leave the dining hall.

There's a short walk before we're given a cavernous suite with an ornate common seating area with doors to four bedrooms. I'm shown to the largest of the four. It's a fantastic room with a canopy bed on one end, a large wooden bathtub in the center, and a reading area at the other end of the ornate room. After my valet leaves, I sit on the bed fighting with myself for being in this position when I hear a small knock on my door.

I open it and see the Queen, her silken nightgown translucent in the light, and displaying her perfectly formed body. Without pausing to give more than a casual glance, I start speaking as if my life depends on it, "Queen Dayna, you flatter me by coming to my rooms. However, I'm no king, and am not worthy of your attention."

She is quick and moves past me into my chambers. Without warning, she simpers and shrugs her shoulders to remove her clothes.

I pull her robe back onto her shoulders and tie it, ignoring her protestations by my continuing verbal rejection. "Surely, you have simply had too much to drink and have wandered from your own room," I coo as I gently direct her to the door.

She huffs and starts to speak her frustration growing, but I say, "Besides, I'm to marry soon. I must consider my own children," trying to use something, anything which she might find less objectionable than being turned away. "I've also had too much to drink. In the human world, this causes problems with performance. You understand, don't you?" I open my door and stand with my hands behind me, waiting for her to depart.

Finally, I have struck a chord, and she replies, "My good dragon, I do understand. It must be frailty with males of all species. I shall keep your problem a tightly guarded secret as I expect you to do with my visit," she warns then giggles with a shake of her head.

"Your Majesty, I'll keep this secret to my grave," I sigh, hoping she'll shut the door and go.

She does.

32

THE BAR

Spar

AFTER ARRIVING IN THE BAR, THE FRIENDLY BADGER, FLINT
and I find a corner that isn't busy and sit. Our waiter, a short fat troll-
like creature, takes our drink order with all of the courteousness of a
dog in a barking contest. His greasy apron isn't surprising as most of
what we've seen in Faery can either be very magical and beautiful or
harsh and dirty.

This strange land's a very different world. Yet, I do kinda like it.
It has rough edges that are quite appealing. I can't say I'd enjoy the
pomp and circumstance that Jared and Peri have to endure. More
power to them, they can have it.

The place we're sitting isn't dark but shadowed and out of the
way of most of the patrons. We aren't speaking since we want to hear
what's going on around us--soldiers to the bone. Not a lot of time goes
by, maybe twenty minutes, before we see a tall skinny Fae with a
heavy robe enter the establishment and discuss something with the
barman.

His hoarse voice gruffs out, "That man at the castle was a

Macbard. He's that Ceorfan Queen's brother, and he's looking for Trix."

The bartender slips a coin to the man and gives him a jerking nod.

My bet is he thinks no one noticed. With a tilt of my head, I gaze up and down at the snitch. He's wearing shiny boots, boots too polished for the type of robe he's got on. As he turns to leave, his robe opens just enough for me to see the colors of the pants the guards are wearing.

I lean close to my partner in this mission. Flint doesn't move.

"Did you see his clothes, he's one of the guards from the castle. He saw Jared and is selling the information. Let's see who else finds out about it. Watch for anyone who leaves abruptly, or takes something from the barman," I say, deliberately keeping my voice low and nonchalantly leaning back against the wall.

Not long after, I hear snippets of conversations pointing to the fact that the guards are sending word to Walter, one of the sad fucks who does Barat's dirty work. When we were sharing information before leaving for our mission, we were told that he's the mark's brother and low and behold, the jerkwad selling information now says, "The Duke is looking for the mage Walter's sister."

Flint winks at me and rises from his wooden chair and trips over the table leg. He stumbles but doesn't go down, then sways and wobbles to the back door of the establishment. He opens the door and leans on the frame opening his fly, he pees standing there. What should typically take only a few seconds, stretches into minutes as he pretends to rest on the door-facing before making his way back to his seat.

I want to laugh. Instead, I grin and pat his shoulder as he finally manages to wrestle his chair into being still enough to plop back into. Next, he leans on the wall, his head falls forward, and he's snoring in seconds.

I'm not sure if he's acting anymore. That little fat gargoyle has many talents, but I haven't seen him on a drunken bender, and I'm interested to see what he does. I proceed to scope the room, keeping up my own charade. Waving a hand to the greasy troll, he comes racing to me. He all but runs into my little table in his haste. I smile, and he jerks away from the smirk, more scared shitless than worried. I forgot, my girl says my smile does that to people. I grin even bigger at the thought, and the waiter sucks in a breath.

I know what he sees. My reflection is in his big shiny eyes. I smirk and pull my shoulders back, my blond mohawk, standing tall and proud, looks fantastic. But I know, it's my terrifying fangs that are the most noticeable feature on my face.

I say, "You sell food, troll?"

He answers, "Yes sir, wh-wh-we have a wh-wh-wonderful stew, fresh bread, and ch-che-cheese ready if you'd like some. It only costs a fiver."

"Sounds great, bring me enough for a big goyle like me. I'll give you extra and a bowl for my friend when he wakes too."

"Yes, yes, yes, will do. I'll bring it shortly," the troll stammers. I catch him glancing, then looking away just as fast from the darkest corner of the restaurant/bar.

My eyes follow where his eyes are now avoiding. Fucking-firetruck, how'd that guy get back there without me seeing him? Is it a gargoyle? I can't make out much, but I can see yellow or goldish skin and a tall mohawk. Maybe not, it's dark as sin back there. I need to get closer. I stand to use Flint's strategy and walk to the back door to take a whiz.

When I turn to make my way over and introduce myself, the dark stranger is nowhere in sight. I pick up several short pieces of information searching for the guy. Then I go to the bar and order some honey mead. I lean down, putting my elbows on the wooden top and wait while the bartender fills my flagon. I get more info that adds up to the fact that the Fae are upset about so many strangers in their restaurant, especially the dark corner chap. One scraggly brownie is weaving across a tabletop, making a loud complaint about how Vincent shouldn't ever be allowed in here.

The man behind the bar shoves my brew toward me. I catch it and take a sip then offer the brownie some for a price. He understands and perches on my arm. I walk over to a still snoozing Flint and sit in my seat.

The brownie climbs off of my arm and bows, saying, "Cravett at yer service, Lord. Hows can I be of service for? Most importantlys, what's am I being paid in return?" His voice is much quieter than it had been seconds ago.

"Well, my name is Spar. I'd like to know if the person in the dark corner a while ago was Vincent. Also, what does he look like, and how can I contact him?"

"Vincent is a hugey gargoyle. He's gots blue-eyed and yellow-gold skin. He's keeps he's hair in a mohawk that be to die for. He's one of those Hewn nomads livin' on his own. He's quiet and of ill-humor and speaks to nobody. He's a loner. And he's doesn't like being touched. Don't mess with he's. I can'ts know how to find he's either. He's private."

"Can you put the word out that I want to talk to him?"

"I can does it, but he's will never come. Now pays me. I'm thirsty."

I hand him the flagon, which is larger than he is, and he tips it up. When the entire contents are gone, he sits down on his ass and burps loud and long. Then says, "Talkin' abouts gettin' the word out. Yous know that everyone here knows yer the Dragon Queen's prince consort and yer's lookin' for Trix? Walter, the mage froms the evil castle, is 'er brother. He's won't let you near 'er."

"Does Walter know that?"

"Yes. Hows does yer think I gots so drunk?" The inebriated little Fae man disappears in a puff of bright twinkles and is gone.

I lean forward and rub my forehead, thinking now that I'm alone. What does this information mean? Okay, so Walter knows gargoyles, the Duke, and a prince consort are in Faery. What's he gonna do? Take crafted and attack? Ask for help saving Trix? Watch?

Greaseball troll brings my food, and I start in on it. It's good despite the place it's been served. I eat and think, and I should be finishing when my thoughts are interrupted. I hear a shrill wolf whistle. I scan the room, and standing in front of the entryway is Peri. My eyes widen, watching her deliver a stiff uppercut to an elf who got out of line and tried to touch her. Kendra's the only woman for me, but I can appreciate my team member. I'm fucking happy now. She made my night.

That tough girl steps over the fallen dickhead and walks tall and proud over to me. She pulls a chair from the empty table next to mine, spins it, and sits with her legs spread around the back. Holy shit, no wonder the idiot whistled.

"Peri, you know you're too sexy for your own good. That was awesome. Can you do it again just for fun," I say laughing my ass off.

"Sure big boy, but I don't want to hurt you. We have to talk about the party," she says with a grin and a wink.

I know 'party' is code for our plans to find Trix and Sass, so I say, "Ah babe, really?"

She kicks the fuck out of my leg under the table and says, "But honey pumpkin, it has to be done, or I might mess it all up, please, for me?" she simpers.

I bounce my eyebrows up and down suggestively and say, "Okay, anything for you sugar-pants. Let's go home so I can get you to myself, at least." I give Flint a little nudge under the table.

He opens the eye closest to me and winks, then closes it again, stretches, and wakes up then says, "Is this my soup?" Thanks, buddy," then in a lower tone, "I'll follow you in a few minutes."

I nod, standing and wrap an arm around Peri and she puts hers around me. We pay little attention to the room of patrons as we leave and return to create our base of operations. We're hoping the people here might be a little bit confused as to who we are.

As soon as we're away from the tavern, I see Steen move off to join us. He's been leaning on a wall of the business next to the bar. I wave him over.

I say, "Peri, I'm going to go over to Barat's castle and take a quick look around, just to be sure Trix isn't there. I'll meet you and Flint in the area we're calling home base. Steen, will you open me a portal to get there?"

"Yes, let's find a secluded spot first," he answers.

Together, we walk into an alley, and he opens the portal then says, "If you aren't back to home base by torp-time, I'm coming to get you."

33

RED TEAM IN THE MEDIA

Kendra

KICK OPENS OUR PORTAL, AND WE STEP THROUGH ONTO THE lush green front lawn of the White House. He sings a light and airy calming song. The stones I now carry within me heighten my magic immensely, all my senses are magnified. The Elite Warrior Guard marches out of the portal, an excellent example of a Ceorfan Warrior parade formation meant to impress whoever is watching.

The auras surrounding the people of this grand establishment and guards, at least the ones whom I can see, are multi-colored. The abundance of a brave yellow is tinted with the curiosity orange. No one is slouching. All are busily doing their jobs.

We're escorted to the front steps where the President and his wife await our arrival. The brief flashes of brilliant white lights of the numerous cameras, mix with the red and blue lights of the security vehicles, causing me an almost phantasmagorical experience. I recognize it's only the press doing their jobs as they report our entrance as well as security keeping us, really the President, safe.

Without missing a step, a breath, or even a heartbeat, I set aside the fantastic imagery and absurd ironies and put on the appropriate smile. I check my team.

Mega, always the general, back straight, power exuding from each movement and unapologetic focus in each facial twitch.

Mica, Kick, and the others mostly gargoyles are on high alert. Their heads turn with every flash, continually watching, preparing for a supposed inevitable attack. Jimmy and Vanessa walk just behind me, nestled protectively between my guard and me.

We climb the steps together, joining the world of the American political elite. The common American man and woman are left to wonder at the possible intrigues unfolding before them. Cameras flash, lighting the area in a sea of white as I greet the president and the first lady.

"Queen Kendra Macbard, we're honored to welcome you and your Ducere and Warrior Guard to the White House. I'm sure you understand, but the press needs its photographs. Would you mind if we wave to the crowd together so they have their pictures?" says the President as he points his hand, palm up to the crowd of press and other dignitaries before us. As he finishes, I hear the First Lady offer her opinion on the pictures by proffering a low, "uuggg."

"We're honored to have been invited...," now leaning closer to the First Lady and lowering my voice conspiratorially, "I agree with you, the photographs are terrible. The press has a way of making me look like a dragon." I grin at my own ironic funny.

The President and First Lady laugh heartily.

After the pomp of our greeting on the front steps of the White House, the President and his gracious wife, lead us into the Oval Office where we're able to have a more relaxed conversation.

I find both the President and his wife are both gracious and charming. Even in this setting, where we're discussing integrating a new race into society. I do think this is more fun than I had believed it would be, and I thoroughly enjoy the banter. They're in full agreement with the plan to integrate the Ceorfan into society and will do what is necessary to make it happen smoothly.

As quick as that, it's over, and the President and his wife are needed elsewhere and leave us. We've been assigned both a guide and security. The guide's job is to keep me entertained between visits with the dignitary of the moment, as I call almost anyone talking to us at any one time.

Guiding us is a big job too because my Red Team is the largest of the three teams. I need gargoyles who will serve as ambassadors, others to help me dress and carry my wardrobe, more to keep me on schedule, and of course, bodyguards. My contingent, while varying in size, depending on the time and requirements, hovers around one-hundred and fifty gargoyles, mages, and Hewn.

Dana has quite a force for digging and building if need be to find the treasure, but not all the drivers, cooks, and trainers that I have to have for various affairs. Jared's team is the smallest since they'll need to be nearly invisible to get in and get out with information on Trix and Sass.

We're still in the Oval Office when a tall, heavy gray-haired man approaches and asks Mica and Kick, who are in front of me if he might shake my hand. Mica tilts his head and bends forward slightly, indicating in the affirmative and makes room for the man to pass. I check his aura, and it's full of blues and turquoise with some movement of yellow that indicates cleverness. He bows and smiles brilliantly.

I remember him... my magic supplies his name; it's Angelis Castle. He's an older, handsome gentleman who moves with an agile grace despite his age. He's sort of cat-like. I reach out my hand to him first and say, "Hello, Ambassador Castle, how do you do this fine evening?"

I read shock, gone as fast as it came, replaced with the slight smile, and a twinkle in his eyes as he answers, "My dear, how could I be anything but thrilled to see the beautiful Ceorfan Queen and her retinue once again?"

Only a small movement of my head and I lock eyes with Mica then Kick and answer, "Indeed, my friend. What are we doing tonight? I understood that we were having a diplomatic meeting with several governments, but if my nose is right, we're also having dinner. The air is full of food smells, and I'm sure the American White House is feeding us seafood to name only one of the dishes. Am I correct?"

"Yes, you are, Queen Kendra. The President asks if you will please indulge him and his wife and stay as their guests for a few days. I'll send a new schedule to your assistant if you assent."

"Ambassador Castle, this is our version of a grand music tour. Yes, of course, we'll stay. We intend to meet the public and make alliances with governments. Most importantly, we intend my people to become a part of society everywhere as soon as possible. However, I need to verify they'll be safe before I allow it."

I reach through the people at my side and take the Count's green goyle arm. He moves closer at my will, as he does, I recognize how well Clifton actually fits in with the ambassadorial teams around us. I introduce Clifton, "Ambassador Castle this is the Count de Treon, my personal assistant, he will work with you and also Duke Findare." Fin also moves forward as I hold out a hand in his direction. "The Duke will be working closely with you as my ambassador."

Angelis Castle perks up, and his eyes widen as he extends a friendly hand to the Count and then to the Duke. A grin comes so naturally to me. But now it's because I've wanted my Ceorfan accepted and this is the realization of that dream. The American ambassador doesn't push me out of the way to get to the others, but he is past me. Fin and Clifton become the spotlight as I take a slight step away.

I duck my head a tiny bit and glance at Mica with a knowing nod. He bobs his own head minutely agreeing. No words are necessary as we both recognize the importance of what has just happened. An actual human ambassador is excited to meet with my Ceorfan Ambassador.

My next thought is, 'where the hell is Sunny.' Since we left Amber safe in Navan with Mason, I need his help with my hair if I'm to look presentable at tonight's state dinner. Without Amber, Sunny is my man for that job. I tap my finger on my chin and wonder if I should call Jamie Serge to help with my wardrobe? He has saved me in the past and always takes his time to make me feel beautiful inside and out. "No," I respond to myself. "This is just dinner, but I do need to call my friend Jamie." I make a mental note to do that tonight. The next few weeks are going to be a whirlwind of activities, and I'll need him for those countries more interested in pomp and circumstance.

A bodyguard walks up to Kick, and they speak with heads bent together for seconds only, then my mage brings the guard with him to stand in front of me.

Kick says, "My lady, they're asking if we're ready to be shown to our rooms. We'll follow this man to them as soon as you're ready."

The guard adds, "You understand that you and your entire retinue will be staying in accommodations across the street in Blair House? They've been specially prepared for you and your cortege. We have bulletproof vans to drive you over."

"Of course, let's go now. And don't be silly we can walk across the street safely, we're Ceorfan." I answer him with a lilting voice, buoyed by the excitement of the evening.

Kick nods, and I understand that he'll use a spell to protect us. Now that I know he will, I can add to it.

The young guard huffs and says, "Ma'am, the lawn is covered with curious onlookers. We've taken precautions, but you never know what could happen." A sense of exasperation causing his final words to register higher.

"The world must come to understand that hurting us isn't easy. Magic is real, and we know how to use it for protection. We are well covered, I promise you."

The guard speaks into a microphone on his lapel, quietly awaits a response, then nods agreeably and begins leading us to our lodgings.

Kick takes position to my right, and Mica takes point with a grouping of five of my Elite Guard around us with Jimmy and Vanessa protectively cradled between. Kick begins his spell song. Mega, who has been casing the room tele-speaks, "I'm right behind you, Edling. Don't worry, we are all accounted for. I'll be posting guards at your door, though."

The Count, having left Ambassador Angelis to our Ambassador Findare, is now close to me as we follow the guard to our quarters. As we walk the short distance across the street from the White House to Blair House, our guard tells us about the accommodations, "The original home was built in 1824 and then purchased by Francis Preston Blair in 1836. In 1858 he built a home next door for his daughter and her husband. The family lived in the property for more than one hundred years. In 1942, it became President Roosevelt's guesthouse and has served in that capacity since. It is made up of four nineteenth-century townhouses which have been connected and built into this one-hundred twenty room, nearly seventy thousand square foot national treasure."

The tour guide portion continues as we walk across the street. I quit paying attention and began looking around. I see several crowds of people and even a few protesters holding signs. I can't read them, so I pay them little mind.

After entering the Blair House and being shown our rooms, I say, "These rooms are gorgeous! They're not what I expected at all." The rooms are beautiful and don't feel like what I would think a government house would look like. The ones we are using are more of an apartment. A nice one at that.

Mega is ordering the guards to their posts and then leaves me to attend his duty. Clifton says, "My lady, the dinner is at nine. You have two hours, plenty of time to rest or talk to the princes.

"Well, I need to change for dinner and look my best. I'm sure there will be more cameras."

"Would you like me to call Sunny and have him come now or in an hour or so?"

"An hour is fine. I need you to contact Jamie, though. I'm going to need some finery and extra care at some of the state functions during this grand tour. Also, Clifton, without Jared here, who is our TASS rep for this roadshow?"

"Already taken care of My Queen. Arden Kelly is here with us, and so is Glen Hughes. The first wants to be known as the court doctor and the last a TASS representative, but if I had to guess, he also has other interests."

Now that's strange. What interests could Glen be thinking of? I stop dead in my tracks, blinking. "Hmmm, well, I need all the friends I can get to pull this venture off."

The Count cocks and eye at me smirks and turns, saying, "I'll be in my room getting ready myself. See you later, My Queen."

I turn slowly, twisting my body to see Mica and Kick staring in my direction. Then Mica flips his head back in a playful mock of Kino and sings, "I'll sing you a song about my lady. Everyone wants her..."

"Keep it up there partner, and I'll show you your lady," I quip.

Kick chuckles, "Darling, you should know that you are beautiful and your position and fame as the Ceorfan Queen will have the suitors after you like kids in a candy shop."

"Maybe, but you both know that Glen is a player, a lady's man, right. He's just a flirt. There aren't going to be any more consorts. I'm happy right now."

Magic twinkles around me as I say this like I made a vow with it, and now it is sure to be so. I know in my bones that this is the case.

The stones are working, and I'm going to need to study their histories so I can get a handle on them and make sure when this happens, I mean for it too. At least I know how to use the magic a little more now. The Healing one... I'm good with it. And Fire is natural for me. It's Air that is frustrating me some. I'll need to work with it more.

In fact, I say, "Kick, let's use the Air stone to dream walk tonight. I want to check on my brothers, Spar and Kino. It'll be interesting to know if it's a better way to share information or not. We can always go back to tablets and phones, but there are places that those won't work. What do you say?"

I think that's a great idea. You want to see if we can bring Mica? I have a thought that if we weave our magic along with the power of the stones, it may be possible... and you do have magic too, brother. What do you think?"

"I love the idea. As soon as the dinner is over, let's do it," I say.

Mica answers, "I'd very much like to try this with you both."

There is a knock on the door, and one of the guards enters pulsing. He says, "I wasn't sure if I should pulse or knock, Your Majesty, your man is here to help you get ready for dinner. Shall I admit him?"

"Yes, by all means, do," I answer.

34

RED TEAM PROBLEM

Kendra

S<small>UNNY DOES A WONDERFUL JOB AS USUAL ON MY HAIR AND</small> makeup. The dress is a cute semi-formal little black dress, perfect for the occasion. The idea that the Ceorfan will be accepted now is forefront in my mind, so I let my dragon out about halfway. Enough of me remains human that I hope there will be more acceptance. Maybe even my people will be respected and not shunned. I hope.

I take Kick's arm and hold back the statements I want to make. Instead, I say, "You look hot in a tux, Dark Angel. Want to come back to my place after this little shindig?"

He doesn't blush, and his face remains blank until he whispers, "I've been thinking about you all day. The thought of bending you over that big chair in our room and having my way with you has crossed my mind more than once."

Mica, who is walking in front of us, turns and winks.

Holy cow, I don't know which was sexier the dirty talk or the wink in agreement. I clench my legs together for a second, then whisper, "You two are going to start something you can't finish."

Kick says, "Don't count on it."

I grin to myself and keep looking straight ahead as the guards in front of Mica stop at the doors to the dining room. It's gorgeous, and just like you see on television, but better.

Ambassador Angelis Castle reaches out a hand with a little bow and says, "Queen Kendra, lovely as always. Let me show you to your table." We're shown to the back of the room well away from the head table. There I spot the rest of my retinue who are already seated. They stand as I get closer.

When I'm near enough to them, Mica pulls out my seat and reaches a big hand for mine to seat me. I stall standing and listen to a couple beside our table.

Just as I reach for him, I hear a curt, "Excuse me, we're walking here." The voice is feminine, and I turn, my eyes widen, and my mouth gapes. The face I see is an attractive middle-aged woman and her older husband. By the way, they both look down their noses at us, it's evident that neither of them has any use for my people or me.

Kill 'em with kindness, Kendra. Kill 'em with kin...

"My dear, if you would not have attempted to cram your arrogant ass into our group, you would not have had your path disrupted," a peevish General Mega says.

Unabashed, they sneer and pivot to walk away. As they do, the male of the couple says, "Come, dear, the smell on this side of the room has become rather odoriferous."

Had we been in any other setting, I would have given my General a high-five for his takedown of the condescending couple. As it is, I have to let it go. But mind to mind I say, *"High five, Megahir. You nailed that bitch for me."*

My dragon is already burning with resentment at being set this far away from the head table. At a dinner where my people are the purported guests of honor. Now I'm practically seething as I watch the two self-important individuals speaking animatedly with one of the support staff while pointing at our table.

"Ambassador Castle, do you know who those two are?" I ask with all the friendliness of an alligator with teeth clenched.

"Yes, I believe they are James and Dominique Qwerty. Their family built an early version of the laserdisc. Frankly, these two are the most useless of their entire family. They wield their wealth like it's some kind of a sword as if they're putting down a peasant uprising," the ambassador says while looking over the top of his glasses at the two. "Excuse me, Kendra, I think I'll enjoy dealing with them."

Before he can leave, I gently take his hand, stopping his march and ask, "Ambassador, if this seating arrangement is an overt slight to my people, I would prefer to leave rather than be demeaned in this way. I won't let my people, or my Guild be treated like proverbial redheaded stepchildren in some political machination. We've been through this before, and I won't stand for it."

"Please, Your Majesty, that isn't the case at all. You are a special guest of the President. Please, this dinner has been planned for months. The seating was negotiated and set well before your Ceorfan Guild was known of. I'll see if there is a possibility of moving you, but there are quite a lot of you, we might have to split you up to accommodate the change."

"No, we'll stay here, together. I didn't understand the protocol for seating, I guess. Still, you should be aware that I don't take slights to my people."

"Yes, Queen Kendra, none are intended. Again, my apologies for the error of not properly informing you of the arrangements. That's my fault, and I take responsibility."

I nod my head to him in gratitude.

"Please, excuse me," he declares the wrinkles on his brow deepening as he turns to leave.

Mica gives me a look, questioning whether or not we are leaving, or should he seat me. I put a hand on him, and he, a gentleman to the core, slides a chair out for me. When I'm seated, facing the front of the enormous room, the rest of my party also sits. Mega tele-speaks,

"*Edling it may be as he says. At least on his part. But I can tell you that he wasn't certain that the seating isn't a deliberate insult. The coordinator was informed to put us closer to the President, and the Ambassador was wondering why we are back here also.*"

I answer, "*Mega, if I must 'make a statement' and leave, do we have enough Elites here to make another grand show like at the last TASS meeting?*"

"*Yes, we do. The honor guard who participated in the parade march is still on the grounds. I'll spread the word to be ready if you so order it,*" he responds.

I concentrate and add magic before I answer, "*Yes, be ready. I will want them to march in through the double doors. Kick will open a portal in the middle of the room where it's less crowded. The parade will march straight through the portal, and we will follow. Kick, I think I added you and Mica to our conversation. Are you able to hear us?*"

"*Yes, darling, I can hear you and will be ready. Kendra, will you add your magic to my magic to make the portal a spectacle?*" Kick says.

"*I will and know just what I want to do,*" I say.

"*You two are just being ornery now!*" Mica exclaims.

I roll my eyes at them and giggle quietly before I get ahold of myself.

The room is filling up, and sure enough, there's a wide swath of empty tables close to us. I ignore it and wait for the perfect timing to address the issue. Before I can, a troop of serving staff flow into the room, carrying plates of food to each table.

When our servers get to us, they are all smiles, and I see that they are genuinely happy to get close to us. Some of them are honored and more than curious and want to know and see us up close and personal. Cheerful yellow abounds in the light around most of them, it isn't just a color for wisdom or other things. I quit looking.

One of the younger waiters bows as he places a plate of colossal lemon garlic shrimp in front of me. He fills my water cup and asks what I would like to drink.

"Wine and lots of it if I'm to make it through this night, please," I smile.

His dark-brown eyes widen, then he grins and says, "Don't worry, Your Majesty. I have you covered. I have a wonderful peach brandy if you would like it? It's sweet and fruity, but not so much that it'll ruin your dinner."

"I love peach brandy. I think you and I will get along just fine," I state.

Kick orders a white Beringer wine, and Mica asks for a dark Irish dry stout.

My waiter leaves and returns with our drinks, while at the same time, most of the Guild are being taken care of by the other wait staff. This might be a nice dinner, anyway. My shoulders rest back in my chair, the relaxation taking hold. Finally, we have a plan. Either this night goes well, or they slight us, and we leave in a showy exit, and the night still goes well.

As the thought fully forms and a smile sashays its way across my mind and probably my face as well, Mega turns to me, "Problem," is all he says before I hear a loud crash followed by...

"You don't fucking own me. I have the fucking right to know!" An unrecognizable waiter is screaming. I watch as another waiter tugs on his arm. This waiter is smaller but is still trying to pull him away from our table. My guards move protectively closer to me.

All eyes on this spectacle, none of us see the carved, gothic gargoyle shaped melon before it bounces off the table and hits me in the chest, covering me with the red entrails of a watermelon.

Immediately, my Ducere and consorts react, encircling me. Moments later, the members of the Guild have also formed up around me, even placing Clifton protectively near me.

The waiter who had begun the shit show by yelling is still shouting and cursing. Others are restraining him. He shakes them loose and runs away.

As I glance toward the front of the room, I see the President, the First Lady, and their entourage being quickly removed from the room. The Secret Service is yelling at everyone to remain in place. That's not happening. We need to leave.

Another melon, similarly sculpted as the first, is thrown towards my table. The little fuck who threw it takes off running. But I saw him and can identify him. As I blithely congratulate my inner park ranger. Vanessa, who's standing beside our table, takes the incoming missile. It hits her square in the face and splatters on her beautiful dress. She's knocked backward and hits the floor, hard. My guards react by increasing their distance from me to create a larger bubble of protection.

I tele-speak, "*Mega I need Jimmy and Vanessa protected. Assign them each a guard.*" As I speak the words, I spot two of my Elite Guard move to find their charges.

Arden is the first to get to Vanessa. He lifts her with ease. She's crying, her face red and blotchy, rivulets of blood run from her nose and there's a cut under her eye. The assigned guard takes a protective position and pushes Arden and Vanessa closer towards me.

I see the second guard looking around, searching the room... why is she... In a flash of sudden comprehension, I yell aloud, "Where's Jimmy?"

Shouts of, "Gargoyles go home!" and "We don't want a Queen!" are almost drowned out by the barrage of "Leave them alone!" all while the crazy waiter is still screaming his vile, bigoted rant.

Ignoring the orders of the Secret Service, my consorts spirit me out the opulent double doors. Our waiter exits the spiraling melee with us. After leaving the room, Kick puts up a hand, and magic flows from him to the server, effectively holding the man away from me.

The kind man speaks, "Queen Kendra, I don't mean any harm. This is your first visit to the White House; I only want to show you back to your rooms." The young man's earnest expression leaves me little doubt as to his sincerity. If his words aren't enough, his blue-colored aura is.

"Thank you, but you need to get to safety also. We're fine and know the way back to the guest house."

I nod to my Elite and tele-comm Mega, *"Find Jimmy then take us to our accommodations, General."*

Mega responds, *"This way."*

When we get outside, the turmoil from the dining hall has already spilled into the streets. Unless this was a coordinated assault? My Ceorfan are getting pounded with all sorts of refuse. Oh, hell, no! I use my donum and press it out to my brothers. The magic of the Air stone takes it to them fast. No sooner had I sent the emergency call, I spy Jared. He's already morphed into his dragon form and flying through a portal to the left of the fighting. He's coming in low, barely off the ground. A storm cloud immediately begins to form, and lightning streaks the sky.

Dana runs through his own portal to the right of the fighting and immediately morphs and takes to the air.

Near where Dana has come through, another portal is fading, and I see Kino. Oddly, I notice my Rockstar has come through from a separate portal as my brother. I wonder why that is, once again, noticing the time dragging effect. This effect is terrific, as it allows me to almost see the situation before it entirely plays out. It allows me to make better decisions. Although, in this case, it's only serving my curiosity.

I join the boys in seconds. As I morph into my dragon body I notice we're live on television again. I guess with the world watching. My brothers fly above those who were throwing items at us. The rain begins to fall.

I tele, *"Jare, Dana, I need you both to roar as loud as you can. On my mark."*

Without waiting too long on their response, I press, *"Mark,"* out to them.

Suddenly and perfectly timed, they both raise their great necks and belch out massive cannons of plasma to the rising storm above us.

The thunderous dissonance shatters every window I can see for blocks around. That's beautiful!

I recognize this group of protesters in no way wants our people in their country. Well, too damn bad we're here. And this is where we're staying. Most of the Ceorfan were here before the American settlers anyway. We just want to live in this world without hiding anymore.

My brothers and I create a ring around our people to protect them. Our wings spread out to cover the Guild and block the few remaining rocks and other detritus still being thrown.

As the storm intensifies, the crowd begins to disperse.

When I spot Jimmy, he's being thrown to the ground. The man doing it is larger than him and obviously has training as a fighter. It's the same asswipe who threw the watermelon and hit Ness. Jimmy must have followed the dirtbag out of the dining hall.

"NO!" I shout and pulse simultaneously.

This isn't the cruel Jessup Cartel or Don Manuel Jessup. These are just misguided inflamed people. Yet, it doesn't matter to my dragon, and I start flaming the area in front of them. My brothers start setting fire on their sides. No way can anyone get close to the Ceorfan Guild. Two Elites Warriors run toward the waiter who is now pounding Jimmy. They peel the bigot away and keep him in custody. Kino rushes forward and picks up Jimmy. He flies with him to the guest house. I smell blood. It's blood from Vanessa, Jimmy, and others in my Guild.

These are my people. The anger is real, and I release it. I arch my long neck and send my flame into the sky, chasing those of my brothers. My wrath made tactile in the form of plasma. That boy had better be okay, or I won't hold back my rage.

I tele-speak to Mega, *"Get the others to safety."*

He answers, *"Yes, My Queen!"*

The Ceorfan don't waste time as our dragons will hold back the crowd. They make it to the housing facility without further injury. My brothers and I fly the short way across the street. I change back to human shape while the boys let me enter safely. I wait in the lobby watching while they morph, Dana first, then Jared.

Then hail begins to fall. The crowd runs for cover.

My little brothers follow me into the lobby.

I urge, "Come to my room, we need to talk about this, and Jare let the hail fall for a while."

He laughs, "Under control, Sis. I'm letting it get to marble size and only one square mile around us. So no one gets hurt."

I laugh a little. Jared is very good with his gift now.

When we get to my room, the television is already on. It's replaying the scenes of the riot and us in full dragon. Somewhat surprisingly, it shows honestly what happened with Vanessa being knocked out and Jimmy being beaten.

The media has done an excellent job telling the story accurately, even mentioning that Vanessa is the daughter of a prominent family, and Jimmy is an adopted son to the Ceorfan. They show a somber view of the ordeal. The phone rings, and it's the President. I let Clifton answer.

After hanging up, he says, "My Queen, the President offers his most humble apologies and his physician if we need them for the young ones."

It will be very distressing to my Guild to find out someone hurt the teens. Children are precious to the Ceorfan people.

I answer, "Count, please tell the President that this isn't something we will fight over. But we also want his full cooperation in understanding how his security forces allowed this to happen. I also want to know how he'll use his bully pulpit to advocate to the American people on behalf of our Guild. If he doesn't, we will act accordingly."

"Yes, Your Majesty," he responds.

"And Clifton, where is Jimmy and Vanessa? Are they alright?" I ask, irritated, I didn't get this information first.

"Both of the children are doing fine. They are with the doctor.

He said he'll be with you soon," the Count says before he leaves, letting Kick and Kino into the room at the same moment.

Jared and Dana are waiting for me so we can talk and decide what to do now. I wave them over to the sofa and ask if they want something to drink.

"What I want to know is where the hell is Spar," I say.

35

THEY LEFT SPAR

Spar

"Spar, get me out of this castle now. It's Kendra," Jared pulses to me. Without a thought, I grab both him and Steen by the hand and run them through the walls, using my gift to pass us through Barat's stone fortress.

When we reach the outside, Steen pulses, "I'll be back before you torp."

At the same time, Jared takes on his dragon form and leaps into the air, taking flight powerfully. Within a heartbeat, Steen opens a portal mid-air, and Jared flies through it. The portal reopens, this time at ground level, and Steen runs through it. Before he makes it through, he pulses, "I am going to warn Flint and Peri. I'll return after I do."

Then, just like that, I'm alone.

"What the fuck! I need to help her too, you shits," I shout at empty air then quiet, so no one in this God-forsaken place hears. I put my hands to my head. Kendra and I are bound by our minds, and I know that she needs help. I also can tell, it's something she can handle. I wish I was with her, but that's not an option now since fucking Jared, my best friend, just left me high and dry.

"I'm gonna whip somebody's ass. I'm gonna whip his dragon ass," I sing, not quite remembering where I heard the phrase before.

Well, they didn't send me here to plant my butt on the ground and eat donuts. The job needs doing, and I'm the goyle here, so it's my job to do it.

As I melt my way back into the castle, I try to follow the same path as the one I used to get my friends out. But, since I was running through the walls and rooms, I get a bit turned around and wind up lost.

I'm in a broad vacant area. Not quite a room, more like a large opening in the hall. Several small cells line the room on opposite sides. A few of the places are more extensive and appear ready to hold more captives. It is hard not to recognize this place for what it is, a dungeon. As I take in my surroundings, my mind wonders if either Kick, Peter, Steen, or Kino had been held in this room.

I begin to search the prison, looking in every area I can get to. On a few occasions, I offer a loud whisper to the darkness, "Trix. My name is Spar. I know that Baratium has ordered your execution. I'm here to find you and take you to safety." No response.

I continue to search. One room I stumble upon has short stubby tables with wash tubs on them, and a drain leading from the tub to the floor where whatever would have been in the tub would have drained. Along the wall nearest the stubby tables stands a large wooden table which is covered with many shiny instruments.

As I gaze at the implements, a sudden convulsion rips through me. My guts twist into a bile retching knot. This is where my brothers were cut so many times. This is where Kick and his friends were forced to torture and be tortured. This is where the pain of a thousand years was visited on my brothers, my friends, my people.

Yesterday's lunch threatens to expel itself forcefully from my gut, as I take in the room with the practiced eye of an investigator. The better I know this room, the more I'll be able to talk to Steen and maybe to be able to understand the three of them and the Cursed.

The shock and disgust behind me, I leave the room. Just down the hall, I find a room with a bed.

"Trix... please, if you are here, I want to help you," I whisper into the darkness. I see movement from the corner of the room, and a dark-skinned Fae woman walks into the dim light from the hall. Even in the darkness, her rainbow-colored hair is hard to miss. She giggles and ducks her head shyly as I stare at her, surprised I found her.

The woman who walks into my view is elegant in her motions and melodic with her amusement. Sensational is the single word I would put on her if I were told to objectify her.

"Are you Trix," I ask, feeling stupid as I do.

"Yes, I am. I wasn't expecting such a luscious piece of meat as a Ceorfan Warrior. You're a warrior, aren't you?" Then, without even the hint of waiting for my reply, she continues, "Do you want to be my pet? I'll call you my pet, how's that gargoyle?"

This seems like a great idea right about now. She uses magic to seduce her targets. In this case, me.

The sexpot takes my pause as a hint that I'm trying to listen, so she tries to calm me by kissing my neck. The beauty pulls herself close, almost on top of me, to reach my most sensitive areas. While she's gorgeous, she isn't Kendra, and I'm not the slightest bit interested. To Trix's complete and utter surprise, I pulled her off of me and set her aside.

"Trix, I'm the prince consort to the Ceorfan Queen. My heart is dragon bound to her. While I'm flattered, I'm here to save your life," I pronounce with conviction.

"What would you attempt to save me from? More importantly, why would you?"

"Kick's very fond of you. He credits you with saving his life. He wants you safe, and the Ceorfan have offered to provide you protection until your safety can be secured," I supply.

"Girl, I understand you have no reason to trust me. But think about this, why would a gargoyle break-in," I emphasize that last word with an extra umph and pause, "to this castle when we know who is here and what he does to gargoyles," I finish almost pleading with her.

She stands, transfixed by something she's looking at... no, not what she sees. It's more like what she thinks in her mind. "Kick's fond of me? He would have me despite what I've done to him?"

Fucking firetruck! I can't believe this. She thinks Kick still wants her. Fuck, shit, fuck, shit, fuck shit, damn! I can't tell her the truth. Kick will just have to deal with this mess when I get her back to Navan. "Well, we haven't specifically spoken about anything so private. He's a private guy. But I know he is fond of you. He has said that much," I say gamely.

The turn of her smile and the tilt of her head gives me all I need to know. She's ready to get out. She takes my hand and starts to pull as if she wants to lead me out. "Trix, I have a gift. I can walk us through these walls to safety. Just hold my hand and stay with me," I say to her.

"Okay, my big blue protector. I'll stay with you," she nearly squeals in delight.

I take her hand and walk to the nearest wall, in the direction, I hope is correct. We pass through.

The first time someone passes through an object with me is usually a little disorienting for them. Generally, I watch them to make sure they don't panic and try to pull away from me. This time is no exception. So as I enter the room, I'm looking back to my new friend and don't notice the two individuals in the room ahead of me.

"Trix, what're you doing here? Ahh, I see you have brought me this gargoyle as an offering to Baratium. Very wise, my sister," Walter slimes the words out of his mouth.

I don't hesitate to pick up my charge, and start to run back through the wall. My front leg makes it into the wall when my muscles are clamped solidly as if each one has a steel vice holding it in place. Then I'm dragged back into the room where Trix wriggles out of my grasp and slides to the floor. When she lands, she looks up into the black eyes of Walter's assistant.

"Bladriell, go and fetch our master. I'm sure he'll want to welcome our newest Crafted creator personally," Walter orders the younger man.

"Gladly," replies the wretched mage.

After Bladriell leaves the room, the older wizard takes up the spell holding me in place. I'm not able to even blink between Bladriell releasing me and Walter re-spelling me.

"Brother, please, you must let us go. This gargoyle has come to save me from Baratium. He is taking me back to Kick. Remember, you said I could have that cute mage?" pleads the dark beauty.

"What? Why would you want to live with them? They are foul creatures of the worst sort," he sniffs back at his sister.

"You didn't think they were so foul when you wanted my friends and me to seduce them and enslave them with our sex. Which is it brother, are they nothing more than repugnant beasts which you have forced your sister to profane herself upon or not? Tell me," she entreats, leaving no room for a correct answer.

"My sweet, sweet sister, please. You must understand. I chose my words, rashly. You understand how Baratium will react if this gargoyle isn't here when he arrives. He'll kill me. You're asking me to die for this gargoyle. You barely know him. Why should I die for him?" the panic rising in the grizzled old guys retort is flung out to his younger sister.

"Brother, I won't see this man die because you will not leave the side of a madman. A madman who has pronounced my death sentence." The steel within the voice of the diminutive satyratrix leaves no doubt as to the sincerity of her words. "Please, brother, free us and leave this place. You can hide... please hide," the pleading in her voice isn't lost on the haggard mage.

Just then, an excited Bladriell returns, and a few steps behind is his master, Baratium.

"My dear, Trix. I'm so glad to see you haven't abandoned me as your brother had told me," he says watching his apprentice, Walter, and after a brief maniacal smile, he turns back to the woman. "This gargoyle, I assume, is your penitence for your earlier betrayal," the fuckwad master hisses. Trix struggles to maintain a satisfied look on her face.

"For now, My Lord," she offers with a deep bow.

"Bladriell, take this creature and prepare him for the Resurgere," vicious master mage says.

No words, just a sneer, and the young shit takes the spell back from Walter and begins to lead me out of the room and to the dungeons where he was earlier in the night.

"Satyratrix, you shall still be punished. However, I've chosen to not kill you since you have returned to me with such a prize. Return to your room and ruminate on your mistakes, and when I call you, explain to me what you believe your punishment should be and why," the old fucktoad says.

Trix smiles and bows her way, respectfully out of the room.

36

WHITE HOUSE

Kendra

THE LOOK ON MY BROTHER'S FACE GOES FROM CONCERN TO 'OH shit' at the speed of light. Now, I'm worried.

Jared starts, "Sissy, Spar's alright, but we're in a bit of a pinch right now. Ok, damn it, he's still in Barat's castle trying to find Trix... I thought we'd be back fast enough that it wouldn't matter. The last anyone saw the satyratrix she was there.

We also think that we've found where Sass might be. She's in Cueva Hallow. We're still working on finding her friend Trix though." Jared spills the beans on Spar as fast as he can.

It's almost like when he was talking to Mom when we were kids. He was always uncomfortable speaking with her, so he always spoke fast. It was like if he said it quickly enough, she couldn't get mad about what he was saying. It didn't work with her and it isn't working with me.

As my brother's words wash over me, I rub my face, hoping that it would stop the fear welling up inside me. "Wait one second, Jared

Kyler Macbard! You left Spar inside that maniac's castle? What in the hell were you thinking?"

"I get it, Sis. But, you called, and I had to get here fast. I was planning on getting right back. In fact, I'm only staying long enough to check on Jimmy and Vanessa. Then, I'm off... okay?" Jared peers at me questioningly.

"Forget it, Jared. I know he's okay right now. Let's go see the kids, then you can leave," I say.

As I start toward the door, I stop and listen. All three of us siblings turn toward the door sensing someone is about to enter. As our heads come around, Arden Kelley pops his head in.

Seeing that we're all looking at him, he tilts his head and says, "Ummm... someday, I need to know how you guys can do that. Anyway, I've just left the teenagers. Ness will have a headache, but there's no concussion. Watch her for a few days. Better yet, give her a dose of dragon healing.

"The boy is more banged up. He has some bruises, a broken rib or two, and a few cuts that would need stitches without your special brand of Dragon Queen healing. We cleaned him up. But he'll need you to do the healing thing on him too," he finishes.

"I'll go right away then. Thank you, Arden," I say, taking a deep breath relaxing my shoulders.

He nods, and I say, "We'll be right back."

Kick says, "I'm going too. I want to see for myself they're alright."

Mica nods and adds, "Not without me."

Kino finishes, "I want to see them also."

Dana says, motioning with his thumb over his shoulder at Jared, "You aren't leaving us behind. We're gonna see that they're good to go before we skedaddle too, Sis."

I jerk my head the direction we're moving and smile. I'm so filled with glee that everyone cares so deeply about the teens. If I weren't so worried about the young ones, I'd laugh. This is the kind of people I want us to be, loyal and caring.

We follow Arden down a carpeted hallway to a room, much like mine but smaller. It still has two bedrooms and a living area with a small kitchenette. It's decorated in blues. The good doctor shows us to the room on the left. I hope to hell he didn't put both teens in the same bed together. My inner mom is showing again.

I tiptoe closer and see Jimmy sound asleep. He looks like a brutally abused rape victim.

My shoulders slump, and I raise a hand, rubbing my forehead, leaning forward. I gaze at my young charge. He looks so vulnerable and small laying there. The results of the beating look much worse than I had expected. Tears glisten in my eyes, but I'm more pissed off than sad knowing that he's so hurt.

My brothers let out quiet growls, but that's all as they stand stiff just inside the doorway. My consorts appear to have similar attitudes. They're also very still, their lips in hard lines.

I look up at Arden with a grimace and say, "That's more than a few bruises and cuts Arden. He looks awful."

The doctor answers, "I did suggest dragon blood, dear friend. There's no damage done to him that won't be healed, and I did give him something for pain. He's a tough kid and said he's okay before he passed out."

Not waiting, I dig a nail into my finger and put a drop of blood on one of his cuts. Kino and Kick both begin to sing a healing and relaxing song under their breath. I add to the melody, and the room swirls with the magic. The cut starts to close before our eyes, and just as quickly, the bruises fade to nothingness. We watch as a few final green spots disappear from view. Jimmy sighs in his sleep and turns over without a groan in pain. The breath I expel in relief is immediate, but my heart still hurts for him.

I place my hand on Arden's arm and say, "Thank you for helping him and Ness. They're like my own. His body looks better, but let's make sure this didn't hurt him emotionally or mentally, okay?"

"Most surely, Kendra. I was talking to him when I was cleaning him up, and he seems to be very much the Ceorfan, resilient and strong that is. I'll show you over to Vanessa now."

When we enter our young lady's room, she's asleep also, looking so small and innocent. She doesn't look as bad as Jimmy, but it breaks my heart to see her swollen face bruised and her cut lip. I hope Clifton called her parents, and they cared enough to at least talk to her on the phone. They've been strangely absent in her life for the last several weeks.

It never hurts me when I dig a claw into my hand. I need to remember to ask Jericho if he knows why not. My guess is, it's because my nails are so sharp and because I'm helping someone.

After I create a drop of blood, I dab it on Ness's swollen lip and the cut under her eye. Then I start the healing song. My consorts add their voices to mine. Almost immediately, she appears better, and before we finish our song, the cut is completely gone, as is the swelling. This working together thing is excellent.

Arden guides us out the door and back into the hall and says, "I'll stay here and keep an eye on them. Don't worry, I'll let you know if there's any problem. Go on, I know you have things you have to discuss. If you need me, I'll be here."

I hug him and say, "Thank you, Arden, you're good for us. I'm glad you're Ceorfan now."

He nods and ducks his head embarrassed. I turn with my consorts and brothers, and we leave Ness's room in a single file and head back to mine. Kino holds the door open for us as we enter.

"Well, we have a lot to discuss. While I deplore the events of this evening, I think it'll drum up some sympathy for the Guild as a whole. At least I hope so. Some good may come out of it. I did give a not so veiled threat that this attack will have consequences if the Americans don't give us their full cooperation on how their security measures failed so miserably. I think I said I wanted the President, personally, to lead the campaign for the inclusion of the Ceorfan Guild. I also warned we'll act accordingly if he doesn't. Guys, what do you think our next move should be?"

Lifting his hands up in the universal gesture, meaning stop, Jared says, "Wait for a second, Sis. I trust you to do the right thing. You have my full support, but I only stayed to see if the kids are okay. Now that I know they are, I have to get back to Fae. I need to go get Spar. I'll be in touch soon. I love you."

I shrug and take a deep breath, reassuring myself that I can do this. My consorts are here and will help. And I do need Jared to go get Spar.

I turn to my brother and say, "I love you too. I know you're in a hurry. So, yes, find my goyle and keep him safe. I mean it, mister," I add as a joke. "I'm sorry I snapped at you earlier. I can sense that he's alright in my mind, but I need him out of there. I know you'll have everything under control. Right?" I add the final word as both a question and a challenge, and I throw in a bit of a teasing growl at the end too. I'm trying to trust here also.

Laughing, he responds, "I'll do it, Sis." Then he punches Dana on the shoulder. "Kick, will you please open a portal to Steen for me."

When that nut is gone, Dana says, "I need'ta git too, Sis. I'm glad the kids are okay. And I have to say donum is working fast and fine as frog's hair. You know, I knew the instant you needed help. Jericho even had the portal open before I could finish askin' for it."

"I never did ask, have you found the treasure?" I query.

"We spoke to Achor, the guy mentioned in that scribbled message on the well lid. The problem is, he'll only talk to you. Just so you know, that dude's as crazy as a bucket of cats in a pond. I'd appreciate it if you'd come back with me. You won't have to stay. But he's adamant he won't spill his guts to anyone but you. Hell, he wouldn't even let us tell him our names! The guy's a loon!" Dana says, eyes wide and pleading.

"Yes, I will. But I need you to hang on a little longer. I've got something to run by you," I finish.

I look to my handsome red goyle standing with me, holding a look of a goyle who isn't leaving. He reaches for me and says, "Beloved, I don't want to leave you in this turmoil. I want to fight with you."

I raise my arms and put them around his neck and look into his eyes and say, "You're the most wonderful goyle. I love you, Rockstar.

If I need you, I'll call. I won't wait. Don't worry, this isn't bad, but if it gets worse, we'll be out of here so fast their heads'll spin."

He presses me close and says, "I'm not sure that helps, but I know you will do what is best. You know, I heard you in my body. It vibrated all over, and I knew you needed me. I opened a portal immediately. I didn't even have to think about the target for it. I believe it reacted to the vibration cast from our bond and your donum."

"Now, that's interesting. I'm not sure why I knew, but I did think that you knew as soon as it happened. I'll do better to send a message with the magic if it happens again. Otherwise, I'll talk to you before morning. Now return to Navan and whatever you were doing to help Dana. And please, keep him out of trouble, okay?"

Before he can answer, Dana chimes in helpfully, "And Loverboy, when you get back to the cave city, check the vault for me. I need to know if I need to add support for the new treasure once we get it. Besides, it's daylight in Turkey, and you'd just have to torp. Delay until it's night, please or get a spell from Jericho if he has one. Thanks, brother."

Dana always has the perfect way to give someone just enough grief, they know they're loved, but not so much as for them to lose face. I smile up at them both, oddly finding myself envying my own life.

Kino pats Dana on the back, maybe a bit too hard, causing him to stumble forward a small half-step. "No problem. I'll get back to you as soon as I can."

Kino steps to me and bends close. I hear a faint song meant just for me. The little tune in my ear makes my body hum with happiness before he stops and backs away. He never takes his eyes off of me as he backs into his own portal and is gone.

We're walking back into the living area when Krag pulses at the door and enters with a woman I've not seen before.

He says, "My Queen, I would like you to meet Terin, daughter of your Royal Mage, Jericho."

37

HEWN IN DC

Kendra

THE DARK LADY BEFORE ME BOWS HER HEAD SLIGHTLY. SHE HAS to be one of the most beautiful women I've ever seen. She's wearing everyday black jeans and a tank. Damn, she wears it well. Her long black hair hangs straight down her back and is held with a silver ponytail holder. Her eyes shine with mystery from the blue, almost purple depths. I know I'm staring, but I'm mesmerized.

"It's nice to meet you, Your Majesty. My father has nothing but good to say about you. I offer my fealty, My Queen, you already have the Hewn at your service and part of the Guild. That's a feat, you know. We haven't trusted to be part of the Ceorfan of Navan in centuries."

"I'm glad to have you and the Hewn. You were always welcome even more so now. Terin, you need to warn the Hewn. The people aren't happy to have us in the world, and it's going to take some adjustment."

"I understand, My Queen. The mess from last night has been in the news everywhere. When you morphed into your dragon with the dragon lords," pausing a moment to look Dana up, then continuing, slowly turning her head but keeping her eyes on him for a fraction longer, "the world loved it. Don't be surprised if you have the support of many who didn't back you yesterday."

"That's good news," I say locking eyes with Mica, Kino, and then Kick in turn. We understand each other.

Terin continues, "I'm here for another reason, though. I brought you the Water stone. It's high time I'm rid of it. The damn thing's just a bauble for me to have to keep up with and lug around. I prefer to pack light and not worry if I lose shit."

As she talks, she takes a velvet bag from her pocket in the side leg of her pants and hands it to me.

I open it. The stone flies to my forehead and sinks in. Instantly, all my consorts are with me in the dream world, we're bound. The Water stone takes me to the lost Ceorfan treasure. I see it clearly, but it is underwater. No wonder it hasn't been found yet. It's so amazing that I twirl around with my princes and laugh. This causes me and them to fly back to our bodies. I think I might be getting the hang of this dream walk thing.

When I open my eyes, Krag is holding me up, and Kick, Mica, and Kino are getting up off of the floor.

Terin is still before me, and I say, "Thank you, Terin, and the Hewn for this precious gift. I feel more complete than I have ever felt."

"It was always yours, I just brought it to you. Now I've got to leave and return to my ship. We're in the middle of serious business, My Queen," Terin says and turns to leave, smiling one more time at Dana.

I let her leave. Turning to my brother I say, "I don't know what that looked like from your point of view, but I was with all my men. We were on this island in a bay, north. I think it was north of Canada. When I first saw it, it was hundreds of years ago, and it was two small islands close to each other with a small strip of water between them. There was a deep shaft and a small square tunnel leading from under the sea. It was blocked off, so no seawater could go through it. Another tunnel, much larger, large enough for a gargoyle, leading from another beach. Both tunnels lead into the shaft. The larger tunnel intersected the shaft at the bottom, and the smaller one crossed the shaft at about ninety feet below its rim.

When I saw it again, in our time, it was a single island. But now, it also has a triangle-shaped swamp. The smaller tunnel has flooded the whole thing. It must have been a booby trap. That's why it's underwater now," I finished, convinced I'd been crystal clear as to both the problem and the location. "That's where the treasure is. Is it possible for you to get to it and get it out?"

"Sissy, I thought some of it was underwater, but wasn't sure about any of the details you just gave me. Come on and talk to that Achor guy with me. I'll take my team, and we can go to this island, and I'll scoop it out of its hidy-place for you," Dana says with all the sincerity of a gold-plated guarantee.

"Okay, Dana. Let me get the Ceorfan back to Navan and safety. I don't want them to torp here. I need to know they're safe before I leave."

We spend the next few hours talking and returning the Guild to the city. I feel much better knowing they're safe from the bigotry when they torp. I can't even think of what would happen if they were stone in front of that wild mob.

When everyone is safe, I turn to my brother and say, "Okay, let's go see your guru. Oh wait, I need to leave someone here to manage the rest of the Ceorfan while I'm gone. Go on, and I'll be there shortly."

Dana grins and heads off through the portal that Kick opens for him, while I organize the few remaining tasks. I leave Mica in charge of the Washington group of goyles. Since he doesn't have to torp at sunset, he can protect them if I don't get back before they torp. I also decide to bring my dark angel with me.

When I'm finally ready, I pull Mica close. I press up to my handsome goyle to say goodbye. He looks down at me with a huge shit-eating grin and says, "Princess, I love you. Try not to burn anyone to a crisp unless you come get me first."

He bends close and nuzzles my neck. Holy crap, there isn't enough time in a day. I need my big goyle. Waiting is such a challenge.

"Will do. I won't be burning and pillaging without my favorite Ranger," I press my lips to his and sigh.

Reluctantly, he let's go of me. I turn to Kick, who opens a portal to meet up with the green team in an area called Anatolia near a large hill named Hisarlik. We're there in an instant. I could get used to using my personal jump stone!

Behind us lie the Dardanelles Strait and the Aegean Sea. In front is the Homeric plane, once a bay which, nearly three thousand years ago, separated warring armies from each other. Looking across this plane, we see the castle Ilioilion standing on the high mound.

I point toward the mound and say, "That's where we'll find Dana's crazy-ass hermit," as I say it and don't even wonder how I know. I jump into the air and transform into my dragon form. Kick follows me, using his father's kilt pin. We begin our flight to the castle walls and my baby brother.

38

WAITING

Dana

W<small>E ARRIVE IN THE CITY AND MAKE OUR WAY THROUGH ITS</small> various paths and past Alexandritana's apple tree. We turn before we get to the ramp, which once led to the great orange head of our former queen, Leta. There we enter the gates which, three-millennia ago, hung between the magnificent topless towers which once protected this castle. I continue on with Peter and the few Ceorfan who can work with me during daylight hours.

With the help of a unique stone created by Jericho, some gargoyles can minimally control when they torp. I've learned from the Royal Mage, that even with this stone, most Ceorfan still can't put off torping at sunset. He told me that even this slight delay is exceedingly rare, and the gift that Mica has is unique to him. That's why I have to leave Kino and most of my other goyles in Navan until sunset.

"Peter, with everything we brought, tents, and all our supplies to dig with, is it possible that you could make our entire camp invisible?"

The thin mage's blonde messy hair blows in the wind. He puts a hand to his chin and says, "I think I know what to do. My gift is the ability to affect light, I can kind of make a light show. I'll bend light to disguise the camp by making it look like the sun is shining here very brightly then later at sunset. Then we can 'on party dude,' bossman. Did I say that correctly?" he asks as sincerely as a child to his parents.

"Close enough. Let's git the work done first, sexpot. Then you can work your magic, and we can 'on party.'"

What there is of the Green Team sets up a camp that looks very much like an architect's dig. I have them recuperate in the tents until the rest of the team and my sister arrive. I brought a cot and lie down with my arms behind my head. I don't sleep, but the rest helps me clear my head and think. I start making lists of the things I need to accomplish. I feel a pulse that I return before sitting up as Kino enters.

"Dana, Duke of Stone, the gargoyles and I are back and ready to help. What would you have us do?"

"Let's git over to the fountain to wait on my sister. I have a nagging suspicion that there's more there than meets the eye."

The team grabs their equipment. It only takes a moment since I had the few gargoyles with me to organize it before we rested. So we troop off to the fountain.

We quickly arrive and are standing beside the 'pond' to wait on Achor and Kendra to come. When I'd left her, I assumed she'd only be a few minutes behind me–I was wrong about that, again.

"Kino, we had time to set up an entire camp, organize our supplies, and rest. Now you and the other gargoyles have gotten back and still no Queen bee. She told you she was comin', right?"

"Yes," Kino answers, unconcernedly.

"Well, where the hell is she?" I say.

"I–" Kino tries to answer before I cut him off.

"No, no need to say anything. I know my Sis. Heck, I'm expecting a portal to open north of the fountain and her to fly through in her dragon form. Then she'll land in all her glory and talk to the crazy Achor dude. But nope, we're waiting! Until she gets off her duff, we're just hanging out, with our butts a flappin' in the breeze. Has anyone even seen the danged hermit?" I say, looking around to see if he's standing nearby... hoping he isn't now that I called him a crazy hermit. Hey, I consider it a win that I didn't call him old... but he is, just sayin'.

"Dana, my brother, you know your sister as well as I. The queen has many irons in the fire. She also can find a way to delay breathing if she sets her mind to it. I'm sure she will be late to her own funeral, which let's hope is hundreds upon hundreds of years on. Let's give her a few more..." Kino says, a touch of exasperation creeping into his voice.

Thud, thud! Right beside me, two solid sounds hit the ground in rapid succession. If I could jump, I may have leaped right out of my skin. But since I can't hop high enough to get my toes off the ground, I barely managed to stay inside of it.

Kick pats me on the shoulder before saying, "Hey guys, how's your night?" a broad grin on his face.

Quickly recovering, I laugh at my earlier startle and ask, "So when is your girlfriend getting here?" with more orneriness than I'd intended.

Kick turns and points to the sky behind us.

Following his direction, I watch as a dark shape blocks the stars, moving north to south. As it gets closer, I begin to make out a form, then finally, it materializes into a fully formed dragon.

I catch a glimpse of Peter as he begins to reminisce, "I never hoped to believe we'd ever have a Ceorfan dragon queen fly these skies again. This is more than a dream, this is life, love, and all that was once good, returning to the place where it all began," Peter says, obvious pride growing in his voice.

Soon the grass around us is blowing in every direction, and dust is flying into the air as Kendra lands near us, transforming into her half-dragon, half-human form immediately as her feet touch the ground.

In a rush, the old hermit, Achor, appears from nowhere and walks up to her, surprising me with his sudden appearance. Before we have a chance to react, he places a hand on each side of her chest, near her shoulders. His shove, while forceful, only causes Kendra to step back. She keeps moving back until her spine is against the wall behind her. It looks like she moves more of her own volition than Achor's touch.

As we see him touch her, both Kino and I react. He grabs hold of one of the hermit's hands and I grab the other. This string bean is strong! Too strong for me to simply pull his arm away. I gape at Kino, and he's having a similar problem. Fear begins to grip me. I worry this hermit may be about to hurt my sister. Kino begins to turn to use his magic as leverage against the man.

"Dana, Kino... please stop. I don't believe this mage has any ill intentions toward me or any of us for that matter. His aurora is all pink, and honestly, my magic would tell me," Kendra explains with a crook of her head to them and a smile to the old hermit.

Well, of course, it's all pink, that explains everything. Let's ignore the fact that he has you pinned, and I can't budge his arm! But like the good baby brother, and the reason why my Sissy always liked me better than Jared, is... I keep my mouth shut and let her finish.

"Let's give him a chance to speak," Kendra asks, using a calming vocal skill I didn't know she possessed until this instant. She's late, and she has this new soothing tone thingy. What the hell. Oh well, it's no biggie. Anyone got a soda pop?

"Thank you, Kendra," the old hermit starts before her red consort cuts him off sharply.

"It is Queen Kendra," Kino says, his tone serious as he steps closer to her.

"I'll be the judge of that if you don't mind, my friend Kokkino Petra Magus, or the red stone," says the hermit as he casts a goofy grin the redhead's way.

My gargoyle brother in law stiffens and raises an eyebrow staring at the old geezer. I kinda wonder myself what this codger is up to.

"What is it on? Are you curious as to how I know your name?" Achor questions with a glint of amusement twinkling in his eyes.

"Well, to be honest, I would like to know. I don't remember you, and you would not let us tell you earlier," Kino answers, his face tilts, and his eyes narrow in surprise before he schools his expression into control.

Now an oddly discomforting smile is plastered on Achor's face. "Dana James Macbard, teal dragon Duke of Stone. I did hear you call me a crazy hermit. I am neither, but I understand why you would think that," he says.

His grin fades as he turns back to Kendra. He removes his hands from her and steps back. "Kendra, you must understand, I protect something wonderfully valuable. Many sorcerers and sorceresses have attempted to steal this treasure using many means, as you can imagine. I was tasked by my Queen, Leta, to protect it. I'll continue to do so until I am utterly destroyed, or I deliver it unto its rightful owner, the true Queen of the Ceorfan. Are you that Queen?" he asks without a hint of mockery.

Oh shit, that old bastard is in for it now. I'm just gonna sit back and enjoy the shit show and try to not laugh too loud.

39

TESTING A QUEEN

Kendra

IF I WASN'T SO PISSED ALREADY, I MIGHT GIVE THIS LITTLE FART a break. However, right now, I rake my hands through my hair, getting it out of my face before I give him the what for. Then he says my grandmother's name, and I calm a fraction to listen for a minute. He better get to the point before I lose it, though.

The old hermit is serious. His body is still, straight, and unmoving as he says with a hint of steel, "I was tasked by my Queen, Leta to protect it. I will continue to do so until I am utterly destroyed, or I deliver it unto its rightful owner, the true Queen of the Ceorfan. Are you that Queen? You should know that if you claim to be a descendant of the Tarragon Queen and you aren't, you will die and no amount of magic, dragon or otherwise, can save you. If you are who you say you are, the fountain will open."

My mind is flooded with memories that are both mine and not mine. They're my grandmother's lifetimes. Undeniably, these echoes of the past are mine. After being etched, it's all part of me. The future queen will inherit them when her time comes.

I step forward to Achor. He's strong because he's an ancient Tarragon, a relative even if we've only met. One who's been standing guard for more than two thousand years, protecting Queen Leta's treasure from all who would steal it from the rightful owners.

Everyone else is on guard and eagerly awaiting my response. With care and lots of patience, I place my hands on his chest and let knowledge flow from my lips, "My brave and loyal soldier. My most trusted advisor and General. I owe you an eternal debt, and I shall begin to repay it with this... Achor Antilleese, my General, I'm Kendra Macbard, Queen of the Ceorfan. From this moment forward, I release you from your vow of servitude to our people. You are now free to walk the earth, free from any oath you made to me or any Ceorfan. You, my loyal friend, have served your duty. As your queen, I will ensure your name is written in the Halls of History along with your brave and magnanimous deeds."

Magic swirls around the circle of Ceorfan. It's soft and warm, like sinking into a hot tub with sore muscles. The air ripples with a rainbow of light that fades into the man before us.

Achor sinks to his knees. His shoulders slump as he shakes, and he begins to cry.

"My Queen, I have waited for more than two-millennia to hear those words. I have heard many attempts to release me from my eternal oath, but none have ever offered release as you have just done. I know you are my one and true queen. I vow to serve and protect you from this day until my last," he says with joy flooding through him like a broken dam.

"My friend, it's the other way around. I'll serve and protect you," I insist.

He nods getting up the great burden finally lifted from his shoulders

"Achor, will you please lead us one final time to the magical barrier that I need to clear? After it's closed, my brother and consort, with their team, will move the treasure to the Ceorfan city. It's called Navan, and is in America. When they get the treasure moved you're welcome to come along, if you're willing to go?" I suggest as I pat his back grinning.

I glance around and notice the entire Ceorfan contingent, including my brother, have stood transfixed. Some of them are focused on me, others on Achor. Only one in the group has a look other than amazement--Dana. He's looking directly into my eyes and a goofy grin on his lips that light up his eyes like he just saw Santa for the first time.

"Sissy, I have to hand it to ya. You got this queening shit down pat," He says as he pats me on the back and walks toward the now open fountain, turning Achor and placing a firm hand on his shoulder.

Under my breath, I mumble, "Oh yeah, I got it. I almost fried the little pissant."

My baby brother chuckles, then turns and says, "Hey Achor, I'm real sorry for sayin' you were crazy and all that. I was the crazy one. I should've learned by now to not question someone's story without knowin' their journey," Dana said it loudly so that everyone who heard him call Achor crazy and hermit would listen to his apology.

My brothers are that way. If they hurt someone in public and they are wrong, they will apologize in public. We believe it's the right thing to do.

That's the cue to get to work. Dana leads the way, and we follow the passage under the fountain down a long tunnel. He feels the rocks as we go and tells us our depth. At a depth of ninety feet, we stop. There's a shimmering forcefield in front of us. I step forward and walk through it. As soon as I do, it collapses. As everyone except Achor starts to move forward again, I hold up my hand in the universal 'stop' gesture. Looking around, I find Achor in the darkness.

"My Queen Kendra, I believe you are the true Queen of the Ceorfan. However, my belief does not constitute the end of your tests. It is just the beginning. I warned you that if you fail, no amount of magic can save you... this is where the application of that meets reality. You must continue on alone. If you do not continue, or if you turn around and attempt to flee, you will die a full and complete death. Should anyone attempt to travel this path with you, they will also be met with certain death."

"You piece of shit," my blue-eyed brother says, obviously preparing for a beat down of the ancient guard.

Interrupting him before he can begin his roll, I say, "Dana, this is why I am here. We knew this before we entered this chamber. Wait here." Then I turn to face the darkness before me.

Before I take my first step, I hear Achor, "Kendra, your stones are the key."

No shit Sherlock. I step into the darkness, and a torch immediately lights my path, and I hear the unmistakable sounds of a charm flashing into existence behind me. When I turn, I see the same shimmering forcefield as what I'd come through at the beginning of this labyrinth.

"How in the name of bat shit crazy do I keep getting myself into these messes?" I ask aloud, somewhat exasperated.

Unexpectedly, I hear Dana yell out, "I've been wondering about that myself, Sis!"

"Ass-hat!" I reply. I only hear his laugh in return. I can't see him, and he can't see me. The underground echo must amplify the sounds making us hear each other.

After nearly two hundred yards, I come to a small side corridor, I take it. It isn't lit. But as I walk the path, torches flare and light my way. When I reach a dead-end about twenty-five feet down, I find what I am looking for. It's an enchanted stone which I can tell controls a flood tunnel. If I'm not able to shut this off this tunnel will flood. By extension, I'll drown and die.

As if on cue, the stone vaporizes, and a torrent of water rushes in. The force is so great, it knocks me off my feet and forces me back down the side tunnel all the way to its entrance. It is only when I reach this junction, where the main passageway is broader, that I'm able to stand against the water. When I do, I see that the way is open back to where I started, but another shield is up, keeping the water from flowing the direction I was going before I made my turn into the side passage.

"Damn, these force shield spells will hold the water in. That means, when it reaches the other shield, the water will begin to rise... I have until it is filled to figure out this problem."

For some reason, I feel no panic, no gut-wrenching terror.

"Come on, kid. This is a problem you can solve. How do you put a stopper in a rush of water when you can't push anything against the water?" I mull this over to myself out loud. Then pausing to consider the question, I notice the water is already at my ankles. It causes cold chills up my legs.

I begin my trudge back to the source of the water, hoping that by the time I arrive, I'll have an answer to the obvious question. The closer I get to the geyser, the more difficult it is for me to move. A problem made all the more difficult by the rising tide. My buoyancy makes my body want to float downstream again.

Suddenly it hits me. I need to make myself ignore the water. It can't affect me if I decide it can't. No sooner had I made the decision, then I was able to walk upstream without difficulty, despite the water being at chest level.

By the time I return to the source, the water is at neck level, and despite my decision that the water doesn't have an effect on me, as it hits my face, I choke. Ok, so you can still drown in this. Find the fix.

Quickly, I look around, and when I do, I see a stone not sitting flat against the wall. It's just above the outflow of water. I push on it. As soon as my hand touches it, it moves back and falls into the stream of water, blocking the flow.

Immediately, I'm standing in front of my great-grandmother Helen.

"Kendra, I have known you since before you were born. I once traveled great distances across the water from Sparta to Illium. I created this Water stone that you might one day find this treasure and secure a future for your people. Know that I always loved my daughter, your grandmother Leta. She was forcefully taken from me.

Please, someday, go to the Halls of History and learn the truth of those events."

With that, the vision ends, and I find myself standing on the other side of the force shield, a wall of water at my back, and my body and clothing dry.

"Well, suck my dick and call me a reindeer! That was kinda fun!" I yell out to nobody except myself before breaking out laughing.

I've been around my baby brother too much. I'm starting to act like him. After my laughing subsides, but still giggling from channeling my inner Dana, I recommence my search. I still have to lift the shield spells blocking me from returning to my family and friends. Oh, and allow them to come here to move the treasure. That is, after all, why we're here!

After less than ten yards down the main tunnel, I reach a large chamber. This room is more than fifty feet each direction and as black as a viper. Since I can see little in front of me, I back up a step and pause. I decide to retrieve one of the torches and turn around to grab one. When I pull it out of the wall, it immediately extinguishes itself, and another relights in its original place on the wall.

"Ok, so I can't take a light with me... what else you got?" Again, speaking to a bunch of nothing. I try lighting an article of clothing. Every time I do, as soon as I walk away, it puts itself out and reforms, unharmed. I return to the room to try to figure out a new plan.

I throw a rock into the darkness in front of me, hoping I hear it hit solid ground. Of course, it doesn't.

You have to get to the other side. And there's no other way but forward. "Fly!" I scream, and I immediately push my dragon form forward... nothing. Crap!

I can't fly, I can't see. I guess the way this one will kill me is I'll beat my head against the wall and die of a concussion. Or maybe I'll get so frustrated, I'll just jump... "Wait, that's it. I'll simply walk across. I need to focus on the Air stone. Doing so should allow me to be able to walk through the air as if it is solid. I command the air, not the other way around!"

Testing a Queen | 229

No sooner had I made my choice than I step into the air. The air which I command. As I ordered, the air became solid under my feet. As I travel across the gap, I look down and spot a pit of fire far below. As soon as my feet touch the other side, my mind flashes to another vision.

"Kendra, I have known you since before your birth. I am your great-great-grandmother, Leda. When I was married to the King of Sparta, Zeus coveted my body. I loved my husband and did not desire Zeus. The king of the gods did not care. I ran, and he chased me. I transformed from one animal to another until I settled on a great goose. Hoping I had finally flown across the sky far enough, I landed in a cave and slept. When I awoke, Zeus had found me and had his way with me. Kendra, I loved your great-grandmother Helen. I tried to protect her. Promise me you will, someday, visit your Halls of History and learn more about my life."

After her vision, I find myself on the other side of the void, the great room now well-lit from below.

My body is shaking with anticipation, wondering what my next trial will be. I pause to take stock of my situation and relish in my victories. I watch my own shadow in front of me. It's growing more intense. Confused, I turned around. The room is getting brighter, and the only light is from below. I carefully make my way to the edge of the void and peer down. The pit of fire once so far down, its light couldn't reach the top, has now become a roaring inferno. The flames are growing bigger and brighter by the second.

"Shit, can't a girl catch a break?" I yell into the growing sun. Kendra, you should run now.

As I'm running, I replay the water and air trials. What have I learned? Well, I discovered I have control over them. That's what. Could it be that direct? Could it be that simple?

I notice a light ahead. This light is bright, and it's in another great room. Unfortunately, there's a shimmering veil between me and my safety. The flame is now igniting the atmosphere in the corridor behind me. I slow my pace, then stop and turn. When I do, I command the fire to extinguish. It does.

When I turn back, the shield charm in front of me has disappeared. I enter the room and find what must be the treasure vault. For a time, I stand transfixed with the vast wealth before me. Gold, silver, and jewels fill the room. There are many such rooms attached, each similarly filled. Each room appears to be the same size. All except one. This room is filled with scrolls. It must contain tens of thousands of manuscripts, parchments, and books.

After a few minutes, Dana, Kino, and the other gargoyles run into the room. Dana sees me first and yells, "You kick ass, Sissy!"

I laugh with him before I ask, "Did you have any problems finding me?"

"Nope, we followed a flood of retreating water. We saw it wash into a great big hole in the ground. I had the rock in there morph into a bridge, and we came straight here." By the time Dana has finished speaking, Achor enters the treasure vault, unsmiling.

I watch as Dana picks up a bar of gold that must have weighed... My donum screams, stop! It's too late, as he collapses in agony.

I rush to him, but by the time I get there. My baby brother's hand is badly damaged. The skin is flaking off with a sizzling type of condition. Kino's quickly by his side, singing a pain-relieving spell. Based on my brother's screams, it is barely helping. My Rockstar looks to me. I immediately know he is chanting his most potent spell. Steen is also there, working some sort of magic, sweat already beading on his forehead from the exertion.

"Achor, what's happened to him? Can you help?" I plead.

"Kendra, I cannot speak as to the cause or condition. At the outset, I told you all that I could," genuine sadness in his voice.

I drag a claw across my palm and drip blood on Dana's wound. Terror is squeezing my chest, preventing me from taking a full breath. I gasp what little air I can into my lungs. I hate him hurting. My blood runs over his hand and does absolutely nothing. Holy hell, what do I do now?

I pause and think again. It might really be that simple, and I haven't used the healing stone yet. I command healing over my brother, and the magic pours into him. I have to ask one day what it looks like to the others. To me, it is like bright glitter and sand floating where I send it, then sinking in when it meets my target. The damage to my brother's hand is reversing. The skin growing back clean and unscarred.

Everything stops, and my grandmother Leta is before me.

She says, "Kendra, you have done well, my granddaughter. We are proud of you and love you very much. You have us etched in your being but don't know us until you bring up a memory. If you go watch the histories, you will see and know more. As it is, you are a great queen and will do well for our people. Promise me you will, someday, visit your Halls of History and learn more about my life."

I feel them, and she's right, I don't know them yet. "It's what I want to do also grandmothers. I promise I'll go and study about you all in the Halls of History soon," I respond.

I come back to myself as Dana blows a breath out loudly and says, "That did it, Sis, I'm better. You used all the stones, didn't you?"

I giggled a bit and answered, "I did and saw our grandmothers, they helped me. You and Jare need to go with me to the Halls and watch the histories of them one day. They're really amazing women."

"You ain't so bad yourself."

I glance over his shoulder as I notice the treasure. We've found wealth beyond any that I could have imagined. I can't help but turn in a circle to gaze at the wonder before me. I sing and use my healing magic on the entire room's contents, pushing it with the air and cleaning it with water and purifying it with fire. It only takes seconds, and the treasure isn't poisonous to touch anymore.

There's no way for me to quit staring at the now clean and wondrous horde of treasure in front of me.

"My Queen, here we have stored two hundred tons of gold, five hundred tons of silver, and more diamonds, rubies, opals, pearls, and other precious stones than there are grains of sand on the beaches outside the castle," Anchor says with a wide grin taking over his visage. His body is jumping like a rabbit bounding through a field.

I'm not even going to pretend I'm paying attention to him. I recognize some of what I'm seeing but am drawn to the wall of parchments before me. There are rolled documents that make the Hall of History look like a local library. I can't help it and reach out for them, touching the historical records. When I pull one out, I find I can read it easily. It's a scroll of ancient spells and recipes, both chemical and alchemical, a treasure indeed.

The old hermit notices I'm not paying attention and quiets. He needs to be rolled into the Ceorfan Guild and asked to assist Dana on the treasure hunt. He knows how to disarm all of the magical traps and doesn't need me to be present for any other hoard. Apparently, this is the only treasure which required my personal action to deactivate the traps. He and the Duke of Stone should be able to easily work together to bring the rest of the treasure to Navan.

"It's getting close to sunrise brother. Watch over the gargoyles when they torp, okay? I need to get back to the White House and check on the teens and our status in the world."

He nods and reaches an arm out to hug me then releases me to go say my goodbyes to Kino, who is close and already looking through the same parchments I'd been drawn to. I put my hands on either side of my rockstar's waist, and he pivots, wrapping his arms around me and lifts me to him.

I giggle, rub my nose on his, and say, "I love you, beloved. I hate to leave and can't wait until we can all be together again. If anything bad happens, use magic. If it doesn't, use it to contact me anyway."

He rubs his nose on mine back and says, "Beloved, I miss you and think of you always. I won't tell you what I'm thinking there are too many people watching here for that, but you never leave my thoughts. We never did get to try that dream walk together. I'll be ready when you want to try."

He sets me back on my feet and kisses me softly, then backs away and poses turning to stone. The magic from the torp rushes into me, and I feel refreshed. I lock eyes with my brother then wave before I open my own portal and leave. "Be sneaky, and don't let anyone here see you taking the treasure home... did you feel that?"

He says, "Yes, I think Jared is mad. You think he's alright?"

I pause then say, "I can't be sure, but I'll meet you in Fae if it gets bad enough. Our donum will let us know if he needs help. Until then, I have to get back. I know you can handle this, but try to rest a little baby brother."

He chuckles, "So bossy, Sis. See you soon. I'll have this cleared out and in the vaults in the city in no time. And I'll be invisible doing it."

I open my own portal the way I had when I got here, and I'm back at the apartment across from the White House in a heartbeat.

40

IT'S NOT GOOD

Jared

WELL, KENDRA AND DANA HAVE A LOT TO DO. IT WAS HARD TO leave them, but I need to get my job here taken care of. My sister has a lot on her plate. I want to get my tasks completed so I can get back to help her as soon as possible. I'm walking in Faery trying to get to the blue team's base camp. I must be close.

So far, it doesn't look like too many people want to welcome the Ceorfan Guild with open arms, except maybe the Fae. I keep a steady pace but I'm concentrating on how to fix this situation.

Without paying a bit of attention I bump into Flint. He holds onto me to keep from falling and shushes me with a finger to his lips. I scan the area to figure out what he's cautious about.

The gargoyle points. I see it now. The troll from the tavern is stalking his way through the trees, looking for something. I sneak over and put a hand on his mouth.

I warn, "Keep quiet troll, or this dragon Duke will slit your throat without missing a beat. I'm going to move my hand from your greasy face. You won't come out of this in one piece if you shout or try to run. Understand?"

I've tried practicing some of Kendra's persuasion vocal tactics. I'm not nearly as accomplished as her, but I'm pretty good at adding enough magic to my meaning to get my point across.

The grimy fellow shakes his head vigorously, agreeing to do as I say. I peel my hand away with disgust and wipe it on his pants.

"Tell me why you're here troll," I demand.

"I came to sell some information. If you want it, that is, I can always just go back the way I came, but I thought you might want to know where Trix is," the greasy troll boasts like he is the one in charge.

The stupid usually think they're in charge. That is until they meet a dragon. Then they often realize they've been mistaken about a great many things in their wretched little lives.

Flint waves Peri and Steen over and we all stand listening as the greasy troll continues, "Well, is it worth something to you?"

Flint rushes the troll and has him on the ground choking him and says, "We don't have to pay the likes of you. Spill your guts, or I'll do it for you." The fat gargoyle is speedy as crap. I'm not really surprised, but it's a treat to watch him move.

Flint keeps his hand where it is and languidly turns his head to me, "Duke Jared Macbard, what would you have me do with this piece of sphincter grease," obviously taking his time ensuring the troll begins to fear for his worthless life.

I pause and look at the troll who looks at me, eyes wide in stunned disbelief at his sudden turn of circumstance. A heartbeat passes, and the troll's eyes grow even wider when I don't immediately call off Flint, who by now has a smirk on his face as he recognizes he and I are playing the same game with the troll.

"Flint, let's give this troll the benefit of the doubt. Let him talk. But be ready to slit his throat if he wastes any more of my time," I warn.

After Flint removes his hand, the troll is so shocked that he stammers, "Yes, yes, yes, I just wanted to tell you for free that Trix has been hiding in town in a brownie's house who takes in the homeless until they can get on their feet. If you want me to, I can show you the way, but we will have to go now. They make the residents leave and help with farming during the daylight hours."

Flint looks to me, I reply to the troll, "No, we don't want to get you in trouble with the politics around here. Just tell us the way and what it looks like, then be on your way."

The little ass tells us all we need to know and leaves. I flip him a silver coin that he catches out of the air as he walks away. The sun is about to rise, and we have to get going. But before we move, we decide on our next steps.

Peri says, "I think I should go try and find Trix. You two need to get Spar from Barat's castle." She points at Flint and Steen as she talks.

"I told Spar if I don't return for him before torp time, he was to hide in a specific area of the basement, and I'd retrieve him. I don't want to wait any longer. It's too dangerous to leave a gargoyle in that castle, and this is the Queen's gargoyle," Steen concludes, putting another very fine point on what has already become a dangerous situation.

When Kendra called for help, Steen, Spar, and I were in Barat-shit's castle looking for Trix. We had only just begun our search when I was drawn to my sister's side. Spar took Steen and me through the castle walls where Steen masked a portal, and I flew through. Steen then had to find Flint and Peri and let them know what had happened. We had just gotten back together when that troll interrupted us.

"You're the best one to find the satyratrix, Peri." I agree.

"I won't take a chance taking two gargoyles into that castle right before its time for them to torp. Flint, you go with Peri. Steen, you stay with them and get them to a safe place to torp. After you do, come to the fuckhead's castle. If I haven't found Spar and gotten back out, you sneak in to help."

I cut off the protests as they begin, "Goyles, we don't have time for this debate. I've made up my mind. If you argue, you won't have time to check the brownie's house for Trix. Go now, no more debate," I end, leaving no room for further discussion.

As they are highly trained soldiers who work in Navan's Combat Information Center (CIC), they turn on a dime and out of sight in quick time.

41

SHE HELPED

Spar

WELL, DOESN'T THIS SUCK LIKE DONKEY-BALLS IN A MILKSHAKE. A few minutes ago, I was rescuing Trix. Now I'm standing, solid as a teenage erection, in a carved stone basin. The basin sits on top of a stubby wooden table.

Beside me is a creepy mage telling me, "Your flesh is strong, Spar Megason. Yes... yes. I do know who your father is. He's a powerful gargoyle. He's filth. I'm happy I'll be the one to tear your flesh from your body. Oh, I could spell you so you wouldn't feel anything. I'd still get what my master wants. But, without your agony, I wouldn't enjoy this nearly as much." His wheezy laugh would have cracked me up had I been able to, you know, laugh. But I can't because the little shit froze me up like a popsicle.

I'm pretty sure this is where Kino and the other Cursed, as they are called, were held and tortured hundreds of years ago. The Cursed are the Ceorfan gargoyles who were captured and cut to pieces in the Resurgere process, which Baratium uses to create his Crafted army robots.

I'm in what appears to be a laboratory, and I'm stiff as stone, but not torped. I'm not scared because Jared knows where I am. I *am* pissed, though. I should have watched where I was going when I was pulling Trix through the walls. My time in the military and as a Park Ranger drilled into my head, entering a room, or rounding a corner is the most dangerous.

I better look for my own way out. Yeah, I know for a fact that Jare will be back for me. He'd never leave me here to be tortured by this fuckwad. If he has to melt this castle to its foundation, I won't stay here much longer. I can feel it. I have known my dragon buddy for too long.

"I don't know if you understand the Resurgere process gargoyle. I am told it can be qui... aaagggghhh," Bladriell gags out before collapsing onto the floor.

As soon as he does, the binding spell releases. I almost fall, as I was in mid-step when the demented little shit, deactivated my muscles, essentially solidifying me.

Lucky for me, I've got great reflexes. I push off hard from my planted foot and flip forward, head over heal, and land on my feet. Even though I stuck the landing, I can only give it a six. With my legs spread wide, I looked more like a bullfrog flipping over than a gymnast.

I turn to see what happened to that piece of shit, Bladriell. I see the diminutive Trix standing there with a cattle prod in one hand and a club in her other. The satisfied sneer that lifts the corners of her mouth in a 'don't fuck with this bitch' posture reminds me of my Honey girl at home.

"Quick Spar, come with me," the brave and terrified Trix says.

I shake my head and take a half step away before she says, "No, we're not going your way again. Let me lead us out, I can do it. Trust me. They have alarm spells in places I can't always know about, but I know what to look for to find them."

The pleading look in her eyes is all the convincing I need... well, that and the crumpled, bloodied body of shit-head Bladriell at my feet.

Smiling at the little Fae, I wave a hand forward, including a full gesticular bow. Trix takes off, fast. I really have to try to keep up with her. We run up one corridor, then up a set of stairs at the end of it. There we turn and run to the other end of another hall and up another set of stairs. Weaving back and forth several times, I barely notice when she slows. She does so with no warning, and I struggle to not trample the Fae woman.

"Quiet, we are passing near Baratium's upper chambers. This is where he likes to work or lie in his druid sleep," she says staring at the wall beside her not taking the time to face me.

Just as she steps into the hallway, an alarm sounds. Barat throws open the door from inside his room and spots her. Fury fills his eyes; malice runs off of him in waves. Walter, his minion is standing beside him, watching, horror carved into his ruined expression.

His master starts to wave his hand... and the ceiling crashes down, just missing them. I hear Walter yell incoherently. Then it's ass-rat Baratium's turn. He's screaming orders to Walter then summons Bladriell.

"Good luck with that," I laugh.

I look up into the new skylight blasted into the top of the castle. There I see my brother, Jared dragon form and all blasting away with his massive electrical fire. He's conjured a great storm that he's using with an unbelievable effect. The maelstrom is demolishing the rest of the castle as well.

Walter and Master McFuckerstuff join together and cast a massive shield spell to cover themselves from the growing devastation above them. As the destruction grows. So does their shield. I watch in awe as the great blue dragon rips the castle to the ground. Just as I knew he would.

I pulse to him, "Jared, I'm here. I'm safe. Destroy these two. I have Trix. And I'm pretty sure she killed the other one while she was rescuing me."

For a moment, less than a single heartbeat, Jared pauses. I could feel the happiness as he pulses a return message telling me to be prepared. That narrowest of windows is all the opportunity Baratium needs. He leaves the unified shield spell and sends a killing spell directly at Trix. She has no chance to escape, no time to plead for mercy. One moment she's full of hope. A hope of saving me and herself. The promise of a future free of torment and abuse. The next, she has fallen, a beautiful unattended marionette, lying lifeless at my feet.

Her death hits me like a hammer blow to the chest. I'm stunned and unable to breathe. I pulse back to Jared, "Hurry, destroy Barat now! He just murdered Trix."

Anger is pumping into each thump of my pulse. I fly into the opening of the ceiling made by the devastation.

This time, there's no hesitation, Jared launches an attack unlike any I have ever imagined, and it's aimed directly at Baratium. It isn't spread to eventually get them both. No, this one is targeting only one evil mastermind mage. I watch as lightning bolts streak into the barrier as the dragon takes a mighty breath and roars down his thunderous lightning plasma fire onto the shield above Barat. The shell around the two of them shrinks. Soon each one is forced into creating their own pocket shield around their own body. I can tell Jared's running out of breath. I watch as his chest pushes every bit of power left into the destruction below.

A hole opens in Baratium's shield. The little plasma left burns the hand Barat is using for his magic, and the remaining shield collapses. Barat's hand begins to melt and is quickly consumed to the elbow. The mighty blue dragon takes a breath and begins the final exhale.

I see a shuffling form emerge from a shadow where Trix had fallen. I have a brief, irrational hope that she had somehow survived the deadly curse of the armless fuck-mage. Bladriell stumbles from the shadow and into the hall. When he sees his master, he activates some sort of magic I've never seen. In a twinkle, they're both gone.

I pulse a stop to Jared and yell out to Walter, still cowering beneath his shield spell. Like it had worked so well for his boss.

"He killed her, Walter. That murderous piece of shit you have followed around for millennia stopped in the middle of our fight and murdered your sister." I await his response. All I hear is crying.

"And he'll kill me too. You don't have a clue to his depravity," he screams in agony. He jumps up. With his shield in place he runs into the surrounding woods screaming like a crazy man.

I start after him, and Jared says, "Don't Spar, let him go. Let's get back to the others and regroup. I need to think about what we need to do next."

That stops me, but I have to get Trix's body. She wasn't a friend, but she did help me and Kick. I won't leave her like so much refuse. What was her brother thinking?

My stare at my best friend is understood by years of being together. He nods, and I fly into the debris of the castle. I flick large pieces of stone off the dead satyratrix's body. It flies off like a movie prop rock. When I get to her, she is breathing, and I have hope that she might be able to live. If only Kendra were here.

When I reach her and start to lift her, she groans in pain and says, "Tell Walter that he's the only one I could ever depend on, and I love him. I'm sorry, gargoyle. I wanted to be good..." One last gulping death rattle, and she's gone.

"You did just fine, Trix," I squeeze out of my tight throat.

There isn't anything to do but gather her up and carry her away from the destruction around me.

When we land, Flint, Peri, and Steen are waiting for us. They rush forward.

Steen gently takes the beautiful corpse and lays her on the soft grass. No one speaks. Instead, we get to work on her grave. The mage opens the ground. Peri has wrapped Trix in one of her blankets in that short time. I place her in the hollow, and we all stand quietly.

Jared says, "We didn't know her, and she was not well received in this land. However, the little we know of her, she was someone who wanted to do right. She saved Spar's life and is deserving of at least kind words over her grave. Would anyone like to say something?"

Steen takes a small step forward, and Jared nods and bows his head.

The bald mage says, "Trix, I hope you have found your rest in the Otherworld. You did right by Spar. But before that, you did help my brother Kick, and I won't let your name be forgotten. I'll petition the Queen to add your name in the Halls of History."

We stand for a moment of silence before Jared bobs his head to Steen, and the mage sings a soft low melody. The body is covered, and the grave mound grows over with flowers, a red rose bush at the head of the mound. I noticed a nice boulder and retrieved it to set it behind the roses. No words are necessary, and the mage writes; Trix, satyratrix of the isle, sister to Walter the mage; she gave all saving Ceorfan from Baratium.

The anger I felt earlier is calming into slow-burning coal. This won't go unpunished. I need to talk to Jared, and he needs to tell me how Kendra is. I feel she's okay, but I need details before my anger flames out of control.

Jared sees the question in my look, he puts an arm around my shoulders, and says, "Come on gargoyle. Let's tell the others what happened and make a new plan from the guest house of your American President. There's no reason to stay in Faery now."

Not waiting, Steen opens a portal, and we are in my baby's room. I can smell her, and I need her. I walk away from the others to find her.

42

BACK IN AMERICA

Kendra

THE PORTAL THAT KICK HAD OPENED LEADING FROM THE treasure vault closes behind me. It's late. I pause and take a moment trying to get my bearings. It's around nine pm in the capital of America. That is unless my dragon sense is off. It's not.

Traveling by portal is the best way to travel; it's fast, and it's instantaneous and has the added benefit of not having to be subjected to the airport TSA.

Kick, let's go of my hand as we get our corporal bodies into my apartment at the guest housing the U.S. government provided. I stop before colliding into my big ranger consort, Mica, who is waiting right in front of me. I reach for him dragging Kick into a hug with us. I'm brimming over with news and excitement, but want to tell him while in his arms.

"Mica, our people are so stinking rich we'll never be without. I have to tell you about it, but no sleep is catching up with me. Do you mind laying down with me and talking? It's night here, and I'm beat."

Kick isn't waiting for us and plops down on the bed where he takes off his shoes. Mica sits on it too.

"Yes, Princess, it is night. I'll lay down with you. Tell me, was it amazing? Is Kino alright? I bet it's daytime there where the treasure is. Is Red in a safe place to torp?" my big goyle asks.

"Yes, he's just fine. He's been working non-stop. When it's torp time in Navan, he's in Turkey and vice versa. It won't take them more than a day or so to magic all the treasure to Navan's vaults. There's a lot, or it wouldn't take so long. They have to be quick, though, because while we know the treasure is ours, Turkey would lay a claim... especially if they knew how much it is."

There's a knock at the door followed by pulses. The guards are letting me know the American ambassador is here and wants to speak with me. I giggle and glance at my consorts.

Jerking up one shoulder I say, "Well, no sleep for the wicked. Let's start our day, and I'll find time to nap later."

I open the door and recognize Ambassador Castle's not happy face. He says, "Your Majesty, the President, and members of the cabinet have requested a meeting with you tonight. I know it isn't on the schedule. I sent the request to Duke Findare, and he refused me, saying you will not negotiate terms until you have eaten breakfast."

I cock an eyebrow, knowing full well that Fin was stalling for me so I could return.

Not inviting the ambassador into my rooms but leaving him standing in the hallway with my door wide open I ask, "So you don't think I should have breakfast? I should go to your meeting right away. Are you telling me that food will be supplied in the conference room then, or do I need to suck it up and fast until the Americans have what they need?"

He stiffens and begins to stammer, "Ma'am, I suppose we could, umm, could bring you breakfast, or dinner if you would like," he offers gamely while looking genuinely uncomfortable.

Kick is putting his shoes back on, and Mica shifts to see me better.

The ambassador is in an unenviable position. He's trying to get me to a meeting as soon as possible without upsetting his boss or me.

"Not dinner, I'm Ceorfan, my breakfast is after sunset, and it's late now as it is. I understand that you're telling me you want me to go into this meeting, being one of the few females who will be there, *and* you're expecting me to eat in front of a room full of men? Not acceptable," I finish, making the ambassador even more uncomfortable.

"Ma'am–" the ambassador starts.

"Your Majesty, if you don't mind," Mica interrupts, standing up to his full imposing height.

Ambassador Castle blurts, raising his hands. "I meant no offense, sir, but proper etiquette in greeting a member of royalty is to first greet them with using their honorifics, and thereafter, in this case, ma'am." He regains some of his composure standing straighter with the explanation, hoping that satisfies my consort.

Mica continues, "Once again. You want us to conform to your etiquette or whatever you call it. I call it common decency. Your people don't seem to have enough of it to allow the simple courtesy of our queen eating in private before she attends your meeting. One she wasn't warned about, to begin with. Talk about hypocrisy," a now visibly frustrated Mica exclaims, raising his hands' palms up. "In fact, did you know our queen was working all of yesterday and all of last night? She hasn't slept in at least thirty hours. She will be there–"

I touch Mica gently on the arm, and he stops talking. My goyle gazes into my eyes, melting my heart with the care I see in his own. He didn't stop because I'm the queen, and he is sworn to obey me. He stops because he loves me and respects me enough to let me speak for myself.

I say, "Ambassador Castle, I understand this meeting to be of vital importance. Otherwise, it wouldn't have been called so quickly. Knowing that, in all good conscience, I wouldn't help my people if I go to the meeting before I sleep. I can be a grumpy dragon. Please, I need to sleep at least a few hours and have something to eat first. If you agree, we can make this a dinner meeting in the morning. Dinner for me, that is. As long as everyone is eating and I have some sleep, I'd be happy to attend. Sir, I'm honestly trying not to be difficult. I understand the President has his agenda, as I'm sure he understands we have one as well. This is a small issue. If we can't work through this, how are we ever going to tackle the larger issues facing our two nations."

"Your Majesty, I stand corrected on every point. In my haste to deliver you to the meeting, I ignored protocol.

"Prince Consort Mica, thank you for correcting me. I'll take your lesson and learn from it to become a better ambassador between our respective nations. May I suggest we meet in the White House meeting room at twelve-thirty tomorrow afternoon for lunch and the meeting with the respective officials?" he finishes with a bow.

"That's fine with me. I also need to know the purpose of the meeting so I can bring my appropriate staff with me," I request. A sense of exhaustion works its way through my words as I stifle a yawn.

"This is regarding the events of last evening. It also concerns the issues surrounding the integration of your nation into the greater nations of the world. I also believe we will discuss NATO and U.N. membership," he finishes without a hint of the bombshell he just dropped into my lap.

Mica always lets me know he thinks I'd be great at poker. I try not to disappoint him as I leave my face blank and tired. Well, the worn-out part I don't have to fake.

"Thank you, ambassador, I'll see you at twelve-thirty tomorrow afternoon," I answer as I close the door.

I reach for my tablet and tap a message to Clifton and Findare about the meeting. An idea hits me as I press send, and I pulse at the same time. Now I can rest. I receive an answering pulse informing me the ambassador is well away from my suite from my guards.

In those seconds, I have time to process a thought and turn to my consorts, "What the hell? They want us to join NATO! No way, no how, not gonna happen! Our military defends us. Our people defend the defenseless. That ethos is incompatible with joining any military union."

A portal opens inside my room, and Spar bursts through to give me a great big blue hug and a passionate kiss. I'm so sleepy I could melt into him and fall apart in his arms. He feels so good my heart skips a beat knowing he's here and safe from that mad murdering mage.

Jared and the other gargoyles of the blue team with Flint and Peri walk in right behind him, noticeably less enthusiastic. I watch my brother, and my heart sinks. Then I check the auras of others, they're blue and purple with grey in the light around them. Sadness leaks out of them.

"What happened?" I ask.

"Trix was killed by Barat before we could save her. I'm sorry, Sis... more than I can say. She was helping Spar escape when she was murdered."

I gaze up into my consort's sky-blue eyes and ask, "Are you okay? I was afraid for you. But I was certain you were okay. You're strong enough to handle almost anything. It didn't keep me from wanting to be with you, though."

"I was pissed when Jared left me in Faery! When I knew you were in a battle, I wanted to help. But, just like you, babe, I knew you were okay. What happened anyway?" Spar asks.

I explain to Spar and the others everything that happened with both the red and green teams. By the time I finish, Jared's eyes are as large and unfocused as I've ever seen them.

"Sis, do you realize how much that treasure is worth," and not even pausing to take a breath before continues, "The gold alone is in the trillions of U.S. dollars! This makes our nation one of the wealthiest in the world. Our people won't have to worry about their future. That is, unless some asshat tries to take it from us," he finishes, the shine of excitement dulled with immediate sobriety on the subject.

"I'd like to see them try," I say, steel creeping into my voice with such force that my blue dragon brother eyeballs me to judge my statement. I'm pretty sure he's convinced I mean what I said.

My consorts stiffen, and each agrees. I smile satisfied with their bravado.

"Besides, I've already spoken to Dana, Jericho, and Achor. They've all assured me that we can easily protect the treasure with spells. Our little brother says the treasure vault will be well below Navan in a room that he can make impenetrable," I add.

"Sis, Peter, and I just wanted to stop in and get a quick update. But, the two of us would like to go find Sass. We're pretty sure she's in Cueva Hallow in a homeless shelter. We're heading there now," Jared's says.

"Okay, when you find her, get her to safety. I don't trust Sass enough to take her to Navan yet. Let's see if we can get TASS to help us with a secure location," I say.

"No problem. I know the perfect location, and I'm sure that the two others who know the location too will keep it safe and secret. Besides, I already have a bunch of security, so there won't be a problem with it all of the sudden popping up," Jared says.

I agree with his plan and give him and Peter both a hug before Peter opens a portal to Cueva Hallow.

43

IMPOSSIBLE

Kendra

I FALL ASLEEP BEFORE MY HEAD HAS A CHANCE TO HIT THE pillow. When I wake, Mica's sleeping on one side of me and Kick on the other. My ranger consort has made a habit of sleeping without his underwear on, and last night was no exception. His naked ass is lying on top of the blankets, and I'm torn between smacking it or rubbing my nakedness on him. But when I catch a glimpse of the clock on the wall, there isn't time. It's already eleven o'clock, and I promised to attend a meeting across the street in the White House at twelve-thirty.

So, I do the next best thing to that round ass. I smack it. When he quickly turns over, I seductively climb out of bed over the top of him, pausing just long enough to give him an erection. Shit, maybe I can skip this meeting and lay here all day with my two guys. I reach over and bite the back of Kick's shoulder playfully.

Nope! There's too much work to get finished, and I want to check on the teens later. Today I hope to have an agreement with the President. This should be for formal recognition of the Ceorfan. It should also include the full support of the United States in ensuring our role in the world. If I have to spend this much time in every country, I have my job cut out for me.

I walk to the shower and am deep in thought as I get ready. The meeting I've been requested to attend is with the President of the United States, which will include many of his cabinet secretaries and his military Joint Chiefs. I'm not sure what to expect. However, one of the bombshells dropped on me last night was a presumption that the Ceorfan would align themselves with NATO.

"I have nothing against NATO as a human construct. I understand it does many wonderful things. But there's no way in hell I'll let any of our people ever be controlled by a foreign military power. I have little faith that our special abilities won't be misused if given a chance. Anyway, I have an idea they'll be like some of the TASS members before we put the royal foot down." I grin at my little joke. No one else did. I should give up trying to be funny.

Stepping out of the water and into the steamy bathroom, Mica hands me a towel, and Kick gets into the shower.

My dark angel says, "We'll be ready when you are darling, but hurry, Sunny is waiting in the sitting room to do your hair."

Mica pops my ass and grins as I scoot by him. I give him a sly look over my shoulder then wrap the towel tight to go get dressed.

I do hurry, and so do they. We have on our finest business attire, even though Sunny brought a crown for my hair. My face is done up to the nines before we're out the door.

As we walk out I tele-speak to Mega, who I spot waiting outside the main building door.

"How are you awake, General?"

"The Royal Mage came up with some magic, but it won't last. All of us are spelled for today."

I say, "Marvelous, let's get this show on the road then."

He has two squads of Elite Warriors and Hewn standing in a perfect wedge formation. As I walk toward the units, the center opens. Now the wedge has wings to either side with me in the middle and my Ducere guarding the rear.

I'm not risking another scratch on one of my people, so I've already told my people we'll be entering the conference room via a portal.

I say, "Duke Findare, will you please go ahead of us and announce us so security doesn't panic?"

He answers, "Yes, Your Majesty, I've already messaged Ambassador Castle our plans. I will, however, ensure they are prepared. See you there, My Lady."

Kick opens a portal for him, and he's gone.

I smile at my mage. His grin in return is enough to light my inner dragon. I have to stop thinking like this just before important meetings!

"I think that's enough time. Kick, if you please," I say. I don't feel I even need to speak in sentences around my consorts anymore. They seem to instinctively understand what I want.

Kick pulls out his small jump stone and jumps our entire formation into the center of the conference room. Apparently, Ambassador Castle was prepared for this jump, because the center of the room has been cleared.

Before anyone has a chance to speak, Mega commands, "Protection status Alpha!"

Suddenly, the wings of the wedge protecting me spread to cover the main entrance. The six Ceorfan take up positions with two on each side of the large double doors and two standing directly in the center. The two in the center face the doors while the other four face the conference room attendees.

Six additional Ceorfan move from the point of the wedge to protect an art niche. When I look at it using my magic, I can tell it's a second exit. These gargoyles guard the hidden door in the same manner as the ones guarding the large double doors.

The remaining twenty men, form up in an echelon formation to my right and left, forming wings behind me. Fitting that its wings and I'm a dragon. I'd need to ask Mega if he intended that imagery.

My Ceorfan are fast. Much faster than a human. They were in position before the President's security team had a chance to react. One particularly obnoxious member of the President's security tried to shove Mica out of the way. Mica didn't budge. He only turns and lifts the poor fellow up by the back of his jacket and sets him down further away. No comment is needed.

Angelis Castle, I guess trying to shortcut any further difficulties, reaches out his hand toward me. Then he pauses and tilts a look to Mica in question. Mica nods his permission to touch me, and the ambassador releases his held breath before taking my hand.

He says, "Your Majesty, please follow me to your seats."

"With pleasure, Ambassador."

The shuffle of paper and scrapping of feet and pens is loud to me here. I sit in the seat indicated, Dolo is already seated next to my place, waiting. He gives me a gentle smile. Mica stands behind me, and Mega and Kick sit on the other side of me.

Before the meeting begins, I speak, "Mr. President, honored attendees. I hope you understand, but after the events of yester-evening, my General Mega is taking control of my security. We're not trying to intimidate, nor is this a show of force. It is solely for our protection. Thank you for understanding."

Without comment, the meeting starts with a sharp hammer of the gavel.

The President speaks, "Your Majesty, General Mega, and Prince Consorts, My Cabinet, and I welcome you. Kendra, the awesome display of power as well as the restraint shown by you and your people yesterday was incredible. Only highly trained, highly disciplined warriors would have been able to act with the same restraint." When he finishes, the Ceorfan Guild receives a standing ovation.

We accept the accolades with what I hope is graciousness and dignity. Unfortunately, that was the end of the pleasantries. The first topic on their list is the formal acceptance of the Ceorfan into NATO.

"Mr. President, while I thank you for the kind invitation, on behalf of my people, I respectfully decline. I won't let my Guild be placed under the command of any foreign power for any reason. However, we'll be happy to help any country or organization which is in legitimate need of assistance."

I hope I come across as dignified as I'm hoping to be. But by the shocked looks on the other side of the table, I don't think I did. I tap my foot, and the jiggle helps calm my nerves.

"Queen Macbard, am I to understand you're turning down our invitation?" a clearly surprised Ambassador Castle asks.

"Yes, sir. You understood me correctly. Frankly, I'm surprised that the first official act you wish my people to perform is one of subordination," I say without a hint of malice.

"Queen Macbard, you're asking a great deal of this country. I don't see that offering to have a mutual protection pact is something that's out of line," the President says, his face reddening.

"I see where you're confused, Mr. President. All we're asking for is for the United States government to recognize the Ceorfan as a free and independent people. We aren't asking for wealth. Nor military might, we defend ourselves. We're willing to work toward a mutual protection agreement. But that agreement will never be exclusive. We will protect any country or people who are being abused, not just this one."

With that, the room erupts with several cabinet members visibly angry, saying, "Get out of our country if you don't like us," and "What, you think you're better than us?" Similar tone, different words from the other night when we were attacked.

There's little I can do except wait for the storm to pass and try to talk to them when the room is calmer.

I feel my donum begin to awaken. As I do, I know Jared is in trouble, and he's in Cueva Hallow.

I interrupt the room by quickly standing and moving to an open area. "Kick, open a portal to Cueva Hallow, I'll direct it to the correct location. Mr. President, there is an attack in an American town in southeastern New Mexico. I have fighters on the scene with my brother, and more are on the way. We have to go now. I trust we can finish this at a later time." With that, I turn and leap through the portal, transforming as I do.

44

ALL PUT AWAY

Dana

It's taken us two full days to get the majority of the treasure and the various documents out of its millennia-long hiding place and into the vaults beneath Navan. We probably could have done it faster, except Achor was in the cave city, overseeing the protections of the vaults. He's a stickler for detail. The old guru made sure that each portal opening into the vault is protected in front and behind. He didn't want a grain of dust entering that he hasn't personally vouched for and approved in triplicate.

In practice, this means Jericho puts in place a protection charm around the load of material coming into Navan. Then after the spell is in place, Peter opens a portal inside the bubble of the charm. On the other end, the guru then forces it to open inside another bubble of protection before pulling the entire load into the vault in Navan.

These spells are complicated to pull off inside a small area. But pulling one off, while leaving enough of a bubble to allow for a portal to be open inside it, is an incredible feat of magic.

"Hey Kino, this is the last load to portal into Navan. I'm ready if you are," I shout. My red brother-in-law goyle is holding up a hand waving, in a 'come to me' motion.

"Yes, we are almost ready. Standby," Kino pulses back his answer.

I find myself laughing. Why would I try to be heard above all the other noise by yelling, instead of sending a simple pulse? No matter how comfortable I am with being a dragon, I still haven't mastered the simple reflexes that every other Ceorfan has used for thousands of years.

Earlier, while I spoke with Achor about removing the last bit of treasure, he'd said it could prove to be problematic. Since, if the treasure is wholly removed, all of the charms will drop. Although, he's not sure how much can be taken away before that happens. So before the last bit of it is portaled out, I've ordered everyone except Jericho, Steen, and me to leave for Navan.

"Steen, please open the portal to Navan and let the rest of the team transit through. And thanks, my friend."

He nods yes and opens one.

Kino says, "Duke, I'm ready to move out. When this portal closes, it will be just the three of you remaining. Be safe, my brother." He steps through the portal into the treasure vault.

"Okay, Jericho, Steen, let's get this show on the road. Open the final treasure portal, then open one for us to skedaddle through. Remember, the final protections will fall... I don't know exactly how long it'll take, but it'll be soon. Let's get ready," I say.

Neither man speaks to me. Instead, they set to work preparing their final spells. That's when I hear the noise. I make my way to the entrance of the chamber as quickly as my long legs will take me. It's hard to believe a few days before it was full of treasure. As I step in front of the entrance, I'm hit with a spell that binds my muscles together. I can't move a muscle to save my life. Down the tunnel, I spot a mage with one arm and another just behind and beside him. It's Barat. I don't recognize the little turd.

They may have frozen me in place, but they can't keep me from pushing my dragon out. This time the morph is difficult. It feels more like when I first transformed. The pain is excruciating. Still, I know I have to push. Then it flows like melted butter, and in a flash, the morph is complete, and my muscles begin unbinding. Without waiting for a total transformation, I push the little amount of air still in my lungs out with dragon plasma. If I can't stop them with this release, I'm sunk. My muscles have freed themselves enough to take in a deep breath and halt the mages.

Fuck-rat and his shit-minion are forced to stop moving and cast their own protection. The look on their faces tells me neither of them expected to find a dragon waiting on them.

I hear, "Master, there must be three dragons. This isn't the same one who attacked your castle!" the short piece of shit yells to his fucking boss.

Damn right, there are three of us. But, one is all it takes to stomp you, bitches, to a pulp. As the last of my air is depleted, I see the two move aside, and hundreds of crafted rush through the tunnel straight for me.

I pulse to Jericho and Steen, "I'll hold 'em off. You two get out of here. That's an order!"

My body is now free. But in my dragon form, it does me little good in this tight confinement. I can move inches back and some to my left, but that is about it.

After taking in another deep breath, I let go of the biggest fire blast I've ever tried. Even in D.C., both Jared and I had to tone it down. Otherwise, we could have injured the protesters and the nearby onlookers. Had we tried, we'd have killed many of them with the force of our sound waves as they erupted from our combined roar.

"Duke of Stone, we will secure Navan and will return for you," Jericho pulses to me.

"No, I can get out of this hole on my own. I can fly back to Navan. Don't leave it unprotected under any circumstances. Tell Kendra I'm safe and not to come after me. I'll let her know if I need help with my donum," I say.

With that, the two mages step through a portal and disappear.

The Crafted keep coming down the tunnel. It feels like these little bastards are harder to kill than they used to be. Relief washes over me just knowing that my people are safe.

"Ass Rat, this is now between you, your turd friend, and me. Keep sending all of the Crafted pieces of shit you want. I'll flame them to ash, too," I scream into the torment unfolding in front of me.

Suddenly, I feel the earth begin to violently shake, and the tunnel collapses in front of me, forming a wall of rock between me, the evil mages, and their Crafted hoard. I end my plasma stream down the passageway. All I can see in front of me is a pile of burned and smoldering Crafted corpses and a glowing halo of the tunnel. Well, that's a bit of luck. I begin my transformation back into my human form so I can search for a way out.

Thump, bang! The entire cavern collapses on top of me.

45

HEATING UP

Jared

PETER AND I FAILED TO FIND SASS AT ANY OF THE HOMELESS shelters in Cueva Hallow that first night. Unwilling to accept failure as an answer, we return to Navan for a few hours of sleep and are back at the search the next morning.

We return to each of the shelters, this time, however, I have some of my security with me. Since I have personal protection who are either current or former members of a police department or the FBI, I let them lead the hunt inside the various shelters. Once again, we come up empty.

I take Peter to an area where a viaduct crosses a river, in the northern part of the town to eat and try to figure out a new strategy. He's never had a hamburger, and Cueva Hallow has some great local burger stops. We grab one from a joint on Main Street and are soon eating by the water.

Peter takes a bite of his burger and says, "I've never had anything like this before! I'm sure I wouldn't want to eat it every day. Still, this is a nice treat after what happened to us in Faery. We were lucky to have anything to eat at all, much less something so tasty," he adds, a bit more sorrowful at the end.

I shake my head then ask, "Peter, do you have any idea how Sass would try to hide?"

"Jared, I don't. She's a vivacious and energetic Fae. I believe she'd be where the energy is greatest," he answers, raising his head from his food.

I snap my fingers and say, "That gives me an idea! We're going to a local wing and burger joint. It's where lots of local youngsters like to hang out. Sass would fit right in with them."

When we arrive at the establishment, people are running out, screaming about monsters attacking. Peter and I look at each other briefly before running toward the building. We don't make it to the door before we see the first Crafted run from the building covered in blood. It's chasing a young mother who is holding her two small children while trying to escape.

Without pausing, Peter launches an explosive curse and destroys the Crafted with his spell.

I continue inside the business to see if there are any more of the monsters. What I find is a surreal nightmare made from the victims. Many of them are still alive, but there are more Crafted at a side door that's being held closed by surviving patrons. Their task is made more difficult due to the blood on the floor. They hold the door closed with as much power as possible. Their shoes slipping in the slickness on the floor, sliding them back a little at a time.

I turn around and pulse to Peter to get inside to help the wounded before I push out a donum call to Kendra, stressing that we need her in Cueva Hallow, right now! My transformation into my dragon form is fast now, and it happens within seconds. I take to the air and begin to burn the Crafted that are on the outside of the building. I conjure a storm, sans lightning to help make sure I don't inadvertently set the place alight.

After destroying the enemy robots at the door, I fly higher to see if I can find where the monsters came from. Across the street, I spy a retirement home. In front of the home, I see a portal open and Crafted pouring out. The portal closes before I can get to it. Then I notice it open again at a large store next door to the restaurant and another large group of Crafted pouring through.

I pause for a second before I realize the evil minions have been portaled into at least thirteen locations.

I shout, "Peter, get to Navan and bring help back. Bring anyone who doesn't have to torp, or can get a spell stone from Jericho."

"On my way," he says, and steps through a doorway in the air and is gone.

The Crafted are doing as much damage around them as possible. I recognize that the monsters aren't spreading out. They've portaled in and are now encircling a nearby strip mall. I'm guessing that's where they think Sass is. I can't just torch everything like I did in Faery. I have to be precise with my targets. Otherwise, I'll hurt and maybe kill innocent civilians.

By my estimation, there are a thousand of the vile beasts. My best plan is to start with the ones in the open. I don't have time to destroy them all, but I can cut them off. I start laying down dragon plasma fire on the nearby road in a dash, space, dash pattern. Then I set another set that is offset from the first in a space, dash, space pattern with an air gap of about ten feet. I'm hoping that the Crafted aren't intelligent enough to get through the maze while the humans can.

Gliding through the air, I'm able to complete the same process on three sides of the mall. The fourth side is a canal that is full of fast-flowing water. This whole process has taken me about a minute. That should keep the enemy contained in this area.

When I spot another portal open outside of the containment I've just built, my heart skips a beat. Then I see Kendra fly through with Mica and Kick right behind her. Another doorway opens on my other side. Through it, Kino leads the way, followed by Jericho, Steen, and Peter and a few other gargoyles who Jericho either gave a stone to or has spelled not to torp today. They also have brought a battalion of humans, more than five hundred men and women, who've been training to be Elite Warrior Guard for the Guild.

"Sis, I need you to go inside the restaurant and help the wounded. I haven't seen any of the Crafted make it into any of the other buildings," I ask.

She is our queen and, by all rights, should take charge. Since I have the most knowledge of the situation, she doesn't hesitate before landing with Steen to help tend to the wounded.

I can't be sure that Crafted haven't entered any other buildings. My voice is dragon loud when I shout, "Kino, Mica, and Peter keep these monsters from entering the other buildings. The rest of us are on cleanup duty. And be warned, everyone keep an eye out for either Bladriell or Barat. Let's get 'em!"

The Ceorfan mages are opening portals as fast as they can, scooping the Crafted up by the dozens and depositing them only the Creator knows where. I might want to find out where they're sending them soon. I use my dragon fire sparingly, mainly only to protect life and property. In reality, my main job now is to swoop down and grab civilians then land them on the other side of the boundary I've created with my flame.

Sirens begin to wail, the doppler effect making the pitch higher the closer they get. Firetrucks, police, ambulances, and men and women with guns start arriving at the site.

I'm delivering yet another person to the other side of the fire line when an over-eager person with a gun, takes a pot shot at me. Since the bullet will bounce off of me, the only real worry I have is if the idiot with the gun hits the person I'm trying to save. I make a point of landing my rescuee right on top of the guy who shot at me. And remembering Dana's chipped tooth, I kept my mouth shut the whole time. After noticing this, the rescue personnel get the hint that we're the good guys and start helping to save people instead of taking random shots at us.

By now, we've gained the upper hand in the battle. The teams I sent into the buildings are coming back out, and pulsing their reports.

Kino's the first one out. He looks my way and says, "Duke of Storms, the buildings on the north are secure. We have wounded humans. I've stabilized them with my healing songs and taken away as much of their pain as possible. I'm leaving two Elites here to protect this site, and I'm coming to help."

"Kino, Kendra's in the restaurant just to your south. Let's set up the triage there. Bring as many wounded as possible to that location," I pulse back, proud of how quickly our team is coming together to overcome the Crafted.

By now, I can't see any more monsters around the restaurant. So I open a rain shower over the road in that area to cool the flames so humans can assist with triage.

I see Kino take to the air, his great red wings pulling him gracefully higher. He's clutching a small child, one of the wounded who he's carrying to Kendra. As he climbs, I hear a shot ring out. In slow motion, I watch as Kino is hit and tumbles from the sky.

46

IMPOSSIBLE

Dana

I'm blind... well, maybe not, but I can't see anything. And I'm sure at least one of my legs is broken. Also, I'm pinned to the floor by a mountain of rubble. The smell of blood is strong. I feel it's pooled around my head and face. The grit and pebbles around me scratch my flesh. I must have been hit in the head by the falling rock when those fucking mages brought down an avalanche on me. Luckily for me, I was able to halt my transformation just long enough to build a hard shell of granite around me. Hours upon hours of practice made using my gifts as easy as writing a letter. No, I don't write letters. But, you know, I could if I wanted to.

The bump on my head must have really rattled my cage. It takes me several minutes to figure out I'm not really blind, it's just impossibly dark in this little shell of stone I've created. Using my dragon senses, I listen to my surroundings. I can't hear a thing, so I flick a finger through the air, and all the rock and debris around me are gone. I imagined it on the surface outside the city. One of these days I'll have to go see if it's where I think it is. If it is, I'll climb the mountain behind IlioIlion. It should be taller.

I try to put pressure on my leg, and there's no way in hell it's working. The bone is snapped clean in two. My leg is bent at a ninety-degree angle at the center of my shin. Fuck this, I don't have time for this shit. I'll morph full dragon again and heal it. Even in my morphed form, I can control the stone around me and pull the elements away, making a shaft big enough for my big teal body to fly out into the air.

I shoot into freedom in the night sky of the ancient city of the Ceorfan, and my skin crawls. Vibrations take my body, and I know both my brother and sister are in danger and need me. Holy fuck, I'm going to have to fly halfway around the world. Then a portal opens in front of me, and I fly through. Jericho is standing high up in the air in front of a portal he's opened for me. He's in the middle of what appears to be an all-out war.

"What the hell, old man. I leave you alone for a little while, and you've decided to play with fire?" I joke.

He looks at me like I've lost my marbles.

"Just joking Jericho, thank you for opening a portal for me right when I needed it. I think I lost my portal stone in my other suit. What's going on here, and where are my sister and brothers?"

"Now that, Duke of Stone, I have an answer for. Your brother is circling the area, saving humans. Your sister is inside that establishment, helping the wounded being supported by two of her consorts. Spar is in the capital city, torped being guarded by human Elites. And I have given a spell to Kino so that he doesn't have to torp today. In fact, see him there?"

We both look to the sky, and I'm grinning to see the red goyle saving a child. Then there is the pop of a gun, and he begins tumbling through the air toward the ground. The baby is secure in his arms as he hugs him tighter and wraps his wings around them both. I look for something to help and find a pine tree under him. I start to grow the tree and spot Jared whipping the wind up so that he can land softer on the branches. But the pair never make it to the tree.

The queen of the Ceorfan shoots like a shot toward her falling consort and catches him with little effort and carries his bloody body and that of the screaming child to safety. Okay... showoff!

I scan the area looking to see if I can help others. An elderly couple huddled on the ground in the distance caught my eye. There's a Crafted about to splatter them. I raise the dirt in front of the monster and tip him, and all the ones with him fall over. I fly to the couple at the same time. I put my wing over them so I can shield them from my flames. Then I torch the Crafted to cinders. When all the enemies are ashes, I help the people up and set them on a nearby bench to recover.

Whoosh, I feel the scraggly hair on the top of my teal dragon head heat up and glance up. There's my brother. I leap into the air and glide to his side.

Jared says, "Dana, good to see that you're okay. I was worried for a second, then you flew through Jericho's portal. I need you to focus on saving the humans. While you're at it, torch any Crafted you see. I'm looking for the mad fucker controlling them. I'm afraid he's evaded us again."

"Will do bro, I'm on it."

We spent the next several hours burning down all the Crafted and saving humans. Including the idiots with cameras that are videoing every second of this mess.

When we're finally finished, I go check on my, Sis. I morph back to my human shape and find her in a building that we used to call a restaurant in town. I say 'used to' because this building will have to be totally rebuilt.

Kino's lying, unmoving, beside her. Interestingly, I can't see a scratch on him showing he'd just been shot from the sky. I sit beside the red goyle and rest watching her, Kick, and Mica take care of the wounded of this city. Most of the people are walking away with few injuries. But some are out sleeping it off like the gargoyle beside me.

A buxom redheaded lady sits beside me. She's covered in ash and blood; obviously, she's been helping the wounded. I reach out a hand and say, "I'm Dana, can I help you?"

"Maybe Sweetheart, but I know I can help you. My name is Sass, and I know where Baratium of the Fae hides. If you want, I'll tell you."

47

JUST LIKE THAT

Kendra

WE'VE BEEN FIGHTING BARAT'S HORDE, SAVING THE BUSINESS area of Cueva Hallow, and, more importantly, it's people for the better part of the day. Almost everyone is healed. Unfortunately, we couldn't save everyone. There were a few who were killed by the Crafted before we were able to stop them. Luckily, it was only a handful. The rest of my consorts and I have been able to save many. The wounded are all revived and are being taken to their homes or set up in shelters. The governor called a state of emergency, and the President got FEMA involved. They are set up to help with lodging and food where needed.

Everyone is revived, except for my Kino. I'm sitting beside my baby brother and leaning on his shoulder for a second. I raise up and say, "I felt you needed help for a split second. Then you were here, kicking ass and taking names. Are you okay? What was going on?"

"I thought I was a goner, Sis. Barat and a short sawed of shit came to the treasure room and tried to kill me. They collapsed the entire mountain on top of me. Luckily, I've been practicing with my gift. So,

I was ok. I'll give you details as soon as we are all together. But suffice it to say, I singed Rat's butt, and he ran. I don't know where, but I think we can find out. I need you to meet someone. Sis, please meet Sass. She knows how to find Barat."

He points to a lady sitting close to his other side. I've seen her helping us with the wounded. I hold a hand out to her, and we shake. I get a tingle of magic. Since this woman's magic works even in the human realm, she must be a succubus/siren. As I read her, though, I realize she has good intentions.

"It's a pleasure to meet you, Your Majesty."

"Sass, you don't know how happy I am to meet you and to ask for your assistance with Baratium. We're finally closing in on him. Maybe with your information, we could get the clues to finally end that...," I pause, unwilling to risk alienating her by disapproving.

"Fucking asswipe, I believe are the words you are searching for," she finishes for me with a devious grin that only a world-wise woman could pull off.

"Right!" I answer as a portal opens, and several Fae race through, led by Dr. Ogman. They have no hesitation in their decision making. Dr. Ogman begins his triage quickly and efficiently.

I've already tended to the most seriously wounded. Most of them had horrible injuries such as severe head trauma, missing limbs, terrible broken, and crushed bones. Most of the cases, I was only able to cut myself and spread my healing blood across them before running to the next injured. All of these people still need medical assistance. That is what the good doctor, along with the other Fae doctors who volunteered to help the humans.

It takes hours to finally help all of the injured and see that their injuries are fully healed. But, to be honest, it wouldn't have taken that long if I didn't have to keep explaining my blood would *not* contaminate anyone, it'll only heal them. The human doctors wound up working as assistants to the Fae doctors. Their job is to prevent anyone from succumbing to their injuries before I could get to them to help.

In the end, the humans begin to believe in my magical healing powers. Soon they beg me to come to the hospital to help. I agree that I can go and spend an hour or two, but they must be prepared for me to leave on short notice.

After working out the details, we agreed I'd return after I rest. I'll portal into the hospital after hours and attend the most critically sick and injured. The medical staff from the hospital also promised to keep the details of my gift a secret and all trips to the hospitals. My gift of persuasion is kickin' it.

48

TURNING IT AROUND

Walter

For the second time in my life, my heart has been ripped from my chest. Short pants of breath are all I can capture as I do my best to regain control. My body is shaky for lack of food. Right now, I'm subsisting on a volcano of white-hot vengeance.

I sit in my empty laboratory and stare into space, reflecting on my life. I knew long ago that I was fighting on the wrong side. In my defense, I'd been hurt by humans long ago. They killed my David, my life, and reason for existence.

My lover was a kind man who never hurt even the smallest bug. They singled him out and killed him because he refused to fight in a war that pitted families and friends against each other. After that day, I was prepared to lose everything to see the humans destroyed. My love would have never approved. Now my sister Trix has paid the ultimate price for doing the right thing. She was the last of any love left for me in this world.

This time I won't fight for revenge. All of the retribution I've poured out on others has gained me nothing. It's cost me the other of the two most beautiful souls to enter my pathetic life. No, I won't fight for revenge. This time, I'll fight for the right reasons. This time I'll fight for the right to have David and Trix greet me in the afterlife. This time I fight for the most potent force I've ever known. I fight for the reason the Ceorfan Queens sacrificed themselves. I fight for love.

I can't atone for the carnage I've caused in this thousand-year war. I can never atone for the cruelty, malice, hatred, and murder I've visited upon the gargoyles, humans, and even Fae. I also know I'll never survive the final battle, no matter that I wish to help the Ceorfan now. They have every reason to want me dead. I agree with all of their rationales.

However, I want to see my former master destroyed. Today I'll put aside my ill-feeling for my own actions as well as the likely effect on my immortal being. I'll use the one asset I have that no others have, my knowledge of Baratium Mezacain.

The Ceorfan Guild will never accept me if I attempt to tell them what I know. No, they're more likely to kill me on the spot. And if I'm to help save the Ceorfan and human race, I need to start by saving the most essential Ceorfan of all, Queen Kendra Macbard.

One of my many talents is shape-shifting. I'm so adept at it that I can stand in a room with my own family, and they would never recognize me if I have shifted into a new form. In fact, I have done so many times. It is one of the tools we used the day we destroyed the Ceorfan training school. I used this to a significant effect on myself and many other like-minded mages.

If I'm to save the Ceorfan queen, I must first find someone who will willingly take the burden of Barat's destruction. I won't trick anyone into this act. Killing that evil mage comes with a price. He has placed a spell on himself that won't dissipate with his death. In fact, it's activated upon his death. His death will put a curse on his killer. Whoever kills him, like me, must commit to this action knowing there are consequences. The thoughts swirling through my mind sparks the beginning of a plan. I start off on the road to the tavern in the little

Fae town where I'm sure to gather intel for my goal, the Friendly Badger.

It's not cold here, but there is a breeze that whips up my wizard's robes around my legs as I walk. Somehow I missed out on walking here. I arrived without noticing a single landmark, until this minute. The smell of bread and stew cooking wake me up to my surroundings, and my stomach growls.

I can't go in the tavern until I'm disguised, so I walk around between two buildings where it's darkest and shift. The look I change into is a last-minute decision, and I transform into the gargoyle who I saw with Trix when she was killed. She called him, Spar.

I like it in this shape. I move to the edge of the building and pause to listen. I've heard several reports of gargoyles hiding in the shadows of Faery. Maybe one of them will be friendly with this man I'm pretending to be and give the information of Barat's location to the Ceorfan queen.

My cover story is that I'm staying in Faery while I try to find Trix's killers and bring them to justice. I know it seems thin, but the ones who frequent the seedy bar have never been accused of being the brightest stars in the sky. I enter the establishment, brushing by the rough wood of the door, and find a seat.

My table is in one of the darker corners of the bar. I order a drink and food and begin to watch. I watch everyone who enters and leaves. I cast short term tracking spells on the ones who interest me. The spells will dissipate if I decide to not follow up on the contact. There are only two who I feel even slightly interested in by the time the bar closes.

The best thing for my safety is if I ensure I'm the last patron to leave. As I settle my bill with the troll owner, he asks, "Why have you returned? I don't want any more trouble." He has a peculiar frightened air about himself, constantly twitching his eyes to the darkest part of the bar.

I take a chance and grab him by his greasy shirt then slam him face-first into the bar. I don't believe he could have been more surprised than if a fairy had popped out of the top of my head and kissed him on his greasy face. After holding him down for a bit, I stand him back up before I pull him close to me and ask, "I'm looking for Walter Deveros. Tell me where he is, and the rest of your teeth will stay inside your mouth and not embedded in your bar."

"Please, I-I d-d-don't know. He-he-he's been miss-missing for several d- days," the troll stammers.

I find it interesting that my stomach is turning with the acts of violence, mild as they are, that I'm committing against this troll. Before I leave, I'll spell him into a healing trance and also force him to forget all about this attack.

"Fine, when you have any information, you will get it to me. Won't you?" I ask with genuine politeness in my question, sorry for my actions.

"You- you sh-should also ch-ch-check with Vincent," as he points with his chin to the dark corner he was eyeing earlier.

I turn and see nothing. Then, as if emerging from a fog bank into the light of day, a tall, muscular yellow-gold gargoyle with a long mohawk leans forward into the light. He remains seated, a large tankard of brew in his hand.

I make my way to his table and ask, "You're Hewn, aren't you? Never mind, it doesn't matter. My name is Spar. I am Queen Macbard's consort, and I'm looking for Walter Deveros." I pause here waiting for the gargoyle to ask me to sit, or otherwise acknowledge my statement. Nothing.

"Alright, you're the big silent type. At least hear me out. Baratium killed Deveros's sister when she was helping me escape. I owe her a debt I can't repay due to her murder. I want to see if I can convince Walter to turn on Baratium. Maybe, he thinks he owes his sister a debt too. I'm hoping Walter will spill some information on how to kill his master. I also think Walter knows the details of a rumored curse that Baratium has cast upon himself," I say, trying for a long shot at getting his help.

As soon as I referenced the curse, Vincent sits up and finally makes eye contact with me. I have him!

"Have you heard of such a curse," I try to draw the goyle into a conversation.

"Yes, but only rumors and innuendo," he intones.

"I'll tell you what I know if you tell me what you know," I respond.

"Nothing more than if he's killed the person who kills him accepts the curse," he finishes with a small shrug of his muscular shoulders.

"Interesting. I haven't heard that part. All I've been told is the curse is called kýrios psychís or soul master," I say to him with what I hope is honest confusion. "Have you ever heard of the spell?" I ask.

"Yes," he says before leaning back into the shadows and ignoring any further attempts at communication.

I take a stone from my pocket and sit it on the table in front of him. If you hear anything or want to help our people, you can find me with this stone. It'll bring you to me anytime, anywhere. Be sure to know your timing. If you show up where I am during the daylight, you'll torp instantly on arrival. That could be dangerous, depending on where I am at the time." Vincent doesn't move a muscle.

I leave the tavern hoping against hope that he has a scrap of loyalty for his people and will give them the information I just funneled him.

49

SACRIFICE

Kendra

As I sit here in the building we've allotted for healing the residents of Cueva Hallow I rest and tend to my red gargoyle. Ever since I've learned to control my magic, I've learned the way of fate is far more interesting than I had previously understood. Thankfully, fate is working for us. Sass is the very person we've been looking for, and for her to show up offering her help is proof. Thank the Creator for small favors. Even if this one could prove to be huge.

"Sass, if you know who I am. You already know that I plan to kill Barat," I say.

"I'll do whatever I can to help you, Your Majesty. Trix is dead, and I intend to see him hung by his balls for it. She was my best friend--my sister really. What do you want to know?"

"My plan is to destroy him and rid the earth of his minions. That includes Walter Deveros, his second in command. It also includes the other rat, that my consort Kick says, is named Bladriell. Do you think you could speak in a large meeting with several heads of state and share the places you know they could be hiding?"

"I'll do it with relish, My Lady. I'm sure I know where the rats are hiding. You know Walter loved his sister. There's a chance he might turn. The Crafted could be useful too, depending on who's controlling them."

"Turn Walter? That's an interesting thought. I hadn't considered it, but you're right. The problem will be getting the chance to talk to him to turn him. As far as the Crafted are concerned, I've tried to think of a way we could use them for good; but, there's a big risk. They were created in the vilest, evil way I can imagine. Evil is magically imbued in them during their creation. Because of that, they'll remain an evil construct and a danger to humans, Ceorfan, and Fae." I glance at Dana, and he agrees with a nod and wink.

Kick and Peter come over to us and sit on the floor. With the emergency over, all the steam is out of me.

Kino stirs with a groan.

"Beloved, you saved me again. I love you. How is the babe?" he asks.

With a soft grin I answer, "He's with his mother and healthy as can be. I love you too, Rockstar. The minute you were shot, I felt it, like it was me who got the bullet."

"In that case, I'm going to have to limit getting hurt in the future," he says, moving to sit up.

"I agree, no more getting hurt. In fact, none of you get hurt. I think if you do, we have the resources to heal pretty fast now though. Also, I want y'all to meet Sass. She's going to help us nail Barat's skinny ass."

Peter bows his head in her direction and takes her hand, saying, "Sass, thank you for helping today. Will you consider taking a walk with me? I'd like some time alone with you."

She smirks a knowing grin and gets to her feet, smoothing her clothes. Even I have to admire her beauty as she jiggles in all the right places. They leave. It doesn't surprise me when the blonde mage takes her hand. My dark one helps me to my feet just before the sun sets.

Mica, Jared, and Steen drag into the room. They look high on the energy of the battle. My partner is strutting, and my brother is patting him and the bald mage on the back. They all have shit-eating grins as they walk up.

Jared says, "We did it. We cleared out all the rabble that was here. I hate to say that I saw no sign of the master or his flunkies. I have no idea how he got away or where he went."

I reach for Mica's hand, and he closes the gap between us, just managing to squeeze through the others without bumping them out of the way.

I feel my people untorping. Even at a distance where they are in Navan and around the globe the magic is strong. I arch my back and reach for Kick, and Kino to share the energy while my blonde Ranger has his hand on my back.

Dana has his head down and soaking in the feeling too. It must be a dragon thing. Jared's eyes open big as he soaks up the energy. The power is fantastic, and the battle rage needs a bit of release. My brothers and I roar into the night sky, not caring who hears us. I shrug at them when the surge is over, and they stretch and agree that it's a wonderful feeling.

A blue portal opens in front of us, and Spar shoots into the room, followed by the Ceorfan, who were in D.C. when we left. My blue goyle pats all of us, checking us out then says, "Even torped I could tell there was something wrong. What happened here, babe?" he asks with the practiced restraint taught to the special operators in the U.S. Military.

"Can we just go home, and I'll tell you there?" I ask.

"Yes, let's go now," he answers, calm exuding from his aura.

My dark angel opens the portal for us, and we step through into my chambers. Elmer chirps and flies to me, lands on my shoulder, and quickly attaches himself to my shirt. I smooth his soft head, happy. He feels like home.

My cute blue goyle busies himself by pouring coffee. The chefs, always professional, have put out a tray of fruit and cheese for their queen. Knowing my likes, they've also laid out jalapeno cheese bagels and donuts on the table. Spar brings me a cup of coffee.

I sit on the couch with Mica's big self sitting with me and Kick on the arm of the sofa touching me. Kino is in front of me in a chair. His long legs stretched out in front of him, and his right foot is just touching my leg. Spar pulls another chair close and sits with his foot touching my other leg.

There's a pulse at the door from Peter and Sass, when I send a welcome pulse they enter and take a chair at my table. Sass sits on Peter's lap. Then the redhead notices the drinks and food and gets up to get something.

I say, "Guys, we need a plan. Sass will tell us where to find Barat and his followers. When we know where they are, and we have a solid plan to attack, I want them dead. I'm sorry if that sounds too harsh. But we can't allow another attack like the one they pulled off today. All of you have more training in planning these kinds of missions than I do. I really need your input."

Mica is first to answer and says, "Princess, you're right. Let's convene the High Guild and speak with General Mega. He has the most experience in developing tactical missions. After we have our plan prepared, then we can meet with TASS. They'll probably help us. Right now, the American government doesn't seem too keen on helping us. After TASS is on board, we go."

Spar says, "I agree, let's get this planned and executed ASAP."

Kino has his tablet in his hands. He's been concentrating on it, seemingly lost in the digital world it holds. Without taking his eyes from the tablet, he says, "I agree with one addition. The media needs to be involved on some level, look at this." He sits his tablet on the stand on the table and spins it so we can see it. We all squeeze together to watch what has gotten his attention.

As we watch, we see a replay of as the news media are calling it, the Battle for Cueva Hallow. The first are shots from various cell phone cameras before the more traditional cameras arrive.

He turns up the volume, and we hear, "Here is yet another video of Jared Macbard transforming into a dragon just before burning the monstrosities trying to get inside the restaurant, to a crisp. Mr. Macbard isn't the only hero of the day, but he sure made a splash at the beginning of the battle. All this and he's rich too. I guess it must be true about a dragon and his gold.

"But Sylvia, the most amazing aspect of today's battle, is, with all of the horrible injuries suffered, only a handful of people died. Moreover, according to the on-scene doctors, there were horrific injuries healed by the former Federal Park Ranger and Ceorfan Queen, Kendra Macbard. I will have much more on today's amazing rescues, including one from the mother of a small child who was rescued by the red gargoyle Kokino Magnus. He was shot by a, let's call her, an over-enthusiastic person. This is Ralphie Montoya reporting for Channel Sixteen News. Back to you in the studio, Sylvia."

"It looks to me like we've already won the publicity war. I wouldn't be surprised if you don't hear back from the President with an apology pretty quickly," Mica says, grinning from ear to ear.

My tablet rings. I look at it as my man is finishing and turn it around for everyone to see the graphic, 'Ambassador Castle.'

"Yes, Ambassador, how may I help you?" I ask as politely as my mom taught me.

There's a short pause while I listen to the man.

"Ambassador, we've been trying to tell you we're protectors. That's who we are. That's why we can't join your NATO."

His response is short, and I find myself shaking my head.

"Oh, thank you, but for now, we can't return to D.C. We have to make sure this doesn't happen again in another part of the world," I say seriousness in my tone.

I should turn this on speaker, but instead, I'm going to cut it off short until we have a plan.

"If we can find a way, we would be honored to fight along with the brave men and women of the United States military. Sir, this may happen very quickly. Unless your men are with us, I don't know how we..."

He actually interrupts me.

I interrupt right back, "Yes, Ambassador. Thank you, and please give the President the thanks of my people." At the end of the conversation, my mouth hangs open. I press end, my eyes wide. I'm pretty sure I'm breathing too fast. I put a hand on my chest, my heart is racing.

"Beloved, what did he say? We only heard your side?" Kino asks.

"He said the president guy says he agrees to everything the Queen asked for," a nonchalant Sass says with a shrug of her shoulders. Then looking around at all of the quizzical faces, she finishes, "What? Fae have great hearing." As if this simple explanation didn't put an outsized exclamation mark on the day's recent events.

That breaks the dam. I laugh, and I can't stop laughing. That gets the others going until it's now the laughter that's making everyone laugh even harder.

When I finally regain control, I add on to Sass's explanation, "The White House is taking point on spearheading our PR campaign. The President wants no preconditions from us.

"He even apologized, via Castle, for not believing me when I said we only want to help people. He thought it was only a negotiation strategy. He also said he'll introduce a bill in the House, which will set aside a large corner of southeastern New Mexico as a sort of autonomous zone for the Ceorfan. Oh, and he wants to send us special forces to fight under our banner until Baratium is destroyed."

Spar says, "I never thought it'd be so fast. See what a little power will get ya, bro?" He punches my Ranger in the arm and backs away.

Mica answers, "Shut the fuck up, blueberry. You know Kendra can do anything she sets her mind to."

Kino adds, "On that note, I'll call the High Guild for an emergency meeting."

The rest of us all say, "Now," at the same time. The laughing starts again.

50

IT'S SET

Kendra

THE HG WASTES NO TIME IN GETTING TO THE ALLODIUM SO WE can start the meeting. Everyone's here, my brothers, the Hewn representatives, Sass, Mega, many of the Elites, both warriors and mages. Even Achor is here sitting beside Dana. Elmer, left with the other bats for dinner.

What I wouldn't give to have stayed in my room and have a romp with my consorts. I guess the rumor about battle rage inciting lust is correct, at least this time. I feel exhilarated.

The chefs have outdone themselves with the buffet. I follow my nose to the feast and fill a plate before sitting. I notice that Jared and Dana have moved their chairs and added more for my consorts. Mica sits to my right and Spar to my left with Kino beside him and Kick on the other side. They're impressive.

I pulse to Clifton, and he starts the meeting without questions. When he is ready he gives the floor to Duke Findare, our new ambassador to the American government. Fin informs the members about the President's intentions. He asks Jericho to provide a visual from a few newscasts from around the world.

The ancient wizard gets up gracefully, using a small yellow stone placed in the palm of his left hand, he chants a spell. Light bursts from the gem, and in the middle of the floor, scenes of dragons, gargoyles, and mages saving people playout for the HG. We look terrifying and beautiful at the same time. I can't imagine anyone messing with us on purpose. It's no small wonder why some are scared of the Ceorfan people. That battle proves what a madman Barat is and how willing he is to hurt others. The Royal Mage stops singing, and the show ends. He bows with a wistful lift of his lips, takes his seat returning the floor to the good Duke.

Like a pro, Fin explains, "Our people can be seen in public now. However, we must remain on guard and take it slowly. Humans need time to get used to us. No large groups, we need to stress to everyone to travel with at least one partner. General Mega, do you have anything to add?"

Mega says, "Yes, I'll be stationing guards, but if gargoyles torp in plain sight, we will have to have them guarded until I'm sure that humans aren't out to damage or destroy them."

Kick says, "I'll make sure that you have someone from the Warrior Mage Guard for that. It would also help if you can add human Elite Warrior Guards to back them up. We're building our numbers, but as it is, we remain few, as you know."

Mega answers, "I can do that. The humans who are training are loyal and wish to work with us."

My General sits, and Findare says, "My Queen?"

I stand, walking as I speak. "I have a few things I'd like to add before ending this meeting. We have a new member for one. Some of you might remember, Achor. He was a trusted General of my grandmother's and welcome here. His devotion to our people has given us endless resources."

Achor stands and asks, "My Queen, if it pleases you, I have additional information for you and this august body."

I nod for him to continue.

"My friends, how I have longed to stand with you as a citizen of this great community. I was called General by Queen Helen. When she fell, I was charged by Queen Leta with designating and designing hiding places for the Ceorfan treasures as well as the dragon treasures. With the help of our queen, her brother, Duke Dana Macbard, and many of our friends, we have returned the Ceorfan treasure to its rightful owners... the Ceorfan people. This is the single most significant hoard of wealth, and as such, I was left to protect it.

"My Queen, there are more treasure hoards. None are nearly so large. However, they should be collected and returned here as soon as you find it convenient," he indicates he's finished speaking by adding a deep bow. When he stands again, he stares directly at me with the biggest smile I've seen. Obviously, he's quite proud of the ability of the traps and disguises he designed so long ago that still function remarkably well protecting our valuables.

The entire chamber stands. A round of pulse power goes through the room toward the ancient general. He ducks his head, humbled and happy.

I say, "Achor, for your tireless sacrifice over the many centuries, your deeds will be added to the Halls of History. Your work will not be forgotten."

More pulses and applause until the humble General is seated.

"Achor, one question, are any of the other treasures guarded by Ceorfan who we should go and bring home?" I ask.

"There was one other, My Queen. I'm sure of her death. She was protecting the dragon treasure, your treasure. I'm sure you have already had a vision regarding this treasure, haven't you?" he finishes with another smile. The wink to Dana tells me that the two of them have been talking.

"I'm happy to know you're so well informed. Thank you."

I continue in a different direction, "Clifton, please send a note to Jamie Serge. I need clothes and formal wear. We need to continue our tour of the world to make allies and see where we can be of help. I need to dress correctly, and he's the one I want."

He holds up a green finger in the air and asks, "I'll do that, Your Majesty. Also, do you have specific Ceorfan you want in the ambassadorial positions around the world, or is this a decision for the HG?"

"That's definitely a job I hope I can delegate to the HG. I'd like to ask Duke Findare if we can change your position and you'll take the position of Secretary of State? Please, to stand in leadership over the Ceorfan ambassadors? Also, after yesterday, I need more generals around the globe. Krag, will you please fill that supervisory position and work with Mega. I need you both to promote and enlarge our military. In fact, since Achor was my great-grandmother Helen's general, please add him as a general. You three plan and take charge of our defenses."

When all the men agree, I say, "Now, let me introduce Sass to you, Generals. She's going to help us blow Barat's ass out of the water." I hold my hand palm up in her direction. Everyone stares at her waiting for further explanation.

Sass begins, "Queen Kendra Macbard, and the High Guild. I want to thank you for taking me in and keeping me under the protection of the Ceorfan people. I pledge fealty to you, My Queen. I want you to know I feel more welcome in your city than I've ever felt in Faery. They always treated me as a curiosity and never as a person who might actually have feelings," she says and turns to stare directly at Peter.

"My Queen, I have been in the castle of the enemy. This gave me many opportunities to overhear his plans. You'll find Barat, his remaining minions, and whatever Crafted he has left at Ilioiliom on the new moon. He has a spell that will reinvigorate all of those he murdered that day a millennia ago. The day he started the Mage Wars. The ones he will rise won't be alive, and their souls can't be returned. He'll be able to command their reassembled bodies to fight for him though," her voice rising to be heard over the growing din of angry shouts and curses.

She raises her voice and adds, "My Queen, Baratium has also placed a curse on himself. It'll permeate the one who kills him. I don't know what the curse is. I imagine it would be terrible for the one who chooses to kill that brutal pile of bat shit. I'm sorry, My Queen, for using rough language in your presence and to the bat shit I just denigrated."

The joke gets a smattering of laughs. Nevertheless, the mood of the room has changed. It was full of joy only a few minutes ago, then anger swept that away. News about the curse sent morbidity of shock and loss spreading across the room. I smother my feelings about the evil mage, leaving only a sense of loss. Sass sits, her hands in her lap, and her head down as if she caused the problem.

"Sass, thank you for the information," I say, displaying only positive emotions. My people need me as a Queen to show hope. I don't have all the answers for what the Faery lady shared with the members, but I can show strength and not despair.

"Everyone, I feel what you're feeling. I don't want anyone to focus on the curse. My consorts and I will find a solution to it. I already have the beginnings of a plan. Bear with us while we develop it. Trust me. We haven't failed you yet, and this will not be an obstacle to end that streak," I pause and eyeball each person forcing them to look at me to understand the proof of my conviction.

"Let's move to our next speaker," I say.

Krag is stiff in place near the end of the table. It is part of his bearing that gives me the hint he wishes to speak. I give him the floor.

He holds himself tall with his shoulders back then speaks, "My people have asked to return here and will be arriving tonight if permission is granted. I need to know where to put them up. I also have one man, My Queen, who wishes to speak with you alone. He's private. I wouldn't tell you about him if I didn't trust him. He's one of my best spies. Is there somewhere you could meet with him?"

I answer, "Yes, Krag, I'll meet with him at a pool in the hills close to here in an hour. Spar, will you give him the coordinates? Gem, do you mind assigning housing to the Ceorfan Hewn who arrive later? Please, make up your team as you see fit."

My blue consort nods as the Hewn leader walks over to him, and with their heads together, they have a discussion in a quiet, non-intrusive way.

Gem answers, "Of course, it will be my pleasure."

I add to the list, "Kick, will you go get Jimmy, Vanessa, Arden, and Glenn from the capitol? It's more than safe in Cueva Hallow now. Bring them all to Navan if they want to come. They can go on the grand tour with us too. Let it be their choice, though."

He says, "Yes, now, in fact. I'll return as soon as possible." He's gone with a little breeze.

I'm finished and want to go meet the spy in the hills. I sit, and the Count ends the meeting.

While everyone disperses, Mica whispers in my ear, "We're going with you to meet the spy, you know."

"I know."

51

VINCENT

Kendra

As soon as Kick returns from Washington DC, he and my other consorts change into dark gear. We want to get to our location with as little disturbance as possible. My consorts want to be present and will be ready to react if needed. Unlike children, they want to be neither seen nor heard. For this mission, we've decided that flying will give them the best opportunity to remain unseen.

We leave at the launching point just outside the cave's entrance. The desert night air has turned slightly cooler, making it the perfect weather for a vigorous flight to the hole in the wall where I agreed to meet Vincent.

This place holds many fond memories for me, as I'm sure it does for Spar as well. It's a little cave with a spring and an opening to the sky. My love and I came here once to get to know each other again.

We arrived quickly. The scent of wild jasmine is thick in the air. The green leaves and yellow blooms of the bushes rustle in the gentle zephyr. This open cave-like area is far enough off road that the only noise is made by small animals scurrying from one hiding spot to another. In the distance, a coyote's call is answered by its pack.

Kick moves in a circle covering any noise, breathing, coughing... with magic. He doesn't try to hide the sound I create, but he is thorough with the men.

The guys blend into the surrounding scenery. Even though, I saw each one's hiding place, if I wasn't bound to them, I wouldn't have any idea where they are. I sit on a large boulder beside the water and wait, but not for long.

"As dark as it is, and as stealthy as you are, I'm the Queen of the Ceorfan. I know you're there. Come talk to me, please," I ask.

Out of the night steps, a magnificent gargoyle. He reminds me of Spar in size, but he's golden. His mohawk isn't messy like my lover's. His is neat and tall. His aura is full of purple and orange. That means he's a visionary, full of spiritual awareness and adventurous, but there's more. He's highly focused and loyal with touches of pale yellow and cream. I trust him and am proud he's one of my people.

He responds, "They said the Queen is beautiful. Some said your beauty rivals that of your great-grandmother, Helen. For once, it seems the rumors are true. I can sense the power of your magic. Is there any magic you don't hold?"

"I'm sure there is. I'm just getting to know how to use it, so who knows. My name is Kendra." I see he's surprised by the lift of his brow that I gave him my name and don't intend to be called by my title here.

"Kendra, my name is Vincent. Thank you for meeting me. I don't trust the opinion of most people. Krag is one who I place a great deal of trust in. He said I should pledge my allegiance to you. I've taken the time to learn about you, but hadn't made up my mind. I have now. Yesterday, you, your brothers and our people saved that city. I was there, watching. I would have stepped in if I had to but I wasn't needed and I need to stay out of the limelight. The events of that day will live with me. I learned a lot about you. Far more than I could've learned by talking to you or listening to people who know you. You earned my respect. More than that, you have earned my obedience. Kendra, I name you, My Queen, from this day and for all the days to come. I'm your gargoyle in this life and beyond."

He kneels in front of me, and I put a hand on his head, recognizing the old phrase. I give him a pulse and say, "I accept your fealty as one my people and will return the debt with a covering in times of harm."

As the magic of the promise ripples through the air, he stands. I pat the space beside me on the boulder. When he sits, he spills all the information he knows about Barat.

I listen then ask, "Vincent, my general, Mega, can speak mind to mind, and so can I now. Do you mind if I connect to you this way? It'll be easier than a clandestine meeting and will keep you safer."

"That's powerful magic. I've seen it used long ago but not in centuries. I'd like that, please try."

I don't wait and briefly concentrate before speaking to him by tele-speak, *"Can you hear me?"*

He smiles at me and says, *"Yes, how far away will this work?"*

"I'm not sure yet, but we can practice. I want you to meet my consorts if that's alright?"

"Yes, but when we leave here, we need to act like strangers. No talking except this way, if you agree."

I say out loud, "Hey guys, will you come to meet Vincent?"

The first of my consorts to get to him is Spar. In fact, he pushes past Mica to get to the new goyle first. He sticks his arm out and says, "Hello, I'm Spar. I doubt you remember me, but we saw each other in The Friendly Badger in Faery."

Vincent hesitates a moment before takes Spar's forearm in his hand with Spar doing the same. Spar lets go while Vincent retains a tight grip on Spar's. "What do you mean that I wouldn't remember you? We had a lengthy conversation about Walter. How could you forget that? Are you trying to fool me, or our Queen?"

The implied threat, directed at my man, causes my donum to

spark. There's something here, and it's important. I need to find it fast before we lose the trust of this golden goyle.

"What do you mean a conversation? We have never spoken. And for your little threat, I'm not the one you should be threatening. We should be on the same team. If you've got something to say, say it. None of this dancing around the subject," Spar says as he shakes a massive arm free from Vincent.

It's interesting to see these two square off against each other. They're both massive goyles. I'm not going to impose my will. I need these two to work through their issues and fast.

"Mega, can you hear me?"

"Yes, Edling."

My general and I have been practicing with the nous-fārī, mind-speakers. We have gotten to the point that we can communicate no matter the distance between us. I ask, *"I need you to talk to your son, father to son, and get him to calm down. That father figure in you is required to help him quiet, and soon. We've met the Hewn nomad at the hole in the wall. He thinks he knows Spar, but Spar is sure they've never spoken. It's starting sparks between the two. Will you please guide him? We need to find out what this nomad is talking about."*

No sooner had I finished tele-speaking to Mega, Spar takes a step back and says, "I understand you're concerned. I can tell you for a fact that you and I have never spoken. Please, let's figure out who you did speak to."

Vincent immediately relaxes, his shoulders rolling forward ever so slightly, his upturned chin, dropping. "Please, let me see your hair in the light?"

I make a small fire with magic to aid them. The reflection of the light off the sides of the rock walls gives quite a lot of light.

With a question hanging in the air, Spar moves nearer to the flames before turning to face Vincent.

"Do you color your hair?" a now clearly confused spy asks.

I answer for my goyle, "Spar has never colored his hair. That's all-natural."

The newcomer says, "My friends, we have a problem then. Because I spoke with a Spar look-alike in Faery earlier. He was trying to talk me into getting Walter to turn on Baratium.

"I have a photographic memory. You look very much like the person I met, but the differences, while subtle are there. The most obvious is your hair color. Yours is golden while the other's was more an ash blonde color," he ends, hoping that he's said enough.

Kick, who has been sitting without a word, speaks, "It must have been Walter Deveros in disguise. Hey big guy, were you seen in the daylight? If not, the coloring of your hair would have been an easy oversight on the old shifter's part. I can't say for certain, because our captors kept us drugged on opium, but some things from my captivity makes more sense now. Walter might have the ability to transform into other forms. There were times when I was sure Barat was gone, but then I'd see him. It must have been another way of controlling us! That has to be it," Kick explains.

My turn to get involved, I ask, "Vincent, what did this person, who we assume is Walter, tell you?"

"It wasn't a long conversation. Mostly it was a conversation about turning Walter into an asset for you. He said the curse is called kýrios psychís, or soul master. I don't know what it means. He gave me this stone to reach him though," The gold gargoyle pulls the stone out and hands it to me. Before I can take it, Kick grabs it.

"Darling, if this is from the old mage, it could be a clever way to kill or injure you. Let me check it before you handle it," Kick warns.

"You're right, but I read the stone for spells when I saw it. The only spell on that stone is one for communication," I say, placing a hand on his shoulder.

He sighs and says, "I should have known you looked. I just want to keep you safe."

"If it makes you feel better, you hold it for now." I lean into him and give him a kiss for showing me love.

"Well, guys, we now need a solution to this problem. Vincent, thank you for your help. But, my consorts and I need to work through this in private." My expression while friendly is an invitation for him to leave. Without a word, he bows and exits the hole in the wall flying into the night sky.

When he's safely out of earshot, I pivot to face my goyles.

Mica begins by saying, "We have to find that crazy old mage. If he turns on Barat, he could help us find a way around the curse. We can finally be rid of that piece of Fae waste," Mica says, putting a clear exclamation point on the earlier conversation.

"So, how do you think–" Kino starts before Kick cuts him off.

"Kendra, I believe if anyone goes, it should be Peter, Steen, and me. We know that sad asshole best. The three of us are recovered enough to support one another. I believe each of us can defeat him one on one without his helper there to freeze us. The three of us combined can defeat anything he could possibly throw at us, including a trap. This plan also has the advantage of not sending another gargoyle in who could get captured and used," my mage glances at Spar before returning to my gaze. "This is the best option, honestly."

"He makes a valid point, and I can't find fault with his logic or the premise for his prescribed course of action," my rockstar states with a nod of approval thrown in.

The others quickly agree too. After thinking about it, I say, "Okay, Dark Angel, you're a go. I want to hear your plan for meeting with Walter before you go. Deal?"

"It's a deal, darling," Kick says.

I ask, "Kino, will you help me put a protective shield around them to be safe.

Kino answers, "Yes, and I have the best spell for that. Spending my time in that monster's keep made me practice for possible needs in the future."

I pat my red goyle's chest and say, "We're blessed to have your experience Beloved. Kick, contact Peter and Steen, and make your plans. I think we're almost ready to take the fight to Barat."

52

TOUR

Kendra

THE FLIGHT HOME IS QUIET. EVERYONE'S DEEP IN THEIR OWN thoughts at the possibilities raised by the meeting with the spy. The night is warm, not hot like they will be in July and August. The summer nights sometimes stay near one-hundred degrees Fahrenheit. No matter how much I love flying, I'm not looking forward to long flights in that type of heat. My mind wanders from topic to topic, and before I realize it. Before I know it Mica pulses the sentries at the cave entrance for admittance.

We circle, hundreds of feet above, waiting for a return pulse. When the guards return a pulse, it feels different to me.

I say, "Guys, that pulse is strange. Let's sneak up on the guards and find out what's up."

Ever the leader Mica takes charge and says, "Kino with me, Kick with Spar, cover us with invisibility, and we'll hide on each side of the entrance. Princess, if you'll be the bait and land in the front of the cave. I promise we won't let you get hurt. If something is wrong, dragon out."

We're prepared for whatever nefarious activity may be awaiting us when I land near the entrance. I don't see my goyles, but I do feel them. I'm ready, and the tension in my body is set for the worst. The guards are standing near the opening and greet me with that funny pulse again. As I get closer, the others move in with me. I pulse to the guards and see that they're questioning one another about it. What? Now, this is interesting... The guards are human.

I stand straighter, pulse my discovery to my consorts, and say, "Good evening. I was wondering why your return pulse was different? How did you accomplish it?"

The men recognize me. I laugh inwardly as I watch their dawning comprehension. The taller, thin man elbows his fellow guard, a shorter and stouter man, and says, "It's the Queen. These must be her... her... you know, her men!"

I laugh at the comical routine playing out in front of me. Although, I do need to check with Jared about the logic of having 'Dick and Harry,' standing watch at the gate to Navan. Maybe I should get their names... nah, Jared will know how to figure out who is here.

With these two all but falling over themselves, I manage to ask again, "How did you manage to pulse a return to us?"

The shorter one, who I've nicknamed Harry, smacks Dick in the stomach with the back of his hand and answers, "Queen..." Wham! Harry gets a return punch from Dick.

"It's Your Majesty! That's what they told us to say. They never said, call her Queen!" Dick tells his stouter comrade.

If looks could kill, the one Harry is burning through his partner would've ignited a small fire. Dick motions to continue by scooping his hands up toward the other's face.

His partner rolls his eyes before continuing, "Your Majesty," he pauses and glares at his skinny companion. "We have sonar on this, and it recognizes pulses and can return a pulse. The thing is, it's only programmed for admittance codes. It knows how to answer them appropriately. It didn't understand your last. We were trying to figure it out when you stepped into view. Do you mind telling us what you said?" He pointed to a little rectangular box hanging from a parachute cord around his neck. It has a screen to read and buttons on the sides, but not much else that I can see.

My princes are all visible and standing behind me now as I answer, "Well, live and learn. I knew the pulse was different. We had to be sure we weren't walking into a trap. But to your question, when I pulsed back, I was asking, in a limited fashion, if you were friendly."

My big Ranger goyle moves forward, reaches for the contraption, and says, "May I?"

"Of course, Prince Consort," the guard answers, taking off the sonar technology and handing it over.

Mica looks it over.

Kino takes it next then asks, "Does this link to your phones? Is that how you get messages?"

The tall guard answers this time, handing Red his phone and showing him the screen, "Yes sir, that's the app it's linked to right there."

He glances at my angle and with the understanding of brothers. Both sing a low melody. In less than a minute, they hand the phone and box back to the guard and take the other guard's box.

My Beloved says, "Now it will work better for you. If you have a problem in the future, bring it to someone in the Warrior Mage Guard."

Both guards, after accepting their devices, back away, bowing several times as they do, while thanking them. As we enter the cave, we hear them chatter excitedly about getting to meet us.

I grin and continue to my chambers. When I get there, I notice several big blue plastic tubs but don't bother to look in them.

After we settle, Kick calls Peter and Steen to detail their objectives concerning Baratium. They are excited to begin, so they're here quick.

I have to get ready to meet with the President of the United

States again. This time, I hope, with a better outcome. I leave the men sitting around the table drinking and planning.

Clifton, who just arrived says, "My Lady, Jamie Serge, is on his way. Jericho is fetching him to help you ready yourself. He said that these are clothes for your trips to visit the dignitaries of the world." He waves a hand toward the plastic containers I'd noticed.

"I wondered what they were. When Jamie gets here, Clifton bring him in, please. I'm going to get a bath."

My consorts all sit up and quiet when I walk toward the bathroom. Oh, this is good.

I add, Clifton, Peter, Steen, please leave my suite and keep everyone away for at least an hour, please."

"Yes, Your Majesty," my assistant raises his hand to hide his grin and leaves. The two mages close behind.

I turn and drop my top on the floor then take a few steps before shimmying out of my pants, leaving them with the top. I hold my hand over my shoulder without turning and curl my finger at my lovers. The intake of breath is covered quickly by the shifting of chairs as they rush to be with me. I take off running and jump into my pool before they catch up. When I surface, I giggle, watching those clowns peeling off their clothes as quickly as possible. The hour goes by way too fast. We're out of the pool and getting dressed when Clifton pulses at my door then enters with Jamie.

My flesh and blood fairy-godmother gives me a big hug and kisses me on the cheeks.

In his usual slow drawl he says, "You don't know how much I've missed you, Kendra dear. I've been planning and waiting and planning ever since I learned you and your people were going to go public. I mean, it should have always been that way. Nobody should have to live in the closet like that... oops. I wasn't talking about me, sweetheart. I've been out of the closet since birth!" Jamie laughs, and I laugh with him.

If I've ever met anyone more comfortable with who they are than Jamie, I don't know who.

"My dear. I love you, and you don't know how thrilled I am to see how you've changed since we first met," the exuberant designer says.

"Thank you, you helped make me this way. Later today, I have to meet the President again. I want to make a better impression than the one I did the last time. I've heard this one will be more clandestine, so we can avoid protestors."

"Ah, that makes sense," he answers in his signature sing-song lilt and a shake of his head.

I continue, "The same day, I'll meet the British Prime Minister for dinner, and the Scottish... whatever for dessert. Then tomorrow, I'm in Ireland, France, Germany, and Russia. That's just for starters. I need new dresses for each location. Oh my, I'm probably going to spend more time getting ready for these meetings than actually in the meetings. I must be crazy to agree to this!" I end with my words running together and rubbing my face.

"Darling, if there's anything I know, it's queens, and you sweetheart are a queen. I don't know anyone better at representing her people and taking care of others like you. You are going to be amazing! I know it," Jamie says, drawing his words out with a chuckle and a coy motion with his one hand the other on his hip.

I take a deep, cleansing breath, hold it for a count of five, then slowly let it blow out across my lips for another five count. My strength restored, at least temporarily, I say, "Well, we have about a week of this. If I remember right, I end up in Athens. I've always wanted to go there, and their Prime Minister has promised me I'll be guarded. They're closing off several blocks for my safety. Like that matters to a red dragon.

"I'm going to ask my guys to take me there and show me around Greece and Turkey. That's where they're from. Did you know that? That'll be a great way to unwind after this race. What do you think?"

"No, I didn't, I love Greece, it sounds thrilling, dear."

We spent the next hour getting me showroom ready for the meetings later today before we portal to the guest house we had stayed in before and meet with the President.

53

SALVATION

Kendra

THE TEAM OF MAGES, INCLUDING KICK, HAVE RETURNED FROM Faery. They have news to share with the HG. Peter and Steen travel directly to Navan to inform Mega and the HG there. My dark consort came here to Scotland. He's currently rubbing my feet. He removed my heels and is sitting in front of me on a plush stool. Today, I met with the American President, the UK Prime Minister, and First Minister of Scotland. It feels like I've been standing for two days straight. These first three meetings went exceptionally well.

While I was hoping there won't be any, the protests in the capital cities were limited in size. When a jerk tried to assassinate the Prime Minister of the UK, Mica took the bullet for him. He torped to heal and no one else has challenged us. In D.C., the counter-protesters far outnumbered the protesters who soon gave up their half-hearted attempts and left.

My friend, José Brinker, invited us to stay in our old rooms in Fiatril Hall. It feels like a second home as we relax after a day of public relations.

"Oooh, Dark Angel that feels good," I groan wiggling my toes and lean back on Mica's hard chest. His arms automatically come around to hold me. We wait on Kick to tell us how the trip to Faery to speak with Walter went.

"I'm glad I hope it helps. Do you want the good news or the bad news first?" he asks.

Spar answers for me, "Give us the bad first, Romeo."

Kino chuckles at the jab, and so does Mica. I feel his chest bounce with his mirth.

Kick sits up and says, "Shut-up and listen then. When we got there, we went straight to Barat's castle. You guys said Jared wrecked it. It was worse than wrecked, it was a disaster. The first thing I thought of when I saw it was a volcano had erupted from below. Stones were thrown out as if they were a discarded child's toy. Many were melted into great pools of black glass. Still, others had been shattered as if an explosion went off everywhere inside the stone all at once. The memories of the place were sort of hard on us for the first few minutes. Even though we were satisfied with the fact that it had been destroyed, we just sort of stood there and gaped. The raw power which hit that place must have been incredible to see."

Spar interrupts, "It was," looking into the distance as if reviewing the event on a faraway movie theater.

My mage pauses politely for the blue goyle to have his say. After a moment, he continues, "Guys, if the Duke of Storms can cause that much destruction, it must truly be amazing what our gal can do. Anyway, after we got over the shock of the destruction, we raised a glass to our friends and family who were lost and tortured there. Then we started a spell to locate Walter. We found him. He was inside one of the outbuildings that had escaped the carnage."

When he pauses I ask, "Did he try to attack you?

The others sit up a little straighter and I feel my ranger tense behind me.

The dark mage answers, "No, we protected ourselves before going. It was weird to see him, though. He isn't the imposing wizard who captured us and commanded so much misery. He's thin and withered. He looks ancient and was alone. That mad wizard told us Barat and Baladriell are gone. They went to Illiolion. In fact, he let us know exactly where he thinks they are, in an underground bunker near the old city.

"There *is* a problem. He told us more about the curse on Barat and what it'll do to the person who kills him. While the Hewn are right, it must be done on the new moon, six days from now, the person who kills him will, by default, agree to accept his soul curse. Apparently, the curse twists the person infected by it. They slowly turn from who they are into the essence of Barat. If that person lives long enough, they'll become like him. It might even change their DNA."

The room is quiet. For five long heartbeats, not a voice is heard. In my mind, I do hear a voice. It tells me that I must be the one to kill Barat. If anyone has a chance to accept this spell, then destroy it, it'll be me.

Spar asks, "What's the good news?"

Kick turns toward him and says, "Barat-ass doesn't know we're coming. The city is familiar territory to the Ceorfan. It's our homeland. We'll be the home team. Best of all, this time, we'll be at-bat with dragons batting two, three, and four, in our lineup." The mirthless grin that Kick holds onto indicates the distance he's prepared to run in this coming battle.

"If we're to be ready, we need to start now," a stern-looking Kino says without staring anyone in the eye.

"I'm assuming you have a plan, Charlie," deadpans Spar, echoing an extinct TV show from the 1980s.

"I do indeed," replies Kick, just as straight-faced.

I SPENT the next several days attending meeting after meeting. Meeting at least three world leaders each day, then planning with my goyles until early in the morning, before sleeping for four or five hours before starting again. Ending Rats-ass is the only priority now. My consorts agree.

It's late when I return to Navan via a portal. After our trip to Scotland, we decided it was best to return to our city each night instead of adding a layer of risk of protecting any sleeping goyles. Since our trips are almost instantaneous, this is a risk easily avoided.

Mica and Kick have been attending meetings with me. At the same time, Kino and Spar remain here to continue working on the plan after they un-torp. My Ranger and mage head off to grab us some food.

I return to my room with Jamie to get my outfits ready for tomorrow. I enter my chamber only to find it empty. This is odd. I wonder where Kino and Spar are?

The ever-positive Jamie says, "My dear, Kendra, I'm worried about you, you're overworked and an under-slept dragon. If you don't get more sleep, I won't know what to do with your eyes tomorrow. They're going to look like two whales humping on your face."

I huff and ask. "Do I look awful?"

After seeing the hurt I try to cover, he takes me gently in a hug saying, "Dear, I'm sorry. I'm a rotten old hag sometimes. It's not you, I'm just tired. Really, I'm tired *for* you. You're doing all the work. I get lots of sleep. Please, forgive me," he pleads letting go of me and stepping back.

"Jamie, I don't need to forgive you. You're amazing, as always. I know you are trying to help. Please, just trust me for a few more days. This business with that murderer will be done soon. Then I won't have to be in such a rush to get stuff finished and everything in order," I say. I cover the annoyance on my face for having slipped up and giving a clue to my secret of taking the soul curse.

"Kendra, dear, why are you in a rush to finish stuff? What's the rush? This will all be... unless? No! No, no, no!" Jamie says, tears welling up in his brown eyes.

"What are you going on about?" I ask, pushing every ounce of conviction into my tone as I can, using my gift of persuasion. If I can't convince him that nothing's wrong. I'll play hell with my princes, letting me anywhere near Baratium.

"You're going to sacrifice yourself, like the last queen. You're going to do that to end him permanently, aren't you?" he asks and sniffs as great drops of tears stain his purple silk shirt.

"Jamie, I have no plans to hurt myself. My people need me. They're stronger with a dragon queen. Look, even Amber is going to have a baby. It's been centuries since a child has been born to a Ceorfan gargoyle. I can't take that from them. Please, Jamie, listen to me." I think I'm even convincing myself to come up with a different plan. No, I have to do this and protect the others. I watch as his aura changes from shades of blue to flashing distressed reds then back to the blues as my words begin to sway him and then ultimately convince him.

"Oh pshaw, see what I've turned into? I think I really do need to get some extra sleep tonight. Do you mind if I go to bed now? I'm sorry, I've ruined your entire evening with my rant," he finishes as he dries his tears on his bright yellow silk hanky.

"Don't be silly. You haven't ruined a thing. We're friends. If friends can't talk to one another, what's the point?" I ask, laying it on thick and adding a light undertone hoping to add positive reinforcement to my ability. I'll continue to push the story that I'm not planning anything sacrificial.

"Thank you, love. I'm off to bed. I'll see you tomorrow. Sleep well, I love you," he adds. He leans in for a hug and a kiss on both cheeks.

"I love you too," I say to his back as he makes his way out of my room and heads toward his.

54

PLANS

Kendra

I'm not using my tablet or phone much anymore. It is simpler to tele-speak to everyone since I've found I can do it, I do. As soon as Jamie's out of my room, I reach out with my mind to Duke Findare and say, *"Fin, will you please call for an HG meeting in ten minutes. I need to find my consorts, and I'll be right there."*

"My Queen, the Count de Treon, has the meeting scheduled in thirty minutes. He asked the Prince Consorts to leave you alone so you can sleep for a short time. He told me it is called a nap of power, and it helps return vigor quickly. Is this so?"

I chuckle and answer, *"In a manner of speaking. It worked pretty well when I was just Kendra, the Park Ranger. As a dragon queen, it will be the same as a full night's sleep or torp. Tell Clifton I said, thank you."*

"I will. The Count said he will be there to wake you exactly seven minutes before the meeting."

I lie down on my bed, feeling alone. My pet, Elmer, lands on my shirt and chirps. Oddly enough, his chirping is enough to push me over the edge, and I fall asleep in seconds.

Mica

All of us Prince Consorts are in the cafeteria. Kick and I haven't had a chance to eat all day, and this is breakfast for Spar and Kino. They've piled their plates high with food. Kick has hash browns, biscuits, gravy and scrambled eggs. Apparently, he'd had it once in Cueva Hallow, and it's now his favorite meal. Each of them is shoveling in food, expecting to get to the allodium for the HG meeting. Then we receive a group message from Mega.

He says, "Ok guys, she is asleep. The meeting is being moved to an hour from now."

I respond for all of us, "Thanks, Commander. We'll be ready."

The guys all nod to me that they understand and let my answer stand as their own.

"So, what do we do now?" I ask.

Without a heartbeat between the end of his question, Spar pipes up, "I have something I need to talk about, but not here. We need to find an out of the way place."

Kick says, "Ok, the jail cell you guys had me in when you captured me, it's out of the way. Let's go there to talk in private." Kick watches Spar. I bet memories of the day he was placed there float in his mind, because the day he was captured, Kick landed a back-kick that struck Spar in... a delicate place. The grimace on big blue's face says he remembers the same thing.

The other two are on the same page and drop their silverware onto their trays at the same time.

I push my plate away saying, "I'm ready now."

To which, the unanimous response is, "Let's go."

We make our way down below the great city to its lowest levels.

Here, the wall sconces render the impotent luminescence into a sphere of brightness surrounding the lamps. The darkness eats its dissipating glow. Since these areas of Navan are rarely frequented by anyone but maintenance workers and security forces who carry their own powerful flashlights, the ambient lighting is ominous. The diluted light causes many Ceorfan to avoid this area. Maybe because of something as simple as being afraid of monsters. This is one reason why Dana chose to leave the jail in this area when he rebuilt and reinforced it. It keeps the looky-loos at bay.

The smell of guano, combined with the dim lighting, makes this an ideal location for hidden agendas. There was a time, not long ago, when humans wanted to use the bat waste for fertilizer. During that time, enormous amounts were removed and sold by gargoyles appearing as men. That time passed quickly, and the Guild returned to their way of magically disposing of it. Based on the smell, it seems like it needs tending to.

We four turn one final corner, and the narrow passageway opens into a large room. It's fifty feet long, if not more. At the far end, it opens to the left, making the place look like a giant 'L.' Unlike the path lighting, this room is well lit from all sides. There aren't any shadows.

There are six jail cells in this room, and Spar moves to the one where Peter had been held before turning to face the other three, "Guys, I know we each have a physical tie to her. I'm mind bound to her. I know Kendra's hiding something. I just don't know what it is. She's has it pushed way down inside of her," he says pushing his mess of a mohawk out of his eyes.

"I'm not gonna disagree with you, brother. I'll add, though, that her heart feels off. It's like it's light and heavy at the same time. I've been thinking it's because she's been doing so much. Now I'm not so sure," I say.

"I feel energy, unlike any other in her body since I have known her. This energy is obviously building and is preparing to explode. I cannot figure out when or where. I feel the time is getting closer, however," Kino adds his green eyes squinted in thought.

Without looking up, Kick says, "Her spirit is burdened. It's in a rush to finish the unfinishable. I believe she is preparing to sacrifice herself in the destruction of Baratium Mezacain. We must stop her." The gravity of what he's just told the others lifts his eyes to meet the others.

"Yeah, good luck with that, Romeo," I say, rubbing my face with a hand.

"Right. Our beloved cannot be forced into any direction against her will. The only chance we have is to say nothing until we take action," Red states emphatically.

"Any ideas then?" I ask.

"I have one," the dark mage says, almost mumbling.

"Well spit it out," the blue mohawk touting gargoyle demands.

"Spar, you need to be the one to reach Baratium first. You have to try to kill him," the mage answers, his shoulders slumping, and his head sagging with the burden of what he has just told them.

Kino erupts in angry protest, "She lost him once, never again," Kokkino, the Lord and heir of Duke Findare pulls authority into his voice and growls.

"It should be me, I deserted her once. None of you have ever betrayed her. She can lose me, but none of you," I add.

Spar stands and raises his arms and says, "Kick, I'll gladly give my life to save her. But why do you think it should be me? What's your logic? I don't have a problem giving my life for her. She's always been, my love. I'll gladly go to my grave, protecting her. I just don't get how you could, this easily, cast me as the sacrifice," Spar queries his brother consort with pointed questions.

The dark mage answers, "Because I don't think it'll be you or any of us who ultimately will kill him." This time when he speaks up, it isn't with the voice of doom he used earlier when he named Spar the sacrifice. This time it's the voice of one who has a nagging premonition that's yet to be revealed.

"It's my fucking duty, and I won't shirk it. Let's get back to the allodium and decide more after we have more information," Mega's son spits out as he turns and leaves.

We follow him not knowing how to respond, yet knowing we won't let him sacrifice himself.

55

BEGINNING OF THE END

Kendra

I'M AWAKENED WITH THE GENTLE PULSING AT MY DOOR. IT'S Clifton. *Those twenty-three minutes went by very fast!* I return a pulse to him that I'm awake and will be there in five minutes. I admit I feel more refreshed than I'd expected. *I may have to take more naps of power!*

When I arrive at my allodium for the meeting, I'm met at the door by all my consorts. Big gorgeous Ceorfan, each one different but hot as Hades. Each one greets me with a kiss, the next more passionate than the last. The guys are trying to outdo one another and take my attention away from my problems. I giggle. I'm content with my choice of consorts. I won't regret my decision to protect them either.

"Clifton, will you please call the meeting to order. I'd like to take the floor immediately if you will," I say.

After he calls for order, he introduces me, all pomp gone from his voice. He knows this meeting is for planning the final battle.

"By now, each of you knows that we know where Baratium is

located. We are sure his acolyte, Bladriell as well as all of his crafted are at this location too. We know they're hiding in caves beneath Ilioiliom. We are here to lay the trap to catch this fuckwad in," I land the last part with extra force and the seriousness the matter deserves.

The plan grows, modifies, shrinks and refolds many times over the next few hours. Until several hours later, we're left with a solid plan. One which I believe will minimize risk and still allow me to get close enough to destroy our enemy once and for all. It consists of three phases.

"General Mega, will you outline the plan one time in its entirety? We need to be sure everyone is clear," High Guild member Trevor asks.

Mega says, "Certainly Marquess, phase one starts with Jericho. He will portal onto the plane outside Ilioiliom near where we expect Barat to exit his underground hiding place. Steen and Peter will portal to the other side of the area. If you're looking down on it you'll see Jericho, the team of Steen and Peter and Barat forming a triangle. Barat will be at the 'bottom' point. Jericho has developed a spell to block the evil mage from using a portal to escape. This includes his using a jump stone. Once the spell is in place phase two will be initiated.

"Phase two will begin with Kino and Kick. They'll open portals for the dragon dukes, Jared and Dana. Afterward, they'll take up positions above and between Barat and their charges. In this case, the Duke of Storms will be charged with protecting Jericho. While the Duke of Stone is responsible for protecting Peter and Steen. After the dragons are in place, the two Princes will then open more portals. This time to give access to the Hewn and Ceorfan gargoyles. Who will exit in a pattern designed to keep Barat from moving Crafted toward the mages who have him spelled? The humans who have trained to be the Elite as well as the special forces who we trust also have a job. They will portal behind Barat closing the loop and effectively eliminating his ability to escape.

"Then phase three launches. When the last phase two portals

close. Our red prince and the mage consorts will open one more. On the ground for Mica and Spar to run through. Our queen can open her own. She will open it in the air and shoot through to the field. They're the attack force. They will kill our longtime foe."

I find myself nodding. It's our job to get close enough to kill that piece of shit. Well, it's mine anyway. I have no intention of letting anyone but me take on that soul curse. If it's on me, I know I can find a way to beat it... at least that's what I'm hoping.

Mega adds, "Are there any questions?"

No one moves. We're ready and itching to go.

56

STARTING

Kendra

David, before his resurgere and brought back as Spar, once told me that no plan survives contact with the enemy. He was an Army Ranger and had fought on almost every continent in the world. His knowledge of battle tactics was exceptional. Since undergoing the resurgere process and gaining the experience of his father, General Mega, that tactical know-how has grown.

Unfortunately for us, this night will prove if our first contact with our enemy will force us to abandon our tactical plan. We must become "flexible," I believe, is the word that Mega is using. Having planned for almost any eventuality, we were smugly executing every phase of our plans when the unthinkable happens.

Barat, Bladriell, and the Crafted were indeed underground. But when the evil wizards were spelled into not moving, the Crafted didn't follow them out of a single exit as we had presumed they would. Instead, they flooded from more than twenty different passageways. They overwhelmed the battlefield.

On sheer gut instincts, my brothers lay down a great burst of dragon plasma. Their fire blasts forth with a thunderous roar. It sounds like a train with as much impetus. My younger brother spits flame at the evil wooden robots giving our baby brother room to maneuver straight for the underground openings. He closes off several of them with a flick of his great teal blue tail.

Thousands of the wooden monsters that have taken the field are fighting on autopilot. They have been given orders with a spell from their master and won't stop until he recalls the magic or they're destroyed. Still, the break in the lines of beasts makes room for the Hewn and Ceorfan alike to enter the battle.

The fighting rages in intensity. Both my brothers are attacking at every point. The aim is to fend off Crafted from our people. One benefit of this is, it allows my attack team to reach Barat. They're a smaller force, and hard to defeat.

I send a message to everyone in tele-speak, *"Keep the focus of the battle on you two and I'll take my team and get closer to the fuckers, and we'll blow their asses away and be done with this fight here and now!"*

Jared screeches from on high, *"Go get them, Sis. We can hold off the Crafted for a while and draw attention until you get there."*

In the heat of the moment Mega tele-comms, *"My Queen, the Ceorfan mages are holding them with a spell, but it won't last for long. Go and use your magic and flame an end to our misery and kill the scum."*

"We're on our way. It'll be over soon. I promise," I respond.

Throughout history, many overmatched armies lost. They lose not because they were defeated tactically. They lost because they didn't see the moment for what it was. A moment to seize history and bend it to their will.

I won't make that mistake. Today, I'll kill both of those murdering thugs. I'll accept the curse and find a way to destroy it. I've had to fight through tougher afflictions. This time, I have all of my stones. My magic is far greater than I had at my disposal before. It has to be me taking the hex. It's the only way I can ensure none of the Guild will suffer anymore.

As I circle in the night sky, the wind is blowing over my wings in a heatwave. It feels good. I watch my consorts fight, destroying Crafted as fast as they can reach one. I have power. Which I can only guess is being supplied by my grandmothers. I drive my massive dragon-wings down. Forceful strokes, push me forward, my trajectory set to release my burning plasma in front of my consorts. My objective is to open a way for them to reach Barat.

Something's off. I pause. A shock of fear rips through my chest. Unable to breathe, I stop burning the vile beasts in front of me. Where the fuck is Spar? I search, looking for him. He was with us before we portaled. Where is he now?

I pulse and receive nothing in response. I reach my mind out for him. Again, nothing. My mind races. I gasp for air and roar. All he had to do was run through the portal with the others. What happened?

57

TWISTED

Spar

ACCORDING TO THE PLAN OF OUR QUARTET OF CONSORTS, KINO will open Kendra's portal to the battlefield. At the same time, Kick will open one into Faery for me. Both glowing gateways open together. I run through mine, as it slams shut behind me. I assume my dark brother opened the other one to the battle and has already gone through. My hope is that he, the red musician, and the Ranger are through and on the battlefield. Most importantly, I hope Kendra hasn't noticed I'm missing.

I have a simple job. Find Walter and convince him to return with me to kill Barat. My wish is that he'll want the privilege to avenge his sister. I want to convince him that I'll be the one to kill his former master... that I'll be the one to take the curse. I'm hoping Walter will decide to save me from the hex. I might be giving him too much credit, but he owes me. I was trying to save his sister from his master. It's a thin hope. But, it is what it is.

Either way, I'll have to ask him to open a portal for me. If he isn't going to help, I'll need it placed so I wind up behind the battle. This will allow me to sneak in close to Barat. I'll kill that piece of shit so Kendra can't. I argued with my brothers to have this task, as did each of them. My winning argument boiled down to the only trump card we have to play. Walter loved his sister. I was trying to save her when she was murdered. She was protecting me. That's the leverage we have. Yes, I know it sucks monkey balls. I also know it has very little chance of working.

It's a dark moonless night in Faery. The inky blackness will provide a perfect backdrop for flying. Kick put me on a path I followed with Jared when we were here for the first time. I'm not sure how Trix's brother will react when he sees me. I decide to stay out of sight until I choose to be seen.

When I reach the castle, I'm again amazed at the destruction visited on this giant stone edifice. The damage is incredible to behold. I realize that even with all the power that Jared used to inflict this kind of carnage on this place, Kendra can do far worse. I mustn't allow Barat any chance at perverting her power to his means if she takes his curse. More importantly, I must find a way to guard her, to forever protect her against any possible harm from that murderous fuckwad. My love for her is all the motivation I need. If I can't convince the mage, Walter, to kill Barat before Kendra has the chance, I'll have to take care of him myself.

I find him in the same out-building where Kick, Peter, and Steen had found him hiding. I remain in the shadows and announce my presence, "Walter, my name is Spar. We didn't have a chance to meet earlier. I was in Faery to save Trix."

"What do you want, Ceorfan?" he moans out of the darkness. I can just make him out due to my enhanced gargoyle vision.

"I want to say I'm sorry your sister was murdered. I want to help you, and explain what happened. We learned Baratium was planning to kill her only a few days ago. Kick asked us to save her. We planned to rescue her and bring her to Navan. I was part of that mission. I am so sorry we failed. She was a good woman."

The sounds of a man crying are all the acknowledgment I receive to know that I had been heard and understood.

I step into the open and press on, "Walter, did you know that Trix died while trying to save me? We both... I mean, she and I thought that she'd killed Bladriell with a club and a cattle prod. Do you know what that means? She wanted away from Baratium. She found happiness in hopes of being with Kick again. She was saving me so I could save her. She loved you. Today, I'm asking for, from the love your sister had for you, repayment. Payment you owe for those you tortured for your old master. Will you please return with me and kill him?"

The crying continues with audible gasps between his breaths. I hear a moan begin that builds into a scream. Each tone reverberating off the walls of the building. The echo adding an eerie undertone.

I've said my words. Now, I need to give him time to reflect. I hope I've said enough. After a few minutes, the echoes of his moans fade. His breathing becomes more regular. Then he gazes at me.

He says, "Spar, I have hated your kind for more than a thousand years. I willingly helped Baratium destroy the Ceorfan and spread them to the wind. My hate was centered on one of your kind who wronged me. Today, the feelings from that slight are so lost that I can't remember why I was angry.

"My sister was the only friend I had left. My hatred blinded me. Bladriell is a conniving, power-mad mage. He lives for it. He wants Baratium to be killed so he can step into his place. Yes, he's talented. Even though he's nothing to be feared. The soul curse on Baratium is. If I kill him, the curse will fall on me. Over time, I'll become him. With my skills, I'll become just as wicked. You'll accomplish nothing with my sacrifice. I'm sorry."

"Our plan, if you don't return, is that I'll kill him. Then my brothers have sworn to kill me. That'll keep me from becoming a threat in the future. I know this is a lot to ask. If you've reached the end of your rope, help me. Return with me. Kill him. I promise, I'll swiftly and painlessly send you to be with Trix.

"I'll even return your body to Faery. Not that it matters, but you'll be remembered in the Ceorfan Halls of History for your sacrifice," I ask my resolve not wavering. I know I'm asking him to, in effect, kill himself. My hope is that he'll find a place in his heart where Trix lived and use it to help me. Unfortunately, I'm running out of time. I have only moments left to convince him.

"Walter, I'm sorry, but I need an answer now. Barat, Bladriell, and the Crafted bastards are fighting and killing my people right now. While the battle rages, many are dying. I know Kendra won't wait long before she tries to finish him." I waited a few seconds. The temperature seems to have increased significantly. As has the pressure for him to shit or get off the pot.

"Walt–"

"I won't return with you to be killed. I won't become the thing who murdered my beautiful sister. All I'll do for you is return you to the battle. You can make your choice on life or death. Ready yourself," Walter says without a hint of cowardice.

I have no more time. "Walter, please open the portal as close to Baratium as you can, but where I can remain hidden." I prepare myself for what I've already decided to do.

With that, a mottled reddish portal opens in front of me. I sprint through ducking low.

Around me, the noises of the battle flood over me. I'm almost knocked to the ground with the fierceness of its power. I take a step back, widening my stance to balance. Screams of pain are everywhere. I block out the noise. I was trained in the Army when I was human to block the tumult. The fighting slows around me. It's in the slow-motion that I find my bearings. I search for my target. When I find Barat, my anger flares, and my muscles tense.

Fucking firetruck, that smelly cockknob mage deposited me as far from Barat as he could. I'm barely on the battlefield. I reach a hand to my back and feel for my weapon. Kino made me a spear. I have it attached there, ready to draw like a sword. It's still with me. Now, if I can get close enough to use it.

Still, in slo-mo, I check my options. If I take to the air, I can reach him faster, but Kendra will spot me. She'll immediately know what I'm up to. She'll act to stop me. No way these two are getting off the hook today. Today is our chance to end them once and for all. I have to be careful.

I trained as a special operator in the Army Rangers. I mobilized with the world's most elite soldiers during my military service. I only left because an unlucky ricochet took out my knee, which made it impossible for me to deploy. Still, one thing that I remain good at is moving at speed while maintaining stealth. In fact, being a gargoyle has made it easier for me. Even with the nearly full moon in the human realm, my blue coloring will work to my advantage in the darkness of the battle.

In less than a minute, I've worked my way closer to the fighting. Before I stand and actively enter the fight, I'll close the gap between the wicked mage and me.

Jared spots me. While we never spoke of the plan, he's my best friend. I would bet my last hair that he knows what I'm planning. Our eyes meet. I nod to him. He understands. He nods back. That big blue dragon turns and burns a path through the Crafted army. It's my time. I sprint as fast as I can through the center of the robot morons toward my target. Like Alexander the Great charging Darius of Persia. Alexander was outnumbered two to one; yet, he saw his goal and would not be denied. Neither will I.

I'm yards away when I see Kendra. My beautiful girl is magnificence personified, deadly gorgeous. My chest swells with pride. I keep moving to beat her to the scum. She's diving at a right angle to my movement. I gape watching her launch burning scarlet flame right at the two enemy mages. She's closer to them than I am. I know her. Risk is part of her character. Her flame is guttering. Holy fuck, she needs a breath! Yet she doesn't have enough air remaining in her lungs to finish the job. While she is taking in another, I'll be able to get close enough that she won't be able to risk a second attack. If she does, she'll kill me. My baby won't take the chance of hurting me.

I pour on the speed toward the malignant mages. I release the spear from its strap on my back. I see the fear in Bladriell's eyes as they widen in his frozen state. Malevolence flares in Barat's. It's as if he realizes this battle is lost and is placing his faith in his 'secret' curse.

Neither of these mages can handle an actual weapon. They've always used magic. But, today, that is being blocked on many fronts. Their Crafted army is being kept away from them by our Guild. In other words, I have a clear road to their destruction. I should feel lousy killing frozen men. I don't, not even a little.

I'm within ten feet. No slowing down for me. Soon my brothers will kill me. They promised. This is the only way to ultimately end any possibility of Barat returning. Soon, they'll kill me--soon.

I remember the first time I saw Kendra. She was as bold as she was gorgeous. She was explaining to a senior ranger, John Cooper, why he was wrong in a particular training exercise. My girl had only been a Park Ranger for a few months... but she was right. I wonder if he was helping the Jessup Cartel back then? Oh, God, I love her. I can do this for her.

Still sprinting to my goal, I raise my spear. My love and I are bound by our minds. I can speak to her using my thoughts. I only have a second before the curse takes me. None of us know how fast it will act, so I send her, *"Baby, I love you. There's no other way. Goodbye."*

As my spear breaks through the shield freezing the assholes in place. I see I can pierce them both with this single plunge. I detect a flash of terror as they realize their end. Both sets of eyes widen and mouths open. I catch a glimpse of my red dragon queen being held tightly to Kino. His arms wrap around her from the back as she squirms to free herself. Mica and Kick are by her side, along with her brothers. They're all waiting. All stiff, standing in runner's stances waiting for the gun to go off to complete our mission. I love them all.

I can't watch my girl in this much pain, so I turn my head. My spear is within inches of Barat's chest. My race is won. The evil, murderous mages are dead as I finish my thrust.

58

CLEANING UP

Kendra

THIS BATTLE WON'T HANG AT THE JUNCTURE OF VICTORY OR defeat. With three dragons and an army of Ceorfan and human warriors at my back, it's only a matter of when Barat is killed, not if. That is, as long as Jericho's plan for holding Barat and Bladriell works like he says it will.

I portal in above the battle just as planned. Circling, I catch a snippet of Mica, leading the others through the portal on the ground before turning my attention to the tactical situation.

My task, along with my consorts, is pretty straight forward. My brothers and the combined Ceorfan army will draw the wooden monsters away from our target. We're all Ceorfan, humans, gargoyles, dragons, and Hewn. The plan is that my goyles and I will hang out on the periphery. We'll shadow the two mages, mirroring any moves they make until my royal mage freezes them in place.

Primarily, we're waiting on the ground around Barat and his minion to clear for our attack. We considered going straight in. But my concern is that in a melee around the enemy, one of my princes will get close enough to kill them. I won't take that chance. One of them would gladly accept the curse. I'm the only one with the knowledge and expertise to defeat it. I hope.

Except for the lingering question of Spar's location, the battle is progressing precisely as we've drawn it up. Jericho, Peter, and Steen have locked down our quarry from using magic to escape. Our army has blocked them from running or hiding.

Below me, I see another portal open. This one is a mottled reddish colored portal. Okay, I'm sure I need to purge whatever exits it. I turn toward it. When I see Spar exit, the astonishment almost causes me to forget I'm flying. I catch myself in time. Where has he been? Why would he come through that color of a portal? I've never seen one that color before... except maybe I have. I saw it once when Barat, Walter, and Bladriell ran as we arrived. It just doesn't make any sense... unless Spar was with Walter. But why?

I learn I'm finding many more questions than answers. Items that need to remain questions until I end these fuckers.

I watch Jared lay down a path of burning lightning, clearing away many Crafted. Then I notice Spar follow Jared's flame as it clears a path... he starts running toward Barat. There are no more of Barat's army in his way.

His plan has become apparent. The horror of this discovery sends panic through me. My breath comes in pants as my heart speeds up. It's obvious why my blue goyle didn't join the battle with the others. He was with Walter. My guess is he was trying to get Walter to destroy his former master. Spar must have failed. Now the job has fallen on him. Tears begin to flood my eyes, and my vision blurs. These aren't tears of sadness or anger. They're born of pending loss. Fuck no! I buried him once as David. I'm not doing it again. I'll get to Barat first.

I dive at a right angle to Spar and quickly overtake him. I send torrents of my red plasma toward the putrid pieces of shit. Then I spot my brothers. They realize what I'm doing. They turn to stop me. They won't make it.

My flames hit the combined shield of Barat and his minion Bladriell. The force of my fire is reaching the end of its fiery exhalation. As I force the final gasps from my lungs, I see the blotchy brownish red portal open again. This time on a nearby hill. That location offers a perfect view of the battle unfolding beneath Walter. It allows him an ideal vantage point from which to help his master. I'll deal with you in a few minutes, you backstabbing piece of garbage.

As I take in another breath, I continue to watch Walter. He's moving his arms as if his gesticulations are meant to explain something grand.

To the right of Barat, I spy something moving fast. It's Spar. Hell, I'm too late. If I try to finish off Barat, I'd also kill my love. My heart breaks as I hear Spar in my mind. *"Baby, I love you. There is no other way. Goodbye."*

Spar raises a spear, one that I've never seen before. One that clearly has been spelled by Kino. I can see his magic. As my blue goyle begins to ram the weapon home, my world collapses. I'm going to fall from the sky. I'm only aloft because Kino has reached me and is holding me up. I have to get to my first love. So I start to resist my redhead's tightening arms. Mica and Kick are here. Now my brothers are too. They are waiting for the kill to be complete and stare at my consort on the ground.

Since becoming Queen, I've been able to slow time in any battle. It has become second nature for that gift to take hold and help guide me through the struggle. This time, it only serves to torture me as I watch the spear descend. He will be changed. This selfless act of purification will make him evil. How can I bear it? He's my first love, my first consort. The spear pierces the shield protecting Barat.

Another ruddy portal opens. This one in front of the still moving Spar. My confusion is almost tactile as I see Vincent step through. He blocks the spear thrust and pushes my love aside. The force of the shove has my blue warrior stumbling and going down on a knee.

In my growing confusion, I hear my new friend say, "I've got this,

Spar. You take care of her." At that, the spy turns and slaughters both Baratium Mezacain and Bladriell in a sudden and ferocious attack.

The portal that Walter had opened has remained open for the seconds it's taken to kill Barat, and for Vincent to accept the curse. Before he steps into the portal again, he pauses and looks directly at me. In what I can only describe as true satisfaction, he smiles at me. Then he steps through the portal while holding my gaze the entire time. The portal closes, and he's gone.

Kino, still holding me, lowers me to the ground. Mica reaches for me, and I hold him close. My dark angel puts a hand on my shoulder.

The fantastic scene which just unfolded before me has taken my breath away. While I'm not happy the spy took the curse, he returned my life to me. I transform, letting go of my princes and run to Spar. I leap toward him, taking him in my arms and crying into his shoulder. His embrace is intense and filled with joy at avoiding the loss which he'd been resigned to.

My other consorts have surrounded us, ensuring nothing gets close enough to hurt either of us. It shouldn't have been a worry, though. The remaining Crafted no longer have a controlling force directing them, making them easy targets. My Ceorfan basically push the last of them over where they became inert. We win.

59

HAPPILY EVER AFTER

Kendra

CLEANING UP THE MESS LEFT BY THE BATTLE IS ACTUALLY easier than after most squirmishes. My brother dragons torch the wooden monster pieces of leftover Crafted. They swoop through the air, making loops and flip out to singe the remains in their typical fun-loving attitudes. Little bits of ash float in the air in their wakes. I notice that when one teal tail got too far ahead of the blue one, however, a flame shoots forth, and our baby brother yelps and flies a bit faster. I hate to think of the revenge he'll visit on Jared for the hot tail.

The Ceorfan mages restore the grass, flowers, and call the wildlife back to the area.

I help with many of the wounded since their injuries are more severe than anything the Fae or humans can care for. In an amusing twist, Jared has to get his personal security detail involved to keep those with minor injuries away. Apparently, they want to have the 'magic blood of a dragon' flowing through their veins. I guess it is a sort of a status symbol for some. Others hope it will lead to a healthier and longer life. I think it just might, but I'm not making any promises.

There is some business to take care of also. I tele-speak, saying, *"Mega, I'll leave the battlefield to you and the other generals. TASS will need a report, and so will the Earth and Faery governments. I'd like to do those in person."*

Mega answers, *"We have this under control, Chuisle mo chroi. Take my son and your princes out of this ruin. Make our allies happy and feel safe. We'll be home before sunrise."*

"Will do, General. See you at home."

I know my loves will hear me, so I shout into the air, "Hey, guys, let's go. This is under control, and I need José Brinker to know the madman is dead and no longer a threat. Where's Clifton?"

Kick points to an area of the walls surrounding the old city of my grandmother's. I grin and watch the Count dig an ancient stone from the wall. What is he doing? He puts a hand into the void and brings out a beautiful knife. Uh oh, that's magical; I spot the purples in the light surrounding it. One can only hope it's safe. I intensify my inspection and verify it's safe; the weapon is spelled to bring happiness to couples.

My consorts and I walk over to him, and I say, "Nice bauble, you've found, Clifton."

"I want to give it to Morgan, as an engagement present. I hid it here long ago, it's time I get on with my life. I don't intend to waste a minute anymore, not doing what I want to do to be happy."

My princes are standing at my sides, waiting. I take the nearest hand to me, which happens to be Mica's and say, "I couldn't agree more. Are you ready? I need to do queen stuff."

"Lead on then," he answers.

A glance to my dark angel, and he opens a portal for us to Scotland.

We don't bother announcing ourselves and barge right into the castle. Then we go straight to José's office and knock on his door. In the middle of the night, he should be in bed like most humans, but he's working. He calls to come in, so we enter and give him the news.

The committee chairman of one of the most influential groups in the world jumps up and hugs me, saying, "Thank you! I knew you would do it, Kendra Macbard! I'm calling a special meeting."

I giggle and say light-heartedly, "So glad you have faith in me. I'm going to let you give the good news. I have to go tell our other allies before some of my Ducere princes turn to stone. I'll send the details to your tablet later."

"Thank you, you saved us. I'm honored to know you and your people."

"Goodnight José, I'll see you soon," I give him a quick hug and we're on our way to Faery to talk to Dag and Dayna.

We take more time with the Fae royalty than I thought we might. They gave us a delightful welcome and received the news well even though they don't like to hear of bloodshed. In turn, they gave us the fantastic news that they are expecting but to keep it secret until they are a few months down the road. I'm so happy I can't even say, but we hugged a lot.

When we leave the Faery castle, I say, "Can we just go home. I'm tired and feel a little sick to my stomach? Clifton, will you call the governments of the Earth and let them know that Barat is dead?"

My assistant answers, "Yes, I'll get right on it."

All my consorts are close to me and touching in some way when Mica says, "What's wrong, princess? Do you want me to carry you?"

Spar says, "Soon as we get home, you need to see Dr. Ogman and Jericho."

Kino is singing under his breath, his brow knit in concern.

Kick opens a portal. As soon as we're through, we're in my chambers. Elmer flies to me and latches onto my shirt front. I pet him, and the Count excuses himself to tend to business.

Kick takes my hand and leads me to the bed and says, "Darling, please let me look at you."

I let him he, is a physician after all, and has helped me before.

However, I can only take so much fussing. I do take the cup of water my red Ducere prince hands me. I'm very thirsty. After a while, I'm pronounced healthy, but they want Jericho and the good Dr. Ogman to look me over later. I might let them, but my eyes are closing. I need to sleep. Before I drift off, I feel the Elite Warrior Guild return and it helps me relax even further. Mica wraps his arms around me, and I snuggle into him and fall asleep.

60

HE'S HERE

Kendra

I AWAKEN WITH A START. WHAT WAS THAT? I LISTEN AND HEAR A scream. Surprised, Mica and Kick, who've been asleep with me, are up, searching for the problem. I must have slept all day because it's night again, and Spar and Kino are untorped.

I hear another screech and know it's Amber. It takes no thought, and I'm flying to her chamber. Mason is standing in the front area, wringing his small hands and pacing. He stops when I pulse to enter and says, "It's time already. We knew that gargoyles have fast pregnancies, but we're still surprised. Dr. Ogman is with her. She's here."

In a little cave to the side of the bigger room, I glimpse a bed with my Ducere maid in the throes of labor. Her body contorts with a pain that she is trying to control but losing the battle. My consorts stay behind out of respect for their fellow warrior. They get comfortable in a seating area, and Mason comes in to help his mate.

I sit on the bed opposite the poor distressed gargoyle and the doctor who says, "It's only a while longer now. The baby is in position and ready to be born."

My hand goes for Amber's when she moans in pain. I instinctively start to sing. Mason has his hands on his wife's shoulder.

My spell wraps around her, and she smiles and relaxes then says, "Doc, I have to push now."

He positions her legs and says, "The babe is crowning. I see the head, you can push now. Mason, you can hold her shoulder up and let her push into your hands. Now Amber, breathe and hold then big push. Push push push."

I sing, she pushes, and in minutes the good doctor is holding up a beautiful baby boy to present to his parents.

We're all crying and laughing at the same time. I leave the new family alone and go announce the child's arrival to my princes. We are all smiles when the Dr. walks over to us and says, "My Queen, do you think you can be at all Guild births? I'm sure there will be many more. You made that one hundred percent easier than it could have been."

"I'll do my best, Doctor," I say.

"I'll leave Amber in the capable hands of Mason and her nurse. But before I go, how are you?"

Spar answers for me, saying, "She was sick earlier, can you look at her?"

I huff and say, "Really, I'm just fine."

Dr. Ogman says, "Please sit, my lady. He takes out a stone and waves it over me. It turns yellow, and he smiles.

I ask, "What is it?"

He answers, "It seems we're to have a royal birth in our near future. Your Majesty, you're pregnant. I want you to eat well and drink plenty of water. I'll need to see you in the Alexandritana Clinic later this week."

I nod, the rest of my body frozen, although I do manage a slow blink. Mica picks me up and is swinging me around. All my consorts are grinning like loons and patting each other on the back.

I gulp, put my hand to my mouth, then say, "Baby, stop, I'm getting sick."

He sets me down, and the fawning begins. I'm not going to do this. I open my mouth to protest but hear Amber call for us. Mason is at the entrance and waves us in to see her.

Somehow the big blue guy slips in first. Amber lets him hold the baby. You can't imagine that goofy grin looking cute on a gargoyle, but he's mine, and I definitely do. Kino gets to hold the baby next. While he holds him, Spar is singing a kids' song about a teapot to him and making a teapot spout. Oh goodness, this is going to be fun having one of our own. If I don't laugh myself to death.

I ask, "Have you two decided on a name for the baby yet?"

Mason grins and answers, "Yes, Edling, we have. His name is Michael after my best friend, who was killed in the mage wars."

"That's a wonderful name. I think we should let them have some privacy now, guys."

Kino returns their baby and says, "If you need anything, let me know."

We leave, and Mica turns on last time and says, "Nice job gravel bits. Nice job."

We go back to my, really our chambers, and discuss our own good news before we get ready for the HG meeting tonight.

61

TERMINUS DEBRIEF

Kendra

THE ROOM IS SILENT AS I ENTER THE ALLODIUM. MY MEN ARE already here and seated. I take my chair and glance around at my people. The faces of contentment are all the reward I need for anything that arises in the future.

I start, "Clifton, please call the meeting to order. Also, as seems to be my standard operating procedure here lately, I'd like to have the floor as soon as you've finished with your introduction."

He answers, "Yes, Your Majesty. I open this meeting of the High Guild. Madam Secretary, will you please read the minutes."

The minutes of the previous meeting are quickly approved. While they were from a High Guild meeting only a few days ago, they may as well have been from another life. The action items are complete or no longer relevant. I've never been one to enjoy this aspect of our meetings, and my mind begins to wander. I hear my name, and my mind returns to reality. When I look up and see everyone staring at me, it becomes apparent this wasn't the first time I was called.

"Edling, are you alright, my lady?" he says.

I blink a smile then start, "Better than ever, before we get too deep into battle details and politics, I have a couple of announcements. Mason and Amber have delivered a beautiful baby boy who they named Michael."

Happy pulses surround the room with excitement.

Then I glance at my princes, and together, we pulse that we're also pregnant. We pulse so that all Navan will know at the same time. The room explodes in glee. Pulses cover my body with love and pride. When it settles down, I can't wipe the grin off my face and say, "Thank you, we're happy. Now to get down to business."

I need a contingent to go into Faery and converse with Walter Deveros. He was last seen with a Hewn gargoyle, who I intend to protect, named Vincent. The mage took the Ceorfan to Faery by portal after the battle. I see both of them as allies to our people. The mage has redeemed himself and deserves a second chance. We need to enlist his help to care for our goyle as he has taken on the soul curse of Barat. Walter will need to keep us informed if he changes so we can combat the problem.

"Any volunteers?"

Jadite, my Ducere warrior, stands up and says, "My Queen, I wish this mission."

We ask Mega and his generals then put it to a vote which passes unanimously.

Clifton asks if there is any other business, and my brothers both hold up a hand. Okay, what could they be up to?

After being recognized, Jared stands and says, "I don't have business per se, but I do have an announcement. I have asked my girlfriend to be my wife, and we will be married in the summer. I'm making her a June bride."

After much congratulations and Dana takes the floor and surprises us again when he says, "I'm not making no speech. I'm getting married too. That's it."

You could have knocked me over with a feather. How far we've come in so short a time. Our whole lives are different, and we live in a different world. I can only hope that it's similar to how we live. With lots of love and tolerance. One where love your neighbor is really a meaningful way of life and practiced. I lean back in my seat, reaching for my loves' hands and rest. I don't have to ever be alone again.

I'm content. I don't see our story ending. This is just the beginning. I can't wait to see what happens.

GLOSSARY

(This short glossary is not a complete character list. More a list of terms we think you might want to remember and a few main characters.)

- **Amber** - Elite Warrior specializes in undercover surveillance. Mate to Mason.
- **Bladriell** - An evil helper to Walter and underling of the enemy mage Barat.
- **Ceorfan** - (Key-or-fan) Carved or born grotesques, gargoyles and dragons. Anyone different who wants to become family and is accepted by the Guild.
- **Chiroptera** - Hand Wing or Little Wing, usually a hand with four fingers located at the top of many wings.
- **Chuisle mo chroí** - means Pulse of my heart. It is what the Ceorfan Guild calls Kendra their queen.
- **CIC** - Combat Information Center. The defense center the Ceorfan use in alert or emergency situations.
- **Crafted** - Evil mindless robot created gargoyles made from wood and magic.

- **Cursed** – The Ceorfan who were captured and tortured in the Mage Wars.
- **Dana Macbard** - (Dan-uh) Brother of Kendra and Jared Macbard. Aqua dragon, Duke of Stone.
- **Donum** - A gift, the knowing that the dragon breed has when there is a need between family members or guild. It can show up as a feeling or thoughts similar to ESP.
- **DRT** - Defense and Reaction Team of the Elite Warriors Guild.
- **Ducere** - Small specialize team of the Elite Warriors Guard. The Ceorfan Special Forces.
- **Edling** - Noble child, heir.
- **Ef** - An effigy or statue of a gargoyle.
- **Elite Warrior Guard** - The warriors/soldiers of the Ceorfan race.
- **Findare** - Took over as temporary king in the interim between viable queens.
- **Flint** - Elite Warrior undercover agent. Member of the Ducere.
- **Gortanik** - A Mage who had been held prisoner of Barat and infiltrated Navan. His nickname is Kick and he is helping the Ceorfan find Barat.
- **Grotesques** - People of the Ceorfan Race that look like what humans call gargoyles.
- **Guild** - The word is used for the race of the Ceorfan people.
- **High Guild** - The advisors to the Ruler of the Ceorfan.
- **Jared Macbard** - Brother of Kendra and Dana Macbard. Blue dragon, Duke of Storms.
- **Jericho** - Mage. Trusted member of the High Guild.
- **Kokkino Petra – Kino** - (Key-no) Mega's third in command of the Elite Guard. Nephew to Findare. Love of Kendra, Consort of the Queen.

- **Mage** - Human with the ability to perform spells of magic.
- **Mage Jar** - A glass jar of liquid lighting used and powered by the magic, in Navan.
- **Mason** - Elite Warrior specializes as a thief and undercover surveillance. Mate to Amber.
- **Megahir/Mega** - (Mega-here) Commander of the Elite Warrior Guard.
- **Mica Jacobs** - (Mike-ah) Second in command of the Elite Guard. Love of Kendra and her partner as a Federal Park Ranger, Consort of the Queen.
- **Navan** - (Nuh-van)The cave city of the entire guild of Ceorfan people.
- **Nous-fārī** - mind-speakers, Ceorfan with the gift of telepathy.
- **Pulse** - An echo pulse is a form of communication between the Ceorfan Guild. Similar to the sonar pulses of bats.
- **Resurgere** - 'Restore our family' literally, when a gargoyle has an ingot carved from his body in the seconds prior to hardening into a torpified state to sleep and heal, for the purpose of giving it willingly to another in exchange for a bone of their own body. Each party is implanted with the other's stone or bone.
- **Spar** Megason - Resurgere gave him a new life from David's body he becomes Mega's son. Love of Kendra, Consort of the Queen.
- **Torpefy/Torp/Torped** - Past tense: torpefied. Meaning: make (someone or something) numb, paralyzed, or lifeless. This is an early 19th century word from Latin [torpefacere], 'be numb or sluggish'. It is when gargoyles turn to stone in the daylight
- **Vincent** - A Ceorfan Hewn warrior who is a spy

dedicated to the Queen's service after a clandestine meeting with her.

- **Walter** - A mage who is a minion of the evil Baratium Mezacain.

ACKNOWLEDGMENTS

Thank you, fans and readers of our books. We appreciate each and every one of you. You are our prize. Please, if you enjoyed the book consider leaving a review. It means more than you can imagine! But if you really hate it... please pass.

The next gargoyle book will be a while coming, but it will be called Vincent. I hope you like that we get to continue with the Ceorfan in a new series. There will be a few more that are novellas and short stories.

I want to add a special thank you to **Kayla Poe** who won a giveaway in a takeover and has named our character **Angeles Castle** who is the acting liaison between the Ceorfan Guild and the American government. Also much thanks to **Felicity Morgan** for naming **James and Dominique Qwerty**, the uppity couple who disparage the Ceorfan Guild.

Also we give a special thanks to our friend **Walter Walker-Carr**. He is the inspiration for the mage in this book and My Tormented Mage called Walter Deveros. He loved the villain. He was a brave soul who lost his fight with cancer in 2019. He gave the world a wonderful example of love.

Thank you to our family, who is always supportive and helpful.
All our friends who are precious to us. Miki and Mine!
Christina and Brenda, you are the best PA's ever!
We love you all. Thank you for your support!

— Miki & Garrett Ward

OTHER BOOKS BY MIKI AND GARRETT WARD

The Ceorfan Gargoyles Series

Carved

Etched

Hewn

The Ceorfan Gargoyles Novellas

My Tormented Mage

Shivers Series

We See You

Double Mirror

Elser Books are stand alone

Flesh and Bold

Stand Alone from Miki Ward

My Phantom Queen

FIND US

Miki & Mine, Guys and Goyles Group
https://bit.ly/2CpH3BM

Miki's FB Author page
https://bit.ly/2yMlVSG

Garrett's FB Author page
https://bit.ly/2P3USwv
Bookbub
https://bit.ly/2J3FRFh
Amazon
Amazon Author Page - Follow Miki
https://amzn.to/2Ey3qrk

Amazon Author Page - Follow Garrett
https://amzn.to/2yNYOr7

www.ingramcontent.com/pod-product-compliance
Lightning Source LLC
Chambersburg PA
CBHW071215250626
47159CB00001B/323